BEST FAIRY STORIES
OF THE WORLD

BEST FAIRY STORIES OF THE WORLD

With an introduction by
MARCUS CLAPHAM

MACMILLAN COLLECTOR'S LIBRARY

This edition first published by Collector's Library 2010

Reissued by Macmillan Collector's Library 2016
an imprint of Pan Macmillan
20 New Wharf Road, London N1 9RR
Associated companies throughout the world
www.panmacmillan.com

ISBN 978-1-5098-2663-6

1 3 5 7 9 8 6 4 2

A CIP catalogue record for this book is available from the British Library.

Casing design and endpaper pattern by Andrew Davidson
Typeset by Antony Gray
Printed and bound in China by Imago

Visit www.panmacmillan.com to read more about all our books
and to buy them. You will also find features, author interviews and
news of any author events, and you can sign up for e-newsletters
so that you're always first to hear about our new releases.

Introduction

These days, fairies do not have a particularly good reputation. Quite apart from any sexual connotation, fairies are generally imagined as small, winsome humanoids with lacy wings, such as appeared in the cleverly faked Cottingley Fairies photographs published in 1920. An examination of these shows that the cardboard cut-outs used to represent the fairies bore a marked resemblance to the images depicted by Richard Doyle in his illustrations in *In Fairyland: A Series of Pictures from the Elf World*, published in 1869. It is, perhaps, no coincidence that the Cottingley Fairies were championed by the creator of Sherlock Holmes, Sir Arthur Conan Doyle, who was Richard Doyle's nephew.

But the history of fairies goes far beyond the sentimentalised Victorian and Edwardian beings characterised by Tinker Bell in *Peter Pan*. The word itself is derived from the Latin *fata* or fate, and is expressed as *fée* in French or 'fay' in English, and it came to denote a person with magical powers – Morgan Le Fay, for instance. Fairies could take many forms, from witches and elves to giants, dwarves, sprites, wizards, ogres, leprechauns and pixies. Some were good, some evil and others morally ambivalent, like the donor of the beans in 'Jack and the Beanstalk'. The development of the concept of fairies owes much to folklore, and the mixture of folk tales and the literary tradition that emerged in the Renaissance, from *The Decameron* and *The Canterbury Tales* to *The*

Faerie Queen and *Le Morte D'Arthur*, contributed to the canon that we know today. By the end of the seventeenth century, stories were becoming more formalised, with the collections of Madame d'Aulnoy and Charles Perrault in France and *The Pentameron* in Italy. The next great collection came over a century later and was *Nursery and Household Tales* by Jakob and Wilhelm Grimm, who were philologists rather than folklorists. It was the oral tradition that interested them, and they insisted on the importance of the tales to the German cultural tradition. In the middle of the nineteenth century a Dane, Hans Christian Andersen, produced a series of fairy tales, some original, some a re-telling of folk tales, all of them written in a simple and attractive style that has been matched, perhaps, only by Oscar Wilde in *The Happy Prince and Other Tales*. The last classical collector of fairy stories was a Scot, Andrew Lang, who drew together stories from around the world in twelve 'coloured' fairy books – from *The Blue Fairy Book*, *The Red Fairy Book* and *The Green Fairy Book* right up to *The Mauve Fairy Book* – and these remain a rich source of world-wide fairy stories.

Most of the stories in this book are re-told in the European style, but many have antecedents far older than the European version. A form of 'Cinderella' first appeared in ninth-century China in the *Yu Young Ts Tsu (Miscellany of Forgotten Lore)*. In Europe, the first Cinderella-type story is found in *The Pentameron*, and the version most familiar to us today comes from Perrault's *Cendrillon* (as well as d'Aulnoy's *Finetta, the Cinder-girl*), though whether he took the story from a source of his own or whether he based it on folk tradition is not known. The Grimm brothers con-

6

structed their version, *Aschenputtel*, from a series of Hessian tales; this is much darker and involves self-mutilation by the ugly sisters.

Common themes running through fairy tales were recognised by a Finn, Antii Aarne, who published a classification of folktales in 1910. This was enlarged and expanded by the American folklorist Stith Thompson, and his 1961 catalogue established the widely recognised Aarne–Thompson categorisation of folk and fairy tales. Briefly, the catalogue is divided into: Supernatural Opponents (for example, 'Little Red Riding-Hood'); Supernatural or Enchanted Relatives (for example, 'Cinderella'); Supernatural Tasks (for example, the labours of Hercules); Supernatural Helpers (for example, 'Rumpelstiltskin') and Others (for example, 'Snow White').

If one looks beyond the conventional narrative of fairy tales, a darker but more socially useful pattern can be discovered. Perhaps this is best explained in Bruno Bettelheim's remarkable book *The Uses of Enchantment*. In it he demonstrates the importance of fairy tales to childhood development. Using Freudian analysis, he shows how for children the stories can help explain often conflicting anxieties, which may be feelings of smallness, helplessness or insignificance, or the fear of strangers and the mysteries of the outside world. For instance, 'Hansel and Gretel' deals with the fear of parental desertion and the need to develop independence and overcome hardship. In 'Little Red Riding Hood', Bettelheim observes that the heroine is more mature, more questioning than Hansel and Gretel, and that she is caught up in the conflicts of puberty in which the Wolf can be seen as the selfish, asocial, violent and potentially destructive male, while the huntsman of the Grimm version (not in this anthology) represents the unselfish, social, thoughtful and protective qualities that may also be seen in the male character.

Bettelheim is particularly illuminating when discussing the role of the stepmother in fairy stories. He proposes that since as a child grows older the formerly all-nurturing mother becomes another separate and demanding creature ('make your bed', 'tie your shoelaces', 'tidy your room'), the 'stepmother' concept enables a young child to rationalise the transition from being totally provided for to having to assume a more mature and responsible position in the household.

It takes nothing away from the old fairy and folk tales to analyse them and to see them as a mirror which reflects aspects of an inner world, and the necessary passage from immaturity to maturity. Several of the stories are quite straightforward in this respect: 'Jack and the Beanstalk' (with all its phallic connotations), 'Dick Whittington' and 'Puss in Boots' all depict the necessity for young males to make their way in the world. 'Puss in Boots' shares with 'The Valiant Little Tailor' a sub-text of bluff, if not outright lying, though perhaps Puss can be seen as the imaginary friend who accompanies many young children for a period, so that his exaggerations and deceits remove blame from the protagonist. Thus, in an unthreatening way, do children become aware of what Thomas Traherne called 'the dirty devices of this world'. Others have even more direct messages. The story of 'The Three Little Pigs' demonstrates not only the fatal consequences of unpreparedness, but also the necessity of guile for ultimate reward. Violent ends are frequent, and the demise of two of the little pigs, a troll and several giants are set apart from reality either through anthropomorphism or because the stories belong to 'once upon a time . . .', 'many years ago . . .', or 'in a far country . . .'

There are straightforwardly didactic stories too, teaching fortitude ('The Steadfast Tin Soldier'), unselfishness ('The Little Match Girl') and the penalties of being too curious ('Blue Beard').

Drawn from around the world, these tales share common themes and, in general, come from an oral tradition. Many themes are older than religion; indeed, religion plays little part in most fairy tales, which is why they were discouraged by Puritans on both sides of the Atlantic. It is this universality that commends the stories with all their simplicity and complexities to the modern world.

Further reading

Aesop, *Fables*, Collector's Library, London, 2006

Andersen, *The Ilustrated Tales*, CRW Publishing, London, 2005

Bettelheim, *The Uses of Enchantment*, Random House, New York, 1976

Giambattista, *Il Pentamerone*, Naples, 1674

D'Aulnoy, *Contes des Fées*, Paris, 1697

Grimm, *Grimms' Fairy Tales*, Collector's Library, London, 2004

Lang, *Fairy Books*, Longmans, London, 1889–1912

Perrault, *Les Contes de ma mère l'Oie*, Paris, 1697

Thompson, *Motif-Index of Folk-Literature*, Bloomington, 1932–6

Zipes, *The Oxford Companion to Fairy Tales*, Oxford, 2000

CONTENTS

CONTENTS

CONTENTS

Aladdin and the Wonderful Lamp

There once lived a poor tailor, who had a son called Aladdin, a careless, idle boy who would do nothing but play all day long in the streets with little idle boys like himself. This so grieved the father that he died; yet, in spite of his mother's tears and prayers, Aladdin did not mend his ways.

One day, when he was playing in the streets as usual, a stranger asked him his age, and if he were not the son of Mustapha the tailor. 'I am, sir,' replied Aladdin; 'but he died a long time ago.'

On this the stranger, who was a famous African magician, fell on his neck and kissed him, saying: 'I am your uncle, and knew you from your likeness to my brother. Go to your mother and tell her I am coming.'

Aladdin ran home, and told his mother of his newly found uncle.

'Indeed, child,' she said, 'your father had a brother, but I always thought he was dead.'

However, she prepared supper, and bade Aladdin seek his uncle, who came laden with wine and fruit. He presently fell down and kissed the place where Mustapha used to sit, bidding Aladdin's mother not to be surprised at not having seen him before, as he had been forty years out of the country. He then turned to Aladdin, and asked him his trade, at which the boy hung his head, while his mother burst into tears. On learning that Aladdin was idle and would learn no trade, he offered to take a shop for him and stock it with merchandise. Next day he bought Aladdin a fine suit of clothes, and took him all over the city, showing him the sights, and brought him home at nightfall to his mother, who was overjoyed to see her son so fine.

Next day the magician led Aladdin into some beautiful gardens a long way outside the city gates. They sat down by a fountain, and the magician pulled a cake from his girdle, which he divided between them. They then journeyed onwards till they almost reached the mountains. Aladdin was so tired that he begged to go back, but the magician beguiled him with pleasant stories, and led him on in spite of himself.

At last they came to two mountains divided by a narrow valley.

'We will go no farther,' said the false uncle. 'I will show you something wonderful; only do you gather up sticks while I kindle a fire.'

When it was lit the magician threw on it a powder he had about him, at the same time saying some magical words. The earth trembled a little and opened in front of them, disclosing a square flat stone with a brass ring in the middle to raise it by. Aladdin tried to run away, but the magician caught him and gave him a blow that knocked him down.

'What have I done, uncle?' he said piteously; whereupon the magician said more kindly: 'Fear nothing, but obey me. Beneath this stone lies a treasure which is to be yours, and no one else may touch it, so you must do exactly as I tell you.'

At the word treasure, Aladdin forgot his fears, and grasped the ring as he was told, saying the names of his father and grandfather. The stone came up quite easily and some steps appeared.

'Go down,' said the magician; 'at the foot of those steps you will find an open door leading into three large halls. Tuck up your gown and go through them without touching anything, or you will die instantly. These halls lead into a garden of fine fruit trees. Walk on till you come to a niche in a terrace where stands a lighted lamp. Pour out the oil it contains and bring it to me.'

He drew a ring from his finger and gave it to Aladdin, bidding him prosper.

Aladdin found everything as the magician had said, gathered some fruit off the trees, and, having got the lamp, arrived back at the mouth of the cave. The magician cried out in a great hurry: 'Make haste and give me the lamp.' This Aladdin refused to do until he was out of the cave. The magician flew into a terrible passion, and throwing some more powder on the fire, he said something, and the stone rolled back into its place.

The magician left Persia for ever, which plainly showed that he was no uncle of Aladdin's but a cunning magician who had read in his magic books of a wonderful lamp, which would make him the most powerful man in the world. Though he alone knew where to find it, he could only receive it from the hand of another. He had picked out the foolish Aladdin for this purpose, intending to get the lamp and kill him afterwards.

For two days Aladdin remained in the dark, crying and lamenting. At last he clasped his hands in prayer, and in so doing rubbed the ring, which the magician had forgotten to take from him. Immediately an enormous and frightful genie rose out of the earth, saying: 'What wouldst thou with me? I am the Slave of the Ring, and will obey thee in all things.'

Aladdin fearlessly replied: 'Deliver me from this place!' whereupon the earth opened, and he found himself outside. As soon as his eyes could bear the light he went home, but fainted on the threshold. When he came to himself he told his mother what had passed, and showed her the lamp and the fruits he had gathered in the garden, which were in reality precious stones. He then asked for some food.

'Alas! child,' she said, 'I have nothing in the house, but I have spun a little cotton and will go and sell it.'

Aladdin bade her keep her cotton, for he would sell the lamp instead. As it was very dirty she began to rub it, that it might fetch a higher price. Instantly a hideous genie appeared, and asked what she would have. She fainted away, but Aladdin, snatching the lamp, said boldly: 'Fetch me something to eat!'

The genie returned with a silver bowl, twelve silver plates containing rich meats, two silver cups, and two bottles of wine. Aladdin's mother, when she came to herself, said: 'Whence comes this splendid feast?'

'Ask not, but eat,' replied Aladdin.

So they sat at breakfast till it was dinner-time, and Aladdin and his mother talked about the lamp. She begged him to sell it, and have nothing to do with devils.

'No,' said Aladdin, 'since chance has made us aware of its virtues, we will use it and the ring likewise, which I shall always wear on my finger.' When they had eaten all the genie had brought, Aladdin sold one of the silver plates, and so on till none were left. He then had recourse to the genie, who gave him another set of plates, and thus they lived for many years.

One day Aladdin heard an order from the sultan

proclaiming that everyone was to stay at home and close his shutters while the princess, his daughter, went to and from the bath. Aladdin was seized by a desire to see her face, which was very difficult, as she always went veiled. He hid himself behind the door of the bath, and peeped through a chink. The princess lifted her veil as she went in, and looked so beautiful that Aladdin fell in love with her at first sight. He went home so changed that his mother was frightened. He told her he loved the princess so deeply that he could not live without her, and meant to ask her in marriage of her father. His mother, on hearing this, burst out laughing, but Aladdin at last prevailed upon her to go before the sultan and carry his request. She fetched a napkin and laid in it the magic fruits from the enchanted garden, which sparkled and shone like the most beautiful jewels. She took these with her to please the sultan, and set out, trusting in the lamp. The grand-vizier and the lords of council had just gone in as she entered the hall and placed herself in front of the sultan. He, however, took no notice of her. She went every day for a week, and stood in the same place.

When the council broke up on the sixth day the sultan said to his vizier: 'I see a certain woman in the audience-chamber every day carrying something in a napkin. Call her next time, that I may find out what she wants.'

Next day, at a sign from the vizier, she went up to the foot of the throne, and remained kneeling till the sultan said to her: 'Rise, good woman, and tell me what you want.'

She hesitated, so the sultan sent away all but the vizier, and bade her speak freely, promising to forgive her beforehand for anything she might say. She then told him of her son's violent love for the princess.

'I prayed him to forget her,' she said, 'but in vain; he threatened to do some desperate deed if I refused to go and ask your majesty for the hand of the princess. Now I pray you to forgive not me alone, but my son Aladdin.'

The sultan asked her kindly what she had in the napkin, whereupon she unfolded the jewels and presented them.

He was thunderstruck, and turning to the vizier said: 'What sayest thou? Ought I not to bestow the princess on one who values her at such a price?'

The vizier, who wanted her for his own son, begged the sultan to withhold her for three months, in the course of which he hoped his son would contrive to make him a richer present. The sultan granted this, and told Aladdin's mother that, though he consented to the marriage, she must not appear before him again for three months.

Aladdin waited patiently for nearly three months, but after two had elapsed his mother, going into the city to buy oil, found everyone rejoicing, and asked what was going on.

'Do you not know,' was the answer, 'that the son of the grand-vizier is to marry the sultan's daughter tonight?'

Breathless, she ran and told Aladdin, who was overwhelmed at first, but presently bethought him of the lamp. He rubbed it, and the genie appeared, saying: 'What is thy will?'

Aladdin replied: 'The sultan, as thou knowest, has broken his promise to me, and the vizier's son is to have the princess. My command is that tonight you bring hither the bride and bridegroom.'

'Master, I obey,' said the genie.

Aladdin then went to his chamber, where, sure enough at midnight the genie transported the bed containing the vizier's son and the princess.

'Take this new-married man,' he said, 'and put him outside in the cold, and return at daybreak.'

Whereupon the genie took the vizier's son out of bed, leaving Aladdin with the princess.

'Fear nothing,' Aladdin said to her; 'you are my wife, promised to me by your unjust father, and no harm shall come to you.'

The princess was too frightened to speak, and passed the most miserable night of her life, while Aladdin lay down beside her and slept soundly. At the appointed hour the genie fetched in the shivering bridegroom, laid him in his place, and transported the bed back to the palace.

Presently the sultan came to wish his daughter good-morning. The unhappy vizier's son jumped up and hid himself, while the princess would not say a word, and was very sorrowful.

The sultan sent her mother to her, who said: 'How comes it, child, that you will not speak to your father? What has happened?'

The princess sighed deeply, and at last told her mother how, during the night, the bed had been carried into some strange house, and what had passed there. Her mother did not believe her in the least, but bade her rise and consider it an idle dream.

The following night exactly the same thing happened, and next morning, on the princess's refusing to speak, the sultan threatened to cut off her head. She then confessed all, bidding him ask the vizier's son if it were not so. The sultan told the vizier to ask his son, who owned the truth, adding that, dearly as he loved the princess, he had rather die than go through another such fearful night, and wished to be separated from her. His wish was granted, and there was an end of feasting and rejoicing.

When the three months were over, Aladdin sent his mother to remind the sultan of his promise. She stood in the same place as before, and the sultan, who had forgotten Aladdin, at once remembered him, and sent for her. On seeing her poverty the sultan felt less inclined than ever to keep his word, and asked the vizier's advice, who counselled him to set so high a value on the princess that no man living could come up to it.

The sultan then turned to Aladdin's mother, saying: 'Good woman, a sultan must remember his promises, and I will remember mine, but your son must first send me forty basins of gold, brimful with jewels, carried by forty black slaves, led by as many white ones, splendidly dressed. Tell him that I await his answer.' The mother of Aladdin bowed low and went home, thinking all was lost.

She gave Aladdin the message, adding: 'He may wait long enough for your answer!'

'Not so long, mother, as you think,' her son sais. 'I would do a great deal more than that for the princess.'

He summoned the genie, and in a few moments the eighty slaves arrived, and filled up the small house and garden.

Aladdin made them set out to the palace, two and two, followed by his mother. They were so richly dressed, with such splendid jewels in their girdles, that everyone crowded to see them and the golden basins they carried on their heads.

*He summoned the genie, and in a few moments the
eighty slaves arrived*

They entered the palace, and, after kneeling before
the sultan, stood in a half-circle round the throne
with their arms crossed, while Aladdin's mother
presented them to the sultan.

He hesitated no longer, but said: 'Good woman,
return and tell your son that I wait for him with open
arms.'

She lost no time in telling Aladdin, bidding him make haste. But Aladdin first called the genie. 'I would like a scented bath,' he said, 'a richly embroidered habit, a horse surpassing the sultan's, and twenty slaves to attend me. Besides this, six slaves, beautifully dressed, to wait on my mother; and lastly, ten thousand pieces of gold in ten purses.'

No sooner said than done. Aladdin mounted his horse and passed through the streets, the slaves strewing gold as they went. Those who had played with him in his childhood knew him not, he had grown so handsome.

When the sultan saw him he came down from his throne, embraced him, and led him into a hall where a feast was spread, intending to marry him to the princess that very day.

But Aladdin refused, saying, 'I must build a palace fit for her,' and took his leave.

Once home he said to the genie: 'Build me a palace of the finest marble, set with jasper, agate and other precious stones. In the middle you shall build me a large hall with a dome, its four walls of massy gold and silver, each side having six windows, whose lattices, all except one, which is to be left unfinished, must be set with diamonds and rubies. There must be stables and horses and grooms and slaves; go and see about it!'

The palace was finished by next day, and the genie carried him there and showed him all his orders faithfully carried out, even to the laying of a velvet carpet from Aladdin's palace to the sultan's. Aladdin's mother then dressed herself carefully, and walked to the palace with her slaves, while he followed her on horseback. The sultan sent musicians with trumpets and cymbals to meet them, so that the air resounded with music and cheers. She was taken to the princess, who saluted her and treated her with great honour. At night the princess said goodbye to her father, and set out on the carpet for Aladdin's palace, with his mother at her side, and followed by the hundred slaves. She was charmed at the sight of Aladdin, who ran to receive her.

'Princess,' he said, 'blame your beauty for my boldness if I have displeased you.'

She told him that, having seen him, she willingly obeyed her father in this matter. After the wedding had taken place Aladdin led her into the hall, where a feast was spread, and she supped with him, after which they danced till midnight.

Next day Aladdin invited the sultan to see the palace. On entering the hall with the four-and-twenty windows, with their rubies, diamonds, and emeralds, he cried: 'It is a world's wonder! There is only one thing that surprises me. Was it by accident that one window was left unfinished?'

'No, sir, by design,' returned Aladdin. 'I wished your majesty to have the glory of finishing this palace.'

The sultan was pleased, and sent for the best jewellers in the city. He showed them the unfinished window, and bade them fit it up like the others.

'Sir,' replied their spokesman, 'we cannot find jewels enough.'

The sultan had his own fetched, which they soon used, but to no purpose, for in a month's time the work was not half done. Aladdin, knowing that their task was vain, bade them undo their work and carry the jewels back, and the genie finished the window at his command. The sultan was surprised to receive his jewels again and visited Aladdin, who showed him the window finished. The sultan embraced him, the envious vizier meanwhile hinting that it was the work of enchantment.

Aladdin had won the hearts of the people by his gentle bearing. He was made captain of the sultan's armies, and won several battles for him, but remained modest and courteous as before, and lived thus in peace and content for several years.

But far away in Africa the magician remembered Aladdin, and by his magic arts discovered that Aladdin, instead of perishing miserably in the cave, had escaped, and had married a princess, with whom he was living in great honour and wealth. He knew that the poor tailor's son could only have accomplished this by means of the lamp, and travelled night and day till he reached the capital of China, bent on Aladdin's ruin. As he passed through the town he heard people talking everywhere about a marvellous palace.

'Forgive my ignorance,' he asked, 'what is this palace you speak of?'

'Have you not heard of Prince Aladdin's palace,' was the reply, 'the greatest wonder of the world? I will direct you if you have a mind to see it.'

The magician thanked him who spoke, and having seen the palace knew that it had been raised by the genie of the lamp, and became half mad with rage. He determined to get hold of the lamp, and again plunge Aladdin into the deepest poverty.

Unluckily, Aladdin had gone a-hunting for eight days, which gave the magician plenty of time. He bought a dozen copper lamps put them into a basket, and went to the palace, crying: 'New lamps for old!' followed by a jeering crowd.

26

The princess, sitting in the hall of four-and-twenty windows, sent a slave to find out what the noise was about. She came back laughing, so that the princess scolded her.

'Madam,' replied the slave, 'who can help laughing to see an old fool offering to exchange fine new lamps for old ones?'

Another slave, hearing this, said: 'There is an old one on the cornice there which he can have.'

Now this was the magic lamp, which Aladdin had left there, as he could not take it out hunting with him. The princess, not knowing its value, laughingly bade the slave take it and make the exchange.

She went and said to the magician: 'Give me a new lamp for this.'

He snatched it and bade the slave take her choice, amid the jeers of the crowd. Little he cared, but left off crying his lamps, and went out of the city gates to a lonely place, where he remained till nightfall, when he pulled out the lamp and rubbed it. The genie appeared, and at the magician's command carried him, together with the palace and the princess in it, to a lonely place in Africa.

Next morning the sultan looked out of the window towards Aladdin's palace and rubbed his eyes, for it was gone. He sent for the vizier, and asked what had become of the palace. The vizier looked out too, and was lost in astonishment. He again put it down to enchantment, and this time the sultan believed him, and sent thirty men on horseback to fetch Aladdin in chains. They met him riding home, bound him, and forced him to go with them on foot. The people, however, who loved him, followed, armed, to see that he came to no harm. He was carried before the sultan,

The magican snatched the lamp

who ordered the executioner to cut off his head. The executioner made Aladdin kneel down, bandaged his eyes, and raised his scimitar to strike.

At that instant the vizier, who saw that the crowd had forced their way into the courtyard and were scaling the walls to rescue Aladdin, called to the executioner to stay his hand. The people, indeed, looked so threatening that the sultan gave way and ordered Aladdin to be unbound, and pardoned him in the sight of the crowd.

Aladdin now begged to know what he had done.

'False wretch!' said the sultan, 'come hither,' and showed him from the window the place where his palace had stood.

Aladdin was so amazed that he could not say a word.

'Where is my palace and my daughter?' demanded the sultan. 'For the first I am not so deeply concerned, but my daughter I must have, and you must find her or lose your head.'

Aladdin begged for forty days in which to find her, promising if he failed to return and suffer death at the sultan's pleasure. His prayer was granted, and he went forth sadly from the sultan's presence. For three days he wandered about like a madman, asking everyone what had become of his palace, but they only laughed and pitied him. He came to the banks of a river, and knelt down to say his prayers before throwing himself in. In so doing he rubbed the magic ring he still wore.

The genie he had seen in the cave appeared, and asked his will.

'Save my life, genie,' said Aladdin, 'and bring my palace back.'

'That is not in my power,' said the genie; 'I am only the slave of the ring; you must ask the slave of the lamp.'

'Even so,' said Aladdin; 'but thou canst take me to the palace, and set me down under my dear wife's window.' He at once found himself in Africa, under the window of the princess, and fell asleep out of sheer weariness.

He was awakened by the singing of the birds, and his heart was lighter. He saw plainly that all his misfortunes were owing to the loss of the lamp, and vainly wondered who had robbed him of it.

That morning the princess rose earlier than she had done since she had been carried into Africa by the magician, whose company she was forced to endure once a day. She, however, treated him so harshly that he dared not live there altogether. As she was dressing, one of her women looked out and saw Aladdin. The princess ran and opened the window, and at the noise she made Aladdin looked up. She called to him to come to her, and great was the joy of these lovers at seeing each other again.

After he had kissed her Aladdin said: 'I beg of you, princess, in God's name, before we speak of anything else, for your own sake and mine, tell me what has become of an old lamp I left on the cornice in the hall of four-and-twenty windows, when I went a-hunting.'

'Alas!' she said, 'I am the innocent cause of our sorrows,' and told him of the exchange of the lamp.

'Now I know,' cried Aladdin, 'that we have to thank the African magician for this! Where is the lamp?'

'He carries it about with him,' said the princess. 'I know, for he pulled it out of his breast to show me. He wishes me to break my faith with you and marry him, saying that you were beheaded by my father's command. He is forever speaking ill of you, but I only reply by my tears. If I persist, I doubt not that he will use violence.'

Aladdin comforted her, and left her for a while. He changed clothes with the first person he met in the town, and having bought a certain powder returned to the princess, who let him in by a little side door.

'Put on your most beautiful dress,' he said to her, 'and receive the magician with smiles, leading him to believe that you have forgotten me. Invite him to sup with you, and say you wish to taste the wine of his country. He will go for some, and while he is gone I will tell you what to do.'

She listened carefully to Aladdin, and when he left arrayed herself gaily for the first time since she left China. She put on a girdle and headdress of diamonds, and seeing in a glass that she looked more beautiful than ever, received the magician, saying to his great amazement: 'I have made up my mind that Aladdin is dead, and that all my tears will not bring him back to me, so I am resolved to mourn no more, and have therefore invited you to sup with me; but I am tired of wines from China and would fain taste those of Africa.'

The magician flew to his cellar, and the princess put the powder Aladdin had given her in her cup. When he returned she asked him to drink her health in the wine of Africa, handing him her cup in exchange for his as a sign she was reconciled to him.

Before drinking the magician made her a speech in praise of her beauty, but the princess cut him short saying: 'Let me drink first, and you shall say what you will afterwards.' She set her cup to her lips and kept it there, while the magician drained his to the dregs and fell back lifeless.

The princess then opened the door to Aladdin, and flung her arms round his neck, but Aladdin put her away, bidding her to leave him, as he had more to do. He then went to the dead magician, took the lamp out of the bosom of his garment, and bade the genie carry the palace and all in it back to China. This was done, and the princess in her chamber only felt two little shocks, and little thought she was at home again.

The sultan, who was sitting in his closet, mourning for his lost daughter, happened to look up, and rubbed his eyes, for there stood the palace as before!

He hastened thither, and Aladdin received him in the hall of the four-and-twenty windows, with the princess at his side. Aladdin told him what had happened, and showed him the dead body of the magician, that he might believe. A ten days' feast was proclaimed, and it seemed as if Aladdin might now live the rest of his life in peace; but it was not to be.

The African magician had a younger brother, who was, if possible, more wicked and more cunning than himself. He travelled to China to avenge his brother's death, and went to visit a pious woman called Fatima, thinking she might be of use to him. He entered her cell and clapped a dagger to her breast, telling her to rise and do his bidding on pain of death. He changed clothes with her, coloured his face like hers, put on her veil and murdered her, that she might tell no tales. Then he went towards the palace of Aladdin, and all the people thinking he was the holy woman, gathered round him, kissing his hands and begging his blessing. When he got to the palace there was such a noise going on round him that the princess bade her slave look out of the window and ask what was the matter. The slave said it was the holy woman, curing people by her touch of their ailments, whereupon the princess, who had long desired to see Fatima, sent for her. On coming to the princess the magician offered up a prayer for her health and prosperity. When she had thanked him the princess made him sit by her, and begged him to stay with her always. The false Fatima, who wished for nothing better, consented, but kept his veil down for fear of discovery. The princess showed him the hall, and asked him what he thought of it.

'It is truly beautiful,' said the false Fatima. 'In my mind it wants but one thing.'

But when the magician came near, Aladdin, seizing his dagger, pierced him to the heart

'And what is that?' said the princess.

'If only a roc's egg,' replied he, 'were hung up from the middle of this dome, it would be the wonder of the world.'

After this the princess could think of nothing but a

33

roc's egg, and when Aladdin returned from hunting he found her in a very ill humour. He begged to know what was amiss, and she told him that all her pleasure in the hall was spoilt for the want of a roc's egg hanging from the dome.

'It that is all,' replied Aladdin, 'you shall soon be happy.'

He left her and rubbed the lamp, and when the genie appeared commanded him to bring a roc's egg. The genie gave such a loud and terrible shriek that the hall shook.

'Wretch!' he cried, 'is it not enough that I have done everything for you, but you must command me to bring my master and hang him up in the midst of this dome? You and your wife and your palace deserve to be burnt to ashes; but this request does not come from you, but from the brother of the African magician whom you destroyed. He is now in your palace disguised as the holy woman – whom he murdered. He it was who put that wish into your wife's head. Take care of yourself, for he means to kill you.' So saying the genie disappeared.

Aladdin went back to the princess, saying his head ached, and requesting that the holy Fatima should be fetched to lay her hands on it. But when the magician came near, Aladdin, seizing his dagger, pierced him to the heart.

'What have you done?' cried the princess. 'You have killed the holy woman!'

'Not so,' replied Aladdin, 'but a wicked magician,' and told her of how she had been deceived.

After this Aladdin and his wife lived in peace. He succeeded the sultan when he died, and reigned for many years, leaving behind him a long line of kings.

Ali Baba and the Forty Thieves

In a town in Persia there dwelt two brothers, one named Cassim, the other Ali Baba. Cassim was married to a rich wife and lived in plenty, while Ali Baba had to maintain his wife and children by cutting wood in a neighbouring forest and selling it in the town. One day, when Ali Baba was in the forest, he saw a troop of men on horseback, coming towards him in a cloud of dust. He was afraid they were robbers, and climbed into a tree for safety. When they came up to him and dismounted, he counted forty of them. They unbridled their horses and tied them to trees. The finest man among them, whom Ali Baba took to be their captain, went a little way among some bushes, and said: 'Open, Sesame!' so plainly that Ali Baba heard him. A door opened in the rocks, and having made the troop go in, he followed them, and the door shut again of itself. They stayed some time inside, and Ali Baba, fearing they might come out and catch him, was forced to sit patiently in the tree. At last the door opened again, and the forty thieves came out. As the captain went in last he came out first, and made them all pass by him; he then closed the door, saying: 'Shut, Sesame!' Every man bridled his horse and mounted, the captain put himself at their head, and they returned as they came.

Then Ali Baba climbed down and went to the door concealed among the bushes, and said: 'Open, Sesame!' and it flew open. Ali Baba, who expected a dull, dismal place, was greatly surprised to find it large

He went in and the door shut behind him

and well lighted, hollowed by the hand of man in the form of a vault, which received the light from an opening in the ceiling. He saw rich bales of merchandise – silk, stuff-brocades, all piled together, and gold and silver in heaps, and money in leather purses. He went in and the door shut behind him. He did not look at the silver, but brought out as many bags of gold as he thought his asses, which were browsing outside, could carry, loaded them with the bags, and hid it all with faggots. Using the words: 'Shut, Sesame!' he closed the door and went home.

Then he drove his asses into the yard, shut the gates, carried the money-bags to his wife, and emptied them out before her. He bade her keep the secret, and he would go and bury the gold. 'Let me first measure it,' said his wife. 'I will go and borrow a measure from someone, while you dig the hole.' So she ran to the wife of Cassim and borrowed a measure. Knowing Ali Baba's poverty, the sister was curious to find out what sort of grain his wife wished to measure, and artfully put some suet at the bottom of the measure. Ali Baba's wife went home and set the measure on the heap of gold, and filled it and emptied it often, to her great content. She then carried it back to her sister, without noticing that a piece of gold was sticking to it, which Cassim's wife perceived directly her back was turned. She grew very curious, and said to Cassim when he came home: 'Cassim, your brother is richer than you. He does not count his money, he measures it.' He begged her to explain this riddle, which she did by showing him the piece of money and telling him where she found it. Then Cassim grew so envious that he could not sleep, and went to his brother in the morning before sunrise. 'Ali Baba,' he said, showing him the gold piece, 'you pretend to be poor and yet you measure gold.' By this Ali Baba perceived that through his wife's folly Cassim and his wife knew their secret, so he confessed all and offered Cassim a share. 'That I expect,' said Cassim; 'but I must know where to find the treasure, otherwise I will discover all, and you will lose all.' Ali Baba, more out of kindness than fear, told him of the cave, and the very words to use. Cassim left Ali Baba, meaning to be beforehand with him and get the treasure for himself. He rose early next morning, and set out with three mules loaded with great chests. He soon found the place, and the door in the rock. He said: 'Open, Sesame!' and the door opened and shut behind him. He could have feasted his eyes all day on the treasures, but he now hastened to gather together as much of it as possible; but when he was ready to go he could not remember what to say for thinking of his great riches. Instead of 'Sesame', he said: 'Open, Barley!' and the door remained fast. He named several different sorts of grain, all but the right one, and the door still stuck fast. He was so frightened at the danger he was in that he had as much forgotten the word as if he had never heard it.

About noon the robbers returned to their cave, and saw Cassim's mules roving about with great chests on their backs. This gave them the alarm; they drew their sabres, and went to the door, which opened on their captain's saying: 'Open, Sesame!' Cassim, who had heard the trampling of their horses' feet, resolved to sell his life dearly, so when the door opened he leaped out and threw the captain down. In vain, however, for the robbers with their sabres soon killed him. On entering the cave they saw all the bags laid ready, and could not imagine how anyone had got in without knowing their secret. They cut Cassim's body into four quarters, and nailed them up inside the cave, in order to frighten anyone who should venture in, and went away in search of more treasure.

As night drew on Cassim's wife grew very uneasy,

and ran to her brother-in-law, and told him where her husband had gone. Ali Baba did his best to comfort her, and set out to the forest in search of Cassim. The first thing he saw on entering the cave was his dead brother. Full of horror, he put the body on one of his asses, and bags of gold on the other two, and, covering all with some faggots, returned home. He drove the two asses laden with gold into his own yard, and led the other to Cassim's house. The door was opened by the slave Morgiana, whom he knew to be both brave and cunning. Unloading the ass, he said to her: 'This is the body of your master, who has been murdered, but whom we must bury as though he had died in his bed. I will speak with you again, but now tell your mistress I am come.' The wife of Cassim, on learning the fate of her husband, broke out into cries and tears, but Ali Baba offered to let her live with him and his wife if she would promise to keep his counsel and leave everything to Morgiana; whereupon she agreed, and dried her eyes.

Morgiana, meanwhile, sought an apothecary and asked him for some lozenges. 'My poor master,' she said, 'can neither eat nor speak, and no one knows what his distemper is.' She carried home the lozenges and returned next day weeping, and asked for an essence only given to those just about to die. Thus, in the evening, no one was surprised to hear the wretched shrieks and cries of Cassim's wife and Morgiana, telling everyone that Cassim was dead. The day after Morgiana went to an old cobbler near the gates of the town who opened his stall early, put a piece of gold in his hand, and bade him follow her with his needle and thread. Having bound his eyes with a handkerchief, she took him to the room where the body lay, pulled off the bandage, and bade him sew the quarters together, after which she covered his eyes again and led him home. Then they buried Cassim, and Morgiana his slave followed him to the grave, weeping and tearing her hair, while Cassim's wife stayed at home uttering lamentable cries. Next day Ali Baba took possession of the house and gave Cassim's shop to his eldest son.

The forty thieves, on their return to the cave, were much astonished to find Cassim's body gone and some of their money-bags. 'We are certainly discovered,' said the captain, 'and shall be undone if we cannot find out who it is that knows our secret. Two men must have known it; we have killed one, we must now find the other. To this end one of you who is bold and artful must go into the city dressed as a

One of you who is bold and artful must go into the city dressed as a traveller

traveller, and discover whom we have killed, and whether men talk of the strange manner of his death. If the messenger fails he must lose his life, lest we be betrayed.' One of the thieves started up and offered to do this, and after the rest had highly commended him for his bravery he disguised himself, and happened to enter the town at daybreak, just by Baba Mustapha's stall. The thief bade him good-day, saying: 'Honest man, how can you possibly see to stitch at your age?' 'Old as I am,' replied the cobbler, 'I have very good eyes, and will you believe me when I tell you that I sewed a dead body together in a place where I had less light than I have now.' The robber was overjoyed at his good fortune, and, giving him a piece of gold, desired to be shown the house where he stitched up the dead body. At first Mustapha refused, saying that he had been blindfolded; but when the robber gave him another piece of gold he began to think he might remember the turnings if blindfolded as before. This means succeeded; the robber partly led him, and was partly guided by him, right to the house he sought, the door of which the robber marked with a piece of chalk. Then, well pleased, he bade farewell to Baba Mustapha and returned to the forest. By and by Morgiana, going out, saw the mark the robber had made, quickly guessed that some mischief was brewing, and fetching a piece of chalk marked two or three doors on each side, without saying anything to her master or mistress.

The thief, meantime, told his comrades of his discovery. The captain thanked him, and bade him show him the house he had marked. But when they came to it they saw that five or six of the houses were chalked in the same manner. The guide was so confounded that he knew not which one to choose, and when they returned he was at once beheaded for having failed. Another robber was dispatched, and, having won over Baba Mustapha, marked the house in red chalk; but Morgiana being again too clever for them, the second messenger was put to death also. The captain now resolved to go himself, but, wiser than the others, he did not mark the house, but looked at it so closely that he could not fail to remember it. He returned, and ordered his men to go into the neighbouring villages and buy nineteen mules, and thirty-eight leather jars, all empty except one, which was to be full of oil. The captain put one of his men, fully armed, into each, rubbing the outside of the jars with oil from the full vessel. Then the nineteen mules were loaded with thirty-seven robbers in jars, and the jar of oil, and reached the town by dusk. The captain stopped his mules in front of Ali Baba's house, and said to Ali Baba, who was sitting outside for coolness: 'I have brought some oil from a distance to sell at tomorrow's market, but it is now so late that I know not where to pass the night, unless you will do me the favour to take me in.' Though Ali Baba had seen the captain of the robbers in the forest, he did not recognise him in the disguise of an oil merchant. He bade him welcome, opened his gates for the mules to enter, and went to Morgiana to bid her prepare a bed and supper for his guest. He brought the stranger into his hall, and after they had supped went again to speak to Morgiana in the kitchen, while the captain went into the yard under pretence of seeing after his mules, but really to tell his men what to do. Beginning at the first jar and ending at the last, he said to each man: 'As soon as I throw some stones from the window of the chamber where I lie, cut the jars open with your knives and come out, and I will be with you in a trice.' He returned to the house, and Morgiana led him to his chamber. She then told Abdallah, her

He bade him welcome and went to Morgiana to bid her prepare a bed and supper for his guest

fellow-slave, to set on the pot to make some broth for her master, who had gone to bed. Meanwhile her lamp went out, and she had no more oil in the house. 'Do not be uneasy,' said Abdallah; 'go into the yard and take some out of one of those jars.' Morgiana thanked him for his advice, took the oil pot, and went into the yard. When she came to the first jar the robber inside said softly: 'Is it time?'

Any other slave but Morgiana, on finding a man in the jar instead of the oil she wanted, would have screamed and made a noise; but she, knowing the danger her master was in, bethought herself of a plan, and answered quietly: 'Not yet, but presently.' She went to all the jars, giving the same answer, till she came to the jar of oil. She now saw that her master, thinking to entertain an oil merchant, had let thirty-eight robbers into his house. She filled her oil pot, went back to the kitchen, and, having lit her lamp, went again to the oil jar and filled a large kettle full of oil. When it boiled she went and poured enough oil into every jar to stifle and kill the robber inside. When this brave deed was done she went back to the kitchen, put out the fire and the lamp, and waited to see what would happen.

In a quarter of an hour the captain of the robbers awoke, got up, and opened the window. As all seemed quiet, he threw down some little pebbles which hit the jars. He listened, and as none of his men seemed to stir he grew uneasy, and went down into the yard. On going to the first jar and saying, 'Are you asleep?' he smelt the hot boiled oil, and knew at once that his plot to murder Ali Baba and his household had been discovered. He found all the gang was dead, and, missing the oil out of the last jar, became aware of the manner of their death. He then forced the lock of a door leading into a garden, and climbing over several walls made his escape. Morgiana heard and saw all this, and, rejoicing at her success, went to bed and fell asleep.

At daybreak Ali Baba arose, and, seeing the oil jars still there, asked why the merchant had not gone with his mules. Morgiana bade him look in the first jar and see if there was any oil. Seeing a man, he started back in terror. 'Have no fear,' said Morgiana; 'the man cannot harm you: he is dead.' Ali Baba, when he had recovered somewhat from his astonishment, asked what had become of the merchant. 'Merchant!' said she, 'he is no more a merchant than I am!' and she told him the whole story, assuring him that it was a plot of the robbers of the forest, of whom only three were left, and that the white and red chalk marks had something to do with it. Ali Baba at once gave Morgiana her freedom, saying that he owed her his life. They then buried the bodies in Ali Baba's garden, while the mules were sold in the market by his slaves.

The captain returned to his lonely cave, which seemed frightful to him without his lost companions, and firmly resolved to avenge them by killing Ali Baba. He dressed himself carefully, and went into the town, where he took lodgings in an inn. In the course of a great many journeys to the forest he carried away many rich stuffs and much fine linen, and set up a shop opposite that of Ali Baba's son. He called himself Cogia Hassan, and as he was both civil and well dressed he soon made friends with Ali Baba's son, and through him with Ali Baba, whom he was continually asking to sup with him. Ali Baba, wishing to return his kindness, invited him into his house and received him smiling, thanking him for his kindness to his son. When the merchant was about to take his leave Ali Baba stopped him, saying: 'Where are you going, sir, in such haste? Will you not stay and sup with me?' The merchant refused, saying that he had a reason; and, on Ali Baba's asking him what that was, he replied: 'It is, sir, that I can eat no victuals that have any salt in them.' 'If that is all,' said Ali Baba, 'let me tell you that there shall be no salt in either the meat or the bread that we eat tonight.' He went to give this order to Morgiana, who was much surprised. 'Who is this man,' she said, 'who eats no salt with his meat?' 'He is an honest man, Morgiana,' returned her master; 'therefore do as I bid you.' But she could not withstand a desire to see this strange man, so she helped Abdallah to carry up the dishes, and saw in a moment that Cogia Hassan was the robber captain, and carried a dagger under his garment. 'I am not surprised,' she said to herself, 'that this wicked man, who intends to kill my master, will eat no salt with him; but I will hinder his plans.'

She sent up the supper by Abdallah, while she made ready for one of the boldest acts that could be thought on. When the dessert had been served, Cogia Hassan was left alone with Ali Baba and his son, whom he thought to make drunk and then to murder. Morgiana, meanwhile, put on a headdress like a dancing-girl's, and clasped a girdle round her waist, from which hung a dagger with a silver hilt, and said to Abdallah: 'Take your tabor, and let us go and divert our master and his guest.' Abdallah took his tabor and played before Morgiana until they came to the door, where Abdallah stopped playing and Morgiana made a low courtesy. 'Come in, Morgiana,' said Ali

Abdallah began to play and Morgiana to dance

Baba, 'and let Cogia Hassan see what you can do;' and, turning to Cogia Hassan, he said: 'She's my gifted housekeeper.' Cogia Hassan was by no means pleased, for he feared that his chance of killing Ali Baba was gone for the present; but he pretended great eagerness to see Morgiana, and Abdallah began to play and Morgiana to dance. After she had performed several dances she drew her dagger and made passes

47

with it, sometimes pointing it at her own breast, sometimes at her master's, as if it were part of the dance. Suddenly, out of breath, she snatched the tabor from Abdallah with her left hand, and, holding the dagger in her right hand, held out the tabor to her master. Ali Baba and his son put a piece of gold into it, and Cogia Hassan, seeing that she was coming to him, pulled out his purse to make her a present, but while he was putting his hand into it Morgiana plunged the dagger into his heart.

'Unhappy girl!' cried Ali Baba and his son, 'what have you done to ruin us?'

'It was to preserve you, master, not to ruin you,' answered Morgiana. 'See here,' opening the false merchant's garment and showing the dagger; 'see what an enemy you have entertained! Remember, he would eat no salt with you, and what more would you have? Look at him! he is both the false oil merchant and the captain of the forty thieves.'

Ali Baba was so grateful to Morgiana for thus saving his life that he offered her to his son in marriage, who readily consented, and a few days after the wedding was celebrated with greatest splendour.

At the end of a year Ali Baba, hearing nothing of the two remaining robbers, judged they were dead, and set out to the cave. The door opened on his saying: 'Open, Sesame!' He went in, and saw that nobody had been there since the captain left it. He brought away as much gold as he could carry, and returned to town. He told his son the secret of the cave, which his son handed down in his turn, so the children and grandchildren of Ali Baba were rich to the end of their lives.

Baba-Yaga and Vasilisa the Fair

A long time ago there lived a merchant and his wife; they had one child, a girl called Vasilisa. One day the mother placed a little doll in the child's hands, she said, 'My child, I am dying. Take this doll as my blessing. Always keep it with you and never show it to anybody. If anything bad happens to you, give the doll food and ask her for guidance.' Shortly afterwards the mother died.

The merchant soon became lonely and decided to marry again. He married a widow he thought would be a good mother but both she and her two daughters were envious of Vasilisa's beauty. They gave her heavy outdoor work to do, so she would grow thin and her face turn ugly in the wind and the sun.

Despite this, Vasilisa became more beautiful every day. For each day she gave her doll food and asked for advice. Having finished eating, the doll would help with the tasks and even bring Vasilisa herbs to prevent sunburn.

As the years passed, Vasilisa grew ever more beautiful as her stepmother's hatred of her intensified.

Then, while Vasilisa's father was away on business, the stepmother moved the family to the edge of a dense birch forest. This was not just any birch forest, for in this forest lived the terrifying witch, Baba-Yaga. A witch who ate people like others ate chicken.

Every day, the stepmother sent Vasilisa into the forest, but the girl always returned safe and sound with the guidance of her magic doll.

Then one night, the stepmother crept around the house and extinguished all the candles. As the last candle failed, she said in a loud voice.

'It's impossible to finish our work in the darkness. Somebody must go to Baba-Yaga and ask for a light.'

'I'm not going,' said the first stepdaughter, who was stitching lace. 'I can see my needle.'

'And I'm not going,' said the second stepdaughter, who was knitting stockings, 'I can see my needles.'

So Vasilisa was thrown out into the dark forbidding forest. Despite her fear, she fed her magic doll and asked for its advice.

'Don't be afraid, Vasilisa,' said the doll. 'Go to Baba-Yaga and ask her to give you a light.'

All that night, Vasilisa walked nervously through the forest holding the doll who guided her path. Then suddenly, she saw a horseman rushing by. His face and clothes were white and he was riding a white horse. As he passed the first light of dawn appeared across the sky. Then, another horseman came by. His face and clothes were red and he was riding a red horse. As he passed the sun began to rise. Vasilisa had never seen such strange men and she was very surprised.

She walked all day, until at last she came to Baba-Yaga's hut, which loomed forbiddingly on its large chicken legs. A fence made of human bones surrounded the hut. It was crowned with human skulls. The gate had a sharp set of teeth that served as a lock. Vasilisa was terribly afraid.

Suddenly, another horseman galloped by. His face and clothes were black and he was riding a black horse. He rode through the gates and disappeared. As he passed, night descended.

*Baba-Yaga's hut, which stood forbidding
on its large chicken legs*

As the sky darkened the eyes of the skulls began to glow. Their light illuminated the forest. Vasilisa trembled, she wanted to run but her legs would not move. Almost immediately she heard a hideous noise. The earth shook, the trees groaned and there was Baba-Yaga, riding in her mortar. She stopped and sniffed the air.

'I smell a human!' she cried. 'Who is here?'

Vasilisa stepped forward, trembling with fear. She said, 'I am, Vasilisa. My stepmother sent me to you to ask for a light.'

'I know of her,' Baba-Yaga replied. 'Stay with me

51

for a while. If you work well, I will give you light. If you do not, I will cook you and eat you.'

Baba-Yaga commanded the gates to open and rode in. Vasilisa followed and the gates closed fast behind her.

As they entered the hut, Baba-Yaga ordered Vasilisa to bring her what was on the stove. There was enough food to feed ten men; then from the cupboard she collected kvas, mead, beer and wine. Baba-Yaga ate and drank everything. She left Vasilisa nothing but some crusts of bread.

'I'm tired,' Baba-Yaga said. 'Tomorrow, Vasilisa, you must clean the yard, sweep the hut, cook the supper and wash the linen.'

'Then,' she added, 'you must go to the corn bin and separate seed by seed the mildewed corn from the good corn, and mind that you remove all the black bits. If you don't complete these tasks, I will eat you.'

Soon Baba-Yaga started snoring, her long nose rattled against the roof of the hut. Vasilisa took her doll out of her pocket, gave it a crust of bread and said, 'Please help me. Baba-Yaga has given me an impossible task to do and if I fail she will eat me.'

The doll replied, 'Don't be afraid, Vasilisa, eat your supper and go to bed. Mornings are wiser than evenings.'

Although Vasilisa woke early the next morning, Baba-Yaga was already up. Vasilisa went to the corn bin and found the doll picking out the last black bits. The other tasks were also fulfilled. The doll said, 'All you have to do now is prepare the supper and after that you can rest.' Vasilisa thanked the doll and went to prepare supper. She cooked the food, laid the table and waited.

Presently, the skulls' eyes began to shine, the trees groaned, the earth trembled, and there was Baba-Yaga.

'Have you done what I told you?' she asked Vasilisa.

'See for yourself,' replied the girl.

Baba-Yaga was very upset, for she wanted to eat the girl but the tasks were all completed. Hiding her anger, she said, 'Very good,' and then cried loudly, 'My faithful servants grind the wheat!'

From nowhere three pairs of hands appeared. They took the wheat and vanished.

Baba-Yaga ate the supper and said to Vasilisa, 'Tomorrow you must do the same tasks and then you must go to the storeroom and sort out the dirt from the poppy seeds.'

The next morning Baba-Yaga again rode off in her mortar. Vasilisa, with the help of her doll, finished the tasks. In the evening the old woman came back and checked everything over. Three pairs of hands appeared. They took the bin of poppy seeds and vanished. Baba-Yaga sat down to eat.

'Why,' she said, 'do you sit there so quiet and still?'

'I'm afraid to speak,' said Vasilisa, 'but would you mind if I asked you some questions?'

'Ask if you want,' said Baba-Yaga, 'but remember that not every question has a good answer.'

Vasilisa hesitated, 'It's just that on my way here I saw a white horseman. Who was he?'

'That was my Bright Day,' answered Baba-Yaga.

Vasilisa continued, 'Then I saw a red horseman. Who was he?'

'That was my Red Sun,' answered Baba-Yaga.

'And then a black horseman overtook me while I was standing outside your gate. Who was he?'

'That was my Black Midnight,' answered Baba-Yaga. 'These horsemen are my faithful servants. Have you further questions?'

Vasilisa remembered the three pairs of hands but remained quiet.

'Now I have a question for you. How have you managed to carry out all the work so quickly?'

Vasilisa replied, 'My mother's blessing helped me.'

'I knew it,' said Baba-Yaga. 'You'd better be gone. I will not have people with blessings in my home.'

With that, the old woman pushed Vasilisa out of the hut and through the gate.

Then she took one of the skulls, stuck it on the end of a stick and gave it to the girl, saying: 'Here's a light for your stepmother and her daughters. That's what you came here for, isn't it?'

Vasilia walked all day and by the evening she reached her home. As she approached the gates she was about to throw away the skull, but suddenly she heard a muffled voice say: 'You must keep me, your stepmother and her daughters have need of me.'

The girl carried the skull into the house. As she entered, the skull fixed its eyes on the stepmother and her two daughters. Its eyes burnt them like fire. They tried to hide, but the piercing eyes followed them and never let them out of their sight. By morning nothing was left of the three women except three heaps of ash on the floor. Vasilisa was unharmed.

She buried the skull in the garden and went to find shelter in the nearest town. Here she lodged with an old woman.

One day the old woman gave Vasilisa some flax. With it Vasilisa spun the most beautiful thread, so fine it was like hair. Then she weaved the thread into the most exquisite cloth. It was brilliant white, soft and so beautiful. Vasilisa gave it to the old woman and said: 'Grandmother, you have been so kind to me, sell this cloth and keep the money.'

The old woman looked at it and said, 'My child, this is too fine to sell. I am going to take it to the Tsar.'

So she brought it to the Tsar as a gift. The Tsar thanked the old woman and gave her many presents before sending her home.

Impressed with the beautiful cloth, the Tsar tried to find someone who could make shirts from it. However all the tailors declined the work, as the cloth was too fine for them to handle. In the end the Tsar called the old woman and said, 'You must also know how to sew the cloth as you made it.'

The old woman replied, 'No, your Majesty. It was not my work. It was done by a girl I took in.'

So the Tsar asked the old woman to see if Vasilisa would make the garments. Vasilisa made the shirts and the old woman took them to the Tsar.

As she waited for the old woman to return, one of the Tsar's servants entered. He said loudly, 'His Majesty wishes to see the needlewoman who has made his wonderful clothes.' So Vasilisa went to the palace.

Vasilisa and the Tsar were captivated by each other and eventually they married.

When Vasilisa's father returned, they invited both him and the old woman to come and live at the palace. Also at the palace was the little doll, for Vasilisa carried it around in her pocket until the day she died.

Beauty and the Beast

Once upon a time, in a very far-off country, there lived a merchant who had been so fortunate in all his undertakings that he was enormously rich. As he had, however, six sons and six daughters, he found that he needed every penny to let them all have everything they fancied, as they were accustomed to do.

But one day a most unexpected misfortune befell them. Their house caught fire and was speedily burnt to the ground, with all the splendid furniture, the books, pictures, gold, silver and precious goods it contained; and this was only the beginning of their troubles. Their father, who had until this moment prospered in all ways, suddenly lost every ship he had upon the sea, either by dint of pirates, shipwreck or fire. Then he heard that his clerks in distant countries, whom he trusted entirely, had proved unfaithful; and at last from great wealth he fell into the direst poverty.

All that he had left was a little house in a desolate place at least a hundred leagues from the town in which he had lived, and to this he was forced to retreat with his children, who were in despair at the idea of leading such a different life. Indeed, the daughters at first hoped that their friends, who had been so numerous while they were rich, would insist on their staying in their houses now they no longer possessed one. But they soon found that they were left alone, and that their former friends even attributed their misfortunes to their own extravagance, and showed no intention of offering them any help. So nothing was left for them but to take their departure to the cottage, which stood in the midst of a dark forest, and seemed to be the most dismal place upon the face of the earth. As they were too poor to have any servants, the girls had to work hard, like peasants, and the sons, for their part, cultivated the fields to earn their living. Roughly clothed, and living in the simplest way, the girls regretted unceasingly the luxuries and amusements of their former life; only the youngest tried to be brave and cheerful. She had been as sad as anyone when misfortune overtook her father, but, soon recovering her natural gaiety, she set to work to make the best of things, to amuse her father and brothers as well as she could and to try to persuade her sisters to join her in dancing and singing. But they would do nothing of the sort, and, because she was not as doleful as themselves, they declared that this miserable life was all she was fit for. But she was really far prettier and cleverer than they were; indeed, she was so lovely that she was always called Beauty. After two years, when they were all beginning to get used to their new life, something happened to disturb their tranquillity. Their father received the news that one of his ships, which he had believed to be lost, had come safely into port with a rich cargo. His sons and daughters at once thought that their poverty was at an end, and wanted to set out directly for the town; but their father, who was more prudent, begged them to wait a little, and, though it was harvest time, and he could ill be spared, determined to go himself first, to make enquiries. Only the youngest daughter had any doubt but that they would soon again be as rich as they were before, or at least rich enough to live comfortably in some town where they would find amusement and gay companions once more. So they all loaded their father with commissions for jewels and dresses which it would have taken a fortune to buy; only Beauty, feeling sure that it was of no use, did not ask for anything. Her father, noticing her silence, said: 'And what shall I bring for you, Beauty?'

'The only thing I wish for is to see you come home safely,' she answered.

But this only vexed her sisters, who fancied she was blaming them for having asked for such costly things. Her father, however, was pleased, but as he thought that at her age she certainly ought to like pretty presents, he told her to choose something.

'Well, dear father,' she said, 'as you insist upon it, I beg that you will bring me a rose. I have not seen one since we came here, and I love them so much.'

So the merchant set out and reached the town as quickly as possible, but only to find that his former companions, believing him to be dead, had divided between them the goods which the ship had brought; and after six months of trouble and expense he found himself as poor as when he started, having been able to recover only just enough to pay the cost of his journey. To make matters worse, he was obliged to leave the town in the most terrible weather, so that by the time he was within a few leagues of his home he was almost exhausted with cold and fatigue. Though he knew it would take some hours to get through the forest, he was so anxious to be at his journey's end that he resolved to go on; but night overtook him, and the deep snow and bitter frost made it impossible for his horse to carry him any farther. Not a house was to be seen; the only shelter he could get was the hollow trunk of a great tree, and there he crouched all the night, which seemed to him the longest he had ever known. In spite of his weariness the howling of the wolves kept him awake, and even when at last the day broke he was not much better off, for the falling snow had covered up every path, and he did not know which way to turn.

At length he made out some sort of track, and though at the beginning it was so rough and slippery that he fell down more than once, it presently became easier, and led him into an avenue of trees which ended in a splendid castle. It seemed to the merchant very strange that no snow had fallen in the avenue, which was entirely composed of orange trees, covered with flowers and fruit. When he reached the first court of the castle he saw before him a flight of agate steps, and went up them, and passed through several splendidly furnished rooms. The pleasant warmth of the air revived him, and he felt very hungry; but there seemed to be nobody in all this vast and splendid palace whom he could ask to give him something to assuage his hunger. Deep silence reigned everywhere, and at last, tired of roaming through empty rooms and galleries, he stopped in a room smaller than the rest, where a clear fire was burning and a couch was drawn up closely to it. Thinking that this must be prepared for someone who was expected, he sat down to wait till he should come, and very soon fell into a sweet sleep.

When his extreme hunger wakened him after several hours, he was still alone; but a little table, upon which was a good dinner, had been drawn up close to him, and, as he had eaten nothing for twenty-four hours, he lost no time in beginning his meal, hoping that he might soon have an opportunity of thanking his considerate entertainer, whoever that person might be. But no one appeared, and even after another long sleep, from which he awoke completely refreshed, there was no sign of anybody, though a fresh meal of dainty cakes and fruit was prepared upon the little table at his elbow. As he was naturally timid, the silence began to terrify him, and he resolved to search once more through all the rooms; but it was of no use. Not even a servant was to be seen; there was no sign of life in the palace! He began to wonder what he should do, and to amuse himself by pretending that all the treasures he saw were his own, and considering how he would divide them among his children. Then he went down into the garden, and though it was winter everywhere else, here the sun shone, and the birds sang, and the flowers bloomed, and the air was soft and sweet. The merchant, in ecstasies with all he saw and heard, said to himself: 'All this must be meant for me. I will go this minute and bring my children to share all these delights.'

In spite of being so cold and weary when he reached the castle, he had taken his horse to the stable and fed it. Now he thought he would saddle it for his homeward journey, and he turned down the path which led to the stable. This path had a hedge of roses on each side of it, and the merchant thought he had never seen or smelt such exquisite flowers. They reminded him of his promise to Beauty, and he stopped and had just gathered one to take to her when he was startled by a strange noise behind him. Turning round, he saw a frightful Beast, which seemed to be very angry and said, in a terrible voice: 'Who told you that you might gather my roses? Was it not enough that I allowed you to be in my palace and was kind to you? This is the way you show your gratitude, by stealing my flowers! But your insolence shall not go unpunished.' The merchant, terrified by these furious words, dropped the fatal rose, and, throwing himself on his knees, cried: 'Pardon me, noble sir. I am truly grateful to you for your hospitality, which was so magnificent that I could not imagine that you would be offended by my taking such a little thing as a rose.' But the Beast's anger was not lessened by this speech.

'You are very ready with excuses and flattery,' he cried; 'but that will not save you from the death you deserve.'

'Alas!' thought the merchant, 'if my daughter could only know what danger her rose has brought me into!'

And in despair he began to tell the Beast all his misfortunes, and the reason of his journey, not forgetting to mention Beauty's request.

'A king's ransom would hardly have procured all that my other daughters asked,' he said, 'but I thought that I might at least take Beauty her rose. I beg you to forgive me, for you see I meant no harm.'

The Beast considered for a moment, and then he said, in a less furious tone: 'I will forgive you on one condition – that is, that you will give me one of your daughters.'

'Ah!' cried the merchant, 'if I were cruel enough to buy my own life at the expense of one of my children's, what excuse could I invent to bring her here?'

'No excuse would be necessary,' answered the Beast. 'If she comes at all she must come willingly. On no other condition will I have her. See if any one of them is courageous enough and loves you well enough to come and save your life. You seem to be an honest man, so I will trust you to go home. I give you a month to see if any of your daughters will come back with you and stay here, to let you go free. If none of them is willing, you must come alone, after bidding them goodbye for ever, for then you will belong to me. And do not imagine that you can hide from me, for if you fail to keep your word I will come and fetch you!' added the Beast grimly.

The merchant accepted this proposal, though he did not really think any of his daughters could be persuaded to come. He promised to return at the time appointed, and then, anxious to escape from the presence of the Beast, he asked permission to set off at once. But the Beast answered that he could not go until next day.

'Then you will find a horse ready for you,' he said. 'Now go and eat your supper, and await my orders.'

The poor merchant, more dead than alive, went back to his room, where the most delicious supper was already served on the little table which was drawn up before a blazing fire. But he was too terrified to eat, and only tasted a few of the dishes, for fear the Beast should be angry if he did not obey his orders. When he had finished he heard a great noise in the next room, which he knew meant that the Beast was coming. As he could do nothing to escape his visit, the only thing that remained was to seem as little afraid as possible; so when the Beast appeared and asked roughly if he had supped well, the merchant answered humbly that he had, thanks to his host's kindness. Then the Beast warned him to remember their agreement, and to prepare his daughter exactly for what she had to expect.

'Do not get up tomorrow,' he added, 'until you see

the sun and hear a golden bell ring. Then you will find your breakfast waiting for you here, and the horse you are to ride will be ready in the courtyard. He will also bring you back again when you come with your daughter a month hence. Farewell. Take a rose to Beauty, and remember your promise!'

The merchant was only too glad when the Beast went away, and though he could not sleep for sadness, he lay down until the sun rose. Then, after a hasty breakfast, he went to gather Beauty's rose, and mounted his horse, which carried him off so swiftly that in an instant he had lost sight of the palace and was still wrapped in gloomy thoughts when it stopped before the door of the cottage.

His sons and daughters, who had been very uneasy at his long absence, rushed to meet him, eager to know the result of his journey, which, seeing him mounted upon a splendid horse and wrapped in a rich mantle, they supposed to be favourable. He hid the truth from them at first, only saying sadly to Beauty as he gave her the rose: 'Here is what you asked me to bring you; you little know what it has cost.'

But this excited their curiosity so greatly that presently he told them his adventures from beginning to end, and then they were all very unhappy. The girls lamented loudly over their lost hopes, and the sons declared that their father should not return to this terrible castle, and began to make plans for killing the Beast if it should come to fetch him. But he reminded them that he had promised to go back. Then the girls were very angry with Beauty, and said it was all her fault, and that if she had asked for something sensible this would never have happened, and complained bitterly that they should have to suffer for her folly.

Poor Beauty, much distressed, said to them: 'I have, indeed, caused this misfortune, but I assure you I did it innocently. Who could have guessed that to ask for a rose in the middle of summer would cause so much misery? But as I did the mischief it is only just that I should suffer for it. I will therefore go back with my father to keep his promise.'

At first nobody would hear of this arrangement, and her father and brothers, who loved her dearly, declared that nothing should make them let her go; but Beauty was firm. As the time drew near she divided all her little possessions between her sisters, and said goodbye to everything she loved, and when the fatal day came she encouraged and cheered her father as they mounted together the horse which had brought him back. It seemed to fly rather than gallop, but so smoothly that Beauty was not frightened; indeed, she would have enjoyed the journey if she had not feared what might happen to her at the end of it. Her father still tried to persuade her to go back, but in vain. While they were talking the night fell, and then, to their great surprise, wonderful coloured lights began to shine in all directions, and splendid fireworks blazed out before them; all the forest was illuminated by them, and even felt pleasantly warm, though it had been bitterly cold before. This lasted until they reached the avenue of orange trees, where were statues holding flaming torches, and when they got nearer to the palace they saw that it was illuminated from the roof to the ground, and music sounded softly from the courtyard. 'The Beast must be very hungry,' said Beauty, trying to laugh, 'if he makes all this rejoicing over the arrival of his prey.'

But, in spite of her anxiety, she could not help admiring all the wonderful things she saw.

The horse stopped at the foot of the flight of steps leading to the terrace, and when they had dismounted her father led her to the little room he had been in before, where they found a splendid fire burning, and the table daintily spread with a delicious supper.

The merchant knew that this was meant for them, and Beauty, who was rather less frightened now that she had passed through so many rooms and seen nothing of the Beast, was quite willing to begin, for her long ride had made her very hungry. But they had hardly finished their meal when the noise of the Beast's footsteps was heard approaching, and Beauty clung to her father in terror, which became all the greater when she saw how frightened he was. But when the Beast really appeared, though she trembled at the sight of him, she made a great effort to hide her terror, and saluted him respectfully.

This evidently pleased the Beast. After looking at her he said, in a tone that might have struck terror into the boldest heart, though he did not seem to be angry: 'Good-evening, old man. Good-evening, Beauty.'

The merchant was too terrified to reply, but Beauty answered sweetly: 'Good-evening, Beast.'

'Have you come willingly?' asked the Beast. 'Will you be content to stay here when your father goes away?'

Beauty answered bravely that she was quite prepared to stay.

'I am pleased with you,' said the Beast. 'As you have come of your own accord, you may stay. As for you, old man,' he added, turning to the merchant, 'at sunrise tomorrow you will take your departure. When the bell rings get up quickly and eat your breakfast, and you will find the same horse waiting to take you home; but remember that you must never expect to see my palace again.'

Then, turning to Beauty, he said: 'Take your father into the next room, and help him to choose everything you think your brothers and sisters would like to have. You will find two travelling-trunks there; fill them as full as you can. It is only just that you should send them something very precious as a remembrance of yourself.'

Then he went away, after saying, 'Goodbye, Beauty; goodbye, old man'; and though Beauty was beginning to think with great dismay of her father's departure, she was afraid to disobey the Beast's orders; and they went into the next room, which had shelves and cupboards all round it. They were greatly surprised at the riches it contained. There were splendid dresses fit for a queen, with all the ornaments that were to be worn with them; and when Beauty opened the cupboards she was quite dazzled by the gorgeous jewels that lay in heaps upon every shelf. After choosing a vast quantity, which she divided between her sisters – for she had made a heap of the wonderful dresses for each of them – she opened the last chest, which was full of gold.

'I think, father,' she said, 'that, as the gold will be more useful to you, we had better take out the other things again, and fill the trunks with it.' So they did this; but the more they put in the more room there seemed to be, and at last they put back all the jewels and dresses they had taken out, and Beauty even added as many more of the jewels as she could carry at once; and then the trunks were not too full, but they were so heavy that an elephant could not have carried them!

'The Beast was mocking us,' cried the merchant; 'he must have pretended to give us all these things, knowing that I could not carry them away.'

'Let us wait and see,' answered Beauty. 'I cannot believe that he meant to deceive us. All we can do is to fasten them up and leave them ready.'

So they did this and returned to the little room, where they slept until the bell rang at sunrise. Then, to their astonishment, they found breakfast ready. The merchant ate his with a good appetite, as the Beast's generosity made him believe that he might perhaps venture to come back soon and see Beauty. But she felt sure that her father was leaving her for ever, so she was very sad when the bell rang sharply for the second time, and warned them that the time had come for them to part. They went down into the courtyard, where two horses were waiting, one loaded with the two trunks, the other for him to ride. They were pawing the ground in their impatience to start, and the merchant was forced to bid Beauty a hasty farewell; and as soon as he was mounted he went off at such a pace that she lost sight of him in an instant. Then Beauty began to cry, and wandered sadly back to her own room. But she soon found that she was very sleepy, and as she had nothing better to do she lay down and instantly fell asleep. And then she dreamed that she was walking by a brook bordered with trees, and lamenting her sad fate, when a young prince, handsomer than anyone she had ever seen, and with a voice that went straight to her heart, came and said to her, 'Ah, Beauty! you are not so unfortunate as you suppose. Here you will be rewarded for all you have suffered elsewhere. Your every wish shall be gratified. Only try to find me out, no matter how I may be disguised, as I love you dearly, and in making me happy you will find your own happiness. Be as true-hearted as you are beautiful, and we shall have nothing left to wish for.'

'What can I do, Prince, to make you happy?' said Beauty.

'Only be grateful,' he answered, 'and do not trust too much to your eyes. And, above all, do not desert me until you have saved me from my cruel misery.'

After this she thought she found herself in a room with a stately and beautiful lady, who said to her: 'Dear Beauty, try not to regret all you have left behind you, for you are destined to a better fate. Only do not let yourself be deceived by appearances.'

Beauty found her dreams so interesting that she was in no hurry to awake, but presently the clock roused her by calling her name softly twelve times, and then she got up and found her dressing-table set out with everything she could possibly want; and when her toilet was finished she found dinner was waiting in the room next to hers. But dinner does not take very long when you are all by yourself, and very soon she sat down cosily in the corner of a sofa, and began to think about the charming prince she had seen in her dream.

'He said I could make him happy,' said Beauty to herself. 'It seems, then, that this horrible Beast keeps him a prisoner. How can I set him free? I wonder why they both told me not to trust to appearances? I don't understand it. But, after all, it was only a dream, so why should I trouble myself about it? I had better go and find something to do to amuse myself.' So she got up and began to explore some of the many rooms of the palace.

The first she entered was lined with mirrors, and Beauty saw herself reflected on every side, and thought she had never seen such a charming room. Then a bracelet which was hanging from a chandelier caught her eye, and on taking it down she was greatly surprised to find that it held a portrait of her unknown admirer, just as she had seen him in her dream. With great delight she slipped the bracelet on her arm, and went on into a gallery of pictures, where she soon found a portrait of the same handsome prince, as large as life, and so well painted that as she studied it he seemed to smile kindly at her. Tearing herself away from the portrait at last, she passed through into a room which contained every musical instrument under the sun, and here she amused herself for a long while in trying some of them, and singing until she was tired. The next room was a library, and she saw everything she had ever wanted to read, as well as everything she had read, and it seemed to her that a whole lifetime would not be enough even to read the names of the books, there were so many. By this time it was growing dusk, and wax candles in diamond and ruby candlesticks were beginning to light themselves in every room.

Beauty found her supper served just at the time she preferred to have it, but she did not see anyone or hear a sound, and, though her father had warned her that she would be alone, she began to find it rather dull.

But presently she heard the Beast coming, and wondered tremblingly if he meant to eat her up now.

However, as he did not seem at all ferocious, and only said gruffly: 'Good-evening, Beauty,' she answered cheerfully and managed to conceal her terror. Then the Beast asked her how she had been amusing herself, and she told him all the rooms she had seen.

Then he asked if she thought she could be happy in his palace; and Beauty answered that everything was so beautiful that she would be very hard to please if she could not be happy. And after about an hour's talk Beauty began to think that the Beast was not nearly so terrible as she had supposed at first. Then he got up to leave her, and said in his gruff voice: 'Do you love me, Beauty? Will you marry me?'

'Oh! what shall I say?' cried Beauty, for she was afraid to make the Beast angry by refusing.

'Say yes or no without fear,' he replied.

'Oh! no, Beast,' said Beauty hastily.

'Since you will not, good-night, Beauty,' he said.

And she answered, 'Good-night, Beast,' very glad to find that her refusal had not provoked him. And after he was gone she was very soon in bed and asleep, and dreaming of her unknown prince. She thought he came and said to her: 'Ah, Beauty! why are you so unkind to me? I fear I am fated to be unhappy for many a long day still.'

And then her dreams changed, but the charming prince figured in them all; and when morning came her first thought was to look at the portrait, and see if it was really like him, and she found that it certainly was.

This morning she decided to amuse herself in the garden, for the sun shone, and all the fountains were playing; but she was astonished to find that every place was familiar to her, and presently she came to the brook where the myrtle trees were growing where she had first met the prince in her dream, and that made her think more than ever that he must be kept a prisoner by the Beast. When she was tired she went back to the palace, and found a new room full of materials for every kind of work – ribbons to make into bows, and silks to work into flowers. Then there was an aviary full of rare birds, which were so tame that they flew to Beauty as soon as they saw her, and perched upon her shoulders and her head.

'Pretty little creatures,' she said, 'how I wish that your cage was nearer to my room, that I might often hear you sing!'

So saying she opened a door, and found, to her delight, that it led into her own room, though she had thought it was quite the other side of the palace.

There were more birds in a room farther on, parrots and cockatoos that could talk, and they greeted Beauty by name; indeed, she found them so entertaining that she took one or two back to her room, and they talked to her while she was at supper; after which the Beast paid her his usual visit, and asked her the same questions as before, and then with a gruff 'good-night' he took his departure, and Beauty went to bed to dream of her mysterious prince. The days passed swiftly in different amusements, and after a while Beauty found out another strange thing in the palace, which often pleased her when she was tired of being alone. There was one room which she had not noticed particularly; it was empty, except that under each of the windows stood a very comfortable chair; and the first time she had looked out of the window it had seemed to her that a black curtain prevented her from seeing anything outside. But the second time she went into the room, happening to be tired, she sat down in one of the chairs, and instantly the curtain was rolled aside, and a most amusing pantomime was acted before her: there were dances, and coloured lights, and music, and pretty dresses, and it was all so gay that Beauty was in ecstasies. After that she tried the other seven windows in turn, and there was some new and surprising entertainment to be seen from each of them, so that Beauty never could feel lonely any more.

Every evening after supper the Beast came to see her, and always before saying good-night asked her in his terrible voice: 'Beauty, will you marry me?' And it seemed to Beauty, now she understood him better, that when she said, 'No, Beast,' he went away quite sad.

But her happy dreams of the handsome young prince soon made her forget the poor Beast, and the only thing that at all disturbed her was to be constantly told to distrust appearances, to let her heart guide her, and not her eyes, and many other equally perplexing things, which, consider as she would, she could not understand.

So everything went on for a long time, until at last, happy as she was, Beauty began to long for the sight of her father and her brothers and sisters; and one night, seeing her look very sad, the Beast asked her what was the matter. Beauty had quite ceased to be afraid of him. Now she knew that he was really gentle in spite of his ferocious looks and his dreadful voice. So she answered that she was longing to see her home once more. Upon hearing this the Beast seemed sadly distressed, and cried miserably.

'Ah! Beauty, have you the heart to desert an unhappy Beast like this? What more do you want to make you happy? Is it because you hate me that you want to escape?'

'No, dear Beast,' answered Beauty softly, 'I do not hate you, and I should be very sorry never to see you any more, but I long to see my father again. Only let me go for two months, and I promise to come back to you and stay for the rest of my life.'

The Beast, who had been sighing dolefully while she spoke, now replied: 'I cannot refuse you anything you ask, even though it should cost me my life. Take the four boxes you will find in the room next to your own, and fill them with everything you wish to take with you. But remember your promise and come back when the two months are over, or you may have cause to repent it, for if you do not come in good time you will find your faithful Beast dead. You will not need any chariot to bring you back. Only say goodbye to all your brothers and sisters the night before you come away, and when you have gone to bed turn this ring round upon your finger and say firmly: "I wish to go back to my palace and see my Beast again." '

As soon as Beauty was alone she hastened to fill the boxes with all the rare and precious things she saw about her, and only when she was tired of heaping things into them did they seem to be full.

Then she went to bed, but could hardly sleep for joy. And when at last she did begin to dream of her beloved prince she was grieved to see him stretched upon a grassy bank, sad and weary, and hardly like himself.

'What is the matter?' she cried.

He looked at her reproachfully, and said: 'How can you ask me, cruel one? Are you not leaving me to my death perhaps?'

'Ah! don't be so sorrowful,' cried Beauty; 'I am only going to assure my father that I am safe and happy. I have promised the Beast faithfully that I will come back, and he would die of grief if I did not keep my word!'

'What would that matter to you?' said the prince. 'Surely you would not care?'

'Indeed, I should be ungrateful if I did not care for such a kind Beast,' cried Beauty indignantly. 'I would die to save him from pain. I assure you it is not his fault that he is so ugly.'

Just then a strange sound woke her – someone was speaking not very far away; and opening her eyes she found herself in a room she had never seen before, which was certainly not nearly so splendid as those she was used to in the Beast's palace. Where could she be? She got up and dressed hastily, and then saw that the boxes she had packed the night before were all in the room. While she was wondering by what magic the Beast had transported them and herself to this strange place she suddenly heard her father's voice, and rushed out and greeted him joyfully. Her brothers and sisters were all astonished at her appearance, as they had never expected to see her again, and there was no end to the questions they asked her. She had also much to hear about what had happened to them while she was away, and of her father's journey home. But when they heard that she had only come to be with them for a short time, and then must go back to the Beast's palace for ever, they lamented loudly. Then Beauty asked her father what he thought could be the meaning of her strange dreams, and why the prince constantly begged her not to trust to appearances. After much consideration, he answered: 'You tell me yourself that the Beast, frightful as he is, loves you dearly, and deserves your love and gratitude for his gentleness and kindness; I think the prince must mean you to understand that you ought to reward him by doing as he wishes you to, in spite of his ugliness.'

Beauty could not help seeing that this seemed very probable; still, when she thought of her dear prince who was so handsome, she did not feel at all inclined to marry the Beast. At any rate, for two months she need not decide, but could enjoy herself with her sisters. But though they were rich now, and lived in town again, and had plenty of acquaintances, Beauty found that nothing amused her very much; and she often thought of the palace, where she was so happy, especially as at home she never once dreamed of her dear prince, and she felt quite sad without him.

Then her sisters seemed to have got quite used to being without her, and even found her rather in the way, so she would not have been sorry when the two months were over but for her father and brothers, who begged her to stay, and seemed so grieved at the thought of her departure that she had not the courage to say goodbye to them. Every day when she got up she meant to say it at night, and when night came she put it off again, until at last she had a dismal dream which helped her to make up her mind. She thought she was wandering in a lonely path in the palace gardens, when she heard groans which seemed to come from some bushes hiding the entrance of a cave, and running quickly to see what could be the matter, she found the Beast stretched out upon his side, apparently dying. He reproached her faintly with being the cause of his distress, and at the same moment a stately lady appeared, and said very gravely:

'Ah! Beauty, you are only just in time to save his life. See what happens when people do not keep their promises! If you had delayed one day more, you would have found him dead.'

Beauty was so terrified by this dream that the next morning she announced her intention of going back at once, and that very night she said goodbye to her father and all her brothers and sisters, and as soon as she was in bed she turned her ring round upon her finger, and said firmly, 'I wish to go back to my palace and see my Beast again,' as she had been told to do.

Then she fell asleep instantly, and only woke up to hear the clock saying 'Beauty, Beauty' twelve times in its musical voice, which told her at once that she was really in the palace once more. Everything was just as before, and her birds were so glad to see her! But Beauty thought she had never known such a long day, for she was so anxious to see the Beast again that she felt as if supper-time would never come.

But when it did come and no Beast appeared she was really frightened; so, after listening and waiting for a long time, she ran down into the garden to search for him. Up and down the paths and avenues ran poor Beauty, calling him in vain, for no one answered, and not a trace of him could she find; until at last, quite tired, she stopped for a minute's rest, and saw that she was standing opposite the shady path she had seen in her dream. She rushed down it, and, sure enough, there was the cave, and in it lay the Beast – asleep, as Beauty thought. Quite glad to have found him, she ran up and stroked his head, but, to her horror, he did not move or open his eyes.

'Oh! he is dead; and it is all my fault,' said Beauty, crying bitterly.

But then, looking at him again, she fancied he still breathed, and, hastily fetching some water from the nearest fountain, she sprinkled it over his face, and, to her great delight, he began to revive.

'Oh! Beast, how you frightened me!' she cried. 'I never knew how much I loved you until just now, when I feared I was too late to save your life.'

'Can you really love such an ugly creature as I am?' said the Beast faintly. 'Ah! Beauty, you only came just in time. I was dying because I thought you had forgotten your promise. But go back now and rest, I shall see you again by and by.'

Beauty, who had half expected that he would be angry with her, was reassured by his gentle voice, and went back to the palace, where supper was awaiting her; and afterwards the Beast came in as usual, and talked about the time she had spent with her father, asking if she had enjoyed herself, and if they had all been very glad to see her.

Beauty answered politely, and quite enjoyed telling him all that had happened to her. And when at last the time came for him to go, and he asked, as he had so often asked before, 'Beauty, will you marry me?'

She answered softly, 'Yes, dear Beast.'

As she spoke a blaze of light sprang up before the windows of the palace; fireworks crackled and guns banged, and across the avenue of orange trees, in letters all made of fireflies, was written: 'Long live the Prince and his Bride.'

Turning to ask the Beast what it could all mean, Beauty found that he had disappeared, and in his place stood her long-loved prince! At the same moment the wheels of a chariot were heard upon the terrace, and two ladies entered the room. One of them

Beauty and the Beast

Beauty recognised as the stately lady she had seen in her dreams; the other was also so grand and queenly that Beauty hardly knew which to greet first.

But the one she already knew said to her companion: 'Well, Queen, this is Beauty, who has had the courage to rescue your son from the terrible enchantment. They love one another, and only your consent to their marriage is wanting to make them perfectly happy.'

'I consent with all my heart,' cried the Queen. 'How can I ever thank you enough, charming girl, for having restored my dear son to his natural form?'

And then she tenderly embraced Beauty and the prince, who had meanwhile been greeting the fairy and receiving her congratulations.

'Now,' said the fairy to Beauty, 'I suppose you would like me to send for all your brothers and sisters to dance at your wedding?'

And so she did, and the marriage was celebrated the very next day with the utmost splendour, and Beauty and the prince lived happily ever after.

Blue Beard

There was a man who had fine houses, both in town and country, a deal of silver and gold plate, embroidered furniture, and coaches gilded all over with gold. But this man was so unlucky as to have a blue beard, which made him so frightfully ugly that all the women and girls ran away from him.

One of his neighbours, a lady of quality, had two daughters who were perfect beauties. He desired of her one of them in marriage, leaving to her choice which of the two she would bestow on him. They would neither of them have him, and sent him backwards and forwards from one to the other, not being able to bear the thought of marrying a man who had a blue beard, and what besides gave them disgust and aversion was his having already been married to several wives, and nobody ever knew what became of them.

Blue Beard, to engage their affection, took them, with the lady their mother and three or four ladies of their acquaintance, with other young people of the neighbourhood, to one of his country seats, where they stayed a whole week.

There was nothing then to be seen but parties of pleasure, hunting, fishing, dancing, mirth and feasting. Nobody went to bed, but all passed the night in rallying and joking with each other. In short, everything succeeded so well that the younger daughter began to think the master of the house not to have a beard so very blue, and that he was a mighty civil gentleman.

As soon as they returned home, the marriage was concluded. About a month afterwards, Blue Beard told his wife that he was obliged to take a country journey for six weeks at least, about affairs of very great consequence, desiring her to divert herself in his absence, to send for her friends and acquaintances, to carry them into the country, if she pleased, and to make good cheer wherever she was.

'Here,' said he, 'are the keys of the two great wardrobes, wherein I have my best furniture; these are of my silver and gold plate, which is not every day in use; these open my strong boxes, which hold my money, both gold and silver; these my caskets of jewels; and this is the master-key to all my apartments. But for this little one here, it is the key of the closet at the end of the great gallery on the ground floor. Open them all; go into all and every one of them, except that little closet, which I forbid you, and forbid it in such a manner that, if you happen to open it, you may expect from me anger and resentment which will know no bounds.'

She promised to observe, very exactly, everything he had ordered, whereupon he, after having embraced her, got into his coach and proceeded on his journey.

Her neighbours and good friends did not wait to be sent for by the new married lady, so great was their impatience to see all the rich furniture of her house, not daring to come while her husband was there, because of his blue beard, which frightened them. They ran through all the rooms, closets and wardrobes, which were all so fine and rich that they seemed to surpass one another.

After that they went up into the two great rooms, where was the best and richest furniture; they could

Here,' said he, 'are the keys of the two great wardrobes

not sufficiently admire the number and beauty of the tapestries, beds, couches, cabinets, stands, tables and looking-glasses, in which you might see yourself from head to foot; some of them were framed with glass, others with silver, plain and gilded, the finest and most magnificent ever were seen.

They ceased not to extol and envy the happiness of their friend, who in the meantime in no way diverted herself in looking upon all these rich things, because of the impatience she had to go and open the closet on the ground floor. She was so much pressed by her curiosity that, without considering that it was very uncivil to leave her company, she went down a little back staircase, and with such excessive haste that she had twice or thrice like to have broken her neck.

82

Coming to the closet-door, she made a stop for some time, thinking upon her husband's orders, and considering what unhappiness might attend her if she was disobedient; but the temptation was so strong she could not overcome it. She then took the little key, and opened it, trembling, but could not at first see anything plainly, because the windows were shut. After some moments she began to perceive that the floor was all covered over with clotted blood, on which lay the bodies of several dead women, ranged against the walls. (These were all the wives whom Blue Beard had married and murdered, one after another.) She thought she should have died for fear, and the key, which she pulled out of the lock, fell out of her hand.

After having somewhat recovered from her surprise, she took up the key, locked the door and went upstairs into her chamber to compose herself; but she could not, she was so much frightened. Having observed that the key of the closet was stained with blood, she tried two or three times to wipe it off, but the blood would not come out; in vain did she wash it, and even rub it with soap and sand; the blood still remained, for the key was magical and she could never make it quite clean; when the blood was gone off from one side, it came again on the other.

Blue Beard returned from his journey the same evening, and said he had received letters upon the road, informing him that the affair he went about was ended to his advantage. His wife did all she could to convince him she was extremely glad of his speedy return.

Next morning he asked her for the keys, which she gave him, but with such a trembling hand that he easily guessed what had happened.

'What!' said he, 'is not the key of my closet among the rest?'

'I must certainly have left it above upon the table,' said she.

'Fail not to bring it to me presently,' said Blue Beard.

After several goings backwards and forwards she was forced to bring him the key. Blue Beard, having very attentively considered it, said to his wife, 'How comes this blood upon the key?'

'I do not know,' cried the poor woman, paler than death.

'You do not know!' replied Blue Beard. 'I very well know. You were resolved to go into the closet, were you not? Mighty well, madam; you shall go in, and take your place among the ladies you saw there.'

Upon this she threw herself at her husband's feet, and begged his pardon with all the signs of true repentance, vowing that she would never more be disobedient. She would have melted a rock, so beautiful and sorrowful was she; but Blue Beard had a heart harder than any rock!

'You must die, madam,' said he, 'and that presently.'

'Since I must die,' answered she (looking upon him with her eyes all bathed in tears), 'give me some little time to say my prayers.'

'I give you,' replied Blue Beard, 'half a quarter of an hour, but not one moment more.'

When she was alone she called out to her sister, and said to her: 'Sister Anne' (for that was her name), 'go up, I beg you, upon the top of the tower, and look if my brothers are not coming over; they promised me that they would come today, and if you see them, give them a sign to make haste.'

Her sister Anne went up upon the top of the tower, and the poor afflicted wife cried out from time to time: 'Anne, sister Anne, do you see anyone coming?'

And sister Anne said: 'I see nothing but the sun, which makes a dust, and the grass, which looks green.'

In the meanwhile Blue Beard, holding a great sabre in his hand, cried out as loud as he could bawl to his wife: 'Come down instantly, or I shall come up to you.'

'One moment longer, if you please,' said his wife, and then she cried out very softly, 'Anne, sister Anne, dost thou see anybody coming?'

And sister Anne answered: 'I see nothing but the sun, which makes a dust, and the grass, which is green.'

'Come down quickly,' cried Blue Beard, 'or I will come up to you.'

'I am coming,' answered his wife; and then she cried, 'Anne, sister Anne, dost thou not see anyone coming?'

'I see,' replied sister Anne, 'a great dust, which comes on this side here.'

'Are they my brothers?'

'Alas! no, my dear sister, I see a flock of sheep.'

'Will you not come down?' cried Blue Beard

'One moment longer,' said his wife, and then she cried out: 'Anne, sister Anne, dost thou see nobody coming?'

'I see,' said she, 'two horsemen, but they are yet a great way off.'

'God be praised,' replied the poor wife joyfully; 'they are my brothers; I will make them a sign, as well as I can, for them to make haste.'

Then Blue Beard bawled out so loud that he made the whole house tremble. The distressed wife came down, and threw herself at his feet, all in tears, with her hair about her shoulders.

'God be praised,' replied the poor wife joyfully;
'they are my brothers.'

'This signifies nothing,' says Blue Beard; 'you must die'; then, taking hold of her hair with one hand, and lifting up the sword with the other, he was going to take off her head. The poor lady, turning about to him, and looking at him with dying eyes, desired him to afford her one little moment to recollect herself.

'No, no,' said he, 'recommend thyself to God,' and was just ready to strike . . .

At this very instant there was such a loud knocking at the gate that Blue Beard made a sudden stop. The gate was opened, and presently entered two horsemen, who, dismounting and drawing their swords, ran directly to Blue Beard. He knew them to be his wife's brothers, one a dragoon, the other a musketeer, so that he ran away immediately to save himself; but the two brothers pursued so close that they overtook him before he could get to the steps of the porch, when they ran their swords through his body and left him dead. The poor wife was almost as dead as her husband, and had not strength enough to rise and welcome her brothers.

Blue Beard had no heirs, and so his wife became mistress of all his estate. She made use of one part of it to marry her sister Anne to a young gentleman who had loved her a long while; another part to buy captains' commissions for her brothers, and the rest to marry herself to a very worthy gentleman, who made her forget the ill time she had passed with Blue Beard.

On the steps of the porch they ran their swords through him

The Bunyip

Long, long ago, far, far away on the other side of the
world, some young men left the camp where they
lived to get some food for their wives and children.
The sun was hot, but they liked heat, and as they
went they ran races and tried who could hurl his spear
the farthest, or was cleverest in throwing a strange
weapon called a boomerang, which always returns to
the thrower. They did not get on very fast at this rate,
but presently they reached a flat place that in time of
flood was full of water, but was now, in the height of
summer, only a set of pools, each surrounded with a
fringe of plants, with bulrushes standing in the inside
of all. In that country the people are fond of the roots
of bulrushes, which they think as good as onions, and
one of the young men said that they had better collect
some of the roots and carry them back to the camp. It
did not take them long to weave the tops of the
willows into a basket, and they were just going to
wade into the water and pull up the bulrush roots
when a youth suddenly called out: 'After all, why
should we waste our time in doing work that is only
fit for women and children? Let them come and get
the roots for themselves; but we will fish for eels and
anything else we can get.'

This delighted the rest of the party, and they all
began to arrange their fishing lines, made from the
bark of the yellow mimosa, and to search for bait for
their hooks. Most of them used worms, but one, who
had put a piece of raw meat for dinner into his skin

wallet, cut off a little bit and baited his line with it, unseen by his companions.

For a long time they cast patiently, without receiving a single bite; the sun had grown low in the sky, and it seemed as if they would have to go home empty-handed, not even with a basket of roots to show; when the youth, who had baited his hook with raw meat, suddenly saw his line disappear under the water. Something, a very heavy fish he supposed, was pulling so hard that he could hardly keep his feet, and for a few minutes it seemed either as if he must let go or be dragged into the pool. He cried to his friends to help him, and at last, trembling with fright at what they were going to see, they managed between them to land on the bank a creature that was neither a calf nor a seal, but something of both, with a long, broad tail. They looked at each other with horror, cold shivers running down their spines; for though they had never beheld it, there was not a man amongst them who did not know what it was – the cub of the awful Bunyip!

All of a sudden the silence was broken by a low wail, answered by another from the other side of the pool, as the mother rose up from her den and came towards them, rage flashing from her horrible yellow eyes. 'Let it go! let it go!' whispered the young men to each other; but the captor declared that he had caught it, and was going to keep it. 'He had promised his sweetheart,' he said, 'that he would bring back enough meat for her father's house to feast on for three days, and though they could not eat the little Bunyip, her brothers and sisters should have it to play with.' So, flinging his spear at the mother to keep her back, he threw the little Bunyip on to his shoulders, and set out for the camp, never heeding the poor mother's cries of distress.

By this time it was getting near sunset, and the plain was in shadow, though the tops of the mountains were still quite bright. The youths had all ceased to be afraid, when they were startled by a low rushing sound behind them, and, looking round, saw that the pool was slowly rising, and the spot where they had landed the Bunyip was quite covered. 'What could it be?' they asked one of another; 'there was not a cloud in the sky, yet the water had risen higher already than they had ever known it do before.' For an instant they stood watching as if they were frozen, then they turned and ran with all their might, the man with the Bunyip running faster than all. When he reached a high peak overlooking all the plain he stopped to take breath, and turned to see if he was safe yet. Safe! why only the tops of the trees remained above that sea of water, and these were fast disappearing. They must run fast indeed if they were to escape. So on they flew, scarcely feeling the ground as they went, till they flung themselves on the ground before the holes scooped out of the earth where they had all been born. The old men were sitting in front, the children were playing, and the women chattering together, when the little Bunyip fell into their midst, and there was scarcely a child among them who did not know that something terrible was upon them. 'The water! the water!' gasped one of the young men; and there it was, slowly but steadily mounting the ridge itself. Parents and children clung together, as if by that means they could drive back the advancing flood; and the youth who had caused all this terrible catastrophe, seized his sweetheart, and cried: 'I will climb with you to the top of that tree, and there no waters can reach us.' But, as he spoke, something cold touched him, and quickly he glanced down at his feet. Then with a shudder he saw that they were feet no longer, but bird's claws. He looked at the girl he was clasping, and beheld a great black bird standing at his side; he turned to his friends, but a flock of great awkward flapping creatures stood in their place He put up his hands to cover his face, but they were no longer hands, only the ends of wings; and when he tried to speak, a noise such as he had never heard before seemed to come from his throat, which had suddenly become narrow and slender. Already the water had risen to his waist, and he found himself sitting easily upon it, while its surface reflected back the image of a black swan, one of many.

Never again did the swans become men; but they are still different from other swans, for in the night-time those who listen can hear them talk in a language that is certainly not swans' language; and there are even sounds of laughing and talking, unlike any noise made by the swans whom we know.

The little Bunyip was carried home by its mother, and after that the waters sank back to their own channels. The side of the pool where she lives is always shunned by everyone, as nobody knows when she may suddenly put out her head and draw him into her mighty jaws. But people say that underneath the black waters of the pool she has a house filled with beautiful things, such as mortals who dwell on the earth have no idea of. Though how they know I cannot tell you, as nobody has ever seen it.

The Cat's Elopement

Once upon a time there lived a cat of marvellous beauty, with a coat as soft and shining as silk, and wise green eyes, that could see even in the dark. His name was Gon, and he belonged to a music teacher, who was so fond and proud of him that he would not have parted with him for anything in the world.

Now not far from the music master's house there dwelt a lady who possessed a most lovely little pussy cat called Koma. She was such a little dear altogether, and blinked her eyes so daintily, and ate her supper so tidily, and when she had finished she licked her pink nose so delicately with her little tongue, that her mistress was never tired of saying, 'Koma, Koma, what should I do without you?'

Well, it happened one day that these two, when out for an evening stroll, met under a cherry tree, and in one moment fell madly in love with each other. Gon had long felt that it was time for him to find a wife, for all the ladies in the neighbourhood paid him so much attention that it made him quite shy; but he was not easy to please, and did not care about any of them. Now, before he had time to think, Cupid had entangled him in his net, and he was filled with love towards Koma. She fully returned his passion, but, like a woman, she saw the difficulties in the way, and consulted sadly with Gon as to the means of overcoming them. Gon entreated his master to set matters right by buying Koma, but her mistress would not part from her. Then the music master was asked to sell Gon to the lady, but he declined to listen to any such suggestion, so everything remained as before.

At length the love of the couple grew to such a pitch that they determined to please themselves, and to seek their fortunes together. So one moonlight night they stole away, and ventured out into an unknown world. All day long they marched bravely on through the sunshine, till they had left their homes far behind them, and towards evening they found themselves in a large park. The wanderers by this time were very hot and tired, and the grass looked very soft and inviting, and the trees cast cool deep shadows, when suddenly an ogre appeared in this paradise, in the shape of a big, big dog! He came springing towards them, showing all his teeth, and Koma shrieked, and rushed up a cherry tree. Gon, however, stood his ground boldly, and prepared to give battle, for he felt that Koma's eyes were upon him, and that he must not run away. But, alas! his courage would have availed him nothing had his enemy once touched him, for he was large and powerful, and very fierce. From her perch in the tree Koma saw it all, and screamed with all her might, hoping that someone would hear, and come to help. Luckily a servant of the princess to whom the park belonged was walking by, and he drove off the dog, and picking up the trembling Gon in his arms, carried him to his mistress.

So poor little Koma was left alone, while Gon was borne away full of trouble, not in the least knowing what to do. Even the attention paid him by the princess, who was delighted with his beauty and pretty ways, did not console him, but there was no use in fighting against fate, and he could only wait and see what would turn up.

The princess, Gon's new mistress, was so good and kind that everybody loved her, and she would have led a happy life, had it not been for a serpent who had fallen in love with her, and was constantly annoying her by his presence. Her servants had orders to drive him away as often as he appeared; but as they were careless, and the serpent very sly, it sometimes happened that he was able to slip past them, and to frighten the princess by appearing before her. One day she was seated in her room, playing on her favourite musical instrument, when she felt something gliding up her sash, and saw her enemy making his way to kiss her cheek. She shrieked and threw herself backwards, and Gon, who had been curled up on a stool at her feet, understood her terror, and with one

bound seized the snake by his neck. He gave him one bite and one shake, and flung him on the ground, where he lay, never to worry the princess any more. Then she took Gon in her arms, and praised and caressed him, and saw that he had the nicest bits to eat, and the softest mats to lie on; and he would have had nothing in the world to wish for if only he could have seen Koma again.

Time passed on, and one morning Gon lay before the house door, basking in the sun. He looked lazily at the world stretched out before him, and saw in the distance a big ruffian of a cat teasing and ill-treating quite a little one. He jumped up, full of rage, and chased away the big cat, and then he turned to comfort the little one, when his heart nearly burst with joy to find that it was Koma. At first Koma did not know him again, he had grown so large and stately; but when it dawned upon her who it was, her happiness knew no bounds. And they rubbed their heads and their noses again and again, while their purring might have been heard a mile off.

Paw in paw they appeared before the princess, and told her the story of their life and its sorrows. The princess wept for sympathy, and promised that they should never more be parted, but should live with her to the end of their days. By and by the princess herself got married, and brought a prince to dwell in the palace in the park. And she told him all about her two cats, and how brave Gon had been, and how he had delivered her from her enemy the serpent.

And when the prince heard, he swore they should never leave them, but should go with the princess wherever she went. So it all fell out as the princess wished; and Gon and Koma had many children, and so had the princess, and they all played together, and were friends to the end of their lives.

The Cauld Lad of Hilton

At Hilton Hall,* long years ago, there lived a brownie
that was the contrariest brownie you ever knew. At
night, after the servants had gone to bed, it would turn
everything topsy-turvy, put sugar in the salt-cellars,
pepper into the beer, and was up to all kinds of pranks.
It would throw the chairs down, put tables on their
backs, rake out fires, and do as much mischief as could
be. But sometimes it would be in a good temper.

'What's a brownie?' you say. Oh, it's a kind of a
sort of a bogle, but it isn't so cruel as a redcap! What!
you don't know what's a bogle or a redcap! Ah, me!
what's the world a-coming to? Of course a brownie is
a funny little thing, half man, half goblin, with pointed

---

* The ruins of Hylton Castle near Sunderland in England
  are haunted by the ghost of a murdered stable-boy,
  known locally as the Cauld Lad of Hylton. The story
  goes that one night Baron Hylton caught his daughter in
  the arms of the stable-boy, Robert Skelton. The baron
  was so enraged that he killed the stable-boy and threw
  the body into a deep pond. Several months later, the
  body was recovered. The baron was tried for Skelton's
  murder, but was acquitted on the evidence of an old
  farm worker, who said that the baron had ordered the
  boy to remove a tool from the top shelf in the barn, and
  the boy had fallen, seriously wounding himself in the
  process; the baron had tended the wounds, but the boy
  had died. Soon afterwards, strange events began to occur
  in the castle.

ears and a hairy hide. When you bury a treasure, you scatter over it blood drops of a newly slain kid or lamb, or, better still, bury the animal with the treasure, and a brownie will watch over it for you, and frighten everybody else away.

Where was I? Well, as I was a-saying, the brownie at Hilton Hall would play at mischief, but if the servants laid out for it a bowl of cream, or a knuckle cake spread with honey, it would clear away things for them, and make everything tidy in the kitchen.

One night, however, when the servants had stopped up late, they heard a noise in the kitchen, and, peeping in, saw the brownie swinging to and fro on the jack chain, and saying:

> 'Woe's me! woe's me!
> The acorn's not yet
> Fallen from the tree,
> That's to grow the wood,
> That's to make the cradle,
> That's to rock the bairn,
> That's to grow to the man,
> That's to set me free.
> Woe's me! woe's me!'

So they took pity on the poor brownie, and asked the nearest henwife what they should do to send it away. 'That's easy enough,' said the henwife, and told them that a brownie that's paid for its service, in aught that's not perishable, goes away at once. So they made a cloak of Lincoln green, with a hood to it, and put it by the hearth and watched. They saw the brownie come up, and seeing the hood and cloak, put them on, and frisk about, dancing on one leg and saying: 'I've taken your cloak, I've taken your hood; The Cauld Lad of Hilton will do no more good.'

And with that it vanished, and was never seen or heard of afterwards.

Childe Rowland

Childe Rowland and his brothers twain
　　Were playing at the ball,
And there was their sister Burd Ellen
　　In the midst, among them all.

Childe Rowland kicked it with his foot
　　And caught it with his knee;
At last as he plunged among them all
　　O'er the church he made it flee.

Burd Ellen round about the aisle
　　To seek the ball is gone,
But long they waited, and longer still,
　　And she came not back again.

They sought her east, they sought her west,
　　They sought her up and down,
And woe were the hearts of those brethren,
　　For she was not to be found.

So at last her eldest brother went to the Warlock Merlin and told him all the case, and asked him if he knew where Burd Ellen was. 'The fair Burd Ellen,' said the Warlock Merlin, 'must have been carried off by the fairies, because she went round the church "widdershins" – the opposite way to the sun. She is now in the Dark Tower of the King of Elfland; it would take the boldest knight in Christendom to bring her back.'

'If it is possible to bring her back,' said her brother, 'I'll do it, or perish in the attempt.'

'Possible it is,' said the Warlock Merlin, 'but woe to the man or mother's son that attempts it, if he is not well taught beforehand what he is to do.'

The eldest brother of Burd Ellen was not to be put off, by any fear of danger, from attempting to get her back, so he begged the Warlock Merlin to tell him what he should do, and what he should not do, in going to seek his sister. And after he had been taught, and had repeated his lesson, he set out for Elfland.

> But long they waited, and longer still,
>   With doubt and muckle pain,
> But woe were the hearts of his brethren,
>   For he came not back again.

Then the second brother got tired and sick of waiting, and he went to the Warlock Merlin and asked him the same as his brother. So he set out to find Burd Ellen.

> But long they waited, and longer still,
>   With muckle doubt and pain,
> And woe were his mother's and brother's heart,
>   For he came not back again.

And when they had waited and waited a good long time, Childe Rowland, the youngest of Burd Ellen's brothers, wished to go, and went to his mother, the good queen, to ask her to let him go. But she would not at first, for he was the last of her children she now had, and if he was lost, all would be lost. But he begged, and he begged, till at last the good queen let him go, and gave him his father's good brand that never struck in vain. And as she girt it round his waist, she said the spell that would give it victory.

So Childe Rowland said goodbye to the good queen, his mother, and went to the cave of the War-lock Merlin. 'Once more, and but once more,' he said to the Warlock, 'tell how man or mother's son may rescue Burd Ellen and her brothers twain.'

'Well, my son,' said the Warlock Merlin, 'there are but two things, simple they may seem, but hard they are to do. One thing to do, and one thing not to do. And the thing to do is this: after you have entered the land of Fairy, whoever speaks to you, till you meet the Burd Ellen, you must out with your father's brand and off with their head. And what you've not to do is this: bite no bit, and drink no drop, however hungry or thirsty you be; drink a drop, or bite a bit, while in Elfland and never will you see Middle Earth again.'

So Childe Rowland said the two things over and over again, till he knew them by heart, and he thanked the Warlock Merlin and went on his way. And he went along, and along, and along, and still farther along, till he came to the horse-herd of the King of Elfland feeding his horses. These he knew by their fiery eyes, and knew that he was at last in the land of Fairy. 'Canst thou tell me,' said Childe Rowland to the horse-herd, 'where the King of Elfland's Dark

Tower is?' 'I cannot tell thee,' said the horse-herd, 'but go on a little farther and thou wilt come to the cow-herd, and he, maybe, can tell thee.'

Then, without a word more, Childe Rowland drew the good brand that never struck in vain, and off went the horse-herd's head, and Childe Rowland went on farther, till he came to the cow-herd, and asked him the same question. 'I can't tell thee,' said he, 'but go on a little farther, and thou wilt come to the henwife, and she is sure to know.' Then Childe Rowland out with his good brand, that never struck in vain, and off went the cow-herd's head. And he went on a little farther, till he came to an old woman in a grey cloak, and he asked her if she knew where the Dark Tower of the King of Elfland was. 'Go on a, little further,' said the henwife, 'till you come to a round green hill, surrounded with terrace-rings, from the bottom to the top; go round it three times, widdershins, and each time say:

> Open, door! open, door!
> And let me come in;

and the third time the door will open, and you may go in.' And Childe Rowland was just going on, when he remembered what he had to do; so he out with the good brand, that never struck in vain, and off went the henwife's head.

Then he went on, and on, and on, till he came to the round green hill with the terrace-rings from top to bottom, and he went round it three times, widder-shins, saying each time:

> Open, door! open, door!
> And let me come in.

And the third time the door did open, and he went in, and it closed with a click, and Childe Rowland was left in the dark.

It was not exactly dark, but a kind of twilight or gloaming. There were neither windows nor candles, and he could not make out where the twilight came from, if not through the walls and roof. These were rough arches made of a transparent rock, encrusted with sheep-silver and rock spar and other bright stones. But though it was rock, the air was quite warm, as it always is in Elfland. So he went through this passage till at last he came to two wide and high folding-doors which stood ajar. And when he opened them, there he saw a most wonderful and glorious sight. A large and spacious hall, so large that it seemed to be as long, and as broad, as the green hill itself. The roof was supported by fine pillars, so large and lofty, that the pillars of a cathedral were nothing to them. They were all of gold and silver, with fretted work, and between them and around them, wreaths of flowers, composed of what do you think? Why, of diamonds and emeralds and all manner of precious stones. And the very keystones of the arches had for ornaments clusters of diamonds and rubies and pearls and other precious stones. And all these arches met in the middle of the roof, and just there, hung by a gold chain, was an immense lamp made out of one great pearl, hollowed out and quite transparent. And in the middle of this was a, huge carbuncle, which kept spinning round and round, and this was what gave light by its rays to the whole hall, which seemed as if the setting sun was shining on it.

The hall was furnished in a manner equally grand, and at one end of it was a glorious couch of velvet, silk and gold, and there sat Burd Ellen, combing her golden hair with a silver comb. And when she saw Childe Rowland she stood up and said:

> 'God pity ye, poor luckless fool,
>   What have ye here to do?
> Hear ye this, my youngest brother,
>   Why didn't ye bide at home?
> Had you a hundred thousand lives
>   Ye couldn't spare any a one.
> But sit ye down; but woe, oh woe,
>   That ever ye were born,
> For come the King of Elfland in,
>   Your fortune is forlorn.'

Then they sat down together, and Childe Rowland told her all that he had done, and she told him how their two brothers had reached the Dark Tower, but had been enchanted by the King of Elfland, and lay there entombed as if dead. And then after they had talked a little longer Childe Rowland began to feel hungry from his long travels, and told his sister Burd Ellen how hungry he was and asked for some food, forgetting all about the Warlock Merlin's warning.

Burd Ellen looked at Childe Rowland sadly, and shook her head, but she was under a spell, and could not warn him. So she rose up, and went out, and soon brought back a golden basin full of bread and milk. Childe Rowland was just going to raise it to his lips, when he looked at his sister and remembered why he had come all that way. So he dashed the bowl to the ground, and said: 'Not a sup will I swallow, nor a bit will I bite, till Burd Ellen is set free.'

Just at that moment they heard the noise of someone approaching, and a loud voice was heard saying:

'Fee, fi, fo, fum,
I smell the blood of a Christian man,
Be he dead, be he living, with my brand,
I'll dash his brains from his brain-pan.'

And then the folding-doors of the hall were burst open, and the King of Elfland rushed in.

'Strike then, bogle, if thou darest,' shouted out Childe Rowland, and rushed to meet him with his good brand that never yet did fail. They fought, and they fought, and they fought, till Childe Rowland beat the King of Elfland down on to his knees, and caused him to yield and beg for mercy. 'I grant thee mercy,' said Childe Rowland, 'if you release my sister from thy spells and raise my brothers to life and let us all go free.' 'I agree,' said the Elfin king, and rising up he went to a chest from which he took a phial filled with a blood-red liquor. With this he anointed the ears, eyelids, nostrils, lips and fingertips of the two brothers, and they sprang at once into life, and declared that their souls had been away, but had now returned. The Elfin king then said some words to Burd Ellen, and she was disenchanted, and they all four passed out of the hall, through the long passage, and turned their back on the Dark Tower, never to return again. And they reached home, and were restored to the good queen, their mother, and Burd Ellen never went round a church widdershins again.

Cinderella

Once there was a gentleman who married, for his second wife, the proudest and most haughty woman that was ever seen. She had, by a former husband, two daughters of her own humour, who were, indeed, exactly like her in all things. He had likewise, by another wife, a young daughter, but of unparalleled goodness and sweetness of temper, which she took from her mother, who was the best creature in the world.

No sooner were the ceremonies of the wedding over but the stepmother began to show herself in her true colours. She could not bear the good qualities of this

pretty girl, and the less because they made her own daughters appear the more odious. She employed her in the meanest work of the house: she scoured the dishes, tables, and scrubbed madam's chamber, and those of her daughters; she lay up in a sorry garret, upon a wretched straw bed, while her sisters lay in fine rooms, with floors all inlaid, upon beds of the very newest fashion, and where they had looking-glasses so large that they might see themselves at their full length from head to foot.

The poor girl bore all patiently, and dared not tell her father, who would have sent her away; for his wife governed him entirely. When she had done her work, she used to go into the chimney-corner, and sit down among cinders and ashes, which made her commonly be called Cinderwench; but the younger sister, who was not so rude and uncivil as the elder, called her Cinderella. However, Cinderella, notwithstanding her mean apparel, was a hundred times handsomer than her sisters, though they were always dressed very richly.

It happened that the king's son gave a ball, and invited all persons of fashion to it. Our young misses were also invited, for they cut very grand figures among the quality. They were mightily delighted at this invitation, and wonderfully busy in choosing out such gowns, petticoats and head-clothes as might become them. This was a new trouble to Cinderella; for it was she who ironed her sisters' linen, and plaited their ruffles; they talked all day long of nothing but how they should be dressed.

'For my part,' said the elder, 'I will wear my red velvet suit with French trimming.'

'And I,' said the younger, 'shall have my usual petticoat; but then, to make amends for that, I will put on my gold-flowered manteau, and my diamond stomacher, which is far from being the most ordinary one in the world.'

They sent for the best tire-woman they could get to make up their headdresses and adjust their double pinners, and they had their red brushes and patches from Mademoiselle de la Poche.

Cinderella was likewise called up to them to be consulted in all these matters, for she had excellent notions, and advised them always for the best, nay, and offered her services to dress their heads, which they were very willing she should do. As she was doing this, they said to her: 'Cinderella, would you not be glad to go to the ball?'

'Alas!' said she, 'you only mock me; it is not for such as I am to go thither.'

'Thou art in the right of it,' replied they; 'it would make the people laugh to see a Cinderwench at a ball.'

Anyone but Cinderella would have dressed their heads awry, but she was very good, and dressed them perfectly well They were almost two days without eating, so much were they transported with joy. They broke above a dozen laces in trying to be laced up close, that they might have a fine slender shape, and they were continually at their looking-glasses. At last the happy day came; they went to court, and Cinderella watched as long as she could, and when she had lost sight of them, she fell a-crying.

Her godmother, who saw her all in tears, asked her what was the matter.

'I wish I could – I wish I could – ' she was not able to speak the rest, being interrupted by her tears and sobbing.

This godmother of hers, who was a fairy, said to her, 'Thou wishest thou couldst go to the ball; is it not so?'

'Y–es,' cried Cinderella, with a great sigh.

'Well,' said her godmother, 'be but a good girl, and I will contrive that thou shalt go.' Then she took her into her chamber, and said to her, 'Run into the garden, and bring me a pumpkin.'

Cinderella went immediately to gather the finest she could get, and brought it to her godmother, not being able to imagine how this pumpkin could make her go to the ball. Her godmother scooped out all the inside of it, having left nothing but the rind; which done, she struck it with her wand, and the pumpkin was instantly turned into a fine coach, gilded all over with gold.

She then went to look into her mousetrap, where she found six sleek mice, all alive, and ordered Cinderella to lift up a little the trap-door; then, giving each mouse, as it came out, a little tap with her wand, she turned every one into a fine horse, and altogether they made a very fine set of six horses of a beautiful mouse-coloured dapple grey. Being at a loss for a coachman, Cinderella said, 'I'll go and see if there is a rat in the rat-trap – we may make a coachman of him.'

'Thou art in the right,' replied her godmother; 'go and look.'

Cinderella brought the trap to her, and in it there were three huge rats. The fairy made choice of one of the three which had the largest beard, and, having touched him with her wand, she turned him into a fat, jolly coachman, who had the smartest whiskers eyes ever beheld. After that, she said to Cinderella: 'Go again into the garden, and you will find six lizards behind the watering-pot, bring them to me.'

She had no sooner done so but her godmother turned them into six footmen, who skipped up immediately behind the coach, with their liveries all bedaubed with gold and silver, and clung as close behind each other as if they had done nothing else their whole lives. The fairy then said to Cinderella: 'Well, you see here an equipage fit to go to the ball with; are you not pleased with it?'

She ordered Cinderella to lift up a little the trap-door

'Oh! yes,' cried she; 'but must I go thither as I am, in these nasty rags?'

Her godmother only just touched her with her wand, and, at the same instant, her clothes were turned into cloth of gold and silver, all beset with jewels. This done, she gave her a pair of glass slippers, the prettiest in the whole world. Being thus decked out, Cinderella got up into her coach; but her godmother, above all things, commanded her not to stay till after midnight, telling her, at the same time, that if she stayed one moment longer, the coach would be a pumpkin again, her horses mice, her coachman a rat, her footmen lizards, and her clothes become just as they were before.

She promised her godmother she would not fail to leave the ball before midnight; and then away she drove, scarce able to contain herself for joy. The king's son, who was told that a great princess, whom nobody knew, was come, ran out to receive her; he gave her his hand as she alighted out of the coach, and led her into the ball, among all the company. There was immediately a profound silence, they left off dancing, and the violins ceased to play, so attentive was everyone to contemplate the singular beauties of the unknown newcomer. Nothing was then heard but a confused noise of: 'Ha! how handsome she is! Ha! how handsome she is!'

The king himself, old as he was, could not help watching her, and telling the queen softly that it was a long time since he had seen so beautiful and lovely a creature.

All the ladies were busied in considering her clothes and headdress, that they might have some made next day after the same pattern, provided they could meet with such fine material and as able hands to make them.

The king's son conducted her to the most honourable seat, and afterwards took her out to dance with him; she danced so very gracefully that they all more and more admired her. A fine collation was served up, whereof the young prince ate not a morsel, so intently was he busied in gazing on her.

She went and sat down by her sisters, showing them a thousand civilities, giving them part of the oranges and citrons which the prince had presented her with, which very much surprised them, for they did not know her. While Cinderella was thus amusing her sisters, she heard the clock strike eleven and three-quarters, whereupon she immediately made a curtsy to the company and hasted away as fast as she could.

When she got home she ran to seek out her godmother, and, after having thanked her, she said she could not but heartily wish she might go next day to the ball, because the king's son had desired her to.

As she was eagerly telling her godmother all that had passed at the ball, her two sisters knocked at the door, which Cinderella ran and opened.

'How long you have stayed!' cried she, gaping, rubbing her eyes and stretching herself as if she had been just waked out of her sleep; she had not, however, the least inclination to sleep, even now.

'If thou hadst been at the ball,' said one of her sisters, 'thou wouldst have marvelled indeed! There came thither the finest princess, the most beautiful ever was seen with mortal eyes; she showed us a thousand civilities, and gave us oranges and citrons.'

Cinderella seemed very indifferent in the matter; indeed, she asked them the name of that princess; but they told her they did not know it, and that the king's son was very uneasy on her account and would give all the world to know who she was. At this Cinderella, smiling, replied: 'She must, then, be very beautiful indeed; how happy you have been! Could not I see her? Ah! dear Miss Charlotte, do lend me your yellow suit of clothes which you wear every day.'

'Ay, to be sure!' cried Miss Charlotte; 'lend my clothes to such a dirty Cinderwench as thou art! I should be a fool.'

Cinderella, indeed, expected well such answer, and was very glad of the refusal; for she would have been sadly put to it if her sister had lent her what she asked for jestingly.

The next day the two sisters were at the ball, and so was Cinderella, but dressed more magnificently than before. The king's son was always by her, and never ceased his compliments and kind speeches to her; to whom all this was so far from being tiresome that she quite forgot what her godmother had recommended to her; so that she, at last, counted the clock striking twelve when she took it to be no more than eleven; she then rose up and fled, as nimble as a deer. The prince followed, but could not overtake her. She left behind one of her glass slippers, which the prince took up most carefully. She got home but quite out of breath, and in her nasty old clothes, having nothing left her of all her finery but one of the little slippers, fellow to that she had dropped. The guards at the palace gate were asked if they had seen a princess go out. They said they had seen nobody go out but a young girl, very meanly dressed, who had more the air of a poor country wench than a gentlewoman.

When the two sisters returned from the ball Cinderella asked them if they had been well diverted, and if the fine lady had been there.

They told her: Yes, but that she hurried away immediately when it struck twelve, and with so much haste that she dropped one of her little glass slippers, the prettiest in the world, which the king's son had taken up; that he had done nothing but look at her all the time at the ball, and that most certainly he was very much in love with the beautiful person who owned the glass slipper.

She left behind one of her glass slippers

What they said was very true; for a few days after the king's son caused it to be proclaimed, by sound of trumpet, that he would marry her whose foot the slipper would just fit. They whom he employed began to try it upon the princesses, then the duchesses and all the court, but in vain; it was brought to the two sisters, who did all they possibly could to thrust their foot into the slipper, but they could not effect it. Cinderella, who saw all this, and knew her slipper, said to them, laughing: 'Let me see if it will not fit me.'

Her sisters burst out a-laughing, and began to banter her. The gentleman who was sent to try the slipper looked earnestly at Cinderella, and, finding her very handsome, said it was but just that she should try, and that he had orders to let everyone make trial.

He obliged Cinderella to sit down, and, putting the slipper to her foot, he found it went on very easily, and fitted her as if it had been made of wax. The astonishment her two sisters were in was excessively great, but still abundantly greater when Cinderella pulled out of her pocket the other slipper, and put it on her other foot. Thereupon, in came her god-mother, who, having touched with her wand Cinderella's clothes, made them richer and more magnificent than any of those she had before.

And now her two sisters found her to be that fine, beautiful lady whom they had seen at the ball. They threw themselves at her feet to beg pardon for all the ill-treatment they had made her undergo. Cinderella took them up, and, as she embraced them, cried that she forgave them with all her heart, and desired them always to love her.

She was conducted to the young prince, dressed as she was; he thought her more charming than ever, and, a few days after, married her. Cinderella, who was no less good than beautiful, gave her two sisters lodgings in the palace, and that very same day matched them with two great lords of the court.

Connla and the Fairy Maiden

Connla of the Fiery Hair was son of Conn of the Hundred Fights. One day as he stood by the side of his father on the height of Usna, he saw a maiden clad in strange attire coming towards him.

'Whence comest thou, maiden?' said Connla.

'I come from the Plains of the Ever Living,' she said, 'there where there is neither death nor sin. There we keep holiday always, nor need we help from any in our joy. And in all our pleasure we have no strife. And because we have our homes in the round green hills, men call us the Hill Folk.'

The king and all with him wondered much to hear a voice when they saw no one. For save Connla alone, none saw the fairy maiden.

'To whom are you talking, my son?' said the king.

Then the maiden answered, 'Connla speaks to a young, fair maid, whom neither death nor old age awaits. I love Connla, and now I call him away to the plain of pleasure, Moy Mell, where Boadag is king for aye, nor has there been complaint or sorrow in that land since he has held the kingship. Oh, come with me, Connla of the Fiery Hair, ruddy as the dawn with thy tawny skin. A fairy crown awaits thee to grace thy comely face and royal form. Come, and never shall thy comeliness fade, nor thy youth, till the last awful day of judgement.'

The king in fear at what the maiden said, which he heard though he could not see her, called aloud to his druid, Coran by name.

connla and the fairy maiden

'Oh, Coran of the many spells,' he said, 'and of the cunning magic, I call upon thy aid. A task is upon me too great for all my skill and wit, greater than any laid upon me since I seized the kingship. A maiden unseen has met us, and by her power would take from me my dear, my comely son. If thou help not, he will be taken from thy king by woman's wiles and witchery.'

Then Coran the druid stood forth and chanted his spells towards the spot where the maiden's voice had been heard. And none heard her voice again, nor could Connla see her longer. Only as she vanished before the druid's mighty spell, she threw an apple to Connla.

For a whole month from that day Connla would take nothing, either to eat or to drink, save only from that apple. But as he ate it grew again and always kept whole. And all the while there grew within him a mighty yearning and longing after the maiden he had seen.

But when the last day of the month of waiting came, Connla stood by the side of the king his father on the plain of Arcomin, and again he saw the maiden come towards him, and again she spoke to him.

' 'Tis a glorious place, forsooth, that Connla holds among short-lived mortals awaiting the day of death. But now the folk of life, the ever-living ones, beg and bid thee come to Moy Mell, the plain of pleasure, for they have learnt to know thee, seeing thee in thy home among thy dear ones.'

When Conn the king heard the maiden's voice he called to his men aloud and said, 'Summon swift my druid Coran, for I see she has again this day the power of speech.'

Then the maiden said: 'Oh, mighty Conn, fighter of a hundred fights, the druid's power is little loved; it has little honour in the mighty land, peopled with so many of the upright. When the Law will come, it will do away with the druid's magic spells that come from the lips of the false black demon.'

Then Conn the king observed that since the maiden came Connla his son spoke to none that spake to him. So Conn of the hundred fights said to him, 'Is it to thy mind what the woman says, my son?'

' 'Tis hard upon me,' then said Connla; 'I love my own folk above all things; but yet, but yet a longing seizes me for the maiden.'

When the maiden heard this, she answered and said, 'The ocean is not so strong as the waves of thy longing. Come with me in my curragh, the gleaming, straight-gliding crystal canoe. Soon we can reach Boadag's realm. I see the bright sun sink, yet far as it is, we can reach it before dark. There is, too, another land worthy of thy journey, a land joyous to all that seek it. Only wives and maidens dwell there. If thou wilt, we can seek it and live there alone together in joy.'

When the maiden ceased to speak, Connla of the Fiery Hair rushed away from them and sprang into the curragh, the gleaming straight-gliding crystal canoe. And then they all, king and court, saw it glide away over the bright sea towards the setting sun. Away and away, till eye could see it no longer, and Connla and the fairy maiden went their way on the sea, and were no more seen, nor did any know where they came.

The History of Dick Whittington

Dick Whittington was a very little boy when his father and mother died; so little, indeed, that he never knew them, nor the place where he was born. He strolled about the country as ragged as a colt, till he met with a wagoner who was going to London, and who gave him leave to walk all the way by the side of his wagon without paying anything for his passage. This pleased little Whittington very much, as he wanted to see London badly, for he had heard that the streets were paved with gold, and he was willing to get a bushel of it; but how great was his disappointment, poor boy! when he saw the streets covered with dirt instead of gold, and found himself in a strange place, without a friend, without food and without money.

Though the wagoner was so charitable as to let him walk up by the side of the wagon for nothing, he took care not to know him when he came to town, and the poor boy was, in a little time, so cold and hungry that he wished himself in a good kitchen and by a warm fire in the country.

In his distress he asked charity of several people, and one of them bid him, 'Go to work for an idle rogue.'

'That I will,' said Whittington, 'with all my heart; I will work for you if you will let me.'

The man, who thought this savoured of wit and impertinence (though the poor lad intended only to show his readiness to work), gave him a blow with a stick which broke his head so that the blood ran down. In this situation, and fainting for want of food, he laid himself down at the door of one Mr Fitzwarren, a merchant, where the cook saw him, and, being an ill-natured hussy, ordered him to go about his business or she would scald him. At this time Mr Fitzwarren came from the Exchange, and began also to scold at the poor boy, bidding him to go to work.

Whittington answered that he should be glad to work if anybody would employ him, and that he should be able if he could get something to eat, for he had had nothing for three days, and he was a poor country boy, and knew nobody, and nobody would employ him.

He then endeavoured to get up, but he was so very weak that he fell down again, which excited so much compassion in the merchant that he ordered the servants to take him in and give him some meat and drink, and let him help the cook to do any dirty work that she had to set him about. People are too apt to reproach those who beg with being idle, but give themselves no concern to put them in the way of getting business to do, or considering whether they are able to do it, which is not charity.

But we return to Whittington, who could have lived happy in this worthy family had he not been bumped about by the cross cook, who must be always roasting and basting and who when the spit was idle employed her hands upon poor Whittington! At last Miss Alice, his master's daughter, was informed of it, and then she took compassion on the poor boy, and made the servants treat him kindly.

Besides the crossness of the cook, Whittington had another difficulty to get over before he could be happy. He had, by order of his master, a flock-bed placed for him in a garret, where there was a number of rats and mice that often ran over the poor boy's nose and disturbed him in his sleep. After some time, however, a gentleman who came to his master's house gave Whittington a penny for brushing his shoes. This he put into his pocket, being determined to lay it out to the best advantage; and the next day, seeing a woman in the street with a cat under her arm, he ran up to know the price of it. The woman (as the cat was a good mouser) asked a deal of money for it, but on Whittington's telling her he had but a penny in the world, and that he wanted a cat badly, she let him have it.

This cat Whittington concealed in the garret, for fear she should be beat about by his mortal enemy the cook, and here she soon killed or frightened away the rats and mice, so that the poor boy could now sleep as sound as a top.

Soon after this the merchant, who had a ship ready to sail, called for his servants, as his custom was, in order that each of them might venture something to try their luck; and whatever they sent was to pay neither freight nor custom, for he thought justly that God Almighty would bless him the more for his readiness to let the poor partake of his fortune.

All the servants appeared but poor Whittington, who, having neither money nor goods, could not think of sending anything to try his luck; but his good friend Miss Alice, thinking his poverty kept him away, ordered him to be called.

She then offered to lay down something for him,

but the merchant told his daughter that would not do, it must be something of his own. Upon which poor Whittington said he had nothing but a cat which he had bought for a penny that was given him. 'Fetch thy cat, boy,' said the merchant, 'and send her.' Whittington brought poor puss and delivered her to the captain, with tears in his eyes, for he said he should now be disturbed by the rats and mice as much as ever. All the company laughed at the adventure except Miss Alice, who pitied the poor boy, and gave him something to buy another cat.

While puss was beating the billows at sea, poor Whittington was severely beaten at home by his tyrannical mistress the cook, who used him so cruelly, and made such game of him for sending his cat to sea, that at last the poor boy determined to run away from his place, and having packed up the few things he had, he set out very early in the morning on All-Hallows day. He travelled through Holloway, which was then a village within sight of the great city, and at the foot of the steep hill that led up to the village of Highgate he sat down on a stone to consider what course he should take; but while he was thus ruminating, Bow bells, of which there were only six, began to ring; and he thought they seemed to say: 'Turn again, Whittington, thrice Lord Mayor of London.'

'Lord Mayor of London!' said he to himself, 'what would not one endure to be Lord Mayor of London, and ride in such a fine coach? Well, I'll go back again, and bear all the pummelling and ill-usage of Cicely rather than miss the opportunity of being Lord Mayor!' So home he went, and happily got into the house and about his business before Mrs Cicely made her appearance.

'Turn again, Whittington, thrice Lord Mayor of London.'

We must now follow Miss Puss to the coast of Africa. How perilous are voyages at sea, how uncertain the winds and the waves, and how many accidents attend a naval life!

The ship that had the cat on board was long beaten at sea, and at last, by contrary winds, driven on a part of the coast of Barbary which was inhabited by Moors unknown to the English. These people received our countrymen with civility, and therefore the captain, in order to trade with them, showed them the patterns of the goods he had on board, and sent some of them to the king of the country, who was so well pleased that he sent for the captain and the factor to come to his palace, which was about a mile from the sea. Here they were placed, according to the custom of the country, on rich carpets, flowered with gold and silver; and the king and queen being seated at the upper end of the room, dinner was brought in, which consisted of many dishes; but no sooner were the dishes put down but an amazing number of rats and mice came from all quarters and devoured all the meat in an instant.

The factor, in surprise, turned round to the nobles and asked if these vermin were not offensive. 'Oh! yes,' said they, 'very offensive; and the king would give half his treasure to be freed of them, for they not only destroy his dinner, as you see, but they assault him in his chamber, and even in bed, so that he is obliged to be watched while he is sleeping, for fear of them.'

The factor jumped for joy; he remembered poor Whittington and his cat, and told the king he had a creature on board the ship that would despatch all these vermin immediately. The king's heart heaved so high at the joy which this news gave him that his turban dropped off his head. 'Bring this creature to me,' said he; 'vermin are dreadful in a court, and if she will perform what you say I will load your ship with gold and jewels in exchange for her.' The factor, who knew his business, took this opportunity to set forth the merits of Miss Puss. He told his majesty that it would be inconvenient to part with her, as, when she was gone, the rats and mice might destroy the goods in the ship – but to oblige his majesty he would fetch her. 'Run, run,' said the queen; 'I am impatient to see the dear creature.'

Away flew the factor, while another dinner was providing, and returned with the cat just as the rats and mice were devouring that also. He immediately put down Miss Puss, who killed a great number of them.

The king rejoiced greatly to see his old enemies

The factor called, 'Pussy, pussy, pussy!' and she came to him.

destroyed by so small a creature, and the queen was highly pleased, and desired the cat might be brought near that she might look at her. Upon which the factor called, 'Pussy, pussy, pussy!' and she came to him. He then presented her to the queen, who started back, and was afraid to touch a creature who had made such havoc among the rats and mice; however, when the factor stroked the cat and called, 'Pussy, pussy!' the queen also touched her and cried, 'Putty, putty!' for she had not learned English.

He then put her down on the queen's lap, where she, purring, played with her majesty's hand, and then sang herself to sleep.

The king, having seen the exploits of Miss Puss, bargained with the captain and factor for the whole ship's cargo, and then gave them ten times as much for the cat as all the rest amounted to. On which, taking leave of their majesties and other great personages at court, they sailed with a fair wind for England, whither we must now attend them.

The morn had scarcely dawned when Mr Fitzwarren arose to count over the cash and settle the
business for that day. He had just entered the
counting-house, and seated himself at the desk, when
somebody came, tap, tap, at the door. 'Who's there?'
said Mr Fitzwarren. 'A friend,' answered the other.
'What friend can come at this unseasonable time?' 'A
real friend is never unseasonable,' answered the other.
'I come to bring you good news of your ship *Unicorn*.'
The merchant bustled up in such a hurry that he
forgot his gout; instantl opened the door, and who
should be seen waiting but the captain and factor,
with a cabinet of jewels, and a bill of lading, for which
the merchant lifted up his eyes and thanked heaven
for sending him such a prosperous voyage. Then they
told him the adventures of the cat, and showed him
the cabinet of jewelswhich they had brought for Mr
Whittington. Upon which he cried out with great
earnestness, but not in the most poetical manner:

'Go, send him in, and tell him of his fame,
And call him Mr Whittington by name.'

It is not our business to animadvert upon these
lines; we are not critics, but historians. It is sufficient
for us that they are the words of Mr Fitzwarren; and
though it is beside our purpose, and perhaps not in
our power to prove him a good poet, we shall soon
convince the reader that he was a good man, which
was a much better character; for when some who
were present told him that this treasure was too much
for such a poor boy as Whittington, he said: 'God
forbid that I should deprive him of a penny; it is his
own, and he shall have it to a farthing.' He then
ordered Mr Whittington in, who was at this time

cleaning the kitchen and would have excused himself from going into the counting-house, saying the room was swept and his shoes were dirty and full of hob-nails. The merchant, however, made him come in, and ordered a chair to be set for him. Upon which, thinking they intended to make sport of him, as had been too often the case in the kitchen, he besought his master not to mock a poor simple fellow, who intended them no harm, but let him go about his business. The merchant, taking him by the hand, said: 'Indeed, Mr Whittington, I am in earnest with you, and sent for you to congratulate you on your great success. Your cat has procured you more money than I am worth in the world, and may you long enjoy it and be happy!'

At length, being shown the treasure, and convinced by them that all of it belonged to him, he fell upon his knees and thanked the Almighty for his providential care of such a poor and miserable creature. He then laid all the treasure at his master's feet, who refused to take any part of it, but told him he heartily rejoiced at his prosperity, and hoped the wealth he had acquired would be a comfort to him, and would make him happy. He then applied to his mistress, and to his good friend Miss Alice, who refused to take any part of the money, but told him she heartily rejoiced at his good success, and wished him all imaginable felicity. He then thanked the captain, factor and the ship's crew for the care they had taken of his cargo. He likewise distributed presents to all the servants in the house, not forgetting even his old enemy the cook, though she little deserved it.

After this Mr Fitzwarren advised Mr Whittington to send for the necessary people and dress himself like a gentleman, and made him the offer of his house to live in till he could provide himself with a better.

Now it came to pass when Mr Whittington's face was washed, his hair curled, and he dressed in a rich suit of clothes, that he turned out a genteel young fellow; and, as wealth contributes much to give a man confidence, he in a little time dropped that sheepish behaviour which was principally occasioned by a depression of spirits, and soon grew a sprightly and good companion, insomuch that Miss Alice, who had formerly pitied him, now fell in love with him.

When her father perceived they had this good liking for each other he proposed a match between them, to which both parties cheerfully consented, and the Lord Mayor, Court of Aldermen, Sheriffs, the Company of Stationers, the Company of Mercers and a number of eminent merchants attended the ceremony, and were elegantly treated at an entertainment made for that purpose.

History further relates that they lived very happy, had several children and died at a good old age. Mr Whittington served as Sheriff of London and was three times Lord Mayor. In the last year of his mayoralty he entertained King Henry V, after his conquest of France, upon which occasion the king, in consideration of Whittington's merit, said: 'Never had prince such a subject;' which being told to Whittington at the table, he replied: 'Never had subject such a king.' His majesty conferred the honour of knighthood on him soon after.

Sir Richard many years before his death constantly fed a great number of poor citizens, built a church and a college to it, with a yearly allowance for poor scholars, and near it erected a hospital.

He also built Newgate for criminals, and gave liberally to St Bartholomew's Hospital and other public charities. And even to this day there stands a great and mighty hospital at the foot of Highgate Hill near where he heard the bells summoning him to return to London. Also around that place are many reminders of the good and faithful cat that brought this tale to such a happy end.

The Dream of Owen O'Mulready

There was a man long ago living near Ballaghadereen named Owen O'Mulready, who was a workman for the gentleman of the place, and was a prosperous, quiet, contented man. There was no one but himself and his wife Margaret, and they had a nice little house and enough potatoes in the year, in addition to their share of wages, from their master. There wasn't a want or anxiety on Owen, except one desire, and that was to have a dream – for he had never had one.

One day when he was digging potatoes, his master – James Taafe – came out to his ridge, and they began talking, as was the custom with them. The talk fell on dreams, and said Owen that he would like better than anything if he could only have one.

'You'll have one tonight,' says his master, 'if you do as I tell you.'

'Musha, I'll do it, and welcome,' says Owen.

'Now,' says his master, 'when you go home tonight, draw the fire from the hearth, put it out, make your bed in its place and sleep there tonight, and you'll have enough of dreaming before the morning.'

Owen promised to do this. When, however, he began to draw the fire out, Margaret thought that he had lost his senses, so he explained everything James Taafe had said to him, had his own way, and they went to lie down together on the hearth.

Not long was Owen asleep when there came a knock at the door. 'Get up, Owen O'Mulready, and go with a letter from the master to America.'

Owen got up, and put his feet into his boots, saying to himself, 'It's late you come, messenger.'

He took the letter, and he went forward and never tarried till he came to the foot of Sliabh Charn, where he met a cow-boy, and he herding cows.

'The blessing of God be with you, Owen O'Mulready,' says the boy.

'The blessing of God and Mary be with you, my boy,' says Owen. 'Everyone knows me, and I don't know anyone at all.'

'Where are you going this time of night?' says the boy.

'I'm going to America, with a letter from the master; is this the right road?' says Owen.

'It is; keep straight to the west; but how are you going to get over the water?' says the boy.

'Time enough to think of that when I get to it,' replied Owen.

He went on the road again, till he came to the brink of the sea; there he saw a crane standing on one foot on the shore.

'The blessing of God be with you, Owen O'Mulready,' says the crane.

'The blessing of God and Mary be with you, Mrs Crane,' says Owen. 'Everybody knows me, and I don't know anyone.'

'What are you doing here?'

Owen told her his business, and that he didn't know how he'd get over the water.

'Leave your two feet on my two wings, and sit on my back, and I'll take you to the other side,' says the crane.

'What would I do if tiredness should come on you before we got over?' says Owen.

'Don't be afraid, I won't be tired or wearied till I fly over.'

Then Owen went on the back of the crane, and she arose over the sea and went forward, but she hadn't flown more than halfway, when she cried out, 'Owen O'Mulready get off me; I'm tired.'

'That you may be seven times worse this day twelve months, you rogue of a crane,' says Owen. 'I can't get off you now, so don't ask me.'

'I don't care,' replied the crane, 'if you'll rise off me a while till I'll take a rest.'

With that they saw threshers over their heads, and Owen shouted, 'Och! Thresher, thresher, leave down your flail at me, that I may give the crane a rest!'

The thresher let down the flail, but when Owen took a hold with his two hands, the crane went from him laughing and mocking.

'My share of misfortunes go with you!' said Owen. 'It's you've left me in a fix hanging between the heavens and the water in the middle of the great sea.'

It wasn't long till the thresher shouted to him to leave go the flail.

'I won't let it go,' said Owen. 'Shan't I be drowned?'

'If you don't let it go, I'll cut the whang.'

'I don't care,' says Owen; 'I have the flail;' and with that he looked away from him, and what should he see but a boat a long way off.

'O sailor, dear sailor, come,

come; perhaps you'll take my lot of bones,' said Owen.

'Are we under you now?' says the sailor.

'Not yet, not yet,' says Owen.

'Fling down one of your shoes, till we see the way it falls,' says the captain.

Owen shook one foot, and down fell the shoe.

'Uill, uill, puil, uil liu – who is killing me?' came a scream from Margaret in the bed. 'Where are you, Owen?'

'I didn't know whether 'twas you were in it, Margaret.'

'Indeed, then it is,' says she, 'who else would it be?'

She got up and lit the candle. She found Owen halfway up the chimney, climbing by the hands on the crook, and he black with soot! He had one shoe on, but the point of the other had struck Margaret, and 'twas that which awoke her.

Owen came down off the crook and washed himself, and from that day on there was no envy on him ever to have a dream again.

Earl Mar's Daughter

One fine summer's day Earl Mar's daughter went into the castle garden, dancing and tripping along. And as she played and sported she would stop from time to time to listen to the music of the birds. After a while as she sat under the shade of a green oak tree she looked up and spied a sprightly dove sitting high up on one of its branches. She looked up and said: 'Coo-my-dove, my dear, come down to me and I will give you a golden cage. I'll take you home and pet you well, as well as any bird of them all.' Scarcely had she said these words when the dove flew down from the branch and settled on her shoulder, nestling up against her neck while she smoothed its feathers. Then she took it home to her own room.

The day was done and the night came on and Earl Mar's daughter was thinking of going to sleep when, turning round, she found at her side a handsome young man. She was startled, for the door had been locked for hours. But she was a brave girl and said: 'What are you doing here, young man, to come and startle me so? The door was barred these hours ago; how ever did you come here?'

'Hush! hush!' the young man whispered. 'I was that cooing dove that you coaxed from off the tree.'

'But who are you then?' she said quite low; 'and how came you to be changed into that dear little bird?'

'My name is Florentine, and my mother is a queen, and something more than a queen, for she knows magic and spells, and because I would not do as she wished she turned me into a dove by day, but at night her spells lose their power and I become a man again. Today I crossed the sea and saw you for the first time and I was glad to be a bird that I could come near you. Unless you love me, I shall never be happy more.'

'But if I love you,' says she, 'will you not fly away and leave me one of these fine days?'

'Never, never,' said the prince; 'be my wife and I'll be yours for ever. By day a bird, by night a prince, I will always be by your side as a husband, dear.'

So they were married in secret and lived happily in the castle and no one knew that every night Coo-my-dove became Prince Florentine. And every year a little son came to them as bonny as bonny could be. But as each son was born Prince Florentine carried the little thing away on his back over the sea to where the queen his mother lived and left the little one with her.

Seven years passed thus and then a great trouble came to them. For the Earl Mar wished to marry his daughter to a noble of high degree who came wooing her. Her father pressed her sore but she said: 'Father dear, I do not wish to marry; I can be quite happy with Coo-my-dove here.'

Then her father got into a mighty rage and swore a great big oath, and said: 'Tomorrow, so sure as I live and eat, I'll twist that birdie's neck,' and out he stamped from her room.

'Oh, oh!' said Coo-my-dove; 'it's time that I was away,' and so he jumped upon the window-sill and in a moment was flying away. And he flew and he flew till he was over the deep, deep sea, and yet on he flew till he came to his mother's castle. Now the queen his mother was taking her walk abroad when she saw the pretty dove flying overhead and alighting on the castle walls.

'Here, dancers come and dance your jigs,' she called, 'and pipers, pipe you well, for here's my own Florentine, come back to me to stay for he's brought no bonny boy with him this time.'

'No, mother,' said Florentine, 'no dancers for me and no minstrels, for my dear wife, the mother of my seven boys, is to be wed tomorrow, and sad's the day for me.'

'What can I do, my son?' said the queen, 'tell me, and it shall be done if my magic has power to do it.'

'Well then, mother dear, turn the twenty-four dancers and pipers into twenty-four grey herons, and let my seven sons become seven white swans, and let me be a goshawk and their leader.'

'Alas! alas! my son,' she said, 'that may not be; my magic reaches not so far. But perhaps my teacher, the spaewife of Ostree, may know better.' And away she hurries to the cave of Ostree, and after a while comes out as white as white can be and muttering over some burning herbs she brought out of the cave. Suddenly Coo-my-dove changed into a goshawk and around him flew twenty-four grey herons and above them flew seven cygnets.

Without a word or a goodbye off they flew over the deep blue sea which was tossing and moaning. They flew and they flew till they swooped down on Earl Mar's castle just as the wedding party were setting out for the church. First came the men-at-arms and then the bridegroom's friends, and then Earl

Mar's men, and then the bridegroom, and lastly, pale and beautiful, Earl Mar's daughter herself. They moved down slowly to stately music till they came past the trees on which the birds were settling. A word from Prince Florentine, the goshawk, and they all rose into the air, herons beneath, cygnets above, and goshawk circling above all. The weddineers wondered at the sight when, swoop! the herons were down among them scattering the men-at-arms. The swanlets took charge of the bride while the goshawk dashed down and tied the bridegroom to a tree. Then the herons gathered themselves together into one featherbed and the cygnets placed their mother upon them, and suddenly they all rose in the air bearing the bride away with them in safety towards Prince Florentine's home. Surely a wedding party was never so disturbed in this world. What could the weddineers do? They saw their pretty bride carried away and away till she and the herons and the swans and the goshawk disappeared, and that very day Prince Florentine brought Earl Mar's daughter to the castle of the queen his mother, who took the spell off him and they lived happy ever afterwards.

East of the Sun and West of the Moon

Once upon a time there was a poor husbandman who had many children and little to give them in the way either of food or clothing. They were all pretty, but the prettiest of all was the youngest daughter, who was so beautiful that there were no bounds to her beauty.

So once – it was late on a Thursday evening in autumn, and wild weather outside, terribly dark, and raining so heavily and blowing so hard that the walls of the cottage shook again – they were all sitting together by the fireside, each of them busy with something or other, when suddenly someone rapped three times against the window-pane.

The man went out to see what could be the matter, and when he got out there stood a great big white bear.

'Good-evening to you,' said the White Bear.

'Good-evening,' said the man.

'Will you give me your youngest daughter?' said the White Bear; 'if you will, you shall be as rich as you are now poor.'

Truly the man would have had no objection to be rich, but he thought to himself: 'I must first ask my daughter about this,' so he went in and told them that there was a great white bear outside who had faithfully promised to make them all rich if he might but have the youngest daughter.

She said no, and would not hear of it; so the man went out again, and settled with the White Bear that

She seated herself on his back with her bundle and they departed

he should come again next Thursday evening, and get her answer. Then the man persuaded her, and talked so much to her about the wealth that they would have, and what a good thing it would be for herself, that at last she made up her mind to go, and washed and mended all her rags, made herself as smart as she could, and held herself in readiness to set out. Little enough had she to take away with her.

Next Thursday evening the White Bear came to fetch her. She seated herself on his back with her bundle, and thus they departed. When they had gone a great part of the way, the White Bear said: 'Are you afraid?'

'No, that I am not,' said she.

'Keep tight hold of my fur, and then there is no danger,' said he.

And thus she rode far, far away, until they came to a great mountain. Then the White Bear knocked on it, and a door opened, and they went into a castle where there were many brilliantly lighted rooms which shone with gold and silver, likewise a large hall in which there was a well-spread table, and it was so magnificent that it would be hard to make anyone understand how splendid it was. The White Bear gave her a silver bell, and told her that when she needed anything she had but to ring this bell, and what she wanted would appear. So after she had eaten, and night was drawing near, she grew sleepy after her journey, and thought she would like to go to bed. She rang the bell, and scarcely had she touched it before she found herself in a chamber where a bed stood ready made for her, which was as pretty as anyone could wish to sleep in. It had pillows of silk, and curtains of silk fringed with gold, and everything that was in the room was of gold or silver, but when she had lain down and put out the light, a man came and lay down beside her, and behold it was the White Bear, who cast off the form of a beast during the night. She never saw him, however, for he always came after she had put out her light, and went away before daylight appeared.

So all went well and happily for a time, but then she began to be very sad and sorrowful, for all day long she had to go about alone; and she did so wish to go home to her father and mother and brothers and sisters. Then the White Bear asked what it was that she wanted, and she told him that it was so dull there in the mountain, and that she had to go about all alone, and that in her parents' house at home there were all her brothers and sisters, and it was because she could not go to them that she was so sorrowful.

'There might be a cure for that,' said the White Bear, 'if you would but promise me never to talk with your mother alone, but only when the others are there too; for she will take hold of your hand,' he said, 'and will want to lead you into a room to talk with you alone; but that you must by no means do, or you will bring great misery on both of us.'

So one Sunday the White Bear came and said that they could now set out to see her father and mother, and they journeyed thither, she sitting on his back, and they went a long, long way, and it took a long, long time; but at last they came to a large white farmhouse, and her brothers and sisters were running about outside it, playing, and it was so pretty that it was a pleasure to look at it.

'Your parents dwell here now,' said the White Bear; 'but do not forget what I said to you, or you will do much harm both to yourself and me.'

'No, indeed,' said she, 'I shall never forget;' and as soon as she was at home the White Bear turned round and went back again.

There were such rejoicings when she went in to her parents that it seemed as if they would never come to an end. Everyone thought that they could never be sufficiently grateful to her for all she had done for them. Now they had everything that they wanted, and everything was as good as it could be. They all asked her how she was getting on where she was. All was well with her too, she said; and she had everything that she could want. What other answers she gave I cannot say, but I am pretty sure that they did not learn much from her. But in the afternoon, after they had dined at midday, all happened just as the White

Bear had said. Her mother wanted to talk with her alone in her own chamber. But she remembered what the White Bear had said, and would on no account go. 'What we have to say can surely be said at any time,' she answered. But somehow or other her mother at last persuaded her, and she was forced to tell the whole story. So she told how every night a man came and lay down beside her when the lights were all put out, and how she never saw him, because he always went away before it grew light in the morning, and how she continually went about in sadness, thinking how happy she would be if she could but see him, and how all day long she had to go about alone, and it was so dull and solitary. 'Oh!' cried the mother, in horror, 'you are very likely sleeping with a troll! But I will teach you a way to see him. You shall have a bit of one of my candles, which you can take away with you hidden in your breast. Look at him with that when he is asleep, but take care not to let any tallow drop upon him.'

So she took the candle, and hid it in her breast, and when evening drew near the White Bear came to fetch her away. When they had gone some distance on their way, the White Bear asked her if everything had not happened just as he had foretold, and she could not but own that it had. 'Then, if you have done what your mother wished,' said he, 'you have brought great misery on both of us.' 'No,' she said, 'I have not done anything at all.' So when she had reached home and had gone to bed it was just the same as it had been before, and a man came and lay down beside her, and late at night, when she could hear that he was sleeping, she got up and kindled a light, lit her candle, let her light shine on him, and saw him, and he was

144

the handsomest prince that eyes had ever beheld, and she loved him so much that it seemed to her that she must die if she did not kiss him that very moment. So she did kiss him; but while she was doing it she let three drops of hot tallow fall upon his shirt, and he awoke. 'What have you done now?' said he; 'you have brought misery on both of us. If you had but held out for the space of one year I should have been free. I have a stepmother who has bewitched me so that I

*It seemed to her that she must die if she did not
kiss him that very moment*

am a white bear by day and a man by night; but now all is at an end between you and me, and I must leave you, and go to her. She lives in a castle which lies east of the sun and west of the moon, and there too is a princess with a nose which is three ells long, and she now is the one whom I must marry.'

She wept and lamented, but all in vain, for go he must. Then she asked him if she could not go with him. But no, that could not be. 'Can you tell me the way then, and I will seek you – that I may surely be allowed to do!'

'Yes, you may do that,' said he; 'but there is no way thither. It lies east of the sun and west of the moon, and never would you find your way there.'

When she awoke in the morning both the prince and the castle were gone, and she was lying on a small green patch in the midst of a dark, thick wood. By her side lay the selfsame bundle of rags which she had brought with her from her own home. So when she had rubbed the sleep out of her eyes, and wept till she was weary, she set out on her way, and thus she walked for many and many a long day, until at last she came to a great mountain. Outside it an aged woman was sitting, playing with a golden apple. The girl asked her if she knew the way to the prince who lived with his stepmother in the castle which lay east of the sun and west of the moon, and who was to marry a princess with a nose which was three ells long. 'How do you happen to know about him?' enquired the old woman; 'maybe you are she who ought to have had him.' 'Yes, indeed, I am,' she said. 'So it is you, then?' said the old woman; 'I know nothing about him but that he dwells in a castle which is east of the sun and west of the moon. You will be a long time in getting to it, if ever you get to it at all; but you shall have the loan of my horse, and then you can ride on it to an old woman who is a neighbour of mine: perhaps she can tell you about him. When you have got there you must just strike the horse beneath the left ear and bid it go home again; but you may take the golden apple with you.'

So the girl seated herself on the horse, and rode for a long, long way, and at last she came to the mountain, where an aged woman was sitting outside with a gold carding-comb. The girl asked her if she knew the way to the castle which lay east of the sun and west of the moon; but she said what the first old woman had said: 'I know nothing about it, but that it is east of the sun and west of the moon, and that you will be a long time in getting to it, if ever you get there at all; but you shall have the loan of my horse to an old woman who lives the nearest to me: perhaps she may know where the castle is, and when you have got to her you may just strike the horse beneath the left ear and bid it go home again.' Then she gave her the gold carding-comb, for it might, perhaps, be of use to her, she said.

So the girl seated herself on the horse, and rode a wearisome long way onward again, and after a very long time she came to a great mountain, where an aged woman was sitting, spinning at a golden spinning-wheel. Of this woman, too, she enquired if she knew the way to the prince, and where to find the castle which lay east of the sun and west of the moon. But it was only the same thing once again. 'Maybe it was you who should have had the prince,' said the old woman. 'Yes, indeed, I should have been the one,' said the girl. But this old crone knew the way no better than the others – it was east of the sun and west of the moon, she knew that, 'and you will be a long time in getting to it, if ever you get to it at all,' she said; 'but you may have the loan of my horse, and I think you had better ride to the East Wind, and ask him: perhaps he may know where the castle is, and will blow you thither. But when you have got to him you must just strike the horse beneath the left ear, and he will come home again.' And then she gave her the golden spinning-wheel, saying: 'Perhaps you may find that you have a use for it.'

The girl had to ride for a great many days, and for a long and wearisome time, before she got there; but at last she did arrive, and then she asked the East Wind if he could tell her the way to the prince who dwelt east of the sun and west of the moon. 'Well,' said the East Wind, 'I have heard tell of the prince, and of his castle, but I do not know the way to it, for I have never blown so far; but, if you like, I will go with you to my brother the West Wind: he may know that, for he is much stronger than I am. You may sit on my back, and then I can carry you there.' So she seated herself on his back, and they did go so swiftly! When they got there, the East Wind went in and said that the girl whom he had brought was the one who ought to have had the prince up at the castle which lay east of the sun and west of the moon, and that now she was travelling about to find him again, so he had come there with her, and would like to hear if the West Wind knew whereabouts the castle was. 'No,' said the West Wind; 'so far as that have I never blown; but if you like I will go with you to the South Wind, for he is much stronger than either of us, and he has roamed far and wide, and perhaps he can tell you what you want to know. You may seat yourself on my back, and then I will carry you to him.'

So she did this, and journeyed to the South Wind, neither was she very long on the way. When they had got there, the West Wind asked him if he could tell her the way to the castle that lay east of the sun and west of the moon, for she was the girl who ought to marry the Prince who lived there. 'Oh, indeed!' said the South Wind, 'is that she? Well,' said he, 'I have wandered about a great deal in my time, and in all kinds of places, but I have never blown so far as that. If you like, however, I will go with you to my brother, the North Wind; he is the oldest and strongest of all of us, and if he does not know where it is no one in the whole world will be able to tell you. You may sit upon my back, and then I will carry you there.' So she seated herself on his back, and off he went from his house in great haste, and they were not long on the way. When they came near the North Wind's dwelling, he was so wild and frantic that they felt cold gusts a long while before they got there. 'What do you want?' he roared out from afar, and they froze as they heard. Said the South Wind: 'It is I, and this is she who should have had the prince who lives in the castle which lies east of the sun and west of the moon. And now she wishes to ask you if you have ever been there, and can tell her the way, for she would gladly find him again.'

'Yes,' said the North Wind, 'I know where it is. I once blew an aspen leaf there, but I was so tired that for many days afterwards I was not able to blow at all. However, if you really are anxious to go there, and are not afraid to go with me, I will take you on my back, and try if I can blow you there.'

'Get there I must,' said she; 'and if there is any way of going I will; and I have no fear, no matter how fast you go.'

'Very well then,' said the North Wind; 'but you must sleep here tonight, for if we are ever to get there we must have the day before us.'

The North Wind woke her betimes next morning, and puffed himself up, and made himself so big and so strong that it was frightful to see him, and away they went, high up through the air, as if they would not stop until they had reached the very end of the world. Down below there was such a storm! It blew down woods and houses, and when they were above the sea the ships were wrecked by hundreds. And thus they tore on and on, and a long time went by, and then yet more time passed, and still they were above the sea, and the North Wind grew tired, and more tired, and at last so utterly weary that he was scarcely able to blow any longer, and he sank and sank, lower and lower, until at last he went so low that the waves dashed against the heels of the poor girl he was carrying. 'Art thou afraid?' said the North Wind. 'I have no fear,' said she; and it was true. But they were not very, very far from land, and there was just enough strength left in the North Wind to enable him to throw her on to the shore, immediately under the windows of a castle which lay east of the sun and west of the moon; but then he was so weary and worn out that he was forced to rest for several days before he could go to his own home again.

Next morning she sat down beneath the walls of the castle to play with the golden apple, and the first person she saw was the maiden with the long nose, who was to have the prince. 'How much do you want

*'Art thou afraid?' said the North Wind. 'I have no fear,'
said she; and it was true*

for that gold apple of yours, girl?' said she, opening
the window. 'It can't be bought either for gold or
money,' answered the girl. 'If it cannot be bought
either for gold or money, what will buy it? You may
say what you please,' said the princess.

'Well, if I may go to the prince who is here, and be
with him tonight, you shall have it,' said the girl who
had come with the North Wind. 'You may do that,'
said the princess, for she had made up her mind what
she would do. So the princess got the golden apple,
but when the girl went up to the prince's apartment
that night he was asleep, for the princess had so
contrived it. The poor girl called to him, and shook
him, and between whiles she wept; but she could not

wake him. In the morning, as soon as day dawned, in came the princess with the long nose, and drove her out again. In the daytime she sat down once more beneath the windows of the castle, and began to card with her golden carding-comb; and then all happened as it had happened before. The princess asked her what she wanted for it, and she replied that it was not for sale, either for gold or money, but that if she could get leave to go to the prince, and be with him during the night, she should have it. But when she went up to the prince's room he was again asleep, and let her call him or shake him or weep as she would, he still slept on, and she could not put any life in him. When daylight came in the morning, the princess with the long nose came too, and once more drove her away. When day had quite come, the girl seated herself under the castle windows to spin with her golden spinning-wheel, and the princess with the long nose wanted to have that also. So she opened the window, and asked what she would take for it. The girl said what she had said on each of the former occasions – that it was not for sale either for gold or for money, but if she could get leave to go to the prince who lived there, and be with him during the night, she should have it.

'Yes,' said the princess, 'I will gladly consent to that.'

But in that place there were some Christian folk who had been carried off, and they had been sitting in the chamber which was next to that of the prince, and had heard how a woman had been in there who had wept and called on him two nights running, and they told the prince of this. So that evening, when the princess came once more with her sleeping-drink, he pretended to drink, but threw it away behind him, for he suspected that it was a sleeping-drink. So, when the girl went into the prince's room this time he was awake, and she had to tell him how she had come there. 'You have come just in time,' said the prince, 'for I should have been married tomorrow; but I will not have the long-nosed princess, and you alone can save me. I will say that I want to see what my bride can do, and bid her wash the shirt which has the three drops of tallow on it. This she will consent to do, for she does not know that it is you who let them fall on it; but no one can wash them out but one born of Christian folk: it cannot be done by one of a pack of trolls; and then I will say that no one shall ever be my bride but the woman who can do this, and I know that you can.' There was great joy and gladness between them all that night, and the next day, when the wedding was to take place, the prince said, 'I must see what my bride can do.'

That you may do,' said the stepmother.

'I have a fine shirt which I want to wear as my wedding shirt, but three drops of tallow have got upon it which I want to have washed off, and I have vowed to marry no one but the woman who is able to do it. If she cannot do that, she is not worth having.'

Well, that was a very small matter, they thought, and agreed to do it. The princess with the long nose began to wash as well as she could, but the more she washed and rubbed, the larger the spots grew. 'Ah! you can't wash at all,' said the old troll-hag, who was her mother. 'Give it to me.' But she too had not had the shirt very long in her hands before it looked worse still, and the more she washed it and rubbed it, the larger and blacker grew the spots.

So the other trolls had to
come and wash, but the
more they did, the
blacker and uglier grew
the shirt, until at
length it was as black
as if it had been up
the chimney. 'Oh,'
cried the prince, 'not
one of you is good
for anything at all!
There is a beggar
girl sitting outside
the window, and
I'll be bound that
she can wash
better than any of
you! Come in, you
girl there!' he cried.
So she came in.

'Can you wash this shirt
clean?' he cried. 'Oh! I don't know,' she said; 'but I
will try.' And no sooner had she taken the shirt and
dipped it in the water than it was white as driven
snow, and even whiter than that. 'I will marry you,'
said the prince.

Then the old troll-hag flew into such a rage that
she burst, and the princess with the long nose and all
the little trolls must have burst too, for they have
never been heard of since. The prince and his bride
set free all the Christian folk who were imprisoned
there, and took away with them all the gold and silver
that they could carry, and moved far away from the
castle which lay east of the sun and west of the moon.

The Elves and the Shoemaker

There was once a shoemaker, who worked very hard and was very honest, but still he could not earn enough to live upon; and at last all he had in the world was gone, save just leather enough to make one pair of shoes.

Then he cut his leather out, all ready to make up the next day, meaning to rise early in the morning to his work. His conscience was clear and his heart light amidst all his troubles; so he went peaceably to bed, left all his cares to heaven, and soon fell asleep. In the morning after he had said his prayers, he sat himself down to his work, but to his great wonder, there stood the shoes, all ready made, upon the table. The good man knew not what to say or think at such an odd thing happening. He looked at the workmanship; there was not one false stitch in the whole job; all was so neat and true, that it was quite a masterpiece.

The same day a customer came in, and the shoes suited him so well that he willingly paid a price higher than usual for them; and the poor shoemaker, with the money, bought leather enough to make two pairs more.

In the evening he cut out the work, and went to bed early, that he might get up and begin betimes next day; but he was saved all the trouble, for when he got up in the morning the work was done ready to his hand. Soon in came buyers, who paid him handsomely for his goods, so that he bought leather enough for four pair more. He cut out the work again overnight and found it done in the morning, as before; and so it went on for some time: what was got ready in the evening was always done by daybreak; and the good man soon became thriving and well off again.

One evening, about Christmastime, as he and his wife were sitting over the fire chatting together, he said to her, 'I should like to sit up and watch tonight, that we may see who it is that comes and does my work for me.' The wife liked the thought; so they left a light burning, and hid themselves in a corner of the room, behind a curtain that was hung up there, and watched what would happen.

As soon as it was midnight, there came in two little naked dwarfs; and they sat themselves upon the shoemaker's bench, took up all the work that was cut out, and began to ply with their little fingers, stitching and rapping and tapping away at such a rate, that the shoemaker was all wonder, and could not take his eyes off them. And on they went, till the job was quite done, and the shoes stood ready for use upon the table. This was long before daybreak; and then they bustled away as quick as lightning.

The next day the wife said to the shoemaker. 'These little wights have made us rich, and we ought to be thankful to them, and do them a good turn if we can. I am quite sorry to see them run about as they do; and indeed it is not very decent, for they have nothing upon their backs to keep off the cold. I'll tell you what: I will make each of them a shirt, and a coat and waistcoat, and a pair of pantaloons into the bargain; and do you make each of them a little pair of shoes.'

The thought pleased the good cobbler very much; and one evening, when all the things were ready, they laid them on the table, instead of the work that they usually cut out, and then went and hid themselves, to watch what the little elves would do.

About midnight in they came, dancing and skipping, hopped round the room, and then went to sit down to their work as usual; but when they saw the clothes lying for them, they laughed and chuckled, and seemed mightily delighted.

Then they dressed themselves in the twinkling of an eye, and danced and capered and sprang about, as merry as could be; till at last they danced out at the door, and away over the green. The good couple saw them no more; but everything went well with them from that time forward, as long as they lived.

The Story of the Emperor's New Clothes

Many years ago there lived an Emperor who was so fond of new clothes that he spent all his money on them in order to be beautifully dressed. He did not care about his soldiers, he did not care about the theatre; he only liked to go out walking to show off his new clothes. He had a coat for every hour of the day; and just as they say of a king, 'He is in the council-chamber,' they always said here, 'The Emperor is in the wardrobe.'

In the great city in which he lived there was always something going on; every day many strangers came there. One day two impostors arrived who gave themselves out as weavers, and said that they knew how to manufacture the most beautiful cloth imaginable. Not only were the texture and pattern uncommonly beautiful, but the clothes which were made of the stuff possessed this wonderful property that they were invisible to anyone who was not fit for his office, or who was unpardonably stupid.

'Those must indeed be splendid clothes,' thought the Emperor. 'If I had them on I could find out which men in my kingdom are unfit for the offices they hold; I could distinguish the wise from the stupid! Yes, this cloth must be woven for me at once.' And he gave both the impostors much money, so that they might begin their work.

They placed two weaving-looms, and began to make as if they were working, but they had not the

One day two impostors arrived

least thing on the looms. They also demanded the
finest silk and the best gold, which they put in their
pockets, and worked at the empty looms till late into
the night.

'I should like very much to know how far they have got on with the cloth,' thought the Emperor. But he remembered when he thought about it that whoever was stupid or not fit for his office would not be able to see it. Now he certainly believed that he had nothing to fear for himself, but he wanted first to send somebody else in order to see how he stood with regard to his office. Everybody in the whole town knew what a wonderful power the cloth had, and they were all curious to see how bad or how stupid their neighbour was.

'I will send my old and honoured minister to the weavers,' thought the Emperor. 'He can judge best what the cloth is like, for he has intellect, and no one understands his office better than he.'

Now the good old minister went into the hall where the two impostors sat working at the empty weaving-looms. 'Dear me!' thought the wise old minister, opening his eyes wide, 'I can see nothing!' But he did not say so.

Both the impostors begged him to be so kind as to step closer, and asked him what he thought of the beautiful texture and lovely colours. They pointed to the empty loom, and the poor old minister went forward rubbing his eyes; but he could see nothing, for there was nothing there.

'Dear, dear!' thought he, 'can I be stupid? I have never thought so, and nobody must know it! Can I be not fit for my office? No, I must certainly not say that I cannot see the cloth!'

'Have you nothing to say about it?' asked one of the men who was weaving.

'Oh, it is lovely, most lovely!' answered the old minister, looking through his spectacles. 'What a texture! What colours! Yes, I will tell the Emperor that it pleases me very much.'

'Now we are delighted at that,' said both the weavers, and thereupon they named the colours and explained the intricacies of the texture.

The old minister paid great attention, so that he could tell the same to the Emperor when he came back to him, which he did.

The impostors now wanted more money, more silk and more gold to use in their weaving. They put it all in their own pockets, and there came no threads on the loom, but they went on as they had done before, working at the empty loom. The Emperor soon sent another worthy statesman to see how the weaving was getting on, and whether the cloth would soon be finished. It was the same with him as the first one; he looked and looked, but because there was nothing on the empty loom he could see nothing.

'Is it not a beautiful piece of cloth?' asked the two impostors, and they pointed to and described the splendid material which was not there.

'Stupid I am not!' thought the man, 'so it must be my good office for which I am not fitted. It is strange, certainly, but no one must be allowed to notice it.' And so he praised the cloth which he did not see, and expressed to them his delight at the beautiful colours and the splendid texture. 'Yes, it is quite beautiful,' he said to the Emperor. Everybody in the town was talking of the magnificent cloth.

Now the Emperor wanted to see it

himself while it was still on the loom. With a great crowd of select followers, amongst whom were both the worthy statesmen who had already been there before, he went to the cunning impostors, who were now weaving with all their might, but without fibre or thread.

'Is it not splendid!' said both the old statesmen who had already been there. 'See, your majesty, what a texture! What colours!' And then they pointed to the empty loom, for they believed that the others could see the cloth quite well.

'What!' thought the Emperor, 'I can see nothing! This is indeed horrible! Am I stupid? Am I not fit to be Emperor? That were the most dreadful thing that could happen to me. Oh, it is very beautiful,' he said. 'It has my gracious approval.' And then he nodded pleasantly, and examined the empty loom, for he would not say that he could see nothing.

His whole court round him looked and looked, and saw no more than the others; but they said like the Emperor, 'Oh! it is beautiful!' And they advised him to wear these new and magnificent clothes for the first time at the great procession which was soon to take place. 'Splendid! Lovely! Most beautiful!' went from mouth to mouth; everyone seemed delighted over them, and the Emperor gave to the impostors the title of Court Weavers to the Emperor.

Throughout the whole of the night before the morning on which the procession was to take place, the impostors were up and were working by the light of over sixteen candles. The people could see that they were very busy making the Emperor's new clothes ready. They pretended they were taking the cloth from the loom, cut with huge scissors in the air, sewed with needles without thread, and then said at last, 'Now the clothes are finished!'

The Emperor came himself with his most distinguished knights, and each impostor held up his arm just as if he were holding something, and said, 'See! here are the breeches! Here is the coat! Here the cloak!' and so on.

'Spun clothes are so comfortable that one would imagine one had nothing on at all; but that is the beauty of it!'

'Yes,' said all the knights, but they could see nothing, for there was nothing there.

'Will it please your majesty graciously to take off your clothes,' said the impostors, 'then we will put on the new clothes, here before the mirror.'

The Emperor took off all his clothes, and the impostors placed themselves before him as if they were putting on each new item of clothing, and the Emperor turned and bent himself in front of the mirror.

'How beautifully they fit! How well they sit!' said everybody. 'What material! What colours! It is a gorgeous suit!'

'They are waiting outside with the canopy which your majesty is wont to have borne over you in the procession,' announced the master of the ceremonies.

'Look, I am ready,' said the Emperor. 'Doesn't it sit well!' And he turned himself again to the mirror to see if his finery was on all right.

The chamberlains who were used to carry the train put their hands near the floor as if they were lifting up the train; then they made as if they were holding something in the air. They would not have it noticed that they could see nothing.

So the Emperor went along in the procession under the splendid canopy, and all the people in the streets and at the windows said, 'How matchless are the Emperor's new clothes! That train fastened to his dress, how beautifully it hangs!'

No one wished it to be noticed that he could see nothing, for then he would have been unfit for his office, or else very stupid. None of the Emperor's clothes had met with such approval as these had.

'But he has nothing on!' said a little child at last.

'Just listen to the innocent child!' said the father, and each one whispered to his neighbour what the child had said.

'But he has nothing on!' the whole of the people called out at last.

This struck the Emperor, for it seemed to him as if they were right; but he thought to himself, 'I must go on with the procession now. And the chamberlains walked along still more uprightly, holding up the train which was not there at all.

The Fisherman and His Wife

There was once a fisherman who lived with his wife in a pigsty, close by the seaside. The fisherman used to go out fishing all day long, and one day, as he sat on the shore with his rod, looking at the sparkling waves and watching his line, all of a sudden his float was dragged away deep into the water, and in drawing it up he pulled out a great fish. But the fish said, 'Pray let me live! I am not a real fish; I am an enchanted prince. Put me in the water again, and let me go!'

'Oh, ho!' said the man, 'you need not make so many words about the matter; I will have nothing to do with a fish that can talk; so swim away, sir, as soon as you please!' Then he put him back into the water, and the fish darted straight down to the bottom, and left a long streak of blood behind him on the wave.

When the fisherman went home to his wife in the pigsty, he told her how he had caught a great fish, and how it had told him it was an enchanted prince, and how, on hearing it speak, he had let it go again. 'Did you not ask it for anything?' said the wife. 'We live very wretchedly here, in this nasty dirty pigsty; do go back and tell the fish we want a snug little cottage.'

The fisherman did not much like the business: however, he went back to the seashore; and when he got there the water looked all yellow and green. And he stood at the water's edge, and said:

'O man of the sea!
Hearken to me!
My wife Ilsabill
Will have her own will,
And hath sent me to beg a boon of thee!'

Then the fish came swimming to him, and said, 'Well, what is her will? What does your wife want?'

'Ah!' said the fisherman, 'she says that when I had caught you, I ought to have asked you for something before I let you go; she does not like living any longer in the pigsty, and wants a snug little cottage.'

'Go home, then,' said the fish; 'she is in the cottage already!' So the man went home, and saw his wife standing at the door of a nice trim little cottage. 'Come in, come in!' said she. 'Is not this much better than the filthy pigsty we had?' And there was a parlour, and a bedchamber, and a kitchen; and behind the cottage there was a little garden, planted with all sorts of flowers and fruits; and there was a courtyard behind, full of ducks and chickens.

'Ah!' said the fisherman, 'how happily we shall live now!'

'We will try to do so, at least,' said his wife.

Everything went right for a week or two, and then Dame Ilsabill said, 'Husband, there is not nearly room enough for us in this cottage; the courtyard and the garden are a great deal too small; I should like to have a large stone castle to live in. Go to the fish again and tell him to give us a castle.'

'Wife,' said the fisherman, 'I don't like to go to him again, for perhaps he will be angry; we ought to be content with this pretty cottage to live in.'

'Nonsense!' said the wife; 'he will do it very willingly,

I know; go along and try!'

The fisherman went, but his heart was very heavy:
and when he came to the sea, it looked blue and
gloomy, though it was very calm; and he went close
to the edge of the waves, and said:

> 'O man of the sea!
> Hearken to me!
> My wife Ilsabill
> Will have her own will,
> And hath sent me to beg a boon of thee!'

'Well, what does she want now?' said the fish.

'Ah!' said the man, dolefully, 'my wife wants to live in a stone castle.'

'Go home, then,' said the fish; 'she is standing at the gate of it already.'

So away went the fisherman, and found his wife standing before the gate of a great castle. 'See,' said she, 'is not this grand?'

With that they went into the castle together, and found a great many servants there, and the rooms all richly furnished, and full of golden chairs and tables; and behind the castle was a garden, and around it was a park half a mile long, full of sheep, and goats, and hares, and deer; and in the courtyard were stables and cow-houses.

'Well,' said the man, 'now we will live cheerful and happy in this beautiful castle for the rest of our lives.'

'Perhaps we may,' said the wife; 'but let us sleep upon it, before we make up our minds to that.' So they went to bed.

The next morning when Dame Ilsabill awoke it was broad daylight, and she jogged the fisherman with her elbow, and said, 'Get up, husband, and bestir yourself, for we must be king of all the land.'

'Wife, wife,' said the man, 'why should you wish to be the king? I will not be king.'

'Then I will,' said she.

'But, wife,' said the fisherman, 'how can you be king – the fish cannot make you a king!'

'Husband,' said she, 'say no more about it, but go and try! I will be king.'

So the man went away quite sorrowful to think that his wife should want to be king. This time the sea looked a dark grey colour, and was overspread with curling waves with ridges of foam as he cried out:

'O man of the sea!
Hearken to me!
My wife Ilsabill
Will have her own will,
And hath sent me to beg a boon of thee!'

'Well, what would she have now?' said the fish.

'Alas!' said the poor man, 'my wife wants to be king.'

'Go home,' said the fish; 'she is king already.'

Then the fisherman went home; and as he came close to the palace he saw a troop of soldiers, and heard the sound of drums and trumpets. And when he went in he saw his wife sitting on a throne of gold and diamonds, with a golden crown upon her head; and on each side of her stood six fair maidens, each a head taller than the other. 'Well, wife,' said the fisherman, 'are you king?'

'Yes,' said she, 'I am king.'

And when he had looked at her for a long time, he said, 'Ah, wife! What a fine thing it is to be king! Now we shall never have anything more to wish for as long as we live.'

'I don't know how that may be,' said she; 'never is a long time. I am king, it is true; but I begin to be tired of that, and I think I should like to be emperor.'

'Alas, wife! Why should you wish to be emperor?' said the fisherman.

'Husband,' said she, 'go to the fish! I say I will be emperor.'

'Ah, wife!' replied the fisherman, 'the fish cannot make an emperor, I am sure, and I should not like to ask him for such a thing.'

'I am king,' said Ilsabill, 'and you are my slave; so go at once!'

So the fisherman was forced to go; and he muttered as he went along, 'This will come to no good, it is too much to ask; the fish will be tired at last, and then we shall be sorry for what we have done.'

He soon came to the seashore; and the water was quite black and muddy, and a mighty whirlwind blew over the waves and rolled them about, but he went as near as he could to the water's brink, and said:

> 'O man of the sea!
> Hearken to me!
> My wife Ilsabill
> Will have her own will,
> And hath sent me to beg a boon of thee!'

'What would she have now?' said the fish.

'Ah!' said the fisherman, 'she wants to be emperor.'

'Go home,' said the fish; 'she is emperor already.'

So he went home again; and as he came near he saw his wife Ilsabill sitting on a very lofty throne made of solid gold, with a great crown on her head full two yards high; and on each side of her stood her guards and attendants in a row, each one smaller than the other, from the tallest giant down to a little dwarf no bigger than my finger. And before her stood princes, and dukes, and earls; and the fisherman went up to her and said, 'Wife, are you emperor?'

'Yes,' said she, 'I am emperor.'

'Ah!' said the man, as he gazed upon her, 'what a fine thing it is to be emperor!'

'Husband,' said she, 'why should we stop at being emperor? I will be pope next.'

'O wife, wife!' said he, 'how can you be pope? There is but one pope at a time in Christendom.'

'Husband,' said she, 'I will be pope this very day.'

'But,' replied the husband, 'the fish cannot make you pope.'

'What nonsense!' said she; 'if he can make an emperor, he can make a pope. Go and try him.'

So the fisherman went. But when he came to the shore the wind was raging and the sea was tossed up and down in boiling waves, and the ships were in trouble, and rolled fearfully upon the tops of the billows. In the middle of the heavens there was a little piece of blue sky, but towards the south all was red, as if a fierce storm was rising. At this sight the fisherman was dreadfully frightened, and he trembled so that his knees knocked together, but still he went down near to the shore, and said:

> 'O man of the sea!
> Hearken to me!
> My wife Ilsabill
> Will have her own will,
> And hath sent me to beg a boon of thee!'

'What does she want now?' said the fish.

'Ah!' said the fisherman, 'my wife wants to be pope.'

'Go home,' said the fish; 'she is pope already.'

Then the fisherman went home, and found Ilsabill sitting on a throne that was two miles high. And she had three great crowns on her head, and around her stood all the pomp and power of the Church. And on each side of her were two rows of burning lights, of all sizes, the greatest as large as the highest and biggest tower in the world, and the least no larger than a small rush-light.

'Wife,' said the fisherman, as he looked at all this greatness, 'are you pope?'

'Yes,' said she, 'I am pope.'

'Well, wife,' replied he, 'it is a grand thing to be pope; and now you must be content, for you can be nothing greater.'

'I will think about that,' said the wife. Then they went to bed, but Dame Ilsabill could not sleep all night for thinking what she should be next. At last, just as she was falling asleep, morning broke and the sun rose. 'Ha!' thought she, as she woke up and looked at it through the window, 'after all I cannot prevent the sun rising.'

At this thought she was very angry, and wakened her husband, and said, 'Husband, go to the fish and tell him I must be lord of the sun and moon.'

The fisherman was half asleep, but the thought frightened him so much that he started and fell out of bed. 'Alas, wife!' said he, 'can you not be content with being pope?'

'No,' said she, 'I am very uneasy as long as the sun and moon rise without my leave. Go to the fish at once!'

Then the man went shivering with fear; and as he was going down to the shore a dreadful storm arose, so that the trees and the very rocks shook. And all the heavens became black with stormy clouds, and the lightning played and the thunder rolled; and you might have seen in the sea great black waves, swelling up like mountains with crowns of white foam upon their heads. And the fisherman crept towards the sea, and cried out, as well as he could:

> 'O man of the sea!
> Hearken to me!
> My wife Ilsabill
> Will have her own will,
> And hath sent me to beg a boon of thee!'

'What does she want now?' said the fish.

'Ah!' said he, 'she wants to be lord of the sun and moon.'

'Go home,' said the fish, 'to your pigsty again.'

And there they live to this very day.

The Frog Prince

One fine evening, a young princess put on her bonnet and clogs, and went out to take a walk by herself in a wood; and when she came to a cool spring of water, that rose in the midst of it, she sat herself down to rest a while. Now she had a golden ball in her hand, which was her favourite plaything; and she was always tossing it up into the air, and catching it again as it fell. After a time she threw it up so high that she missed catching it as it fell, and the ball bounded away, and rolled along upon the ground, till at last it fell down into the spring. The princess looked into the spring after her ball, but it was very deep, so deep that she could not see the bottom of it. Then she began to bewail her loss, and said, 'Alas! if I could only get my ball again, I would give all my fine clothes and jewels, and everything that I have in the world.'

While she was speaking, a frog put his head out of the water, and said, 'Princess, why do you weep so bitterly?'

'Alas!' said she, 'what can you do for me, you nasty frog? My golden ball has fallen into the spring.'

The frog said, 'I want not your pearls, and jewels, and fine clothes; but if you will love me, and let me live with you and eat from off your golden plate and sleep upon your bed, I will bring you your ball again.'

'What nonsense,' thought the princess, 'this silly frog is talking! He can never even get out of the spring to visit me, though he may be able to get my ball for me, and therefore I will tell him he shall have what asks.' So she said to the frog, 'Well, if you will bring me my ball, I will do all you ask.'

Then the frog put his head down, and dived deep under the water; and after a little while he came up again, with the ball in his mouth, and threw it on to the edge of the spring. As soon as the young princess saw her ball, she ran to pick it up; and she was so overjoyed to have it in her hand again, that she never thought of the frog, but ran home with it as fast as she could. The frog called after her, 'Stay, princess, and take me with you as you said,' but she did not stop to hear a word.

The next day, just as the princess had sat down to dinner, she heard a strange noise – tap, tap – plash, plash – as if something was coming up the marble staircase, and soon afterwards there was a gentle knock at the door, and a little voice cried out and said:

'Open the door, my princess dear,
  Open the door to thy true love here!
  Remember the words that thou and I said
  By the fountain cool, in the greenwood shade.'

Then the princess ran to the door and opened it, and there she saw the frog, whom she had quite forgotten. At this sight she was sadly frightened, and shutting the door as fast as she could came back to her seat. The king, her father, seeing that something had frightened her, asked her what was the matter. 'There is a nasty frog,' said she, 'at the door, that lifted my ball for me out of the spring last evening. I told him that he should live with me here, thinking that he could never get out of the spring; but there he is at the door, and he wants to come in.'

While she was speaking the frog knocked again at the door, and said:

'Open the door, my princess dear,
Open the door to thy true love here!
Remember the words that thou and I said
By the fountain cool, in the greenwood shade.'

Then the king said to the young princess, 'As you have given your word you must keep it; so go and let him in.' She did so, and the frog hopped into the room, and then straight on – tap, tap – plash, plash – from the bottom of the room to the top, till he came up close to the table where the princess sat. 'Pray lift me upon a chair,' said he to the princess, 'and let me sit next to you.' As soon as she had done this, the frog said, 'Put your plate nearer to me, that I may eat from it.' This she did, and when he had eaten as much as he could, he said, 'Now I am tired; carry me upstairs, and put me into your bed.' And the princess, though very unwilling, took him up in her hand, and put him upon the pillow of her own bed, where he slept all night long.

As soon as it was light he jumped up, hopped downstairs, and went out of the house. 'Now, then,' thought the princess, 'at last he is gone, and I shall be troubled with him no more.'

But she was mistaken; for when night came again she heard the same tapping at the door; and the frog came once more, and said:

'Open the door, my princess dear,
Open the door to thy true love here!
Remember the words that thou and I said
By the fountain cool, in the greenwood shade.'

And when the princess opened the door the frog

came in, ate with her and slept upon her pillow as before, till the morning broke. And the third night he did the same.

But when the princess awoke on the following

The princess, though very unwilling, took him up in her hand

morning she was astonished to see, instead of the frog, a handsome prince, gazing on her with the most beautiful eyes she had ever seen, and standing at the head of her bed.

He told her that he had been enchanted by a spiteful fairy, who had changed him into a frog; and that he had been fated so to abide till some princess should take him out of the spring, and let him eat from her plate, and sleep upon her bed for three nights. 'You,' said the prince, 'have broken his cruel charm, and now I have nothing to wish for but that you should go with me into my father's kingdom, where I will marry you, and love you as long as you live.'

The princess, you may be sure, was not long in giving her consent; and even as they spoke, a magnificent coach drove up, drawn by eight beautiful horses, decked with plumes of feathers and golden harness; and behind the coach rode the prince's servant, faithful Heinrich, who had bewailed the misfortunes of his dear master during his enchantment so long and so bitterly that his heart had well-nigh burst. They then took leave of the king, and got into the coach, and all set out, full of joy and merriment, for the prince's kingdom, which they reached safely; and there they lived happily a great many years.

Frost

There was once an old man who had a wife and three daughters. The wife had no love for the eldest of the three, who was her stepdaughter, but was always scolding her. Moreover, she used to make her get up ever so early in the morning, and gave her all the work of the house to do. Before daybreak the girl would feed the cattle and give them to drink, fetch wood and water indoors, light the fire in the stove, give the room a wash, mend the dresses, and set everything in order.

Even then her stepmother was never satisfied, but would grumble away at Marfa, exclaiming: 'What a lazybones! what a slut! Why here's a brush not in its place, and there's something put wrong, and she's left the ashcan inside the house!'

The girl held her peace, and wept; she tried in every way to accommodate herself to her stepmother, and to be of service to her stepsisters. But they, following the example of their mother, were always insulting Marfa, quarrelling with her, and making her cry: that was even a pleasure to them! As for them, they lay in bed late, washed themselves in water got ready for them, dried themselves with a clean towel, and didn't sit down to work till after dinner.

Well, our girls grew and grew, until they grew up and were old enough to be married. The old man felt sorry for his eldest daughter, whom he loved because she was industrious and obedient, never was obstinate, always did as she was bid, and never

179

uttered a word of contradiction. But he didn't know how he was to help her in her trouble. He was feeble, his wife was a scold, and her daughters were as obstinate as they were indolent.

Well, the old folks set to work to consider – the husband how he could get his daughters settled, the wife how she could get rid of the eldest one.

One day she says to him: 'I say, old man! let's get Marfa married.'

'Gladly,' says he, slinking off to the sleeping-place above the stove. But his wife called after him: 'Get up early tomorrow, old man, harness the mare to the sledge, and drive away with Marfa. And, Marfa, get your things together in a basket, and put on a clean shift; you're going away tomorrow on a visit.'

Poor Marfa was delighted to hear of such a piece of good luck as being invited on a visit, and she slept comfortably all night. Early next morning she got up, washed herself, prayed to God, got all her things together, packed them away in proper order, dressed herself in her best things, and looked something like a lass! – a bride fit for any place whatsoever!

Now it was wintertime, and out of doors was a rattling frost. Early in the morning, between daybreak and sunrise, the old man harnessed the mare to the sledge and led it up to the steps. Then he went indoors, sat down on the window-sill, and said: 'Now then! I've got everything ready.'

'Sit down to table and swallow your victuals!' replied the old woman.

The old man sat down to table, and made his daughter sit by his side. On the table stood a pannier; he took out a loaf, and cut bread for himself and his daughter. Meantime his wife served up a dish of old cabbage soup, and said: 'There, my pigeon, eat and be off; I've looked at you quite enough! Drive Marfa to her bridegroom, old man. And look here, old greybeard! drive straight along the road at first, and then turn off from the road to the right, you know, into the forest – right up to the big pine that stands on the hill, and there hand Marfa over to Frost.'

The old man opened his eyes wide, also his mouth, and stopped eating, and the girl began lamenting.

'Now then, what are you hanging your chaps and squealing about?' said her stepmother. 'Surely your bridegroom is a beauty, and he's that rich! Why, just see what a lot of things belong to him, the firs, the pine-tops and the birches, all in their robes of winter bark – ways and means that anyone might envy; and he himself a *bogatir*!'

The old man silently placed the things on the sledge, made his daughter put on a warm pelisse, and set off on the journey. After a time, he reached the forest, turned off from the road; and drove across the frozen snow. When he got into the depths of the forest, he stopped, made his daughter get out, laid her basket under the tall pine, and said: 'Sit here, and await the bridegroom. And mind you receive him as pleasantly as you can.'

Then he turned his horse round and drove off homewards.

The girl sat and shivered. The cold had pierced her through. She would fain have cried aloud, but she had not strength enough; only her teeth chattered. Suddenly she heard a sound. Not far off, Frost was cracking away on a fir. From fir to fir was he leaping, and snapping his fingers. Presently he appeared on that very pine under which the maiden was sitting and from above her head he cried: 'Art thou warm, maiden?'

'Warm, warm am I, dear Father Frost,' she replied.

Frost began to descend lower, all the more cracking and snapping his fingers. To the maiden said Frost: 'Art thou warm, maiden? Art thou warm, fair one?'

The girl could scarcely draw her breath, but still she replied: 'Warm am I, Frost dear: warm am I, father dear!'

Frost began cracking more than ever, and more loudly did he snap his fingers, and to the maiden he said: 'Art thou warm, maiden? Art thou warm, pretty one? Art thou warm, my darling?'

The girl was by this time numb with cold, and she could scarcely make herself heard as she replied: 'Oh! quite warm, Frost dearest!'

Then Frost took pity on the girl, wrapped her up in furs, and warmed her with blankets.

Next morning the old woman said to her husband: 'Drive out, old greybeard, and wake the young couple!'

The old man harnessed his horse and drove off. When he came to where his daughter was, he found she was alive and had got a good pelisse, a costly bridal veil and a pannier with rich gifts. He stowed everything away on the sledge without saying a word, took his seat on it with his daughter, and drove back. They reached home, and the daughter fell at her step-mother's feet. The old woman was thunderstruck when she saw the girl alive, and the new pelisse and the basket of linen.

'Ah, you wretch!' she cries. 'But you shan't trick me!'

Well, a little later the old woman says to her husband: 'Take my daughters, too, to their bridegroom. The presents he's made are nothing to what he'll give them.'

Well, early next morning the old woman gave her girls their breakfast, dressed them as befitted brides, and sent them off on their journey. In the same way as before the old man left the girls under the pine.

There the girls sat, and kept laughing and saying: 'Whatever is mother thinking of! All of a sudden to marry both of us off! As if there were no lads in our village, forsooth! Some rubbishy fellow may come, and goodness knows who he may be!'

The girls were wrapped up in pelisses, but for all that they felt the cold.

'I say, Prascovia! the frost's skinning me alive. Well, if our bridegroom doesn't come quick, we shall be frozen to death here!'

'Don't go talking nonsense, Mashka; as if suitors generally turned up in the forenoon. Why it's hardly dinner-time yet!'

'But I say, Prascovia! if only one comes, which of us will he take?'

'Not you, you stupid goose!'

'Then it will be you, I suppose!'

'Of course it will be me!'

'You, indeed! there now, have done talking stuff and treating people like fools!'

Meanwhile, Frost had numbed the girls' hands, so our damsels folded them under their dress, and then went on quarrelling as before.

'What, you fright! you sleepy-face! you abominable shrew! why, you don't know so much as how to begin weaving; and as to going on with it, you haven't an idea!'

'Aha, boaster! and what is it you know? Why,

nothing at all except to go out to merry-makings and lick your lips there. We'll soon see which he'll take first!'

While the girls went on scolding like that, they began to freeze in downright earnest. Suddenly they both cried out at once: 'Whyever is he so long coming? Do you know, you've turned quite blue!'

Now, a good way off, Frost had begun cracking, snapping his fingers and leaping from fir to fir. To the girls it sounded as if someone was coming.

'Listen, Prascovia! He's coming at last, and with bells, too!'

'Get along with you! I won't listen; my skin is peeling with cold.'

'And yet you're still expecting to get married!'

Then they began blowing on their fingers.

Nearer and nearer came Frost. At length he appeared on the pine, above the heads of the girls, and said to them: 'Are ye warm, maidens? Are ye warm, pretty ones? Are ye warm, my darlings?'

'Oh, Frost, it's awfully cold! we're utterly perished! We're expecting a bridegroom, but the confounded fellow has disappeared.'

Frost slid lower down the tree, cracked away more, snapped his fingers oftener than before.

'Are ye warm, maidens? Are ye warm, pretty ones?'

'Get along with you! Are you blind that you can't see our hands and feet are quite dead?'

Still lower descended Frost, still more put forth his might, and said: 'Are ye warm, maidens?'

'Into the bottomless pit with you! Out of sight, accursed one!' cried the girls – and became lifeless forms.

Next morning the old woman said to her husband:

'Old man, go and get the sledge harnessed; put an armful of hay in it, and take some sheepskin wraps. I dare say the girls are half-dead with cold. There's a terrible frost outside! And, mind you, old greybeard, do it quickly!'

Before the old man could manage to get a bite he was out of doors and on his way. When he came to where his daughters were, he found them dead. So he lifted the girls on to the sledge, wrapped a blanket round them, and covered them up with a bark mat. The old woman saw him from afar, ran out to meet him, and called out ever so loud: 'Where are the girls?'

'In the sledge.'

The old woman lifted the mat, undid the blanket, and found the girls both dead.

Then, like a thunderstorm, she broke out against her husband, abusing him saying: 'What have you done, you old wretch? You have destroyed my daughters, the children of my own flesh and blood, my never-enough-to-be-gazed-on seedlings, my beautiful berries! I will thrash you with the tongs; I will give it you with the stove-rake.'

'That's enough, you old goose! You flattered yourself you were going to get riches, but your daughters were too stiff-necked. How was I to blame? it was you yourself would have it.'

The old woman was in a rage at first, and used bad language; but afterwards she made it up with her stepdaughter, and they all lived together peaceably, and thrived, and bore no malice. A neighbour made an offer of marriage, the wedding was celebrated, and Marfa is now living happily. The old man frightens his grandchildren with stories about Frost, and doesn't let them have their own way.

The Story of Gelert

It was somewhere about 1200, Prince Llewellyn had a castle at Aber, just abreast of us here; indeed, parts of the towers remain to this day. His consort was the Princess Joan; she was King John's daughter. Her coffin remains with us to this day. Llewellyn was a great hunter of wolves and foxes, for the hills of Carnarvonshire were infested with wolves in those days, after the young lambs.

Now the prince had several hunting-houses – sorts of farmhouses – and one of them was at the place now called Beth-Gelert, for the wolves were very thick there at this time. Now the prince used to travel from farmhouse to farmhouse with his family and friends, when going on these hunting parties.

One season they went hunting from Aber, and stopped at the house where Beth-Gelert is now – it's about fourteen miles away. The prince had all his hounds with him, but his favourite was Gelert, a hound who had never let off a wolf for six years.

The prince loved the dog like a child, and at the sound of his horn Gelert was always the first to come bounding up. There was company at the house, and one day they went hunting, leaving his wife and the child, in a big wooden cradle, behind him at the farmhouse.

The hunting party killed three or four wolves, and about two hours before the word passed for returning home, Llewellyn missed Gelert, and he asked his huntsmen: 'Where's Gelert? I don't see him.'

'Well, indeed, master, I've missed him this half-hour.'

And Llewellyn blew his horn, but no Gelert came at the sound.

Indeed, Gelert had got on to a wolf's track which led to the house.

The prince sounded the return, and they went home, the prince lamenting Gelert. 'He's sure to have been slain – he's sure to have been slain! since he did not answer the horn. Oh, my Gelert!' And they approached the house, and the prince went into the house, and saw Gelert lying by the overturned cradle, and blood all about the room.

'What! hast thou slain my child?' said the prince, and ran his sword through the dog.

After that he lifted up the cradle to look for his child, and found the body of a big wolf underneath that Gelert had slain, and his child was safe. Gelert had capsized the cradle in the scuffle.

'Oh, Gelert! Oh, Gelert!' said the prince, 'my favourite hound, my favourite hound! Thou hast been slain by thy master's hand, and in death thou hast licked thy master's hand!' He patted the dog, but it was too late, and poor Gelert died licking his master's hand.

Next day they made a coffin, and had a regular funeral, the same as if it were a human being; all the servants in deep mourning, and everybody. They made him a grave, and the village was called after the dog, Beth-Gelert – Gelert's Grave; and the prince planted a tree, and put a gravestone of slate, though it was before the days of quarries. And they are to be seen to this day.

The Golden Goose

There was a man who had three sons, the youngest of whom was called Simpleton and was despised, mocked and sneered at on every occasion.

It happened that the eldest wanted to go into the forest to hew wood, and before he went his mother gave him a beautiful sweet cake and a bottle of wine in order that he might not suffer from hunger or thirst.

When he entered the forest he met a little grey-haired old man who bade him good-day, and said: 'Do give me a piece of cake out of your pocket, and let me have a draught of your wine; I am so hungry and thirsty.'

But the clever son answered: 'If I give you my cake and wine, I shall have none for myself; be off with you,' and he left the little man standing and went on.

But when he began to hew down a tree, it was not long before he made a false stroke, and the axe cut him in the arm, so that he had to go home and have it bound up. And this was the little grey man's doing.

After this the second son went into the forest, and his mother gave him, like the eldest, a cake and a bottle of wine.

The little old grey man met him likewise, and asked him for a piece of cake and a drink of wine. But the second son, too, said sensibly enough: 'What I give you will be taken away from myself; be off!' and he left the little man standing and went on.

His punishment, however, was not delayed; when he had made a few blows at the tree he struck himself in the leg, so that he had to be carried home.

Then Simpleton said: 'Father, do let me go and cut wood.'

The father answered: 'Your brothers have hurt themselves with it; leave it alone, you do not understand anything about it.'

But Simpleton begged so long that at last he said: 'Just go then, you will get wiser by hurting yourself.' His mother gave him a cake made with water and baked in the cinders, and with it a bottle of sour beer.

When he came to the forest the little old grey man met him likewise, and greeting him, said: 'Give me a piece of your cake and a drink out of your bottle; I am so hungry and thirsty.'

Simpleton answered: 'I have only cinder-cake and sour beer; if that pleases you, we will sit down and eat.'

So they sat down, and when Simpleton pulled out his cinder-cake, it was a fine sweet cake, and the sour beer had become good wine.

So they ate and drank, and after that the little man said: 'Since you have a good heart, and are willing to divide what you have, I will give you good luck. There stands an old tree; cut it down, and you will find something at the roots.' Then the little man took leave of him.

Simpleton went and cut down the tree, and when it

fell there was a goose sitting in the roots with feathers of pure gold. He lifted her up, and taking her with him, went to an inn where he thought he would stay the night.

Now the host had three daughters, who saw the goose and were curious to know what such a wonderful bird might be, and would have liked to have one of its golden feathers.

The eldest thought: 'I shall soon find an opportunity of pulling out a feather,' and as soon as Simpleton had gone out she seized the goose by the wing, but her hand remained sticking fast to it.

The second came soon afterwards, thinking only of how she might get a feather for herself, but she had scarcely touched her sister than she was held fast.

At last the third also came with the like intent, and the others screamed out: 'Keep away; for goodness' sake, keep away!'

But she did not understand why she was to keep away. 'The others are there,' she thought, 'I may as well be there too,' and ran to them; but as soon as she had touched her sister, she remained sticking fast to her. So they had to spend the night with the goose.

The next morning Simpleton took the goose under his arm and set out, without troubling himself about the three girls who were hanging on to it. They were obliged to run after him continually, now left, now right, wherever his legs took him.

In the middle of the fields the parson met them, and when he saw the procession he said: 'For shame, you good-for-nothing girls, why are you running across the fields after this young man? Is that seemly?'

At the same time he seized the youngest by the hand in order to pull her away, but as soon as he touched her he likewise stuck fast, and was himself obliged to run behind.

Before long the sexton came by and saw his master, the parson, running behind three girls. He was astonished at this and called out: 'Hi! Your reverence, whither away so quickly? Do not forget that we have a christening today!' and running after him he took him by the sleeve, but was also held fast to it.

While the five were trotting thus, one behind the other, two labourers came with their hoes from the fields; the parson called out to them and begged that they would set him and the sexton free. But they had scarcely touched the sexton when they were held fast, and now there were seven of them running behind Simpleton and the goose.

Soon afterwards he came to a city, where a king ruled who had a daughter who was so serious that no one could make her laugh. So her father had put forth a decree that whosoever should be able to make her laugh should marry her.

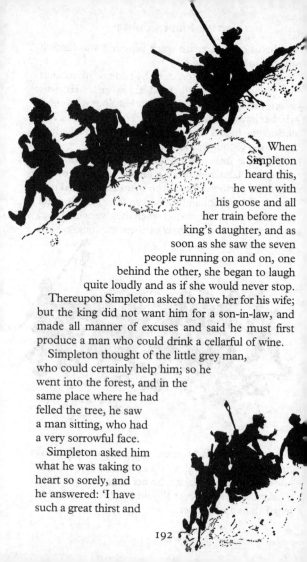

When
Simpleton
heard this,
he went with
his goose and all
her train before the
king's daughter, and as
soon as she saw the seven
people running on and on, one
behind the other, she began to laugh
quite loudly and as if she would never stop.
Thereupon Simpleton asked to have her for his wife;
but the king did not want him for a son-in-law, and
made all manner of excuses and said he must first
produce a man who could drink a cellarful of wine.

Simpleton thought of the little grey man,
who could certainly help him; so he
went into the forest, and in the
same place where he had
felled the tree, he saw
a man sitting, who had
a very sorrowful face.

Simpleton asked him
what he was taking to
heart so sorely, and
he answered: 'I have
such a great thirst and

cannot quench it; cold water I cannot stand, a barrel of wine I have just emptied, but that to me is like a drop on a hot stone!'

'There I can help you,' said Simpleton, 'just come with me and you shall be satisfied.' He led him into the king's cellar, and the man bent over the huge barrels and drank till his loins hurt, and before the day was out he had emptied all the barrels.

Then Simpleton asked once more for his bride, but the king was vexed that such an ugly fellow, whom everyone called Simpleton, should take away his daughter, and he made a new condition; he must first find a man who could eat a whole mountain of bread.

Simpleton did not think long, but went straight into the forest, where in the same place there sat a man who was tying up his body with a strap, and making an awful face, and saying: 'I have eaten a whole ovenful of rolls, but what good is that when one has such a hunger as I? My stomach remains empty, and I must tie myself up if I am not to die of hunger.'

At this Simpleton was glad, and said: 'Get up and come with me; you shall eat yourself full.'

He led him to the king's palace where all the flour in the whole kingdom was collected, and from it he caused a huge mountain of bread to be baked.

The man from the forest stood before it, began to eat, and by the end of one day the whole mountain had vanished.

Then Simpleton for the third time asked for his

bride; but the king again sought a way out, and ordered him to find a ship which could sail on land and on water.

'As soon as you come sailing back in it,' said he, 'you shall have my daughter for wife.'

Simpleton went straight into the forest, and there sat the little grey man to whom he had given his cake. When he heard what Simpleton wanted, he said: 'Since you have given me to eat and to drink, I will give you the ship; and I do all this because you once were kind to me.'

Then he gave him the ship which could sail on land and water, and when the king saw that, he could no longer prevent him from having his daughter.

The wedding was celebrated, and after the king's death, Simpleton inherited his kingdom and lived for a long time contentedly with his wife.

The Golden Harp

Morgan is one of the oldest names in Cymric land. It means one who lives near the sea. Every day, for centuries past, tens of thousands of Welsh folk have looked out on the great blue plain of salt water.

It is just as true, also, that there are all sorts of Morgans. One of these, named Taffy, was like nearly all Welshmen, in that he was very fond of singing. The trouble in his case, however, was that no one but himself loved to hear his voice, which was very disagreeable. Yet of the sounds which he himself made with voice or instrument he was an intense admirer. Nobody could persuade him that his music was poor and his voice rough. He always refused to improve.

Now in Wales, the bard, or poet who makes up his poetry or song as he goes along, is a very important person, and it is not well to offend one of these gentlemen. In French, they call such a person by a very long name – the *improvisateur*.

These poets have sharp tongues and often say hard things about people whom they do not like. If they used whetstones, or stropped their tongues on leather, as men do their razors, to give them a keener edge, their words could not cut more terribly.

Now, on one occasion, Taffy Morgan had offended one of these bards. It was while the poetic gentleman was passing by Taffy's house. He heard the jolly fellow inside singing, first at the top and then at the bottom of the scale. He would drop his voice down on the low notes and then again rise to the highest until it ended in a screech.

Someone on the street asked the poet how he liked the music which he had heard inside.

'Music?' replied the bard with a sneer. 'Is that what Morgan is trying? Why! I thought it was first the lowing of an aged cow, and then the yelping of a blind dog, unable to find its way. Do you call that music?'

The truth was that when the soloist had so filled himself with strong ale that his brain was fuddled, then it was hard to tell just what kind of a noise he was making. It took a wise man to discover the tune, if there was any.

One evening, when Morgan thought his singing unusually fine, and felt sorry that no one heard him, he heard a knock.

Instead of going to the door to enquire, or welcome the visitor, he yelled out 'Come in!'

The door opened and there stood three tired looking strangers. They appeared to be travellers. One of them said: 'Kind sir, we are weary and worn, and would be glad of a morsel of bread. If you can give us a little food, we shall not trouble you further.'

'Is that all?' said Morgan. 'See there the loaf and the cheese, with a knife beside them. Take what you want, and fill your bags. No man shall ever say that Taffy Morgan denied anyone food, when he had any himself.'

Whereupon the three travellers sat down and began to eat.

Meanwhile, without being invited to do so, their host began to sing for them.

Now the three travellers were fairies in disguise.

They were journeying over the country, from cottage to cottage, visiting the people. They came to reward all who gave them a welcome and were kind to them, but to vex and play tricks upon those who were stingy, bad tempered or of sour disposition. Turning to Taffy before taking leave, one of them said: 'You have been good to us and we are grateful. Now what can we do for you? We have power to grant anything you may desire. Please tell us what you would like most.'

At this, Taffy looked hard in the faces of the three strangers, to see if one of them was the bard who had likened his voice in its ups and downs to a cow and a blind dog. Not seeing any familiar face, he plucked up his courage, and said: 'If you are not making fun of me, I'll take from you a harp. And, if I can have my wish in full, I want one that will play only lively tunes. No sad music for me!'

Here Morgan stopped. Again he searched their faces, to see if they were laughing at him and then proceeded.

'And something else, if I can have it; but it's really the same thing I am asking for.'

'Speak on, we are ready to do what you wish,' answered the leader.

'I want a harp, which, no matter how badly I may play, will sound out sweet and jolly music.'

'Say no more,' said the leader, who waved his hand. There was a flood of light, and, to Morgan's amazement, there stood on the floor a golden harp.

But where were the three travellers? They had disappeared in a flash.

Hardly able to believe his own eyes, it now dawned upon him that his visitors were fairies.

He sat down, behind the harp, and made ready to

sweep the strings. He hardly knew whether or not he touched the instrument, but there rolled out volumes of lively music, as if the harp itself were mad. The tune was wild and such as would set the feet of young folks a-going, even in church.

As Taffy's fingers seemed every moment to become more skilful, the livelier the music increased, until the very dishes rattled on the cupboard, as if they wanted to join in. Even the chair looked as if about to dance.

Just then, Morgan's wife and some neighbours entered the house. Immediately, the whole party, one and all, began dancing in the jolliest way. For hours, they kept up the mad whirl. Yet all the while, Taffy seemed happier and the women the merrier.

No telegraph ever carried the news faster, all over the region, that Morgan had a wonderful harp. All the grass in front of the house was soon worn away by the crowds that came to hear and dance. As soon as Taffy touched the harp strings, the feet of everyone, young and old, began shuffling, nor could anyone stop, so long as Morgan played. Even very old, lame and one-legged people joined in. Several old women, whom nobody had ever prevailed upon to get out of their chairs, were cured of their rheumatism. Such unusual exercise was severe for them, but it seemed to be healthful.

A shrewd monk, the business manager of the monastery near by, wanted to buy Morgan's house, set up a sanatorium and advertise it as a holy place. He hoped thus to draw pilgrims to it and get for it a great reputation as a healing place for the lame and the halt, the palsied and the rheumatic. Thus the monastery would be enriched and all the monks get fat.

But Taffy was a happy-go-lucky fellow, who cared little about money and would not sell; for, with his harp, he enjoyed both fun and fame.

One day, in the crowd that stood around his door waiting to begin to hop and whirl, Morgan espied the bard who had compared his voice to a cow and a cur. The bard had come to see whether the stories about the harp were true or not.

He found to his own discomfort what was the fact and the reality, which were not very convenient for him. As soon as the harp music began, his feet began to go up, and his legs to kick and whirl. The more Morgan played, the madder the dance and the wilder the antics of the crowd, and in these the bard had to join, for he could not help himself. Soon they all began to spin round and round on the flagstones fronting the door, as if crazy. They broke the paling of the garden fence. They came into the house and knocked over the chairs and sofa, even when they cracked their shins against the wood. They bumped their heads against the walls and ceiling, and some even scrambled over the roof and down again. The bard could no more stop his weary legs than could the other lunatics.

To Morgan his revenge was so sweet, that he kept on until the bard's legs snapped, and he fell down on top of people that had tumbled from shear weariness, because no more strength was left in them. Meanwhile, Morgan laughed until his jaws were tired and his stomach muscles ached.

But no sooner did he take his fingers off the strings, to rest them, than he opened his eyes in wonder; for in a flash the harp had disappeared.

He had made a bad use of the fairies' gift, and they

were displeased. So both the monk and Morgan felt sorry.

Yet the grass grew again when the quondam harper and singer ceased desolating the air with his quavers. The air seemed sweeter to breathe, because of the silence.

However, the fairies kept on doing good to the people of goodwill, and today some of the sweetest singers in Wales come from the poorest homes.

Goldilocks and the Three Bears

Once upon a time there were three bears, who lived together in a house of their own, in a wood. One of them was a Little Wee Bear, and one was a Middle-sized Bear, and the other was a Great Big Bear. They had each a bowl for their porridge; a little bowl for the Little Wee Bear; and a middle-sized bowl for the Middle-sized Bear; and a great bowl for the Great Big Bear. And they had each a chair to sit in; a little chair for the Little Wee Bear; and a middle-sized chair for the Middle-sized Bear; and a great chair for the Great Big Bear. And they had each a bed to sleep in; a little bed for the Little Wee Bear; and a middle-sized bed for the Middle-sized Bear; and a great bed for the Great Big Bear.

One day, after they had made the porridge for their breakfast, and poured it into their porridge-bowls, they walked out into the wood while the porridge was cooling, that they might not burn their mouths by beginning too soon, for they were polite, well-brought-up bears. And while they were away a little girl called Goldilocks, who lived at the other side of the wood and had been sent on an errand by her mother, passed by the house, and looked in at the window. And then she peeped in at the keyhole, for she was not at all a well-brought-up little girl. Then seeing nobody in the house she lifted the latch. The door was not fastened, because the bears were good bears, who did nobody any harm, and never suspected that anybody would harm them. So Goldilocks

201

opened the door and went in; and well pleased was she when she saw the porridge on the table. If she had been a well-brought-up little girl she would have waited till the bears came home, and then, perhaps, they would have asked her to breakfast; for they were good bears – a little rough or so, as the manner of bears is, but for all that very good-natured and hospitable. But she was an impudent, rude little girl, and so she set about helping herself.

First she tasted the porridge of the Great Big Bear, and that was too hot for her. Next she tasted the porridge of the Middle-sized Bear, but that was too cold for her. And then she went to the porridge of the Little Wee Bear, and tasted it, and that was neither too hot nor too cold, but just right, and she liked it so well that she ate it all up, every bit!

Then Goldilocks, who was tired, for she had been catching butterflies instead of running on her errand, sat down in the chair of the Great Big Bear, but that was too hard for her. And then she sat down in the chair of the Middle-sized Bear, and that was too soft for her. But when she sat down in the chair of the Little Wee Bear, that was neither too hard nor too soft, but just right. So she seated herself in it, and there she sat till the bottom of the chair came out, and down she came, plump upon the ground; and that made her very cross, for she was a bad-tempered little girl.

Now, being determined to rest, Goldilocks went upstairs into the bedchamber in which the Three Bears slept. And first she lay down upon the bed of the Great Big Bear, but that was too high at the head for her. And next she lay down upon the bed of the Middle-sized Bear, and that was too high at the foot for her. And then she lay down upon the bed of the Little Wee Bear, and that was neither too high at the head nor at the foot, but just right. So she covered herself up comfortably, and lay there till she fell fast asleep.

By this time the Three Bears thought their porridge would be cool enough for them to eat it properly; so they came home to breakfast. Now careless Goldilocks had left the spoon of the Great Big Bear standing in his porridge.

'Somebody has been at my porridge!' said the Great Big Bear in his great, rough, gruff voice.

Then the Middle-sized Bear looked at his porridge and saw the spoon was standing in it too.

'Somebody has been at my porridge!' said the Middle-sized Bear in his middle-sized voice.

Then the Little Wee Bear looked at his, and there was the spoon in the porridge-bowl, but the porridge was all gone!

'Somebody has been at my porridge and has finished it all up!' said the Little Wee Bear in his little wee voice.

Upon this the Three Bears, seeing that someone had entered their house, and eaten up the Little Wee Bear's breakfast, began to look about them. Now the careless Goldilocks had not put the hard cushion straight when she rose from the chair of the Great Big Bear.

'Somebody has ben sitting in my chair!' said the Great Big Bear in his great, rough, gruff voice.

And the careless Goldilocks had squatted down the soft cushion of the Middle-sized Bear.

'Somebody has ben sitting in my chair!' said the Middle-sized Bear in his middle-sized voice.

'Somebody has ben sitting in my chair and has sat the bottom through!' said the Little Wee Bear in his little wee voice.

Then the Three Bears thought they had better make further search in case it was a burglar, so they went upstairs into their bedchamber. Now Goldilocks had pulled the pillow of the Great Big Bear out of its place.

'Somebody has been lying in my bed!' said the Great Big Bear in his great, rough, gruff voice.

And Goldilocks had pulled the bolster of the Middle-sized Bear out of its place.

'Somebody has been lying in my bed!' said the Middle-sized Bear in his middle-sized voice.

But when the Little Wee Bear came to look at his bed, there was the bolster in its place!

And the pillow was in its place upon the bolster!

And upon the pillow – ?

There was Goldilocks's yellow head – which was not in its place, for she had no business there.

'Somebody has been lying in my bed – and here she is still!' said the Little Wee Bear in his little wee voice.

Now Goldilocks had heard in her sleep the great, rough, gruff voice of the Great Big Bear; but she was so fast asleep that it was no more to her than the roaring of wind, or the rumbling of thunder. And she had heard the middle-sized voice of the Middle-sized Bear, but it was only as if she had heard someone speaking in a dream. But when she heard the little wee voice of the Little Wee Bear, it was so sharp, and so shrill, that it awakened her at once. Up she started, and when she saw the Three Bears on one side of the bed, she tumbled herself out at the other, and ran to

'Somebody has been lying in my bed – and here she is still!'
said the Little Wee Bear in his little wee voice.

the window. Now the window was open, because
the bears, like good, tidy bears, as they were, always
opened their bedchamber window when they got
up in the morning. So naughty, frightened little
Goldilocks jumped; and whether she broke her neck
in the fall, or ran into the wood and was lost there, or
found her way out of the wood and got whipped for
being a bad girl and playing truant, no one can say.
But the Three Bears never saw anything more of her.

The Goose Girl

The king of a great land died, and left his queen to take care of their only child. This child was a daughter, who was very beautiful; and her mother loved her dearly, and was very kind to her. And there was a good fairy too, who was fond of the princess, and helped her mother to watch over her. When she grew up, she was betrothed to a prince who lived a great way off; and as the time drew near for her to be married, she got ready to set off on her journey to his country. Then the queen her mother packed up a great many costly things: jewels, and gold, and silver; trinkets, and fine dresses, and in short everything that became a royal bride. And she gave her a waiting-maid to ride with her and give her into the bride-groom's hands; and each had a horse for the journey. Now the princess's horse was the fairy's gift, and it was called Falada, and could speak.

When the time came for them to set out, the fairy went into her bedchamber, and took a little knife, and cut off a lock of her hair, and gave it to the princess, and said, 'Take care of it, dear child; for it is a charm that may be of use to you on the road.' Then they all took a sorrowful leave of the princess; and she put the lock of hair into her bosom, got upon her horse, and set off on her journey to her bridegroom's kingdom.

One day, as they were riding along by a brook, the princess began to feel very thirsty: and she said to her maid, 'Pray get down and fetch me some water in my golden cup out of yonder brook, for I want to drink.'

'Nay,' said the maid, 'if you are thirsty, get off yourself, and stoop down by the water and drink; I shall not be your waiting-maid any longer.'

Then she was so thirsty that she got down, and knelt over the little brook, and drank; for she was frightened, and dared not bring out her golden cup; and she wept and said, 'Alas! what will become of me?'

And the lock answered her, and said:

> 'Alas! alas! if thy mother knew it,
> Sadly, sadly, would she rue it.'

But the princess was very gentle and meek, so she said nothing about her maid's ill behaviour, but got upon her horse again.

Then all rode farther on their journey, till the day grew so warm, and the sun so scorching, that the bride began to feel very thirsty again; and at last, when they came to a river, she forgot her maid's previous rude speech, and said, 'Pray get down, and fetch me some water to drink in my golden cup.'

But the maid answered her, and even spoke even more haughtily than before: 'Drink if you will, but I shall not be your waiting-maid.'

Then the princess was so thirsty that she got off her horse, and lay down, and held her head over the running stream, and cried and said, 'What will become of me?'

And the lock of hair answered her again:

> 'Alas! alas! if thy mother knew it,
> Sadly, sadly, would she rue it.'

And as she leaned down to drink, the lock of hair fell from her bosom, and floated away with the water. Now she was so frightened that she did not see it;

but her maid saw it, and was very glad, for she knew it was a charm; and she saw that the poor bride would be in her power, now that she had lost the hair.

So when the bride had done drinking, and would have got upon Falada again, the maid said, 'I shall ride upon Falada, and you may have my horse instead;' so she was forced to give up her horse, and soon afterwards to take off her royal clothes and put on her maid's shabby ones.

At last, as they drew near the end of their journey, this treacherous servant threatened to kill her mistress if she ever told anyone what had happened. But Falada saw it all, and marked it well.

Then the waiting-maid rode on upon Falada, and the real bride rode upon the other horse, and they went on in this way till at last they came to the royal court. There was great joy at their coming, and the prince flew to meet them, and lifted the maid from her horse, thinking she was the one who was to be his wife; and she was led upstairs to the royal chamber; but the true princess was told to stay in the court below.

Now the old king happened just then to have nothing else to do; so he amused himself by sitting at his kitchen window, looking at what was going on; and he saw her in the courtyard. As she looked very pretty, and too delicate for a waiting-maid, he went up into the royal chamber to ask the bride who it was she had brought with her but had thus left standing in the court below.

'I brought her with me for the sake of her company on the road,' said she; 'pray give the girl some work to do, that she may not be idle.'

The old king could not for some time think of any

work for her to do; but at last he said, 'I have a lad who takes care of my geese; she may go and help him.' Now the name of this lad that the real bride was to help in watching the king's geese was Curdken.

But the false bride said to the prince, 'Dear husband, pray do me one piece of kindness.'

'That I will,' said the prince.

'Then tell one of your slaughterers to cut off the head of the horse I rode upon, for it was very unruly, and plagued me sadly on the road.' But the truth was, she was very much afraid lest Falada should someday or other speak, and tell all she had done to the princess. She had her way, and the faithful Falada was killed; but when the true princess heard of it, she wept, and begged the man to nail up Falada's head in a large dark gateway of the city, through which she had to pass every morning and evening, that there she might still see him sometimes. Then the slaughterer said he would do as she wished; and cut off the head, and nailed it up in the dark gateway.

Early the next morning, as she and Curdken went out through the gate, she said sorrowfully: 'Falada, Falada, there thou hangest!' and the head answered:

'Bride, bride, there thou gangest!
Alas! alas! if thy mother knew it,
Sadly, sadly, would she rue it.'

Then they went out of the city, and drove the geese on. And when she came to the meadow, she sat down upon a bank there, and let down her waving locks of hair, which were all of pure silver; and when Curdken saw it glitter in the sun, he ran up, and would have pulled some of the locks out, but she cried:

'Blow, breezes, blow!
Let Curdken's hat go!
Blow, breezes, blow!
Let him after it go!
O'er hills, dales and rocks,
Away be it whirl'd,
Till the silvery locks
Are all comb'd and curl'd!

Then there came a wind so strong that it blew off
Curdken's hat; and away it flew over the hills: and he

was forced to turn and run after it. By the time he came back, she had done combing and curling her hair, and had put it up again safe. Then he was very angry and sulky, and would not speak to her at all; but they watched the geese until it grew dark in the evening, and then drove them homewards.

The next morning, as they were going through the dark gateway, the poor girl looked up at Falada's head, and cried: 'Falada, Falada, there thou hangest!' and the head answered:

> 'Bride, bride, there thou gangest!
> Alas! alas! if they mother knew it,
> Sadly, sadly, would she rue it.'

Then she drove on the geese, and sat down again in the meadow, and began to comb out her hair as before; and Curdken ran up to her, and wanted to take hold of it; but she cried out quickly:

> 'Blow, breezes, blow!
> Let Curdken's hat go!
> Blow, breezes, blow!
> Let him after it go!
> O'er hills, dales and rocks,
> Away be it whirl'd,
> Till the silvery locks
> Are all comb'd and curl'd!'

Then the wind came and blew away his hat; and off it flew a great way, over the hills and far away, so that he had to run after it; and when he came back she had bound up her hair again, and all was safe. So they watched the geese till it grew dark.

In the evening, after they came home, Curdken

went to the old king, and said, 'I cannot have that strange girl to help me to keep the geese any longer.'

'Why?' said the king.

'Because, instead of doing any good, she does nothing but tease me all day long.'

Then the king made him tell him what had happened. And Curdken said, 'When we go in the morning through the dark gateway with our flock of geese, she cries and talks with the head of a horse that hangs upon the wall, and says: 'Falada, Falada, there thou hangest!' and the head answers:

> 'Bride, bride, there thou gangest!
> Alas! alas! if they mother knew it,
> Sadly, sadly, would she rue it.'

And Curdken went on to tell the king what had happened upon the meadow where the geese fed: how his hat was blown away, and how he was forced to run after it, and to leave his flock of geese to themselves.

The old king told the boy to go out again the next day, and when morning came, he placed himself beside the dark gateway, and heard how she spoke to Falada, and how Falada answered. Then he went into the field, and hid himself in a bush by the meadow's side; and he soon saw with his own eyes how they drove the flock of geese; and how, after a little time, she let down her hair that glittered in the sun. And then he heard her say:

> 'Blow, breezes, blow!
> Let Curdken's hat go!
> Blow, breezes, blow!
> Let him after it go!

O'er hills, dales and rocks,
Away be it whirl'd,
Till the silvery locks
Are all comb'd and curl'd!

And soon came a gale of wind, and carried away
Curdken's hat, and away went Curdken after it, while
the girl went on combing and curling her hair. All this
the old king saw, and then he went home without
being seen. When the little goose girl came back in
the evening he called her aside, and asked her why
she behaved as she did; she burst into tears, and said,
'That I must not tell you or any man, or I shall lose
my life.'

But the old king
begged so hard
that she had
no peace till
she had told
him all the
tale, from
beginning
to end,
word for
word. And
it was very
lucky for
her that she did
so, for when she
had done the king
ordered royal clothes
to be put upon her, and gazed on her with wonder,
she was so beautiful. Then he called his son and told
him that he had only a false bride, one who was

merely a waiting-maid, while the true bride stood by. And the young king rejoiced when he saw her beauty, and heard how meek and patient she had been; and without saying anything to the false bride, the king ordered a great feast to be got ready for all his court. The bridegroom sat at the top, with the false princess on one side, and the true one on the other; but nobody recognised her, for her beauty was quite dazzling to their eyes; and she did not seem at all like the little goose girl, now that she had her brilliant dress on.

When they had eaten and drunk, and were very merry, the old king said he would tell them a tale. So he began, and told all the story of the princess, as if it was one that he had once heard; and he asked the true waiting-maid what she thought ought to be done to anyone who would behave thus.

'Nothing better,' said this false bride, 'than that she should be thrown into a cask stuck round with sharp nails, and that two white horses should be put to it, and should drag it from street to street till she was dead.'

'Thou art she!' said the old king; 'and as thou hast judged thyself, so shall it be done to thee.' And the young king was then married to his true wife, and they reigned over the kingdom in peace and happiness all their lives; and the good fairy came to see them, and restored the faithful Falada to life again.

Hansel and Gretel

Hard by a great forest dwelt a poor woodcutter with his wife and the two children of his former marriage. The boy was called Hansel and the girl Gretel. He earned very little, and once when a great famine fell on the land, he could no longer procure even daily bread. Now, when he thought over this by night in his bed, and tossed about in his anxiety, he groaned and said to his wife: 'What is to become of us? How are we to feed our poor children when we no longer have anything even for ourselves?'

'I'll tell you what, husband,' answered the woman, 'early tomorrow morning we will take the children out into the forest to where it is the thickest; there we will light a fire for them, and give each of them one last piece of bread, and then we will go to our work and leave them alone. They will not find the way home again, and we shall be rid of them.'

'No, wife,' said the man, 'I will not do that; how can I bear to leave my children alone in the forest? The wild animals would soon come and tear them to pieces.'

'Oh, you fool!' said she; 'then we must all four die of hunger; you may as well plane the planks for our coffins,' and she left him no peace until he consented.

'But I feel very sorry for the poor children, all the same,' said the man.

The two children had also not been able to sleep for hunger and had heard what their stepmother had said to their father. Gretel wept bitter tears, and said to Hansel: 'Now all is over with us.'

'Be quiet, Gretel,' said Hansel, 'do not distress yourself, I will soon find a way to help us.' And when the old folk had fallen asleep, he got up, put on his little coat, opened the door below and crept outside. The moon shone brightly, and the white pebbles which lay in front of the house glittered like real silver pennies. Hansel stooped and stuffed the little pocket of his coat with as many as he could get in. Then he went back and said to Gretel: 'Be comforted, dear little sister, and sleep in peace, God will not forsake us,' and he lay down again in his bed.

When day dawned, but before the sun had risen, the woman came and awoke the two children, saying: 'Get up, you sluggards! we are going into the forest to fetch wood.' She gave each a little piece of bread, and said: 'There is something for your dinner, but do not eat it up before then, for you will get nothing else.'

Gretel took the bread under her apron, as Hansel had the pebbles in his pocket. Then they all set out together on the way to the forest. When they had walked a short time, Hansel stood still and peeped back at the house, and did so again and again. His father said: 'Hansel, what are you looking at there and staying behind for? Pay attention, and do not forget how to use your legs.'

'Ah, father,' said Hansel, 'I am looking at my little white cat; she is sitting up on the roof, and wants to say goodbye to me.'

The wife said: 'Fool, that is not your little cat, that is the morning sun which is shining on the chimney.'

Hansel, however, had not been looking back at the

The white pebbles glittered like real silver pennies. Hansel
the pocket of his coat with as many as he could get in.

cat, but had been constantly throwing one of the white
pebble-stones out of his pocket on the road.

When they had reached the middle of the forest,
the father said: 'Now, children, pile up some wood,
and I will light a fire that you may not be cold.'

Hansel and Gretel gathered brushwood together, as high as a little hill. The brushwood was lighted, and when the flames were burning very high, the woman said: 'Now, children, lay yourselves down by the fire and rest; we will go into the forest and cut some wood. When we have done, we will come back and fetch you away.'

Hansel and Gretel sat by the fire, and when noon came, each ate a little piece of bread, and as they heard the strokes of the wood-axe they believed that their father was near. It was not the axe, however, but a branch which he had fastened to a withered tree which the wind was blowing backwards and forwards. And as they had been sitting such a long time, their eyes closed with fatigue, and they fell fast asleep. When at last they awoke, it was already dark night.

Gretel began to cry and said: 'How are we to get out of the forest now?'

But Hansel comforted her and said: 'Just wait a little, until the moon has risen, and then we will soon find the way.'

And when the full moon had risen, Hansel took his little sister by the hand, and followed the pebbles which shone like newly-coined silver pieces, and showed them the way.

They walked the whole night long, and by break of day came once more to their father's house. They knocked at the door, and when the woman opened it and saw that it was Hansel and Gretel, she said: 'You naughty children, why have you slept so long in the forest? We thought you were never coming back at all!' The father, however, rejoiced, for it had cut him to the heart to leave them behind alone.

Not long afterwards, there was once more great

dearth throughout the land, and the children heard their mother saying at night to their father: 'Everything is eaten again, we have one half-loaf left, and that is the end. The children must go, we will take them farther into the wood, so that they will not find their way out again; there is no other means of saving ourselves!' The man's heart was heavy, and he thought: 'It would be better for me to share the last mouthful with my children.' The woman, however, would listen to nothing that he had to say, but scolded and reproached him. He who says A must say B likewise, and as he had yielded the first time, he had to do so a second time also.

The children, however, were still awake and had heard the conversation. When the old folk were asleep, Hansel again got up, and wanted to go out and pick up pebbles as he had done before, but the woman had locked the door, and Hansel could not get out. Nevertheless he comforted his little sister, and said: 'Do not cry, Gretel, go to sleep quietly, the good God will help us.'

Early in the morning came the woman, and took the children out of their beds. Their piece of bread was given to them, but it was still smaller than the time before. On the way into the forest Hansel crumbled his in his pocket, and often stood still and threw a morsel on the ground.

'Hansel, why do you stop and look round?' said the father. 'Come on, do.'

'I am looking back at my little pigeon which is sitting on the roof and wants to say goodbye to me,' answered Hansel.

'Fool!' said the woman, 'that is not your little pigeon, that is the morning sun that is shining on the chimney.'

Hansel, however, little by little, threw all the crumbs on the path.

The woman led the children still deeper into the forest, where they had never in their lives been before. Then a great fire was again made, and the mother said: 'Just sit there, you children, and when you are tired you may sleep a little; we are going into the forest to cut wood, and in the evening when we are done, we will come and fetch you away.'

When it was noon, Gretel shared her piece of bread with Hansel, who had scattered his by the way. Then they fell asleep and evening passed, but no one came to the poor children. They did not awake until it was dark night, and Hansel comforted his little sister and said: 'Just wait, Gretel, until the moon rises, and then we shall see the crumbs of bread which I have strewn about; they will show us our way home again.'

When the moon came they set out, but they found no crumbs, for the many thousands of birds which fly about in the woods and fields had picked them all up. Hansel said to Gretel: 'We shall soon find the way,' but they did not find it. They walked the whole night and all the next day too, from morning till evening, but they did not get out of the forest, and they were very hungry for they had had nothing to eat but two or three berries which grew on the ground. And as they were so weary that their legs would carry them no longer, they lay down beneath a tree and fell asleep.

It was now three mornings since they had left their father's house. They began to walk again, but they always came deeper into the forest, and if help did not come soon, they must die of hunger and weariness. When it was midday, they saw a beautiful snow-white bird sitting on a bough, which sang so delightfully that they stood still and listened to it. And when its song was over, it spread its wings and flew away before them, and they followed it until they reached a little house, on the roof of which it alighted; and when they approached the little house they saw that it was built of bread and covered with cakes, but that the windows were of clear sugar. 'We will set to work on that,' said Hansel, 'and have a good meal. I will eat a bit of the roof, and you Gretel, can eat some of the window, it will taste sweet.' Hansel reached up and broke off a little of the roof to try how it tasted, and Gretel leant against the window and nibbled at the panes. Then a soft voice cried from the parlour: 'Nibble, nibble, gnaw. Who is nibbling at my little house?'

The children answered: 'The wind, the wind, the heaven-born wind,' and went on eating without disturbing themselves. Hansel, who liked the taste of the roof, tore down a great piece of it, and Gretel pushed out the whole of one round windowpane and sat down on the ground to enjoy it.

Suddenly the door opened, and a woman as old as the hills, who supported herself on crutches, came hobbling out. Hansel and Gretel were so terribly frightened that they let fall what they had in their hands. The old woman, however, nodded her head, and said: 'Oh, you dear children, who has brought you here? Do come in, and stay with me. No harm shall come to you.'

She took them both by the hand, and led them into her little house. Then good food was set before them, milk and pancakes, with sugar, apples and nuts. Afterwards two pretty little beds were covered with clean white linen, and Hansel and Gretel lay down in them, and thought they were in heaven.

The old woman had only pretended to be so kind; she was in reality a wicked witch, who lay in wait for children, and had only built the little house of bread in order to entice them there. When a child fell into her power, she killed it, cooked and ate it, and that was a feast day with her. Witches have red eyes, and cannot see far, but they have a keen sense of smell like the beasts, and are aware when human beings draw near. When Hansel and Gretel came into her neighbourhood, she laughed with malice, and said mockingly: 'I have them, they shall not escape me!'

Early in the morning before the children were awake, she was already up, and when she saw both of them sleeping and looking so pretty, with their plump and rosy cheeks, she muttered to herself: 'That will be a dainty mouthful!' Then she seized Hansel with her shrivelled hand, carried him into a little stable, and locked him in behind a grated door. Scream as he might, it would not help him. Then she went to Gretel, shook her till she awoke, and cried: 'Get up, lazy thing, fetch some water, and cook something good for your brother; he is in the stable outside, and is to be made fat. When he is fat, I will eat him.' Gretel began to weep bitterly, but it was all in vain, for she was forced to do what the wicked witch commanded.

And now the best food was cooked for poor Hansel, but Gretel got nothing but crab-shells. Every morning the woman crept to the little stable, and cried: 'Hansel, stretch out your finger that I may feel if you will soon be fat.' Hansel, however, stretched out a little bone to her, and the old woman, who had dim eyes, could not

*'Hansel, stretch out your finger that I may
feel if you will soon be fat.'*

see it, and thought it was Hansel's finger, and was
astonished that there was no way of fattening him.

When four weeks had gone by, and Hansel still

remained thin, she was seized with impatience and would not wait any longer. 'Now, then, Gretel,' she cried to the girl, 'stir yourself, and bring some water. Let Hansel be fat or lean, tomorrow I will kill him, and cook him.'

Ah, how the poor little sister did lament when she had to fetch the water, and how her tears did flow down her cheeks! 'Dear God, do help us,' she cried. 'If the wild beasts in the forest had but devoured us, we should at any rate have died together.'

'Just keep your noise to yourself,' said the old woman, 'it won't help you at all.'

Early in the morning, Gretel had to go out and hang up the cauldron with the water, and light the fire.

'We will bake first,' said the old woman, 'I have already heated the oven, and kneaded the dough.' She pushed poor Gretel out to the oven, from which flames of fire were already darting. 'Creep in,' said the witch, 'and see if it is properly heated, so that we can put the bread in.'

Once Gretel was inside, she intended to shut the oven and let her bake in it, and then she would eat her, too. But Gretel saw what she had in mind, and said: 'I do not know how I am to do it; how do I get in?'

'Silly goose,' said the old woman. 'The door is big enough; just look, I can get in myself!' and she crept up and thrust her head into the oven. Then Gretel gave her a push that drove her far into it, and shut the iron door, and fastened the bolt. Oh! Then she began to howl quite horribly, but Gretel ran away and the wicked witch was miserably burnt to death.

Gretel, however, ran like lightning to Hansel, opened his little stable, and cried: 'Hansel, we are saved! The old witch is dead!' Then Hansel sprang like a bird from its cage when the door is opened. How they did rejoice and embrace each other, and dance about and kiss each other! And as they had no longer any need to fear her, they went into the witch's house, and in every corner there stood chests full of pearls and jewels. 'These are far better than pebbles!' said Hansel, and thrust into his pocket whatever could be got in, and Gretel said: 'I, too, will take something home with me,' and filled her pinafore full. 'But now we must be off,' said Hansel, 'that we may get out of the witch's forest.'

When they had walked for two hours, they came to a great stretch of water. 'We cannot cross,' said Hansel, 'I see no foot-plank, and no bridge.'

'And there is alas no ferry,' answered Gretel; 'but a white duck is swimming there: if I ask her, she will help us over.' Then she cried:

'Little duck, little duck, dost thou see,
　Hansel and Gretel are waiting for thee?
　There's never a plank or bridge in sight,
　Take us across on thy back so white.'

The duck came to them, and Hansel seated himself on its back, and told his sister to sit by him. 'No,' replied Gretel, 'that will be too heavy for the little duck; she shall take us across one after the other.' The good little duck did so, and when they were once safely across and had walked for a short time, the forest seemed to be more and more familiar to them, and at length they saw from afar their father's house.

Then they began to run, rushed into the parlour and threw themselves round their father's neck. The man had not known one happy hour since he had left the children in the forest; and the woman, who had been so cruel, was dead.

Gretel emptied her pinafore so that quantities of pearls and precious stones ran about the room, and Hansel threw one handful after another out of his pocket to add to them. Then all anxiety was at an end, and they lived together in perfect happiness.

Henny-Penny

One day Henny-penny was picking up corn in the cornyard when – whack! – something hit her upon the head. 'Goodness gracious me!' said Henny-penny; 'the sky's a-going to fall; I must go and tell the king.'

So she went along and she went along and she went along till she met Cocky-locky. 'Where are you going, Henny-penny?' says Cocky-locky. 'Oh! I'm going to tell the king the sky's a-falling,' says Henny-penny. 'May I come with you?' says Cocky-locky. 'Certainly,' says Henny-penny. So Henny-penny and Cocky-locky went to tell the king the sky was falling.

They went along, and they went along, and they went along, till they met Ducky-daddles. 'Where are you going to, Henny-penny and Cocky-locky?' says Ducky-daddles. 'Oh! we're going to tell the king the sky's a-falling,' said Henny-penny and Cocky-locky. 'May I come with you?' says Ducky-daddles. 'Certainly,' said Henny-penny and Cocky-locky. So Henny-penny, Cocky-locky and Ducky-daddles went to tell the king the sky was a-falling.

So they went along, and they went along, and they went along, till they met Goosey-poosey, 'Where are you going to, Henny-penny, Cocky-locky and Ducky-daddles?' said Goosey-poosey. 'Oh! we're going to tell the king the sky's a-falling,' said Henny-penny and Cocky-locky and Ducky-daddles. 'May I come with you,' said Goosey-poosey. 'Certainly,' said Henny-penny, Cocky-locky and Ducky-daddles. So Henny-penny, Cocky-locky, Ducky-daddles and

Goosey-poosey went to tell the king the sky was a-falling.

So they went along, and they went along, and they went along, till they met Turkey-lurkey. 'Where are you going, Henny-penny, Cocky-locky, Ducky-daddles, and Goosey-poosey?' says Turkey-lurkey. 'Oh! we're going to tell the king the sky's a-falling,' said Henny-penny, Cocky-locky, Ducky-daddles and Goosey-poosey. 'May I come with you? Henny-penny, Cocky-locky, Ducky-daddles and Goosey-poosey?' said Turkey-lurkey. 'Why, certainly, Turkey-lurkey,' said Henny-penny, Cocky-locky, Ducky-daddles, and Goosey-poosey. So Henny-penny, Cocky-locky, Ducky-daddles, Goosey-poosey and Turkey-lurkey all went to tell the king the sky was a-falling.

So they went along, and they went along, and they went along, till they met Foxy-woxy, and Foxy-woxy said to Henny-penny, Cocky-locky, Ducky-daddles, Goosey-poosey and Turkey-lurkey: 'Where are you going, Henny-penny, Cocky-locky, Ducky-daddles, Goosey-poosey, and Turkey-lurkey?' And Henny-penny, Cocky-locky, Ducky-daddles, Goosey-poosey,

H. RYLAND

and Turkey-lurkey said to Foxy-woxy: 'We're going to tell the king the sky's a-falling.' 'Oh! but this is not the way to the king, Henny-penny, Cocky-locky, Ducky-daddles, Goosey-poosey and Turkey-lurkey,' says Foxy-woxy; 'I know the proper way; shall I show it you?' 'Why certainly, Foxy-woxy,' said Henny-penny, Cocky-locky, Ducky-daddles, Goosey-poosey, and Turkey-lurkey. So Henny-penny, Cocky-locky, Ducky-daddles, Goosey-poosey, Turkey-lurkey, and Foxy-woxy all went to tell the king the sky was a-falling. So they went along, and they went along, and they went along, till they came to a narrow and dark hole.

Now this was the door of Foxy-woxy's cave. But Foxy-woxy said to Henny-penny, Cocky-locky, Ducky-daddles, Goosey-poosey, and Turkey-lurkey: 'This is the short way to the king's palace; you'll soon get there if you follow me. I will go first and you come after, Henny-penny, Cocky-locky, Ducky daddles, Goosey-poosey and Turkey-lurkey.' 'Why of course, certainly, without doubt, why not?' said Henny-Penny, Cocky-locky, Ducky-daddles, Goosey-poosey and Turkey-lurkey.

So Foxy-woxy went into his cave, and he didn't go very far but turned round to wait for Henny-penny, Cocky-locky, Ducky-daddles, Goosey-poosey and Turkey-lurkey. So first of all Turkey-lurkey went through the dark hole into the cave. He hadn't got far when, 'Hrumph,' Foxy-woxy snapped off Turkey-lurkey's head and threw his body over his left shoulder. Then Goosey-poosey went in, and, 'Hrumph,' off went her head and Goosey-poosey was thrown beside Turkey-lurkey. Then Ducky-daddles waddled down, and, 'Hrumph,' snapped Foxy-woxy, and Ducky-

daddles' head was off and Ducky-daddles was thrown alongside Turkey-lurkey and Goosey-poosey. Then Cocky-locky strutted down into the cave and he hadn't gone far when, 'Snap, Hrumph!' went Foxy-woxy and Cocky-locky was thrown alongside of Turkey-lurkey, Goosey-poosey and Ducky-daddles.

But Foxy-woxy had made two bites at Cocky-locky, and when the first snap only hurt Cocky-locky, but didn't kill him, he called out to Henny-penny. So she turned tail and ran back home, so she never told the king the sky was a-falling.

How Jack Went to Seek His Fortune

Once on a time there was a boy named Jack, and one morning he started to go and seek his fortune.

He hadn't gone very far before he met a cat.

'Where are you going, Jack?' said the cat.

'I am going to seek my fortune.'

'May I go with you?'

'Yes,' said Jack, 'the more the merrier.'

So on they went, jiggelty-jolt, jiggelty-jolt.

They went a little farther and they met a dog.

'Where are you going, Jack?' said the dog.

'I am going to seek my fortune.'

'May I go with you?'

'Yes,' said Jack, 'the more the merrier.'

So on they went, jiggelty-jolt, jiggelty-jolt. They went a little farther and they met a goat.

'Where are you going, Jack?' said the goat.

'I am going to seek my fortune.'

'May I go with you?'

'Yes,' said Jack, 'the more the merrier.'

So on they went, jiggelty-jolt, jiggelty-jolt.

They went a little farther and they met a bull.

'Where are you going, Jack?' said the bull.

'I am going to seek my fortune.'

'May I go with you?'

'Yes,' said Jack, 'the more the merrier.'

So on they went, jiggelty-jolt, jiggelty-jolt.

They went a little farther and they met a rooster.

'Where are you going, Jack?' said the rooster.

'I am going to seek my fortune.'

'May I go with you?'

'Yes,' said Jack, 'the more the merrier.'

So on they went, jiggelty-jolt, jiggelty-jolt.

Well, they went on till it was about dark, and they began to think of some place where they could spend the night. About this time they came in sight of a house, and Jack told them to keep still while he went up and looked in through the window. And there were some robbers counting over their money. Then Jack went back and told them to wait till he gave the word, and then to make all the noise they could. So when they were all ready Jack gave the word, and the cat mewed, and the dog barked, and the goat bleated, and the bull bellowed, and the rooster crowed, and all together they made such a dreadful noise that it frightened the robbers all away.

And then they went in and took possession of the house. Jack was afraid the robbers would come back in the night, and so when it came time to go to bed he put the cat in the rocking-chair, and he put the dog under the table, and he put the goat upstairs, and he

put the bull down in the cellar, and the rooster flew up on to the roof, and Jack went to bed.

By and by the robbers saw it was all dark and they sent one man back to the house to look after their money. Before long he came back in a great fright and told them his story.

'I went back to the house,' said he, 'and went in and tried to sit down in the rocking-chair, and there was an old woman knitting, and she stuck her knitting-needles into me.' That was the cat, you know.

'I went to the table to look after the money and there was a shoemaker under the table, and he stuck his awl into me.' That was the dog, you know.

'I started to go upstairs, and there was a man up there threshing, and he knocked me down with his flail.' That was the goat, you know.

'I started to go down into the cellar, and there was a man down there chopping wood, and he knocked me over with his axe.' That was the bull, you know.

'But I shouldn't have minded all that if it hadn't been for that little fellow on top of the house, who kept a-hollering, "Chuck him up to me–e! Chuck him up to me–e!" ' Of course that was the cock-a-doodle-do.

Jack and the Beanstalk

There was once upon a time a poor widow who had an only son named Jack, and a cow named Milky-white. And all they had to live on was the milk the cow gave every morning which they carried to the market and sold. But one morning Milky-white gave no milk and they didn't know what to do.

'What shall we do, what shall we do?' said the widow, wringing her hands.

'Cheer up, mother, I'll go and get work somewhere,' said Jack.

'We've tried that before, and nobody would take you,' said his mother; 'we must sell Milky-white and with the money do something – start a shop or something.'

'All right, mother,' says Jack; 'it's market-day today, and I'll soon sell Milky-white, and then we'll see what we can do.'

So he took the cow's halter in his hand, and off he starts. He hadn't gone far when he met a funny-looking old man who said to him: 'Good-morning, Jack.'

'Good-morning to you,' said Jack, and wondered how he knew his name.

'Well, Jack, and where are you off to?' said the man.

'I'm going to market to sell our cow here.'

'Oh, you look the proper sort of chap to sell cows,' said the man; 'I wonder if you know how many beans make five.'

'Two in each hand and one in your mouth,' says Jack, as sharp as a needle.

'Right you are,' said the man, 'and here they are the very beans themselves,' he went on pulling out of his pocket a number of strange-looking beans. 'As you are so sharp,' says he, 'I don't mind doing a swop with you – your cow for these beans.'

'Walker!' says Jack; 'wouldn't you like it?'

'Ah! you don't know what these beans are,' said the man; 'if you plant them overnight, by morning they grow right up to the sky.'

'Really?' says Jack; 'you don't say so.'

'Yes, that is so, and if it doesn't turn out to be true you can have your cow back.'

'Right,' says Jack, and hands him over Milky-white's halter and pockets the beans.

Back goes Jack home, and as he hadn't gone very far it wasn't dusk by the time he got to his door.

'What back, Jack?' said his mother; 'I see you haven't got Milky-white, so you've sold her. How much did you get for her?'

'You'll never guess, mother,' says Jack.

'No, you don't say so. Good boy! Five pounds, ten, fifteen, no, it can't be twenty.'

'I told you you couldn't guess, what do you say to these beans; they're magical, plant them overnight and – '

'What!' says Jack's mother, 'have you been such a fool, such a dolt, such an idiot, as to give away my Milky-white, the best milker in the parish, and prime beef to boot, for a set of paltry beans. Take that! Take that! Take that! And as for your precious beans here they go out of the window. And now off with you to bed. Not a sup shall you drink, and not a bite shall you swallow this very night.'

So Jack went upstairs to his little room in the attic, and sad and sorry he was, to be sure, as much for his mother's sake, as for the loss of his supper.

At last he dropped off to sleep.

When he woke up, the room looked so funny. The sun was shining into part of it, and yet all the rest was quite dark and shady. So Jack jumped up and dressed himself and went to the window. And what do you think he saw? why, the beans his mother had thrown out of the window into the garden had sprung up into a big beanstalk which went up and up and up till it reached the sky. So the man spoke truth after all.

The beanstalk grew up quite close past Jack's window, so all he had to do was to open it and give a jump on to the beanstalk which was made like a big plaited ladder. So Jack climbed and he climbed and he climbed and he climbed and he climbed and he climbed and he climbed till at last he reached the sky. And when he got there he found a long broad road going as straight as a dart. So he walked along and he walked along and he walked along till he came to a great big tall house, and on the doorstep there was a great big tall woman.

'Good-morning, mum,' says Jack, quite polite-like. 'Could you be so kind as to give me some breakfast?' For he hadn't had anything to eat, you know, the night before and was as hungry as a hunter.

'It's breakfast you want, is it?' says the great big tall woman, 'it's breakfast you'll be if you don't move off from here. My man is an ogre and there's nothing he likes better than boys broiled on toast. You'd better be moving on or he'll soon be coming.'

'Oh! please mum, do give me something to eat, mum. I've had nothing to eat since yesterday morning, really and truly, mum,' says Jack. 'I may as well be broiled as die of hunger.'

Well, the ogre's wife wasn't such a bad sort, after all. So she took Jack into the kitchen, and gave him a hunk of bread and cheese and a jug of milk. But Jack hadn't half finished these when thump! thump! thump! the whole house began to tremble with the noise of someone coming.

'Goodness gracious me! It's my old man,' said the ogre's wife, 'what on earth shall I do? Here, come quick and jump in here.' And she bundled Jack into the oven just as the ogre came in.

He was a big one, to be sure. At his belt he had three calves strung up by the heels, and he unhooked them and threw them down on the table and said: 'Here, wife, broil me a couple of these for breakfast. Ah what's this I smell? Fee, fi, fo, fum! I smell the blood of an Englishman. Be he alive, or be he dead, I'll grind his bones to make my bread.'

'Nonsense, dear,' said his wife, 'you're dreaming. Or perhaps you smell the scraps of that little boy you liked so much for yesterday's dinner. Here, go you and have a wash and tidy up, and by the time you come back your breakfast'll be ready for you.'

So the ogre went off, and Jack was just going to jump out of the oven and run off when the woman stopped him. 'Wait till he's asleep,' says she; 'he always has a snooze after breakfast.'

Well, the ogre had his breakfast, and after that he goes to a big chest and takes out of it a couple of bags of gold and sits down counting the pieces till at last his head began to nod and he began to snore till the whole house shook again.

Then Jack crept out on tiptoe from his oven, and as he was passing the ogre he took one of the bags of gold under his arm, and off he pelters till he came to the beanstalk, and then he threw down the bag of gold which of course fell into his mother's garden, and then he climbed down and climbed down till at last he got home and told his mother and showed her

the gold and said: 'Well, mother, wasn't I right about the beans. They are really magical, you see.'

So they lived on the bag of gold for some time, but at last they came to the end of it. So Jack made up his mind to try his luck once more up at the top of the beanstalk. So one fine morning he got up early, and got on to the beanstalk, and he climbed and he climbed and he climbed and he climbed and he climbed and he climbed till at last he got on the road again and came to the great big tall house he had been to before. There, sure enough, was the great big tall woman a-standing on the doorstep.

'Good-morning, mum,' says Jack, as bold as brass, 'could you be so good as to give me something to eat?'

'Go away, my boy,' said the big, tall woman, 'or else my man will eat you up for breakfast. But aren't you the youngster who came here once before? Do you know, that very day, my man missed one of his bags of gold.'

'That's strange, mum,' says Jack. 'I dare say I could tell you something about that but I'm so hungry I can't speak till I've had something to eat.'

Well the big tall woman was that curious that she took him in and gave him something to eat. But he had scarcely begun munching it as slowly as he could when thump! thump! thump! they heard the giant's footstep, and his wife hid Jack away in the oven.

All happened as it did before. In came the ogre as he did before, said: 'Fee, fi, fo, fum!' and had his breakfast off three broiled oxen. Then he said: 'Wife, bring me the hen that lays the golden eggs.' So she brought it, and the ogre said: 'Lay,' and it laid an egg all of gold. And then the ogre began to nod his head, and to snore till the house shook.

Then Jack crept out of the oven on tiptoe and caught hold of the golden hen, and was off before you could say 'Jack Robinson'. But this time the hen gave a cackle which woke the ogre, and just as Jack got out of the house he heard him calling: 'Wife, wife, what have you done with my golden hen?'

And the wife said: 'Why, my dear?'

But that was all Jack heard, for he rushed off to the beanstalk and climbed down like a house on fire. And when he got home he showed his mother the wonderful hen and said, 'Lay,' to it; and it laid a golden egg every time he said, 'Lay.'

Well, Jack was not content, and it wasn't very long before he determined to have another try at his luck up there at the top of the beanstalk. So one fine morning, he got up early, and went on to the beanstalk, and he climbed and he climbed and he climbed and he climbed till he got to the top. But this time he knew better than to go straight to the ogre's house. And when he got near it he waited behind a bush till he saw the ogre's wife come out with a pail to get some water, and then he crept into the house and got into the copper. He hadn't been there long when he heard thump! thump! thump! as before, and in came the ogre and his wife.

'Fee, fi, fo, fum! I smell the blood of an Englishman,' cried the ogre; 'I smell him, wife, I smell him.'

'Do you, my dearie?' says the ogre's wife. 'Then if it's that little rogue that stole your gold and the hen that laid the golden eggs he's sure to have got into the oven.' And they both rushed to the oven. But Jack wasn't there, luckily, and the ogre's wife said: 'There you are again with your Fee, fi, fo, fum!. Why of course it's the laddie you caught last night that I've broiled for your breakfast. How forgetful I am, and how careless you are not to tell the difference between a live un and a dead un.'

So the ogre sat down to the breakfast and ate it, but every now and then he would mutter: 'Well, I could have sworn – ' and he'd get up and search the larder and the cupboards, and everything, only luckily he didn't think of the copper.

After breakfast was over, the ogre called out: 'Wife, wife, bring me my golden harp.' So she brought it and put it on the table before him. Then he said: 'Sing!' and the golden harp sang most beautifully. And it went on singing till the ogre fell asleep, and commenced to snore like thunder.

Then Jack lifted up the copper-lid very quietly and got down like a mouse and crept on hands and knees till he got to the table; then he got up and caught hold of the golden harp and dashed with it towards the door. But the harp called out quite loud: 'Master! Master!' and the ogre woke up just in time to see Jack running off with his harp.

Jack ran as fast as he could, and the ogre came rushing after, and would soon have caught him, only Jack had a start and dodged him a bit and knew where he was going. When he got to the beanstalk the ogre was not more than twenty yards away when suddenly he saw Jack disappear, and when he got up to the end of the road he saw Jack underneath, climbing down for dear life. Well, the ogre didn't like trusting himself to such a ladder, and he stood and waited, so Jack got another start. But just then the harp cried out: 'Master! master!' and the ogre swung himself down on to the beanstalk which shook with his weight. Down climbs Jack, and after him climbed the ogre.

By this time Jack had
climbed down and
climbed down and
climbed down till he
was very nearly home.
So he called out:
'Mother! mother! bring me an
axe, bring me an axe.' And his
mother came rushing out with
the axe in her hand, but when
she came to the beanstalk she
stood stock still with fright for
there she saw the ogre just
coming down below the clouds.

But Jack jumped down and
got hold of the axe and gave a
chop at the beanstalk which cut
it half in two. The ogre felt the
beanstalk shake and quiver so
he stopped to see what was the
matter. Then Jack gave
another chop with
the axe, and the
beanstalk was cut in
two and began to
topple over. Then the
ogre fell down and
broke his crown,
and the beanstalk
came toppling after.

Then Jack showed his mother his golden harp, and
what with showing that and selling the golden eggs,
Jack and his mother became very rich, and he married
a great princess, and they lived happy ever after.

Jack the Giant Killer

When good King Arthur reigned with Guinevere his queen, there lived, near the Land's End in Cornwall, a farmer who had one only son called Jack. Now Jack was brisk and ready; of such a lively wit that none nor nothing could worst him.

In those days, the Mount of St Michael in Cornwall was the fastness of a hugeous giant whose name was Cormoran.

He was full eighteen feet in height, some three yards about his middle, of a grim fierce face, and he was the terror of all the countryside. He lived in a cave amidst the rocky Mount, and when he desired victuals he would wade across the tides to the mainland and furnish himself forth with all that came in his way. The poor folk and the rich folk alike ran out of their houses and hid themselves when they heard the swish-swash of his big feet in the water; for if he saw them, he would think nothing of broiling half a dozen or so of them for breakfast. As it was, he seized their cattle by the score, carrying off half a dozen fat oxen on his back at a time, and hanging sheep and pigs to his waistbelt like bunches of dip-candles. Now this had gone on for long years, and the poor folk of Cornwall were in despair, for none could put an end to the giant Cormoran.

It so happened that one market day Jack, then quite a young lad, found the town upside down over some new exploit of the giant's. Women were weeping, men were cursing, and the magistrates were sitting in council over what was to be done. But none could suggest a plan. Then Jack, blithe and gay, went up to the magistrates, and with a fine courtesy – for he was ever polite – asked them what reward would be given to him who killed the giant Cormoran?

'The treasures of the giant's cave,' quoth they.

'Every whit of it?' quoth Jack.

'To the last farthing,' quoth they.

'Then will I undertake the task,' said Jack, and forthwith set about the business.

It was wintertime, and having got himself a horn, a pickaxe and a shovel, he went over to the Mount in the dark evening, set to work, and before dawn he had dug a pit no less than twenty-two feet deep and nigh as big across. This he covered with long thin sticks and straw, sprinkling a little loose mould over all to make it look like solid ground. So, just as dawn was breaking, he planted himself fair and square on the side of the pit that was farthest from the giant's cave, raised the horn to his lips, and with full blast sounded: 'Tantivy! Tantivy! Tantivy!' just as he would have done had he been hunting a fox.

Of course this woke the giant, who rushed in a rage out of his cave, and seeing little Jack, fair and square blowing away at his horn, as calm and cool as may be, he became still more angry, and made for the disturber of his rest, bawling out, 'I'll teach you to wake a giant, you little whippersnapper. You shall pay dearly for your tantivys. I'll take you and broil you whole for break – '

He had only got this far when crash – he fell into the pit! So there was a break indeed; such a one that it caused the very foundations of the Mount to shake.

But Jack shook with laughter. 'Ho, ho!' he cried,

'how about breakfast now, sir giant? Will you have me broiled or baked? And will no diet serve you but poor little Jack? Faith! I've got you in Lob's pound now! You're in the stocks for bad behaviour, and I'll plague you as I like. Would I had rotten eggs; but this will do as well.' And with that he up with his pickaxe and dealt the giant Cormoran such a most weighty knock on the very crown of his head, that he killed him on the spot.

Whereupon Jack calmly filled the pit with earth again and went to search the cave, where he found much treasure.

Now when the magistrates heard of Jack's great exploit, they proclaimed that henceforth he should be known as Jack the Giant Killer. And they presented him with a sword and belt, on which these words were embroidered in gold:

> Here's the valiant Cornishman,
> Who slew the giant Cormoran.

*   *   *

Of course the news of Jack's victory soon spread over all England, so that another giant named Blunderbore, who lived to the north, hearing of it, vowed if ever he came across Jack he would be revenged upon him. Now this giant Blunderbore was lord of an enchanted castle that stood in the middle of a lonesome forest.

It so happened that Jack, about four months after he had killed Cormoran, had occasion to journey into Wales, and on the road he passed this forest. Weary with walking, and finding a pleasant fountain by the wayside, he lay down to rest and was soon fast asleep.

Now the giant Blunderbore, coming to the well for

water, found Jack sleeping, and knew by the lines embroidered on his belt that here was the far-famed giant killer. Rejoiced at his luck, the giant, without more ado, lifted Jack to his shoulder and began to carry him through the wood to the enchanted castle.

But the rustling of the boughs awakened Jack, who, finding himself already in the clutches of the giant, was terrified; nor was his alarm decreased by seeing the courtyard of the castle all strewn with men's bones.

'Yours will be with them ere long,' said Blunderbore as he locked poor Jack into an immense chamber above the castle gateway. It had a high-pitched, beamed roof, and one window that looked down the road. Here poor Jack was to stay while Blunderbore went to fetch his brother-giant, who lived in the same wood, so that he might share in the feast.

Now, after a time, Jack, watching through the window, saw the two giants tramping hastily down the road, eager for their dinner.

'Now,' quoth Jack to himself, 'my death or my deliverance is at hand.' For he had thought out a plan. In one corner of the room he had seen two strong cords. These he took, and making a cunning noose at the end of each, he hung them out of the window, and as the giants were unlocking the iron door of the gate managed to slip them over their heads without their noticing it. Then, quick as thought, he tied the other ends to a beam, so that as the giants moved on the nooses tightened and throttled them until they grew black in the face. Seeing this, Jack slid down the ropes, and drawing his sword, slew them both.

So, taking the keys of the castle, he unlocked all the doors and freed three beauteous ladies who, tied by their hair, he had found almost starved to death.

'Sweet ladies,' quoth Jack kneeling on one knee – for he was ever polite – 'here are the keys of this enchanted castle. I have destroyed the giant Blunderbore and his brutish brother, and thus have restored to you your liberty. These keys should bring you all else you require.'

So saying he proceeded on his journey to Wales.

*　　*　　*

He travelled as fast as he could; perhaps too fast, for, losing his way he found himself benighted and far from any habitation. He wandered on always in hopes, until on entering a narrow valley he came on a very large, dreary-looking house standing alone. Being anxious for shelter he went up to the door and knocked. You may imagine his surprise and alarm when the summons was answered by a giant with two heads. But though this monster's look was exceedingly fierce, his manners were quite polite. The truth was that he was a Welsh giant, and as such double-faced and smooth, given to gaining his malicious ends by show of false friendship.

So he welcomed Jack heartily in a strong Welsh accent, and prepared a bedroom for him, where he was left with kind wishes for a good rest. Jack, however, was too tired to sleep well, and as he lay awake, he overheard his host muttering to himself in the next room. Having very keen ears he was able to make out these words or something like them:

> 'Though here you lodge with me this night,
> You shall not see the morning light.
> My club shall dash your brains outright.'

'Say'st thou so!' quoth Jack to himself, starting up

at once. 'So that is your Welsh trick, is it? But I will be even with you.' Then, leaving his bed, he laid a big billet of wood among the blankets and, taking one of these to keep himself warm, made himself snug in a corner of the room, pretending to snore, so as to make Mr Giant think he was asleep.

And sure enough, after a little time in came the monster on tiptoe as if treading on eggs, and carrying a big club. Then – Whack! Whack! Whack!

Jack could hear the bed being belaboured until the giant, thinking every bone of his guest's body must be broken, stole out of the room again; whereupon Jack went calmly to bed once more and slept soundly! Next morning the giant couldn't believe his eyes when he saw Jack coming down the stairs fresh and hearty.

'Odds splutter hur nails!' he cried astonished. 'Did ye sleep well? Was there not nothing felt in the night?'

'Oh,' replied Jack, laughing in his sleeve, 'I think a rat did come and give me a few flaps of his tail.'

On this the giant was dumbfounded, and led Jack to breakfast, bringing him a bowl which held at least four gallons of hasty-pudding, and bidding him, as a man of such mettle, eat the lot. Now Jack when travelling wore under his cloak a leathern bag to carry his things withal; so, quick as thought, he hitched this round in front with the opening just under his chin; thus, as he ate, he could slip the best part of the pudding into it without the giant's being any the wiser. So they sat down to breakfast, the giant gobbling down his own measure of hasty-pudding, while Jack made away with his.

'See,' says crafty Jack when he had finished. 'I'll show you a trick worth two of yours,' and with that he up with a carving-knife and ripping up the leathern bag out fell all the hasty-pudding on the floor!

'Odds splutter hur nails!' cried the giant, not to be outdone. 'Hur can do that hurself!' Whereupon he seized the carving-knife, and ripping open his own belly fell down dead.

Thus was Jack quit of the Welsh giant.

* * *

Now it so happened that in those days when gallant
knights were always seeking adventures, King Arthur's
only son, a very valiant prince, begged of his father a
large sum of money to enable him to journey to Wales,
and there strive to set free a certain beautiful lady
who was possessed by seven evil spirits. In vain the
king denied him; so at last he gave way and the prince
set out with two horses, one of which he rode, the
other he had laden with gold pieces. Now after some
days' journey the prince came to a market-town in
Wales where there was a great commotion. On asking
the reason for it he was told that, according to law,
the corpse of a very generous man had been arrested
on its way to the grave, because, in life, it had owed
large sums to the moneylenders.

'That is a cruel law,' said the young prince. 'Go,
bury the dead in peace, and let the creditors come to
my lodgings; I will pay the debts of the dead.'

So the creditors came, but they were so numerous
that by evening the prince had but twopence left for
himself, and could not go farther on his journey.

Now it so happened that Jack the Giant Killer on his
way to Wales passed through the town, and, hearing
of the prince's plight, was so taken with his kindness
and generosity that he determined to be the prince's
servant. So this was agreed upon, and next morning,
after Jack had paid the reckoning with his last farthing,
the two set out together. But as they were leaving the
town, an old woman ran after the prince and called
out, 'Justice! Justice! The dead man owed me twopence these seven years. Pay me as well as the others.'

And the prince, kind and generous, put his hand to
his pocket and gave the old woman the twopence that
was left to him. So now they had not a penny between

them, and when the sun grew low the prince said: 'Jack! Since we have no money, how are we to get a night's lodging?'

Then Jack replied, 'We shall do well enough, master; for within two or three miles of this place there lives a huge and monstrous giant with three heads who can fight four hundred men in armour and make them fly from him like chaff before the wind.'

'And what good will that be to us?' quoth the prince. 'He will for sure chop us up in a mouthful.'

'Nay,' said Jack, laughing. 'Let me go and prepare the way for you. By all accounts this giant is a dolt. Mayhap I may manage better than that.'

So the prince remained where he was, and Jack pricked his steed at full speed till he came to the giant's castle, at the gate of which he knocked so loud that he made the neighbouring hills resound.

On this the giant roared from within in a voice like thunder: 'Who's there?'

Then said Jack as bold as brass, 'None but your poor cousin Jack.'

'Cousin Jack!' quoth the giant astounded. 'And what news with my poor cousin Jack?' For, see you, he was quite taken aback; so Jack made haste to reassure him.

'Dear coz, heavy news, God wot!'

'Heavy news,' echoed the giant, half afraid. 'God wot no heavy news can come to me. Have I not three heads? Can I not fight five hundred men in armour? Can I not make them fly like chaff before the wind?'

'True,' replied crafty Jack, 'but I came to warn you because the great King Arthur's son with a thousand men in armour is on his way to kill you.'

At this the giant began to shiver and to shake. 'Ah!

Cousin Jack! Kind cousin Jack! This is heavy news indeed,' quoth he. 'Tell me, what am I to do?'

'Hide yourself in the vault,' says crafty Jack, 'and I will lock and bolt and bar you in, and keep the key till the prince has gone. So you will be safe.'

Then the giant made haste and ran down into the vault and Jack locked and bolted and barred him in. Then, having him thus secure, he went and fetched his master, and the two made themselves heartily merry over what the giant was to have had for supper, while the miserable monster shivered and shook with fright in the underground vault.

Well, after a good night's rest Jack woke his master in early morn, and having furnished him well with gold and silver from the giant's treasure, bade him ride three miles forward on his journey. So when Jack judged that the prince was pretty well out of the

smell of the giant, he took the key and let his prisoner out. He was half dead with cold and damp, but very grateful; and he begged Jack to let him know what he would be given as a reward for saving the giant's life and castle from destruction, and he should have it.

'You're very welcome,' said Jack, who always had his eyes about him. 'All I want is the old coat and cap, together with the rusty old sword and slippers which are at your bed-head.'

When the giant heard this he sighed, and shook his head. 'You don't know what you are asking,' quoth he. 'They are the most precious things I possess, but as I have promised, you must have them. The coat will make you invisible, the cap will tell you all you want to know, the sword will cut asunder whatever you strike, and the slippers will take you wherever you want to go in the twinkling of an eye!'

So Jack, overjoyed, rode away with the coat and cap, the sword and the slippers, and soon overtook his master; and they rode on together until they reached the castle where the beautiful lady lived whom the prince sought.

Now she was very beautiful, for all she was possessed of seven devils, and when she heard the prince sought her as a suitor, she smiled and ordered a splendid banquet to be prepared for his reception. And she sat on his right hand, and plied him with food and drink.

And when the repast was over she took out her own handkerchief and wiped his lips gently, and said with a smile: 'I have a task for you, my lord! You must show me that kerchief tomorrow morning or lose your head.'

And with that she put the handkerchief in her bosom and said, 'Good-night!'

The prince was in despair, but Jack said nothing till his master was in bed. Then he put on the old cap he had got from the giant, and lo! in a minute he knew all that he wanted to know. So, in the dead of the night, when the beautiful lady called on one of her familiar spirits to carry her to Lucifer himself, Jack was beforehand with her, and putting on his coat of darkness and his slippers of swiftness, was there as soon as she was. And when she gave the handkerchief to the Devil, bidding him keep it safe, and he put it away on a high shelf, Jack just up and nipped it away in a trice!

So the next morning when the beauteous enchanted lady looked to see the prince crestfallen, he just made a fine bow and presented her with the handkerchief.

At first she was terribly disappointed, but as the day drew on, she ordered another and still more splendid repast to be got ready. And this time when the repast was over, she kissed the prince full on the lips and said: 'I have a task for you, my lover. Show me tomorrow morning the last lips I kiss tonight or you lose your head.'

Then the prince, who by this time was head over ears in love, said tenderly, 'If you will kiss none but mine, I will.'

Now the beauteous lady for all she was possessed by seven devils could not but see that the prince was a very handsome young man; so she blushed a little, and said: 'That is neither here nor there: you must show me them, or death is your portion.'

So the prince went to his bed, sorrowful as before; but Jack put on the cap of knowledge and knew in a moment all he wanted to know.

Thus when, in the dead of the night, the beauteous lady called on her familiar spirit to take her to Lucifer himself, Jack in his coat of darkness and his shoes of swiftness was there before her.

'Thou hast betrayed me once,' said the beauteous lady to Lucifer, frowning, 'by letting go my handkerchief. Now will I give thee something none can steal, and so best the prince, king's son though he be.'

With that she kissed the loathly demon full on the lips, and left him. Whereupon Jack, with one blow of the rusty sword of strength, cut off Lucifer's head and, hiding it under his coat of darkness, brought it back to his master.

Thus next morning when the beauteous lady, with malice in her beautiful eyes, asked the prince to show her the lips she had last kissed, he pulled out the demon's head by the horns. On that the seven devils, which possessed the poor lady, gave seven dreadful shrieks and left her. Thus the enchantment being broken, she appeared in all her perfect beauty and goodness.

So she and the prince were married the very next morning. After which they journeyed back to the court of King Arthur, where Jack the Giant Killer, for his many exploits, was made one of the Knights of the Round Table.

*   *   *

This, however, did not satisfy our hero, who was soon on the road again searching for giants. Now he had not gone far when he came upon one, seated on a huge block of timber near the entrance to a dark cave. He was a most terrific giant. His goggle eyes were as coals of fire, his countenance was grim and gruesome; his cheeks, like huge flitches of bacon, were covered with a stubbly beard, the bristles of which resembled rods of iron wire, while the locks of hair that fell on his brawny shoulders showed like curled snakes or hissing adders. He held a knotted iron club, and breathed so heavily you could hear him a mile away. Nothing daunted by this fearsome sight, Jack alighted from his horse and putting on his coat of darkness went close up to the giant and said softly: 'Hallo! is that you? It will not be long before I have you fast by your beard.'

So saying he made a cut with the sword of strength at the giant's head, but, somehow, missing his aim, cut off the nose instead, clean as a whistle! My goodness! How the giant roared! It was like claps of thunder, and he began to lay about him with the knotted iron club, like one possessed. But Jack in his coat of darkness easily dodged the blows, and running in behind, drove the sword up to the hilt into the giant's back, so that he fell stone dead.

Jack then cut off the head and sent it to King Arthur by a wagoner whom he hired for the purpose. After which he began to search the giant's cave to find his treasure. He passed through many windings and turnings until he came to a huge hall paved and roofed with freestone. At the upper end of this was an immense fireplace where hung an iron cauldron, the like of which, for size, Jack had never seen before. It was boiling and gave out a savoury steam; while beside it, on the right hand, stood a big massive table set out with huge platters and mugs. Here it was that the giants used to dine. Going a little farther he came upon a sort of window barred with iron, and looking within beheld a vast number of miserable captives.

'Alas! Alack!' they cried on seeing him. 'Art come, young man, to join us in this dreadful prison?'

'That depends,' quoth Jack; 'but first tell me wherefore you are thus held imprisoned?'

'Through no fault,' they cried at once. 'We are captives of the cruel giants and are kept here and well nourished until such time as the monsters desire a feast. Then they choose the fattest and sup off them.'

On hearing this Jack straightway unlocked the door of the prison and set the poor fellows free. Then, searching the giants' coffers, he divided the gold and silver equally amongst the captives as some redress for their sufferings, and taking them to a neighbouring castle gave them a right good feast.

* * *

Now as they were all making merry over their deliverance, and praising Jack's prowess, a messenger arrived to say that one Thunderdell, a huge giant with two heads, having heard of the death of his kinsman was on his way from the northern dales to be revenged, and was already within a mile or two of the castle, the country folk with their flocks and herds flying before him like chaff before the wind.

Now the castle with its gardens stood on a small island that was surrounded by a moat twenty feet wide and thirty feet deep, having very steep sides. And this moat was spanned by a drawbridge. This, without a moment's delay, Jack ordered should be sawn on both sides at the middle, so as to leave only one plank uncut over which he in his invisible coat of darkness passed swiftly to meet his enemy, bearing in his hand the wonderful sword of strength.

Now though the giant could not, of course, see Jack, he could smell him, for giants have keen noses. Therefore Thunderdell cried out in a voice like his name:

'Fee, fi, fo, fum!
I smell the blood of an Englishman.
Be he alive, or be he dead,
I'll grind his bones to make my bread!'

'Is that so?' quoth Jack, cheerful as ever. 'Then art thou a monstrous miller for sure!'

On this the giant peering round everywhere for a glimpse of his foe, shouted out: 'Art thou, indeed, the villain who hath killed so many of my kinsmen? Then, indeed, will I tear thee to pieces with my teeth, suck thy blood, and grind thy bones to powder.'

'Thou'lt have to catch me first,' quoth Jack, laughing, and throwing off his coat of darkness and putting on his slippers of swiftness he began nimbly to lead the giant a prettydance, he leaping and doubling light as a feather, the monster following heavily like a walking tower, so that the very foundations of the earth seemed to shake at every step. At this game the onlookers nearly split their sides with laughter, until Jack, judging there had been enough of it, made for the drawbridge, ran neatly over the single plank, and reaching the other side waited in teasing fashion for his adversary.

On came the giant at full speed, foaming at the mouth with rage, and flourishing his club. But when he came to the middle of the bridge his great weight, of course, broke the plank, and there he was fallen headlong into the moat, rolling and wallowing like a whale, plunging from place to place yet unable to get out and be revenged.

The spectators greeted his efforts with roars of laughter, and Jack himself was at first too overcome with merriment to do more than scoff. At last, however, he went for a rope,

cast it over the giant's two heads, and so with the help of a team of horses drew them shorewards, where two blows from the sword of strength settled the matter.

*   *

After some time spent in mirth and pastimes, Jack began once more to grow restless, and taking leave of his companions set out for fresh adventures.

He travelled far and fast, through woods, and vales, and hills, till at last he came, late at night, on a lonesome house set at the foot of a high mountain.

He knocked at the door, and it was opened by an old man whose head was white as snow.

'Father,' said Jack, ever courteous, 'can you lodge a benighted traveller?'

'Ay, that will I, and welcome to my poor cottage,' replied the old man.

Whereupon Jack came in, and after supper they sat together chatting in friendly fashion. Then it was that the old man, seeing by Jack's belt that he was the famous Giant Killer, spoke in this wise: 'My son! You are the great conqueror of evil monsters. Now close by there lives one well worthy of your prowess. On the top of yonder high hill is an enchanted castle kept by a giant named Galligantua, who, by the help of a wicked old magician, inveigles many beautiful ladies and valiant knights into the castle, where they are transformed into all sorts of birds and beasts, yea, even into fishes and insects. There they live pitiably in confinement; but most of all do I grieve for a duke's daughter whom they kidnapped in her father's garden,

bringing her hither in a burning chariot drawn by
fiery dragons. Her form is that of a white hind; and
though many valiant knights have tried their utmost
to break the spell and work her deliverance, none
have succeeded; for, see you, at the entrance to the
castle are two dreadful griffins who destroy everyone
who attempts to pass them by.'

Now Jack bethought him of the coat of darkness
which had served him so well before, and he put on
the cap of knowledge, and in an instant he knew
what had to be done. Then the very next morning, at
dawn-time, Jack arose and put on his invisible coat
and his slippers of swiftness. And in the twinkling of
an eye there he was on the top of the mountain! And
there were the two griffins guarding the castle gates –
horrible creatures with forked tails and tongues.

But they could not see him because of the coat of
darkness, so he passed them by unharmed.

And hung to the doors of the gateway he found a
golden trumpet on a silver chain, and beneath it was
engraved in red lettering:

> Whoever shall this trumpet blow
> Will cause the giant's overthrow.
> The black enchantment he will break,
> And gladness out of sadness make.

No sooner had Jack read these words than he blew a loud 'Tantivy! Tantivy! Tantivy!'

Now at the very first note the castle trembled to its vast foundations, and before he had finished the measure, both the giant and the magician were biting their thumbs and tearing their hair, knowing that their wickedness must now come to an end. But the giant showed fight and took up his club to defend himself; whereupon Jack, with one clean cut of the sword of strength, severed his head from his body, and would doubtless have done the same to the magician, but that the latter was a coward, and, calling up a whirl-wind, was swept away by it into the air, nor has he ever been seen or heard of since. The enchantments being thus broken, all the valiant knights and beautiful ladies who had been transformed into birds and beasts and fishes and reptiles and insects returned to their proper shapes, including the duke's daughter, who, from being a white hind, showed as the most beauteous maiden upon whom the sun ever shone. Now, no sooner had this occurred than the whole castle vanished away in a cloud of smoke, and from that moment giants vanished also from the land.

So Jack, when he had presented the head of Galli-gantua to King Arthur, together with all the lords and ladies he had delivered from enchantment, found he had nothing more to do. So as a reward for past services King Arthur bestowed the hand of the duke's daughter upon honest Jack the Giant Killer. So married they were, and the whole kingdom was filled with joy at their wedding. Furthermore, the king bestowed on Jack a noble castle and a magnificent estate, whereon he, his lady and their children lived in great joy and content for the rest of their days.

The Story of King Frost

There was once upon a time a peasant-woman who had a daughter and a stepdaughter. The daughter had her own way in everything, and whatever she did was right in her mother's eyes; but the poor step-daughter had a hard time. Let her do what she would, she was always blamed, and got small thanks for all the trouble she took; nothing was right, everything wrong; and yet, if the truth were known, the girl was worth her weight in gold – she was so unselfish and good-hearted. But her stepmother did not like her, and the poor girl's days were spent in weeping; for it was impossible to live peacefully with the woman. The wicked shrew was determined to get rid of the girl by fair means or foul, and kept saying to her father: 'Send her away, old man; send her away – anywhere so that my eyes shan't be plagued any longer by the sight of her, or my ears tormented by the sound of her voice. Send her out into the fields, and let the cutting frost do for her.'

In vain did the poor old father weep and implore her pity; she was firm, and he dared not gainsay her. So he placed his daughter in a sledge, not even daring to give her a horse-cloth to keep herself warm with, and drove her out on to the bare, open fields, where he kissed her and left her, driving home as fast as he could, that he might not witness her miserable death.

Deserted by her father, the poor girl sat down under a fir tree at the edge of the forest and began to weep silently. Suddenly she heard a faint sound: it was King Frost springing from tree to tree, and cracking his fingers as he went. At length he reached the fir tree beneath which she was sitting, and with a crisp crackling sound he alighted beside her, and looked at her lovely face.

'Well, maiden,' he snapped out, 'do you know who I am? I am King Frost, king of the red-noses.'

'All hail to you, great king!' answered the girl, in a gentle, trembling voice. 'Have you come to take me?'

'Maiden, are you warm?' he replied.

'Quite warm, King Frost,' she answered, though she shivered as she spoke.

Then King Frost stooped down, and bent over the

'MAIDEN ARE YOU WARM?'

girl, and the crackling sound grew louder, and the air seemed to be full of knives and darts; and again he asked: 'Maiden, are you warm? Are you warm, you beautiful girl?'

And though her breath was almost frozen on her lips, she whispered gently, 'Quite warm, King Frost.'

Then King Frost gnashed his teeth, and cracked his fingers, and his eyes sparkled, and the crackling, crisp sound was louder than ever, and for the last time he asked her: 'Maiden, are you still warm? Are you still warm, little love?'

And the poor girl was so stiff and numb that she could just gasp, 'Still warm, O king!'

Now her gentle, courteous words and her uncomplaining ways touched King Frost, and he had pity on her, and he wrapped her up in furs, and covered her with blankets, and he fetched a great box, in which were beautiful jewels and a rich robe embroidered in gold and silver. And she put it on, and looked more lovely than ever, and King Frost stepped with her into his sledge, with six white horses.

In the meantime the wicked stepmother was waiting at home for news of the girl's death, and preparing pancakes for the funeral feast. And she said to her husband: 'Old man, you had better go out into the fields and find your daughter's body and bury her.' Just as the old man was leaving the house the little dog under the table began to bark, saying:

'*Your* daughter shall live to be your delight;
Her daughter shall die this very night.'

'Hold your tongue, you foolish beast!' scolded the woman. 'There's a pancake for you, but you must say:

"*Her* daughter shall have much silver and gold;
   His daughter is frozen quite stiff and cold." '

But the doggie ate up the pancake and barked, saying:

'*His* daughter shall wear a crown on her head;
   Her daughter shall die unwooed, unwed.'

Then the old woman tried to coax the doggie with more pancakes and to terrify it with blows, but he barked on, always repeating the same words. And suddenly the door creaked and flew open, and a great heavy chest was pushed in, and behind it came the stepdaughter, radiant and beautiful, in a dress all glittering with silver and gold. For a moment the stepmother's eyes were dazzled. Then she called to her husband: 'Old man, yoke the horses at once into the sledge, and take my daughter to the same field and leave her on the same spot exactly;' and so the old man took the girl and left her beneath the same tree where he had parted from his daughter. In a few minutes King Frost came past, and, looking at the girl, he said: 'Are you warm, maiden?'

'What a blind old fool you must be to ask such a question!' she answered angrily. 'Can't you see that my hands and feet are nearly frozen?'

Then King Frost sprang to and fro in front of her, questioning her, and getting only rude, rough words in reply, till at last he got very angry, and cracked his fingers, and gnashed his teeth, and froze her to death.

But in the hut her mother was waiting for her return, and as she grew impatient she said to her husband: 'Get out the horses, old man, to go and fetch her home; but see that you are careful not to upset the sledge and lose the chest.'

But the doggie beneath the table began to bark, saying:

'Your daughter is frozen quite stiff and cold,
  And shall never have a chest full of gold.'

'Don't tell such wicked lies!' scolded the woman. 'There's a cake for you; now say: *'Her* daughter shall marry a mighty king.'

At that moment the door flew open, and she rushed out to meet her daughter, and as she took her frozen body in her arms she too was chilled to death.

King O'Toole and His Goose

Och, I thought all the world, far and near, had heerd o' King O'Toole – well, well, but the darkness of mankind is untellible! Well, sir, you must know, as you didn't hear it afore, that there was a king, called King O'Toole, who was a fine old king in the old ancient times, long ago; and it was he that owned the churches in the early days. The king, you see, was the right sort; he was the real boy, and loved sport as he loved his life, and hunting in particular; and from the rising o' the sun, up he got, and away he went over the mountains after the deer; and fine times they were.

Well, it was all mighty good, as long as the king had his health; but, you see, in course of time the king grew old, by raison he was stiff in his limbs, and when he got stricken in years, his heart failed him, and he was lost entirely for want o' diversion, because he couldn't go a-hunting no longer; and, by dad, the poor king was obliged at last to get a goose to divert him. Oh, you may laugh, if you like, but it's truth I'm telling you; and the way the goose diverted him was this-a-way: You see, the goose used to swim across the lake, and go diving for trout, and catch fish on a Friday for the king, and flew every other day round about the lake, diverting the poor king. All went on mighty well until, by dad, the goose got stricken in years like her master, and couldn't divert him no longer, and then it was that the poor king was lost entirely. The king was walkin' one mornin' by the edge of the lake, lamentin' his cruel fate, and thinking

268

of drowning himself, that could get no diversion in life, when all of a sudden, turning round the corner, who should he meet but a mighty decent young man coming up to him.

'God save you,' says the king to the young man.

'God save you kindly, King O'Toole,' says the young man.

'True for you,' says the king. 'I am King O'Toole. Prince and plennypennytinchery of these parts. But how came ye to know that?'

'Oh, never mind,' says St Kavin.

You see it was St Kavin, sure enough – the saint himself in disguise, and nobody else. 'Oh, never mind,' says he, 'I know more than that. May I make bold to ask how is your goose, King O'Toole?'

'Blur-an-agers, how came ye to know about my goose?' says the king.

'Oh, no matter; I was given to understand it,' says St Kavin.

After some more talk the king says, 'What are you?'

'I'm an honest man,' says St Kavin.

'Well, honest man,' says the king, 'and how is it you make your money so aisy?'

'By makin' old things as good as new,' says St Kavin.

'Is it a tinker you are?' says the king.

'No,' says the saint; 'I'm no tinker by trade, King O'Toole; I've a better trade than a tinker,' says he. 'What would you say,' says he, 'if I made your old goose as good as new?'

My dear, at the word of making his goose as good as new, you'd think the poor old king's eyes were ready to jump out of his head. With that the king whistled, and down came the poor goose, just like a hound, waddling up to the poor cripple, her master, and as like him as two peas. The minute the saint clapped his eyes on the goose, 'I'll do the job for you,' says he, 'King O'Toole.'

'By *Jaminee*!' says King O'Toole. 'If you do, I'll say you're the cleverest fellow in the seven parishes.'

'Oh, by dad,' says St Kavin, 'you must say more nor that – my horn's not so soft all out,' says he, 'as to repair your old goose for nothing; what'll you gi' me if I do the job for you?' says St Kavin.

'I'll give you whatever you ask,' says the king; 'isn't that fair?'

'Divil a fairer,' says the saint; 'that's the way to do business. Now,' says he, 'this is the bargain I'll make with you, King O'Toole: will you gi' me all the ground the goose flies over, the first offer, after I make her as good as new?'

'I will,' says the king.

'You won't go back o' your word?' says St Kavin.

'Honour bright!' says King O'Toole.

'Honour bright!' says St Kavin, back agin, 'it's a bargain. Come here!' says he to the poor old goose 'come here, you unfortunate ould cripple, and it's I that'll make you the sporting bird.' With that, my dear, he took up the goose by the two wings – 'Criss o' my cross an you,' says he, markin' her to grace with the blessed sign at the same minute – and throwing her up in the air. 'Whew,' says he, jist givin' her a blast to help her; and with that, my jewel, she took to her heels, flyin' like one o' the eagles themselves, and cutting as many capers as a swallow before a shower of rain.

Well, my dear, it was a beautiful sight to see the king standing with his mouth open, looking at his poor old goose flying as light as a lark, and better than ever she was; and when she lit at his feet, he patted her on the head, and, '*Ma vourneen*,' says he, 'but you are the *darlint* o' the world.'

'And what do you say to me,' says St Kavin, 'for making her the like?'

'By Jabers,' says the king, 'I say nothing beats the art o' man, barring the bees.'

'And do you say no more nor that?' says St Kavin.

'And that I'm beholden to you,' says the king.

'But will you gi'e all the ground the goose flew over?' says St Kavin.

'I will,' says King O'Toole, 'and you're welcome to it,' says he, 'though it's the last acre I have to give.'

'But you'll keep your word true?' says the saint.

'As true as the sun,' says the king.

'It's well for you, King O'Toole, that you said that word,' says he; 'for if you didn't say that word, the devil the bit o' your goose would ever fly agin.'

When the king was as good as his word, St Kavin was pleased with him, and then it was that he made himself known to the king. 'And,' says he, 'King O'Toole, you're a decent man, for I only came here to try you. You don't know me,' says he, 'because I'm disguised.'

'Musha! Then,' says the king, 'who are you?'

'I'm St Kavin,' said the saint, blessing himself.

'Oh, queen of heaven!' says the king, making the sign of the cross and falling down on his knees before the saint. 'Is it the great St Kavin,' says he, 'that I've been discoursing with all this time without knowing it,' says he, 'all as one as if he was a lump of a gossoon? – and so you're a saint?' says the king.

'I am,' says St Kavin.

'By Jabers, I thought I was only talking to a dacent boy,' says the king.

'Well, you know the difference now,' says the saint. 'I'm St Kavin,' says he, 'the greatest of all the saints.'

And so the king had his goose as good as new, to divert him as long as he lived and the saint supported him after he came into his property, as I told you, until the day of his death – and that was soon after; for the poor goose thought he was catching a trout one Friday; but, my jewel, it was a mistake he made – and instead of a trout, it was a thieving horse-eel; and instead of the goose killing a trout for the king's supper, bydad, the eel killed the king's goose – and small blame to him; but he didn't ate her, because he darn't ate what St Kavin had laid his blessed hands on.

The King of the Golden Mountain

There was once a merchant who had only one child, a son, who was very young and barely able to run alone. He had two richly laden ships then making a voyage upon the seas, in which he had embarked all his wealth, in the hope of making great gains, but news came that both were lost. Thus from being a rich man he became all at once so very poor that nothing was left to him but one small plot of land; and there he often went in an evening to take his walk, and ease his mind of a little of his trouble.

One day, as he was roaming along in a brown study, thinking with no great comfort on what he had been and what he now was and was likely to be, all of a sudden there stood before him a little, rough-looking, black dwarf. 'Prithee, friend, why so sorrowful?' said he to the merchant; 'what is it you take so deeply to heart?'

'If you would do me any good I would willingly tell you,' said the merchant.

'Who knows but I may?' said the little man. 'Tell me what ails you, and perhaps you will find I may be of some use.'

Then the merchant told him how all his wealth was gone to the bottom of the sea, and how he had nothing left but that little plot of land.

'Oh, trouble not yourself about that,' said the dwarf; 'only undertake to bring me here, twelve years hence, whatever meets you first on your going home, and I will give you as much as you please.'

The merchant thought this was no great thing to ask; that it would most likely be his dog or his cat, or something of that sort, but forgot his little boy Heinel; so he agreed to the bargain, and signed and sealed the bond to do what was asked of him.

But as he drew near home, his little boy was so glad to see him that he crept behind him, and laid fast hold of his legs, and looked up in his face and laughed.

Then the father started, trembling with fear and horror, and saw what it was that he had bound himself to do; but as no gold was come, he made himself easy by thinking that it was only a joke that the dwarf was playing him, and that, at any rate, when the money came, he should see the bearer, and would not take it in.

About a month afterwards he went upstairs into a lumber-room to look for some old iron, that he might sell it and raise a little money; and there, instead of his iron, he saw a large pile of gold lying on the floor.

At the sight of this he was overjoyed, and forgetting all about his son, went into trade again, and became a richer merchant than before.

Meantime little Heinel grew up, and as the end of the twelve years drew near the merchant began to call to mind his bond, and became very sad and thoughtful; so that care and sorrow were written upon his face.

The boy one day asked what was the matter, but his father would not tell for some time; at last, however, he said that he had, without knowing it, sold him for gold to a little, ugly-looking, black dwarf, and that the twelve years were coming round when he must keep his word.

Then Heinel said, 'Father, don't trouble yourself about that; I shall be too much for the little man.'

When the time came, the father and son went out together to the place agreed upon, and the son drew a circle on the ground and set himself and his father in the middle of it. The little black dwarf soon came, and walked round and round about the circle, but could not find any way to get into it, and he either could not or dared not jump over it.

At last the boy said to him. 'Have you anything to say to us, my friend? What do you want?' Now Heinel had found a friend in a good fairy, that was fond of

him and had told him what to do; for this fairy knew what good luck was in store for him.

'Have you brought me what you said you would?' said the dwarf to the merchant.

The old man held his tongue, but Heinel said again, 'What do you want here?'

The dwarf said, 'I come to talk with your father, not with you.'

'You have cheated and taken in my father,' said the son; 'pray give him up his bond at once.'

'Fair and softly,' said the little old man; 'right is right; I have paid my money, and your father has had it, and spent it; so be so good as to let me have what I paid it for.'

'You must have my consent to that first,' said Heinel, 'so please to step in here, and let us talk.'

The old man grinned, and showed his teeth, as if he should have been very glad to get into the circle if he could. Then at last, after a long talk, they came to terms. Heinel agreed that his father must give him up, and that so far the dwarf should have his way; but, on the other hand, the fairy had told Heinel what fortune was in store for him if he followed his own course; and he did not choose to be given up to his humpbacked friend, who seemed so anxious for his company.

So, to make a sort of drawn battle of the matter, it was settled that Heinel should be put into an open boat that lay on the seashore hard by; that the father should push him off with his own hand, and that he should thus be set adrift, and left to the bad or good luck of wind and weather. Then he took leave of his father, and set himself in the boat, but before it got far off a wave struck it, and it fell with one side low in the water, so the merchant thought that poor Heinel was lost, and went home very sorrowful, while the dwarf went his way, thinking that at any rate he had had his revenge.

The boat, however, did not sink, for the good fairy took care of her friend, and soon raised the boat up again, and it went safely on. The young man sat safe within, till at length it ran ashore upon an unknown land. As he jumped upon the shore he saw before him a beautiful castle, but empty and dreary within, for it was enchanted. 'Here,' said he to himself, 'must I find the prize the good fairy told me of.' So he searched the whole palace through, till at last he found a white snake, lying coiled up on a cushion in one of the chambers.

Now the white snake was an enchanted princess; and she was very glad to see him, and said, 'Are you at last come to set me free? Twelve long years have I waited here for the fairy to bring you hither as she promised, for you alone can save me. This night twelve men will come: their faces will be black, and they will be dressed in chain armour. They will ask what you do here, but give no answer; and let them do what they will – beat, whip, pinch, prick or torment you – bear all; only speak not a word, and at twelve o'clock they must go away. The second night twelve others will come; and the third night twenty-four, who will even cut off your head; but at the twelfth hour of that night their power will be gone, and I shall be free, and will come and bring you the Water of Life, and will wash you with it, and bring you back to life and health.' And all came to pass as she had said; Heinel bore all, and spoke not a word; and the third night the princess came, and fell on his neck and kissed him. Joy and gladness filled the castle, the wedding was celebrated, and he was crowned King of the Golden Mountain.

They lived together very happily, and the queen had a son. And thus eight years had passed over their heads, when the king thought of his father; and he began to long to see him once again. But the queen was against his going, and said, 'I know well that misfortunes will come upon us if you go.' However, he gave her no rest till she agreed. At his going away she gave him a wishing-ring, and said, 'Take this ring, and put it on your finger; whatever you wish it will bring you; only promise never to make use of it to bring me hence to your father's house.' Then he said he would do what she asked, and put the ring on his finger, and wished himself near the town where his father lived.

Heinel found himself at the gates in a moment; but the guards would not let him go in, because he was so strangely clad. So he went up to a neighbouring hill, where a shepherd dwelt, and borrowed his old smock, and thus passed unknown into the town. When he came to his father's house, he said he was his son; but the merchant would not believe him, and said he had had but one son, his poor Heinel, who he knew was long since dead; and as he was only dressed like a poor shepherd, he would not even give him anything to eat. The king, however, still vowed that he was his son, and said, 'Is there no mark by which you would know that I am really your son?'

'Yes,' said his mother, 'our Heinel had a mark like a raspberry on his right arm.' Then he showed them the mark, and they knew that what he had said was true.

He next told them how he was King of the Golden Mountain, and was married to a princess, and had a son seven years old.

But the merchant said, 'That can never be true; he must be a fine king truly who travels about in a shepherd's smock!'

At this the son was vexed; and forgetting his word, turned his ring and wished for his queen and son. In an instant they stood before him; but the queen wept, and said he had broken his word, and bad luck would follow. He did all he could to soothe her, and she at last seemed to be appeased; but she was not so in truth, and was only thinking how she should punish him.

One day he took her to walk with him out of the town, and showed her the spot where the boat was set adrift upon the wide waters. Then he sat himself down, and said, 'I am very much tired; sit by me, I will rest my head in your lap, and sleep a while.' As soon as he had fallen asleep, however, she drew the ring from his finger, and crept softly away, and wished herself and her son at home in their kingdom. And when he awoke he found himself alone, and saw that the ring was gone from his finger. 'I can never go back to my father's house,' said he; 'they would say I am a sorcerer. I will journey forth into the world, till I come again to my kingdom.'

So saying he set out and travelled till he came to a hill where three giants were sharing their father's goods; and as they saw him pass they cried out and said, 'Little men have sharp wits; he shall part the goods between us.' Now there was a sword that cut off an enemy's head whenever the wearer gave the words, 'Heads off!'; a cloak that made the owner invisible, or gave him any form he pleased; and a pair of boots that carried the wearer wherever he wished. Heinel said they must first let him try these wonderful things, then he might know how to set a value upon them. Then they gave him the cloak, and he wished himself a fly, and in a moment he was a fly. 'The cloak is very well,' said he; 'now give me the sword.'

'No,' said they; 'not unless you undertake not to say, "Heads off!" for if you do we are all dead men.' So they gave it him, charging him to try it on a tree. He next asked for the boots also; and the moment he had all three in his power, he wished himself at the Golden Mountain; and there he was at once. So the giants were left behind with no goods to share or quarrel about.

As Heinel came near his castle he heard the sound of merry music; and the people around told him that his queen was about to marry another husband. Then he threw his cloak around him, and passed through the castle hall, and placed himself by the side of the queen, where no one saw him. But when anything to eat was put upon her plate, he took it away and ate it himself; and when a glass of wine was handed to her, he took it and drank it; and thus, though they kept on giving her meat and drink, her plate and cup were always empty.

Upon this, fear and remorse came over her, and she went into her chamber alone, and sat there weeping; and he followed her there. 'Alas!' said she to herself, 'was I not once set free? Why then does this enchantment still seem to bind me?'

'False and fickle one!' said he. 'One indeed came who set thee free, and he is now near thee again; but how have you used him? Ought he to have had such treatment from thee?'

Then he went out and sent away the company, and said the wedding was at an end now that he had come back to his kingdom. But the princes, peers and great men mocked at him. However, he would enter into no parley with them, but only asked them if they would go in peace or not. Then they turned upon him and tried to seize him; but he drew his sword. 'Heads off!' cried he; and with the word the traitors' heads fell before him, and Heinel was once more King of the Golden Mountain.

The Little Match Girl

It was terribly cold; it snowed and was already almost dark, and evening came on, the last evening of the year. In the cold and gloom a poor little girl, bareheaded and barefoot, was walking through the streets. When she left her own house she certainly had had slippers on; but of what use were they? They were very big slippers, and her mother had used them till then, so big were they. The little maid lost them as she slipped across the road, where two carriages were rattling by terribly fast. One slipper was not to be found again, and a boy had seized the other, and run away with it. He said he could use it very well as a cradle, someday when he had children of his own. So now the little girl went with her little naked feet, which were quite red and blue with the cold. In an old apron she carried a number of matches, and a bundle of them in her hand. No one had bought anything of her all day, and no one had given her a farthing.

Shivering with cold and hunger she crept along, a picture of misery, poor little girl! The snowflakes covered her long fair hair, which fell in pretty curls over her neck; but she did not think of that now. In all the windows lights were shining, and there was a glorious smell of roast goose, for it was New Year's Eve. Yes, she thought of that!

In a corner formed by two houses, one of which projected beyond the other, she sat down, cowering. She had drawn up her little feet, but she was still colder, and she did not dare to go home, for she had sold no matches, and did not bring a farthing of money. From her father she would certainly receive a beating, and besides, it was cold at home, for they had nothing over them but a roof through which the wind whistled, though the largest rents had been stopped with straw and rags.

Her little hands were almost benumbed with the cold. Ah! a match might do her good, if she could only draw one from the bundle, and rub it against the wall, and warm her hands at it. She drew one out. R-r-atch! how it sputtered and burned! It was a warm, bright flame, like a little candle, when she held her hands over it; it was a wonderful little light! It really seemed to the little girl as if she sat before a great polished stove, with bright brass feet and a brass cover. How the fire burned! how comfortable it was! but the little flame went out, the stove vanished, and she had only the remains of the burned match in her hand.

A second was rubbed against the wall. It burned up, and when the light fell upon the wall it became transparent like a thin veil, and she could see through it into the room. On the table a snow-white cloth was spread; upon it stood a shining dinner service; the roast goose smoked gloriously, stuffed with apples and dried plums. And what was still more splendid to behold, the goose hopped down from the dish, and waddled along the floor, with a knife and fork in its breast, to the little girl. Then the match went out, and only the thick, damp, cold wall was before her. She lighted another match. Then she was sitting under a beautiful Christmas tree; it was greater and more ornamented than the one she had seen through the glass door last Christmas at the rich merchant's. Thousands of candles burned upon the green branches, and coloured pictures like those in the print shops looked down upon them. The little girl stretched forth her hand towards them; then the match went out. The Christmas lights mounted higher. She saw them now as stars in the sky: one of them fell down, forming a long line of fire.

'Now someone is dying,' thought the little girl, for her old grandmother, the only person who had loved her, and who was now dead, had told her that when a star fell down a soul mounted up to God.

She rubbed another match against the wall; it became bright again, and in the brightness the old grandmother stood clear and shining, mild and lovely.

'Grandmother!' cried the child. 'Oh! take me with you! I know you will go when the match is burned out. You will vanish like the warm fire, the beautiful roast goose, and the great glorious Christmas tree!'

And she hastily rubbed the whole bundle of matches, for she wished to hold her grandmother fast. And the matches burned with such a glow that it became brighter than in the middle of the day; grandmother had never been so large or so beautiful. She took the little girl in her arms, and both flew in brightness and joy above the earth, very, very high, and up there was neither cold, nor hunger, nor care – they were with God!

But in the corner, leaning against the wall, sat in the cold morning hours the poor girl with red cheeks and smiling mouth, frozen to death on the last evening of the Old Year. The New Year's sun rose upon a little corpse! The child sat there, stiff and cold, with the matches of which one bundle was burned. 'She wanted to warm herself,' the people said. No one imagined what a beautiful thing she had seen, and in what glory she had gone in with her grandmother to the New Year's joy.

The Little Mermaid

Far out at sea the water is as blue as the bluest cornflower, and as clear as the clearest crystal; but it is very deep, too deep for any cable to fathom, and if many steeples were piled on the top of one another they would not reach from the bed of the sea to the surface of the water. It is down there that the mermen live.

Now don't imagine that there are only bare white sands at the bottom; oh no! the most wonderful trees and plants grow there, with such flexible stalks and leaves that at the slightest motion of the water they move just as if they were alive. All the fish, big and little, glide among the branches just as, up here, birds glide through the air. The palace of the merman king lies in the very deepest part; its walls are of coral and the long pointed windows of the clearest amber, but the roof is made of mussel shells which open and shut with the lapping of the water. This has a lovely effect, for there are gleaming pearls in every shell, any one of which would be the pride of a queen's crown.

The merman king had been for many years a widower, but his old mother kept house for him; she was a clever woman, but so proud of her noble birth that she wore twelve oysters on her tail, while the other grandees were only allowed six. Otherwise she was worthy of all praise, especially because she was so fond of the little mermaid princesses, her grandchildren. They were six beautiful children, but the youngest was the prettiest of all, her skin was as soft and delicate as a rose leaf, her eyes as blue as the deepest sea, but like all the others she had no feet, and instead of legs she had a fish's tail.

All the livelong day they used to play in the palace in the great halls, where living flowers grew out of the walls. When the great amber windows were thrown open the fish swam in, just as the swallows fly into our rooms when we open the windows, but the fish swam right up to the little princesses, ate out of their hands and allowed themselves to be patted.

Outside the palace was a large garden, with fiery red and deep blue trees, the fruit of which shone like gold, while the flowers glowed like fire on their ceaselessly waving stalks. The ground was of the finest sand, but it was of a blue phosphorescent tint. Everything was bathed in a wondrous blue light down there; you might more readily have supposed yourself to be high up in the air, with only the sky above and below you, than that you were at the bottom of the ocean. In a dead calm you could just catch a glimpse of the sun like a purple flower with a stream of light radiating from its calyx.

Each little princess had her own little plot of garden, where she could dig and plant just as she liked. One made her flower-bed in the shape of a whale, another thought it nice to have hers like a little mermaid; but the youngest made hers quite round like the sun, and she would only have flowers of a rosy hue like its beams. She was a curious child, quiet and thoughtful, and while the other sisters decked out their gardens with all kinds of extraordinary objects which they got from wrecks, she would have nothing besides the rosy flowers like the sun up above, except a statue of a beautiful boy. It was hewn out of the purest white marble and had gone to the bottom from some wreck. By the statue she planted a rosy red weeping willow which grew splendidly, and the fresh delicate branches hung round and over it, till they almost touched the blue sand where the shadows showed violet, and were ever moving like the branches. It looked as if the leaves and the roots were playfully interchanging kisses.

Nothing gave her greater pleasure than to hear about the world of human beings up above; she made her old grandmother tell her all that she knew about ships and towns, people and animals. But above all it seemed strangely beautiful to her that up on the earth the flowers were scented, for they were not so at the bottom of the sea; also that the woods were green, and that the fish which were to be seen among the branches could sing so loudly and sweetly that it was a delight to listen to them. You see the grandmother called little birds fish, or the mermaids would not have understood her, as they had never seen a bird.

'When you are fifteen,' said the grandmother, 'you will be allowed to rise up from the sea and sit on the rocks in the moonlight, and look at the big ships sailing by, and you will also see woods and towns.'

One of the sisters would be fifteen in the following year, but the others – well, they were each one year younger than the other, so that the youngest had five whole years to wait before she would be allowed to

come up from the bottom, to see what things were like on earth. But each one promised the others to give a full account of all that she had seen, and found most wonderful on the first day. Their grandmother could never tell them enough, for there were so many things about which they wanted information.

None of them was so full of longings as the youngest, the very one who had the longest time to wait, and who was so quiet and dreamy. Many a night she stood by the open windows and looked up through the dark blue water which the fish were lashing with their tails and fins. She could see the moon and the stars, it is true, their light was pale but they looked much bigger through the water than they do to our eyes.

When she saw a dark shadow glide between her and them, she knew that it was either a whale swimming above her, or else a ship laden with human beings. I am certain they never dreamt that a lovely little mermaid was standing down below, stretching up her white hands towards the keel.

'When you are fifteen,' said the grandmother, 'you will be allowed . . .'

The eldest princess had now reached her fifteenth birthday, and was to venture above the water. When she came back she had hundreds of things to tell them, but the most delightful of all, she said, was to lie in the moonlight, on a sandbank in a calm sea, and to gaze at the large town close to the shore, where the lights twinkled like hundreds of stars; to listen to music and the noise and bustle of carriages and people, to see the many church towers and spires, and to hear the bells ringing; and just because she could not go on shore she longed for that most of all.

Oh! how eagerly the youngest sister listened, and when, later in the evening, she stood at the open window and looked up through the dark-blue water, she thought of the big town with all its noise and bustle, and fancied that she could even hear the church bells ringing.

The year after, the second sister was allowed to mount up through the water and swim about wherever she liked. The sun was just going down when she reached the surface, the most beautiful sight, she thought, that she had ever seen. The whole sky had looked like gold, she said, and as for the clouds! well, their beauty was beyond description, they floated in red and violet splendour over her head, and far faster than they went, a flock of wild swans flew like a long white veil over the water towards the setting sun; she swam towards it, but it sank and all the rosy light on clouds and water faded away.

The year after that the third sister went up, and being much the most venturesome of them all, swam up a broad river which ran into the sea. She saw beautiful green, vine-clad hills; palaces and country seats peeping through splendid woods. She heard the birds singing, and the sun was so hot that she was often obliged to dive, to cool her burning face. In a tiny bay she found a troop of little children running about naked and paddling in the water; she wanted to play with them, but they were frightened and ran away. Then a little black animal came up, it was a dog, but she had never seen one before; it barked so furiously at her that she was frightened and made for the open sea. She could never forget the beautiful woods, the green hills and the lovely children who could swim in the water although they had no fishes' tails

The fourth sister was not so brave, she stayed in the remotest part of the ocean, and, according to her account, that was the most beautiful spot. You could see for miles and miles around you, and the sky above was like a great glass dome. She had seen ships, but only far away, so that they looked like seagulls. There were grotesque dolphins turning somersaults, and gigantic whales squirting water through their nostrils like hundreds of fountains on every side.

Now the fifth sister's turn came. Her birthday fell in the winter, so that she saw sights that the others had not seen on their first trips. The sea looked quite green, and large icebergs were floating about, each one of which looked like a pearl, she said, but was much bigger than the church towers built by men. They took the most wonderful shapes, and sparkled like diamonds. She had seated herself on one of the largest, and all the passing ships sheered of in alarm when they saw her sitting there with her long hair streaming loose in the wind.

In the evening the sky became overcast with dark clouds; it thundered and lightning flashed, and the huge icebergs glittering in the bright lightning were lifted high into the air by the black waves. All the ships shortened sail, and there was fear and trembling

on every side, but she sat quietly on her floating ice-
berg watching the blue lightning dart in zigzags down
on to the shining sea.

The first time any of
the sisters rose above
the water she was
delighted by the
novelties and beauties
she saw; but once
grown up, and at
liberty to go where she
liked, she became
indifferent and longed for
her home; in the course of a
month or so they all said that
after all their own home in the
deep was best, it was so cosy
there.

Many an evening the five
sisters interlacing their arms
would rise above the water
together. They had lovely
voices, much clearer than any
mortal, and when a storm was

*'Oh! if I were
only fifteen!'*

rising, and they expected ships to be wrecked, they
would sing in the most seductive strains of the wonders
of the deep, bidding the seafarers have no fear of them.
But the sailors could not understand the words, they
thought it was the voice of the storm; nor could it be
theirs to see this Elysium of the deep, for when the
ship sank they were drowned, and only reached the
merman's palace in death. When the elder sisters rose
up in this manner, arm in arm, in the evening, the
youngest remained behind quite alone, looking after

them as if she must weep, but mermaids have no tears and so they suffer all the more.

'Oh! if I were only fifteen!' she said, 'I know how fond I shall be of the world above, and of the mortals who dwell there.'

At last her fifteenth birthday came.

'Now we shall have you off our hands,' said her grandmother, the old queen dowager. 'Come now, let me adorn you like your other sisters!' and she put a wreath of white lilies round her hair, but every petal of the flowers was half a pearl; then the old queen had eight oysters fixed on to the princess's tail to show her high rank.

'But it hurts so!' said the little mermaid.

'You must endure the pain for the sake of the finery!' said her grandmother.

But oh! how gladly would she have shaken off all this splendour, and laid aside the heavy wreath. Her red flowers in her garden suited her much better, but she did not dare to make any alteration. 'Goodbye,' she said, and mounted as lightly and airily as a bubble through the water.

The sun had just set when her head rose above the water, but the clouds were still lighted up with a rosy and golden splendour, and the evening star sparkled in the soft pink sky, the air was mild and fresh, and the sea as calm as a millpond. A big three-masted ship lay close by with only a single sail set, for there was not a breath of wind, and the sailors were sitting about the rigging, on the cross trees and at the mast-heads. There was music and singing on board, and as the evening closed in, hundreds of gaily coloured lanterns were lighted – they looked like the flags of all nations waving in the air. The little mermaid swam right up to the cabin windows, and every time she was lifted by the swell she could see through the transparent panes crowds of gaily dressed people. The handsomest of them all was the young prince with large dark eyes; he could not be much more than sixteen, and all these festivities were in honour of his birthday. The sailors danced on deck, and when the prince appeared among them hundreds of rockets were let off making it as light as day, and frightening the little mermaid so much that she had to dive under the water. She soon ventured up again, and it was just as if all the stars of heaven were falling in showers round about her. She had never seen such magic fires. Great suns whirled round, gorgeous fire-fish hung in the blue air, and all was reflected in the calm and glassy sea. It was so light on board the ship that every little rope could be seen, and the people still better. Oh! how handsome the prince was, how he laughed and smiled as he greeted his guests, while the music rang out in the quiet night.

It got quite late, but the little mermaid could not take her eyes off the ship and the beautiful prince. The coloured lanterns were put out, no more rockets were sent up, and the cannon had ceased its thunder, but deep down in the sea there was a dull murmuring and moaning sound. Meanwhile she was rocked up and down on the waves, so that she could look into the cabin; but the ship got more and more way on, sail after sail was filled by the wind, the waves grew stronger, great clouds gathered, and lightning forked in the distance. Oh, there was going to be a fearful storm! and soon the sailors had to shorten sail. The great ship rocked and rolled as she dashed over the angry sea, the black waves rose like mountains, high enough to overwhelm her, but she dived like a swan through them and rose again and again on their towering crests. The little mermaid thought it a most amusing race, but not so the sailors. The ship creaked and groaned, the mighty timbers bulged and bent under the heavy blows, the water broke over the decks, snapping the main mast like a reed, she heeled over on her side and the water rushed into the hold.

Now the little mermaid saw that they were in danger and she had for her own sake to beware of the floating beams and wreckage. One moment it was so pitch dark that she could not see at all, but when the lightning flashed it became so light that she could see all on board. Every man was looking out for his own safety as best he could, but she more particularly followed the young prince with her eyes, and when the ship went down she saw him sink in the deep sea. At first she was quite delighted, for now he was coming to be with her, but then she remembered that human beings could not live under water, and that only if he were dead could he go to her father's palace. No! he must not die; so she swam towards him all among the drifting beams and planks, quite forgetting that they might crush her.

She dived deep down under the water, and came up again through the waves, and at last reached the young prince just as he was becoming unable to swim any farther in the stormy sea. His limbs were numbed, his beautiful eyes were closed, and he must have died if the little mermaid had not come to the rescue. She held his head above the water and let the waves drive them whithersoever they would.

By daybreak all the storm was over, of the ship not a trace was to be seen; the sun rose from the water in radiant brilliance and his rosy beams seemed to cast a glow of life into the prince's cheeks, but his eyes remained closed. The mermaid kissed his fair and lofty brow, and stroked back the dripping hair; it seemed to her that he was like the marble statue in her little garden, she kissed him again and longed that he might live.

At last she saw dry land before her, high blue mountains on whose summits the white snow glistened as if a flock of swans had settled there; down by the shore were beautiful green woods, and in the foreground a church or temple, she did not

296

quite know which, but it was a building of some sort. Lemon and orange trees grew in the garden and lofty palms stood by the gate. At this point the sea formed a little bay where the water was quite calm, but very deep, right up to the cliffs; at their foot was a strip of fine white sand to which she swam with the beautiful prince, and laid him down on it, taking great care that his head should rest high up in the warm sunshine.

The bells now began to ring in the great white building and a number of young maidens came into the garden. Then the little mermaid swam further off behind some high rocks and covered her hair and breast with foam, so that no one should see her little face, and then she watched to see who would discover the poor prince.

It was not long before one of the maidens came up to him; at first she seemed quite frightened, but only for a moment, and then she fetched several others, and the mermaid saw that the prince was coming to life, and that he smiled at all those around him, though he had never smiled at her; you see he did not know that she had saved him; she felt so sad that when he was led away into the great building she dived sorrowfully into the water and made her way home to her father's palace.

Always silent and thoughtful, she became more so now than ever. Her sisters often asked her what she had seen on her first visit to the surface, but she never would tell them anything.

Many an evening and many a morning she would rise to the place where she had left the prince. She saw the fruit in the garden ripen, and then gathered, she saw the snow melt on the mountain-tops, but she never saw the prince, so she always went home still sadder than before. At home her only consolation was to sit in her little garden with her arms twined round the handsome marble statue which reminded her of the prince. It was all in gloomy shade now, as she had ceased to tend her flowers and the garden had become a neglected wilderness of long stalks and leaves entangled with the branches of the tree.

At last she could not bear it any longer, so she told one of her sisters, and from her it soon spread to the others, but to no one else except to one or two other mermaids who only told their dearest friends. One of these knew all about the prince, she had also seen the festivities on the ship; she knew where he came from and where his kingdom was situated.

'Come, little sister!' said the other princesses, and, throwing their arms round each other's shoulders, they rose from the water in a long line, just in front of the prince's palace.

It was built of light yellow glistening stone, with great marble staircases, one of which led into the garden. Magnificent gilded cupolas rose above the roof, and the spaces between the columns which encircled the building were filled with lifelike marble statues. Through the clear glass of the lofty windows you could see gorgeous halls adorned with costly silken hangings, and the pictures on the walls were a sight worth seeing. In the midst of the central hall a large fountain played, throwing its jets of spray upwards to a glass dome in the roof, through which the sunbeams lighted up the water and the beautiful plants which grew in the great basin.

She knew now where he lived and often used to go there in the evenings and by night over the water; she swam much nearer the land than any of the others dared, she even ventured right up the narrow channel under the splendid marble terrace which threw a long shadow over the water. She used to sit here looking at the young prince who thought he was quite alone in the clear moonlight.

She saw him many an evening sailing about in his beautiful boat, with flags waving and music playing; she used to peep through the green rushes, and if the wind happened to catch her long silvery veil and anyone saw it, they only thought it was a swan flapping its wings.

Many a night she heard the fishermen, who were fishing by torchlight, talking over the good deeds of the young prince; and she was happy to think that she had saved his life when he was drifting about on the waves, half dead, and she could not forget how closely his head had pressed her breast, and how passionately she had kissed him; but he knew nothing of all this, and never saw her even in his dreams.

She became fonder and fonder of mankind, and longed more and more to be able to live among them; their world seemed so infinitely bigger than hers; with their ships they could scour the ocean, they could ascend the mountains high above the clouds, and their wooded, grass-grown lands extended farther than her eye could reach. There was so much that she wanted to know, but her sisters could not give an answer to all her questions, so she asked her old grandmother who knew the upper world well, and rightly called it the country above the sea.

'If men are not drowned,' asked the little mermaid, 'do they live for ever. Do they not die as we do down here in the sea?'

'Yes,' said the old lady, 'they have to die too, and their lifetime is even shorter than ours. We may live here for three hundred years, but when we cease to exist we become mere foam on the water and do not have so much as a grave among our dear ones. We have no immortal souls, we have no future life, we are just like the green seaweed, which once cut down can never revive again! Men, on the other hand, have a soul which lives for ever, lives after the body has become dust; it rises through the clear air, up to the shining stars! Just as we rise from the water to see the land of mortals, so they rise up to unknown beautiful regions which we shall never see.'

'Why have we no immortal souls?' asked the little mermaid sadly. 'I would give all my three hundred years to be a human being for one day, and afterwards to have a share in the heavenly kingdom.'

'You must not be thinking about that,' said the grandmother, 'we are much better off and happier than human beings.'

'Then I shall have to die and to float as foam on the water, and never hear the music of the waves or see the beautiful flowers or the red sun! Is there nothing I can do to gain an immortal soul?'

'No,' said the grandmother; 'only if a human being so loved you that you were more to him than father or mother, if all his thoughts and all his love were so centred in you that he would let the priest join your hands and would vow to be faithful to you here, and to all eternity; then your body would become infused with his soul. Thus and only thus, could you gain a share in the felicity of mankind. He would give you a soul while yet keeping his own. But that can never happen! That which is your greatest beauty in the sea, your fish's tail, is thought hideous up on earth, so little do they understand about it; to be pretty there you must have two clumsy supports which they call legs!'

Then the little mermaid sighed and looked sadly at her fish's tail.

'Let us be happy,' said the grandmother; 'we will hop and skip during our three hundred years of life, it is surely a long enough time, and after it is over, we shall rest all the better in the foamy deep. There is to be a court ball tonight.'

This was a much more splendid affair than we ever see on earth. The walls and the ceiling of the great ballroom were of thick but transparent glass. Several hundreds of colossal mussel shells, rose-red and grass-green, were ranged in order round the sides holding blue lights, which illuminated the whole room and shone through the walls, so that the sea outside was quite lit up. You could see countless fish, great and small, swimming towards the glass walls, some with shining scales of crimson hue, while others were golden and silvery. In the middle of the room was a broad stream of running water, and on this the mermaids and mermen danced to their own beautiful singing. No earthly beings have such lovely voices. The little mermaid sang more sweetly than any of them and they all applauded her. For a moment she felt glad at heart, for she knew that she had the finest voice either in the sea or on land. But she soon began to think again about the upper world; she could not forget the handsome prince and her sorrow in not possessing, like him, an immortal soul. Therefore she stole out of her father's palace, and while all within was joy and merriment, she sat sadly in her little garden. Suddenly she heard the sound of a horn through the water, and she thought, 'Now he is out sailing up there; he whom I love more than father or mother, he to whom my thoughts cling and to whose hands I am ready to commit the happiness of my life. I will dare anything to win him and to gain an immortal soul! While my sisters are dancing in my father's palace, I will go to the sea witch of whom I have always been very much afraid, she will perhaps be able to advise and help me!'

Thereupon the little mermaid left the garden and went towards the roaring whirlpools at the back of which the witch lived. She had never been that way before; no flowers grew there, no seaweed, only the bare grey sands stretched towards the whirlpools, which like rushing mill-wheels swirled round, dragging everything that came within reach down to the depths. She had to pass between these boiling eddies to reach the witch's domain, and for a long way the only path led over warm bubbling mud, which the witch called her 'peat bog'. Her house stood behind this in the midst of a weird forest. All the trees and bushes were polyps, half animal and half plant; they looked like hundred-headed snakes growing out of the sand: the branches were long slimy arms, with tentacles like wriggling worms, every joint of which from the root to the outermost tip was in constant motion. They wound themselves tightly round whatever they could lay hold of and never let it escape. The little mermaid standing outside was quite frightened, her heart beat fast with terror and she nearly turned back; but then she remembered the prince and the immortal soul of mankind and took courage. She bound her long flowing hair tightly round her head, so that the polyps should not seize her by it, folded her hands over her breast, and darted like a fish through the water, in between the hideous polyps which stretched out their sensitive arms and tentacles towards her. She could see that every one of them had something or other, which they had grasped with their hundred arms, and which they held as if in iron bands. The bleached bones of men who had perished at sea and sunk below peeped forth from the arms of some, while others clutched rudders and sea chests, or the skeleton of some land animal; and most horrible of all, a little mermaid whom they had caught and suffocated. Then she came to a large opening in the wood where the ground was all slimy and where some huge fat water snakes were gambolling about. In the middle of this opening was a house built of the bones of the wrecked; there sat the witch, letting a toad eat out of her mouth, just as mortals let a little canary eat sugar. She called the hideous water-snakes her little chickens, and allowed them to crawl about on her unsightly bosom.

'I know very well what you have come here for,' said the witch. 'It is very foolish of you! All the same you shall have your way, because it will lead you into misfortune, my fine princess. You want to get rid of your fish's tail, and instead to have two stumps to walk about upon like human beings, so that the young prince may fall in love with you, and that you may win him and an immortal soul.' Saying this, she gave such a loud hideous laugh that the toad and the snakes fell to the ground and wriggled about there.

'You are just in the nick of time,' said the witch. 'After sunrise tomorrow I should not be able to help you until another year had run its course. I will make you a potion, and before sunrise you must swim ashore with it, seat yourself on the beach and drink it; then your tail will divide and shrivel up to what men call beautiful legs; but it hurts, it is as if a sharp sword were running through you. All who see you will say that you are the most beautiful child of man they have ever seen. You will keep your gliding gait, no dancer will rival you, but every step you take will be as if you were treading upon sharp knives, so sharp as to draw blood. If you are willing to suffer all this I am ready to help you!'

'Yes!' said the little princess with a trembling voice, thinking of the prince and of winning an undying soul.

'But remember,' said the witch, 'when once you have received a human form, you can never be a mermaid again, you will never again be able to dive down through the water to your sisters and to your father's palace. And if you do not succeed in winning the prince's love, so that for your sake he will forget father and mother, cleave to you with his whole heart, let the priest join your hands and make you man and wife, you will gain no immortal soul! The first morning after his marriage with another your heart will break, and you will turn into foam of the sea.'

'I will do it,' said the little mermaid as pale as death.

'But you will have to pay me, too,' said the witch, 'and it is no trifle that I demand. You have the most beautiful voice of any at the bottom of the sea, and I dare say that you think you will fascinate him with it, but you must give me that voice. I will have the best you possess in return for my precious potion! I have to mingle my own blood with it so as to make it as sharp as a two-edged sword.'

'But if you take my voice,' said the little mermaid, 'what have I left?'

'Your beautiful form,' said the witch, 'your gliding gait, and your speaking eyes, with these you ought surely to be able to bewitch a human heart. Well! have you lost courage? Put out your little tongue and I will cut it off in payment for the powerful draught.'

'Let it be done,' said the little mermaid, and the witch put on her cauldron to brew the magic potion. 'There is nothing like cleanliness,' said she, as she scoured the pot with a bundle of snakes; then she punctured her breast and let the black blood drop into the cauldron, and the steam took the most weird shapes, enough to frighten anyone. Every moment the witch threw new ingredients into the pot, and when it boiled the bubbling was like the sound of crocodiles weeping. At last the potion was ready and it looked like the clearest water.

'There it is,' said the witch, and thereupon she cut off the tongue of the little mermaid, who was dumb now and could neither sing nor speak.

'If the polyps should seize you, when you go back through my wood,' said the witch, 'just drop a single drop of this liquid on them, and their arms and fingers will burst into a thousand pieces.' But the little mermaid had no need to do this, for at the mere sight of the bright liquid which sparkled in her hand like a shining star, they drew back in terror. So she soon got past the wood, the bog and the eddying whirlpools.

She saw her father's palace, the lights were all out in the great ballroom, and no doubt all the household was asleep, but she did not dare to go in now that she was dumb and about to leave her home for ever. She felt as if her heart would break with grief. She stole into the garden and plucked a flower from each of her sister's plots, wafted with her hand countless kisses towards the palace, and then rose up through the dark blue water.

The sun had not risen when she came in sight of the prince's palace and landed at the beautiful marble steps. The moon was shining bright and clear. The little mermaid drank the burning, stinging draught, and it was like a sharp, two-edged sword running through her tender frame; she fainted away and lay as if she were dead. When the sun rose on the sea she woke up and became conscious of a sharp pang but just in front of her stood the handsome young prince, fixing his coal-black eyes on her; she cast hers down and saw that her fish's tail was gone, and that she had the prettiest little white legs any maiden could desire, but she was quite naked, so she wrapped her long thick hair around her. The prince asked who she was and how she came there; she looked at him tenderly and with a sad expression in her dark blue eyes, but could not speak. Then he took her by the hand and led her into the palace. Every step she took was, as the witch had warned her beforehand, as if she were treading on sharp knives and spikes but she bore it gladly; led by the prince she moved as lightly as a bubble, and he and everyone else marvelled at her graceful gliding gait.

Clothed in the costliest silks and muslins she was the greatest beauty in the palace, but she was dumb and could neither sing nor speak. Beautiful slaves clad in silks and gold came forward and sang to the prince and his royal parents; one of them sang better than all the others, and the prince clapped his hands and smiled at her; that made the little mermaid very sad, for she knew that she used to sing far better

herself. She thought, 'Oh! if he only knew that for the sake of being with him I had given up my voice for ever!' Now the slaves began to perform, graceful and undulating dances to enchanting music; thereupon the little mermaid lifting her beautiful white arms and raising herself on tiptoe glided on the floor with a grace which none of the other dancers had yet attained. With every motion her grace and beauty became more apparent, and her eyes appealed more deeply to the heart than the songs of the slaves. Everyone was delighted with it, especially the prince, who called her his little foundling, and she danced on and on, notwithstanding that every time her foot touched the ground it was like treading on sharp knives. The prince said that she should always be near him, and she was allowed to sleep outside his door on a velvet cushion.

He had a man's dress made for her, so that she could ride about with him. They used to ride through scented woods, where the green branches brushed her shoulders, and little birds sang among the fresh leaves. She climbed up the highest mountains with the prince, and although her delicate feet bled so that others saw it, she only laughed and followed him until they saw the clouds sailing below them like a flock of birds, taking flight to distant lands.

At home in the prince's palace, when at night the others were asleep, she used to go out on to the marble steps; it cooled her burning feet to stand in the cold sea water, and at such times she used to think of those she had left in the deep.

One night her sisters came arm in arm; they sang so sorrowfully as they swam on the water that she beckoned to them and they recognised her, and told her how she had grieved them all. After that they visited her every night, and one night she saw, a long way out, her old grandmother (who for many years had not been above the water), and the merman king with his crown on his head; they stretched out their hands towards her, but did not venture so close to land as her sisters.

Day by day she became dearer to the prince, he loved her as one loves a good sweet child, but it never entered his head to make her his queen; yet unless she became his wife she would never win an ever-lasting soul, but on his wedding morning would turn to sea foam.

'Am I not dearer to you than any of them?' the little mermaid's eyes seemed to say when he took her in his arms and kissed her beautiful brow.

'Yes, you are the dearest one to me,' said the prince, 'for you have the best heart of them all, and you are fondest of me; you are also like a young girl I once saw, but whom I never expect to see again. I was on board a ship which was wrecked, I was driven on shore by the waves close to a holy temple where several young girls were ministering at a service; the youngest of them found me on the beach and saved my life; I saw her but twice. She was the only person I could love in this world, but you are like her, you almost drive her image out of my heart. She belongs to the holy temple, and therefore by good fortune you have been sent to me, we will never part!'

'Alas! he does not know that it was I who saved his life,' thought the little mermaid. 'I bore him over the sea to the wood, where the temple stands. I sat behind the foam and watched to see if anyone would come. I saw the pretty girl he loves better than me.'

And the mermaid heaved a bitter sigh, for she could not weep.

'The girl belongs to the holy temple, he has said, she will never return to the world, they will never meet again, I am here with him, I see him every day. Yes, I will tend him, love him, and give up my life to him.'

But now the rumour ran that the prince was to be married to the beautiful daughter of a neighbouring king, and for that reason was fitting out a splendid ship. It was given out that the prince was going on a voyage to see the adjoining countries, but it was without doubt to see the king's daughter; he was to have a great suite with him, but the little mermaid shook her head and laughed; she knew the prince's intentions much better than any of the others. 'I must take this voyage,' he had said to her; 'I must go and see the beautiful princess; my parents demand that, but they will never force me to bring her home as my bride; I can never love her! She will not be like the lovely girl in the temple whom you resemble. If ever I had to choose a bride it would sooner be you with your speaking eyes, my sweet, dumb foundling!' And he kissed her rosy mouth, played with her long hair, and laid his head upon her heart, which already dreamt of human joys and an immortal soul.

'You are not frightened of the sea, I suppose, my dumb child?' he said, as they stood on the proud ship which was to carry them to the country of the neighbouring king; and he told her about storms and calms, about curious fish in the deep, and the marvels seen by divers; and she smiled at his tales, for she knew all about the bottom of the sea much better than anyone else.

At night, in the moonlight, when all were asleep, except the steersman who stood at the helm, she sat at the side of the ship trying to pierce the clear water with her eyes, and fancied she saw her father's palace, and above it her old grandmother with her silver crown on her head, looking up through the cross-currents towards the keel of the ship. Then her sisters rose above the water, they gazed sadly at her, wringing their white hands; she beckoned to them, smiled, and was about to tell them that all was going well and happily with her, when the cabin boy approached, and the sisters dived down, but he supposed that the white objects he had seen were nothing but flecks of foam.

The next morning the ship entered the harbour of the neighbouring king's magnificent city. The church bells rang and trumpets were sounded from every lofty tower, while the soldiers paraded with flags flying and glittering bayonets. There was a fête every day, there was a succession of balls and receptions followed one after the other; but the princess was not yet present, she was being brought up a long way off, in a holy temple they said, and was learning all the royal virtues. At last she came. The little mermaid stood eager to see her beauty, and she was obliged to confess that a lovelier creature she had never beheld. Her complexion was exquisitely pure and delicate, and her trustful eyes of the deepest blue shone through their dark lashes.

'It is you,' said the prince, 'you who saved me when I lay almost lifeless on the beach!' And he clasped his blushing bride to his heart. 'Oh! I am too happy!' he exclaimed to the little mermaid.

'A greater joy than I had dared to hope for has come to pass. You will rejoice at my joy, for you love me better than anyone.' Then the little mermaid kissed his hand, and felt as if her heart were broken already.

His wedding morn would bring death to her and change her to foam.

All the church bells pealed and heralds rode through the town proclaiming the nuptials. Upon every altar throughout the land fragrant oil was burnt in costly silver lamps. Amidst the swinging of censers by the priests, the bride and bridegroom joined hands and received the bishop's blessing. The little mermaid dressed in silk and gold stood holding the bride's train, but her ears were deaf to the festal strains; her eyes saw nothing of the sacred ceremony; she was thinking of her coming death and of all that she had lost in this world.

That same evening the bride and bridegroom embarked, amidst the roar of cannon and the waving of banners. A royal tent of purple and gold softly cushioned was raised amidships where the bridal pair were to repose during the calm cool night.

The sails swelled in the wind and the ship skimmed lightly and almost without motion over the transparent sea.

At dusk lanterns of many colours were lighted and the sailors danced merrily on deck. The little mermaid could not help thinking of the first time she came up from the sea and saw the same splendour and gaiety; and she now threw herself among the dancers, whirling, as a swallow skims through the air when pursued. The onlookers cheered her in amazement, never had she danced so divinely; her delicate feet pained her as if they were cut with knives, but she did not feel it, for the pain at her heart was much sharper. She knew that it was the last night that she would breathe the same air as he, and would look upon the mighty deep, and the blue starry heavens; an endless night without thought and without dreams awaited her, who neither had a soul, nor could win one. The joy and revelry on board lasted till long past midnight; she went on laughing and dancing with the thought of death all the time in her heart. The prince caressed his lovely bride and she played with his raven locks, and with their arms entwined they retired to the gorgeous tent. All became hushed and still on board the ship, only the steersman stood at the helm; the little mermaid laid her white arms on the gunwale and looked eastwards for the pink-tinted dawn; the first sunbeam, she knew, would be her death. Then she saw her sisters rise from the water, they were as pale as she was, their beautiful long hair no longer floated on the breeze, for it had been cut off.

'We have given it to the witch to obtain her help, so that you may not die tonight! She has given us a knife, here it is, look how sharp it is! Before the sun rises, you must plunge it into the prince's heart, and when his warm blood sprinkles your feet they will join together and grow into a tail, and you will once more be a mermaid; you will be able to come down into the water to us, and to live out your three hundred years before you are turned into dead, salt, sea-foam. Make haste! You or he must die before sunrise! Our old grandmother is so full of grief that her white hair has fallen off as ours fell under the witch's scissors. Slay the prince and come back to us! Quick! Quick! Do you not see the rosy streak in the sky? In a few moments the sun will rise and then you must die!' Saying this they heaved a wondrous deep sigh and sank among the waves.

The little mermaid drew aside the purple curtain from the tent and looked at the beautiful bride asleep with her head on the prince's breast; she bent over him and kissed his fair brow, looked at the sky where the dawn was spreading fast; looked at the sharp knife, and again fixed her eyes on the prince who, in his dream, called his bride by name; yes! she alone was in his thoughts! – For a moment the knife quivered in her grasp, then she threw it far out among the waves now rosy in the morning light and where it fell the water bubbled up like drops of blood.

Once more she looked at the prince, with her eyes already dimmed by death, then dashed overboard and fell, her body dissolving into foam.

Now the sun rose from the sea and with its kindly beams warmed the deadly cold foam, so that the little mermaid did not feel the chill of death. She saw the bright sun and above her floated hundreds of beauteous ethereal beings through which she could see the white ship and the rosy heavens; their voices were melodious but so spirit-like that no human ear could hear them, any more than an earthly eye could see their forms. Light as bubbles they floated through the air without the aid of wings. The little mermaid perceived that she had a form like theirs, it gradually took shape out of the foam. 'To whom am I coming?' said she, and her voice sounded like that of the other beings, so unearthly in its beauty that no music of ours could reproduce it.

'To the daughters of the air!' answered the others, 'a mermaid has no undying soul, and can never gain one without winning the love of a human being. Her eternal life must depend upon an unknown power. Nor have the daughters of the air an everlasting soul, but by their own good deeds they may create one for themselves. We fly to the tropics where mankind is the victim of hot and pestilent winds, there we bring cooling breezes. We diffuse the scent of flowers all around, and bring refreshment and healing in our train. When, for three hundred years, we have laboured to do all the good in our power we gain an undying soul and take a part in the everlasting joys of mankind. You, poor little mermaid, have with your whole heart struggled for the same thing that we have struggled for. You have suffered and endured, raised yourself to the spirit world of the air; and now, by your own good deeds, you may, in the course of three hundred years, work out for yourself an undying soul.'

Then the little mermaid lifted her transparent arms towards God's sun, and for the first time shed tears.

On board ship all was again life and bustle; she saw the prince with his lovely bride searching for her, they looked sadly at the bubbling foam, as if they knew that she had thrown herself into the waves. Unseen she kissed the bride on her brow, smiled at the prince and rose aloft with the other spirits of the air to the rosy clouds which sailed above. 'In three hundred years we shall thus float into Paradise.'

'We might reach it sooner,' whispered one. 'Unseen we flit into the homes of men where there are children, and every time that we find a good child who gives pleasure to its parents and deserves their love, God shortens our time of probation. The child does not know that when we fly through the room, and when we smile with pleasure at it, one year of our three hundred is taken away. But if we see a naughty or badly disposed child, we can't help shedding tears of sorrow, and every tear adds a day to the time of our probation.'

Little Red Riding Hood

Once upon a time there lived in a certain village a little country girl, the prettiest creature was ever seen. Her mother was excessively fond of her; and her grandmother doted on her still more. This good woman had made for her a little red riding hood; which became the girl so extremely well that everybody called her Little Red Riding Hood.

One day her mother, having made some custards, said to her: 'Go, my dear, and see how thy grandmama does, for I hear she has been very ill; carry her a custard, and this little pot of butter.'

Little Red Riding Hood set out immediately to go to her grandmother, who lived in another village.

As she was going through the wood, she met with Gaffer Wolf, who had a very great mind to eat her up, but he dared not, because of some woodcutters hard by in the forest. He asked her whither she was going. The poor child, who did not know that it was dangerous to stay and hear a wolf talk, said to

him: 'I am going to see my grandmama and carry her a custard and a little pot of butter from my mama.'

'Does she live far off?' asked the Wolf.

'Oh! ay,' answered Little Red Riding Hood; 'it is beyond that mill you see there, at the first house in the village.'

'Well,' said the Wolf, 'and I'll go and see her too. I'll go this way and you go that, and we shall see who will be there soonest.'

The Wolf began to run as fast as he could, taking the nearest way, and the little girl went by that farthest about, diverting herself in gathering nuts, running after butterflies, and making nosegays of such little flowers as she met with. The Wolf was not long before he got to the old woman's house. He knocked at the door – tap, tap.

'Who's there?'

'Your grandchild, Little Red Riding Hood,' replied the Wolf, counterfeiting her voice; 'who has brought you a custard and a little pot of butter sent you by mama.'

The good grandmother, who was in bed, because she was somewhat ill, cried out: 'Pull the bobbin, and the latch will go up.'

The Wolf pulled the bobbin, and the door opened, and then presently he fell upon the good woman and ate her up in a moment, for it was above three days that he had not touched a bit. He then shut the door and went into the grandmother's bed, expecting Little Red Riding Hood, who came some time afterwards and knocked at the door – tap, tap.

'Who's there?'

Little Red Riding Hood, hearing the big voice of the Wolf, was at first afraid; but believing her grand-

mother had got a cold and was hoarse, answered: '
'Tis your grandchild, Little Red Riding Hood, who
has brought you a custard and a little pot of butter
mama sends you.'

The Wolf cried out to her, softening his voice as
much as he could: 'Pull the bobbin, and the latch will
go up.'

Little Red Riding Hood pulled the bobbin, and the
door opened.

The Wolf, seeing her come in, said to her, hiding
himself under the bedclothes: 'Put the custard and

the little pot of butter upon the stool, and come and talk with me.'

Little Red Riding Hood went over to the bed, where, being greatly amazed to see how her grandmother looked in her nightclothes, she said to her:

'Grandmama, what great arms you have got!'

'That is the better to hug thee, my dear.'

'Grandmama, what great legs you have got!'

'That is to run the better, my child.'

'Grandmama, what great ears you have got!'

'That is to hear the better, my child.'

'Grandmama, what great eyes you have got!'

'It is to see the better, my child.'

'Grandmama, what great teeth you have got!'

'That is to eat you up.'

And, saying these words, this wicked wolf fell upon Little Red Riding Hood, and ate her all up.

The Ogre of Rashomon

Long, long ago in Kyoto, the people of the city were terrified by accounts of a dreadful ogre, who, it was said, haunted the Gate of Rashomon at twilight and seized whoever passed by. The missing victims were never seen again, so it was whispered that the ogre was a horrible cannibal, who not only killed the unhappy victims but ate them also. Now everybody in the town and neighbourhood was in great fear, and no one durst venture out after sunset near the Gate of Rashomon.

Now at this time there lived in Kyoto a general named Raiko, who had made himself famous for his brave deeds. Some time before this he had made the country ring with his name, for he had attacked Oeyama, where a band of ogres lived with their chief and instead of wine drank the blood of human beings. He had routed them all and cut off the head of the chief monster.

This brave warrior was always followed by a band of faithful knights. In this band there were five knights of great valour. One evening as the five knights sat at a feast quaffing sake in their rice bowls and eating all kinds of fish, raw and stewed and broiled, and toasting each other's healths and exploits, the first knight, Hojo, said to the others: 'Have you all heard the rumour that every evening after sunset there comes an ogre to the Gate of Rashomon, and that he seizes all who pass by?'

The second knight, Watanabe, answered him, saying: 'Do not talk such nonsense! All the ogres

320

were killed by our chief Raiko at Oeyama! It cannot be true, because even if any ogres did escape from that great killing they would not dare to show themselves in this city, for they know that our brave master would at once attack them if he knew that any of them were still alive!'

'Then do you disbelieve what I say, and think that I am telling you a falsehood?'

'No, I do not think that you are telling a lie,' said Watanabe; 'but you have heard some old woman's story which is not worth believing.'

'Then the best plan is to prove what I say, by going there yourself and finding out yourself whether it is true or not,' said Hojo.

Watanabe, the second knight, could not bear the thought that his companion should believe he was afraid, so he answered quickly: 'Of course, I will go at once and find out for myself!'

So Watanabe at once got ready to go – he buckled on his long sword and put on a coat of armour, and tied on his large helmet. When he was ready to start he said to the others: 'Give me something so that I can prove I have been there!'

Then one of the men got a roll of writing paper and his box of indian ink and brushes, and the four comrades wrote their names on a piece of paper.

'I will take this,' said Watanabe, 'and put it on the Gate of Rashomon, so tomorrow morning you can all go and look at it. I may be able to catch an ogre or two by then!' and he mounted his horse and rode off gallantly.

It was a very dark night, and there was neither moon nor star to light Watanabe on his way. To make the darkness worse a storm came on, the rain fell heavily and the wind howled like wolves in the mountains. Any ordinary man would have trembled at the thought of going out of doors, but Watanabe was a brave warrior and dauntless, and his honour and word were at stake; so he sped on into the night, while his companions listened to the sound of his horse's hoofs dying away in the distance, then shut the sliding shutters close and gathered round the charcoal fire and wondered what would happen – and whether their comrade would encounter one of those horrible Oni.

At last Watanabe reached the Gate of Rashomon, but peer as he might through the darkness he could see no sign of an ogre.

'It is just as I thought,' said Watanabe to himself; 'there are certainly no ogres here; it is only an old woman's story. I will stick this paper on the gate so that the others can see I have been here when they come tomorrow, and then I will take my way home and laugh at them all.'

He fastened the piece of paper, signed by all his four companions, on the gate, and then turned his horse's head towards home.

As he did so he became aware that someone was behind him, and at the same time a voice called out to him to wait. Then his helmet was seized from the back. 'Who are you?' said Watanabe fearlessly. He then put out his hand and groped around to find out who or what it was that held him by the helmet. As he did so he touched something that felt like an arm – it was covered with hair and as big round as the trunk of a tree!

Watanabe knew at once that this was the arm of an ogre, so he drew his sword and cut at it fiercely.

There was a loud yell of pain, and then the ogre dashed in front of the warrior.

Watanabe's eyes grew large with wonder, for he saw that the ogre was taller than the great gate, his eyes were flashing like mirrors in the sunlight, his huge mouth was wide open, and as the monster breathed, flames of fire shot out of his mouth.

The ogre thought to terrify his foe, but Watanabe never flinched. He attacked the ogre with all his strength, and thus they fought face to face for a long time. At last the ogre, finding that he could neither frighten nor beat Watanabe and that he might himself be beaten, took to flight. But Watanabe, determined not to let the monster escape, put spurs to his horse and gave chase.

But though the knight rode very fast the ogre ran faster, and to his disappointment he found himself unable to overtake the monster, who was gradually lost to sight.

Watanabe returned to the gate where the fierce fight had taken place, and got down from his horse. As he did so he stumbled upon something lying on the ground.

Stooping to pick it up he found that it was one of the ogre's huge arms which he must have slashed off in the fight. His joy was great at having secured such a prize, for this was the best of all proofs of his adventure with the ogre. So he took it up carefully and carried it home as a trophy of his victory.

When he got back, he showed the arm to his comrades, who one and all called him the hero of their band and gave him a great feast. His wonderful deed was soon noised abroad in Kyoto, and people from far and near came to see the ogre's arm.

Watanabe now began to grow uneasy as to how he should keep the arm in safety, for he knew that the ogre to whom it belonged was still alive. He felt sure that one day or other, as soon as the ogre got over his scare, he would come to try to get his arm back again. Watanabe therefore had a box made of the strongest wood and banded with iron. In this he placed the arm, and then he sealed down the heavy lid, refusing to open it for anyone. He kept the box in his own room and took charge of it himself, never allowing it out of his sight.

Now one night he heard someone knocking at the porch, asking for admittance. When the servant went to the door to see who it was, there was only an old woman, very respectable in appearance. On being asked who she was and what was her business, the old woman replied with a smile that she had been nurse to the master of the house when he was a little baby. If the lord of the house were at home she begged to be allowed to see him. The servant left the old woman at the door and went to tell his master that his old nurse had come to see him. Watanabe thought it strange that she should come at that time of night, but at the thought of his old nurse, who had been like a foster-mother to him and whom he had not seen for a long time, a very tender feeling sprang up for her in his heart. He ordered the servant to show her in.

The old woman was ushered into the room, and after the customary bows and greetings were over, she said: 'Master, the report of your brave fight with the ogre at the Gate of Rashomon is so widely known that even your poor old nurse has heard of it. Is it really true, what everyone says, that you cut off one of the ogre's arms? If you did, your deed is highly to be praised!'

'I was very disappointed,' said Watanabe, 'that I was not able take the monster captive, which was what I wished to do, instead of only cutting off an arm!'

'I am very proud to think,' answered the old woman, 'that my master was so brave as to dare to cut off an ogre's arm. There is nothing that can be compared to your courage. Before I die it is the great wish of my life to see this arm,' she added pleadingly.

'No,' said Watanabe. 'I am sorry, but I cannot grant your request.'

'But why?' asked the old woman.

'Because,' replied Watanabe, 'ogres are very revengeful creatures, and if I open the box there is no telling but that the ogre may suddenly appear and carry off his arm. I have had a box made on purpose with a very strong lid, and in this box I keep the ogre's arm secure; and I never show it to anyone, whatever happens.'

'Your precaution is very reasonable,' said the old woman. 'But I am your old nurse, so surely you will not refuse to show *me* the arm. I have only just heard of your brave act, and not being able to wait till the morning I came at once to ask you to show it to me.'

Watanabe was very troubled at the old woman's pleading, but he still persisted in refusing. Then the old woman said: 'Do you suspect me of being a spy sent by the ogre?'

'No, of course I do not suspect you of being the ogre's spy, for you are my old nurse,' answered Watanabe.

'Then you cannot surely refuse to show me the arm any longer?' entreated the old woman; 'for it is the great wish of my heart to see for once in my life the arm of an ogre!'

Watanabe could not hold out in his refusal any longer, so he gave in at last, saying: 'Then I will show you the ogre's arm, since you so earnestly wish to see it. Come, follow me!' and he led the way to his own room, the old woman following.

When they were both in the room Watanabe shut the door carefully, and then going towards a big box which stood in a corner of the room, he took off the heavy lid. He then called to the old woman to come near and look in, for he never took the arm out of the box.

'What is it like? Let me have a good look at it,' said the old nurse, with a joyful face.

She came nearer and nearer, as if she were afraid, till she stood right against the box. Suddenly she plunged her hand into the box and seized the arm, crying with a exultant voice which made the room shake: 'Oh, joy! I have got my arm back again!'

And from an old woman she was suddenly transformed into the towering figure of the frightful ogre!

Watanabe sprang back and was unable to move for a moment, so great was his astonishment; but recognising the ogre who had attacked him at the Gate of Rashomon, he determined with his usual courage to put an end to him this time. He seized his sword, drew it out of its sheath in a flash, and tried to cut the ogre down.

So quick was Watanabe that the creature had a narrow escape. But the ogre sprang up to the ceiling, and bursting through the roof, disappeared in the mist and clouds.

In this way the ogre escaped with his arm. The

knight gnashed his teeth with disappointment, but that was all he could do. He waited in patience for another opportunity to dispatch the ogre. But the latter was afraid of Watanabe's great strength and daring, and never troubled Kyoto again. So once more the people of the city were able to go out without fear even at night, and the brave deeds of Watanabe have never been forgotten!

The Story of Pretty Goldilocks

Once upon a time there was a princess who was the prettiest creature in the world. And because she was so beautiful, and because her hair was like the finest gold, and waved and rippled nearly to the ground, she was called Pretty Goldilocks. She always wore a crown of flowers, and her dresses were embroidered with diamonds and pearls, and everybody who saw her fell in love with her.

Now one of her neighbours was a young king who was not married. He was very rich and handsome, and when he heard all that was said about Pretty Goldilocks, though he had never seen her, he fell so deeply in love with her that he could neither eat nor drink. So he resolved to send an ambassador to ask her in marriage. He had a splendid carriage made for his ambassador, and gave him more than a hundred horses and a hundred servants, and told him to be sure and bring the princess back with him. After he had started nothing else was talked of at court, and the king felt so sure that the princess would consent that he set his people to work at pretty dresses and splendid furniture, that they might be ready by the time she came. Meanwhile, the ambassador arrived at the princess's palace and delivered his little message, but whether she happened to be cross that day, or whether the compliment did not please her, is not known. She only answered that she was very much obliged to the king, but she had no wish to be

married. The ambassador set off sadly on his homeward way, bringing all the king's presents back with
him, for the princess was too well brought up to
accept the pearls and diamonds when she would
not accept the king, so she had only kept twenty-five
English pins that he might not be vexed.

When the ambassador reached the city, where
the king was waiting impatiently, everybody was very
much annoyed with him for not bringing the princess,
and the king cried like a baby, and nobody could
console him. Now there was at the court a young
man, who was more clever and handsome than anyone else. He was called Charming, and everyone
loved him, excepting a few envious people who were
angry at his being the king's favourite and knowing all
the state secrets. He happened one day to be with
some people who were speaking of the ambassador's
return and saying that his going to the princess had
not done much good, when Charming said rashly: 'If
the king had sent me to the Princess Goldilocks I am
sure she would have come back with me.'

His enemies at once went to the king and said:
'You will hardly believe, sire, what Charming has
the audacity to say – that if *he* had been sent to the
Princess Goldilocks she would certainly have come
back with him. He seems to think that he is so much
handsomer than you that the princess would have
fallen in love with him and followed him willingly.'
The king was very angry when he heard this.

'Ha, ha!' said he; 'does he laugh at my unhappiness,
and think himself more fascinating than I am? Go,
and let him be shut up in my great tower to die of
hunger.'

So the king's guards went to fetch Charming, who

had thought no more of his rash speech, and carried him off to prison with great cruelty. The poor prisoner had only a little straw for his bed, and but for a little stream of water which flowed through the tower he would have died of thirst.

One day when he was in despair he said to himself: 'How can I have offended the king? I am his most faithful subject, and have done nothing against him.'

The king chanced to be passing the tower and recognised the voice of his former favourite. He stopped to listen in spite of Charming's enemies, who tried to persuade him to have nothing more to do with the traitor. But the king said: 'Be quiet, I wish to hear what he says.'

And then he opened the tower door and called to Charming, who came very sadly and kissed the king's hand, saying: 'What have I done, sire, to deserve this cruel treatment?'

'You mocked me and my ambassador,' said the king, 'and you said that if I had sent you for the Princess Goldilocks you would certainly have brought her back.'

'It is quite true, sire,' replied Charming; 'I should have drawn such a picture of you, and represented your good qualities in such a way, that I am certain the princess would have found you irresistible. But I cannot see what there is in that to make you angry.'

The king could not see any cause for anger either when the matter was presented to him in this light, and he began to frown very fiercely at the courtiers who had so misrepresented his favourite.

So he took Charming back to the palace with him, and after seeing that he had a very good supper he said to him: 'You know that I love Pretty Goldilocks as much as ever, her refusal has not made any difference to me; but I don't know how to make her change her mind; I really should like to send you, to see if you can persuade her to marry me.'

Charming replied that he was perfectly willing to go, and would set out the very next day.

'But you must wait till I can get a grand escort for you,' said the king. But Charming said that he only wanted a good horse to ride, and the king, who was delighted at his being ready to start so promptly, gave him letters to the princess, and bade him good speed. It was on a Monday morning that he set out all alone upon his errand, thinking of nothing but how he could persuade the Princess Goldilocks to marry the king. He had a writing-book in his pocket, and whenever any happy thought struck him he dismounted from his horse and sat down under the trees to put it into the harangue which he was preparing for the princess, before he forgot it.

One day when he had started at the very earliest dawn, and was riding over a great meadow, he

suddenly had a capital idea, and, springing from his horse, he sat down under a willow tree which grew by a little river. When he had written it down he was looking round him, pleased to find himself in such a pretty place, when all at once he saw a great golden carp lying gasping and exhausted upon the grass. In leaping after little flies she had thrown herself high upon the bank, where she had lain till she was nearly dead. Charming had pity upon her, and, though he couldn't help thinking that she would have been very nice for dinner, he picked her up gently and put her back into the water. As soon as Dame Carp felt the refreshing coolness of the water she sank down joyfully to the bottom of the river, then, swimming up to the bank quite boldly, she said: 'I thank you, Charming, for the kindness you have done me. You have saved my life; one day I will repay you.' So saying, she sank down into the water again, leaving Charming greatly astonished at her politeness.

Another day, as he journeyed on, he saw a raven in great distress. The poor bird was closely pursued by an eagle, which would soon have eaten it up, had not Charming quickly fitted an arrow to his bow and shot the eagle dead. The raven perched upon a tree very joyfully.

'Charming,' said he, 'it was very generous of you to rescue a poor raven; I am not ungrateful, some day I will repay you.'

Charming thought it was very nice of the raven to say so, and went on his way.

Before the sun rose he found himself in a thick wood where it was too dark for him to see his path, and here he heard an owl crying as if it were in despair.

'Hark!' said he, 'that must be an owl in great

trouble, I am sure it has gone into a snare'; and he began to hunt about, and presently found a great net which some bird-catchers had spread the night before.

'What a pity it is that men do nothing but torment and persecute poor creatures which never do them any harm!' said he, and he took out his knife and cut the cords of the net, and the owl flitted away into the darkness, but then turning, with one flicker of her wings, she came back to Charming and said: 'It does not need many words to tell you how great a service you have done me. I was caught; in a few minutes the fowlers would have been here – without your help, I should have been killed. I am grateful, and one day I will repay you.'

These three adventures were the only ones of any consequence that befell Charming upon his journey, and he made all the haste he could to reach the palace of the Princess Goldilocks.

When he arrived he thought everything he saw delightful and magnificent. Diamonds were as plentiful as pebbles, and the gold and silver, the beautiful dresses, the sweetmeats and pretty things that were everywhere quite amazed him; he thought to himself: 'If the princess consents to leave all this, and come with me to marry the king, he may think himself lucky!'

Then he dressed himself carefully in rich brocade, with scarlet and white plumes, and threw a splendid embroidered scarf over his shoulder, and, looking as gay and as graceful as possible, he presented himself at the door of the palace, carrying in his arm a tiny pretty dog which he had bought on the way. The guards saluted him respectfully, and a messenger was sent to the princess to announce the arrival of Charming as ambassador of her neighbour the king.

'Charming,' said the princess, 'the name promises well; I have no doubt that he is good-looking and fascinates everybody.'

'Indeed he does, madam,' said all her maids of honour in one breath. 'We saw him from the window of the garret where we were spinning flax, and we could do nothing but look at him as long as he was in sight.'

'Well to be sure,' said the princess, 'that's how you amuse yourselves, is it? Looking at strangers out of the window! Be quick and give me my blue satin embroidered dress, and comb out my golden hair. Let somebody make me fresh garlands of flowers, and give me my high-heeled shoes and my fan, and tell them to sweep my great hall and my throne, for I want everyone to say I am really "Pretty Goldilocks".'

You can imagine how all her maids scurried this way and that to make the princess ready, and how in their haste they knocked their heads together and hindered each other, till she thought they would never have done. However, at last they led her into the gallery of mirrors that she might assure herself that nothing was lacking in her appearance, and then she mounted her throne of gold, ebony and ivory, while her ladies took their guitars and began to sing softly. Then Charming was led in, and was so struck with astonishment and admiration that at first not a word could he say. But presently he took courage and delivered his harangue, bravely ending by begging the princess to spare him the disappointment of going back without her.

'Sir Charming,' answered she, 'all the reasons you have given me are very good ones, and I assure you that I should have more pleasure in obliging you than anyone else, but you must know that a month ago as I was walking by the river with my ladies I took off my glove, and as I did so a ring that I was wearing slipped off my finger and rolled into the water. As I valued it more than my kingdom, you may imagine how vexed I was at losing it, and I vowed never to listen to any proposal of marriage unless the ambassador first brought me back my ring. So now you know what is expected of you, for if you talked for fifteen days and fifteen nights you could not make me change my mind.'

Charming was very much surprised by this answer, but he bowed low to the princess, and begged her to accept the embroidered scarf and the tiny dog he had brought with him. But she answered that she did not want any presents, and that he was to remember what she had just told him. When he got back to his lodging he went to bed without eating any supper, and his little dog, who was called Frisk, couldn't eat

any either, but came and lay down close to him. All night Charming sighed and lamented.

'How am I to find a ring that fell into the river a month ago?' said he. 'It is useless to try; the princess must have told me to do it on purpose, knowing it was impossible.' And then he sighed again.

Frisk heard him and said: 'My dear master, don't despair; the luck may change, you are too good not to be happy. Let us go down to the river as soon as it is light.'

But Charming only gave him two little pats and said nothing, and very soon he fell asleep.

At the first glimmer of dawn Frisk began to jump about, and when he had waked Charming they went out together, first into the garden, and then down to the river's brink, where they wandered up and down. Charming was thinking sadly of having to go back unsuccessful when he heard someone calling: 'Charming, Charming!' He looked all about him and thought he must be dreaming, as he could not see anybody. Then he walked on and the voice called again: 'Charming, Charming!'

'Who calls me?' said he. Frisk, who was very small and could look closely into the water, cried out: 'I see a golden carp coming.' And sure enough there was the great carp, who said to Charming: 'You saved my life in the meadow by the willow tree, and I promised that I would repay you. Take this, it is Princess Goldilocks' ring.' Charming took the ring out of Dame Carp's mouth, thanking her a thousand times, and he and tiny Frisk went straight to the palace, where someone told the princess that he was asking to see her.

'Ah! poor fellow,' said she, 'he must have come to say goodbye, finding it impossible to do as I asked.'

So in came Charming, who presented her with the ring and said: 'Madam, I have done your bidding. Will it please you to marry my master?' When the princess saw her ring brought back to her unhurt she was so astonished that she thought she must be dreaming.

'Truly, Charming,' said she, 'you must be the favourite of some fairy, or you could never have found it.'

'Madam,' answered he, 'I was helped by nothing but my desire to obey your wishes.'

'Since you are so kind,' said she, 'perhaps you will do me another service, for till it is done I will never be married. There is a prince not far from here whose name is Galifron, who once wanted to marry me, but when I refused he uttered the most terrible threats against me, and vowed that he would lay waste my country. But what could I do? I could not marry a frightful giant as tall as a tower, who eats up people as a monkey eats chestnuts, and who talks so loud that anybody who has to listen to him becomes quite deaf. Nevertheless, he does not cease to persecute me and to kill my subjects. So before I can listen to your proposal you must kill him and bring me his head.'

Charming was rather dismayed at this command, but he answered: 'Very well, princess, I will fight this Galifron; I believe that he will kill me, but at any rate I shall die in your defence.'

Then the princess was frightened and said everything she could think of to prevent Charming from fighting the giant, but it was of no use, and he went out to arm himself suitably; and then, taking little Frisk with him, he mounted his horse and set out for Galifron's country. Everyone he met told him what a terrible giant Galifron was, and that nobody dared go near him; and the more he heard, the more frightened he grew. Frisk tried to encourage him by saying: 'While you are fighting the giant, dear master, I will go and bite his heels, and when he stoops down to look at me you can kill him.'

Charming praised his little dog's plan, but knew that this help would not do much good.

At last he drew near the giant's castle, and saw to his horror that every path that led to it was strewn with bones. Before long he saw Galifron coming. His head was higher than the tallest trees, and he sang in a terrible voice:

> 'Bring out your little boys and girls,
> Pray do not stay to do their curls,
> For I shall eat so very many,
> I shall not know if they have any.'

Thereupon Charming sang out as loud as he could to the same tune:

> 'Come out and meet the valiant Charming,
> Who finds you not at all alarming;
> Although he is not very tall,
> He's big enough to make you fall.'

The rhymes were not very correct, but you see he had made them up so quickly that it is a miracle that they were not worse; especially as he was horribly frightened all the time. When Galifron heard these words he looked all about him, and saw Charming standing, sword in hand. This put the giant into a terrible rage, and he aimed a blow at Charming with his huge iron club, which would certainly have killed him if it had reached him, but at that instant a raven perched upon the giant's head, and, pecking with its strong beak and beating with its great wings, so confused and blinded him that all his blows fell harmlessly upon the air, and Charming, rushing in, gave him several strokes with his sharp sword so that he fell to the ground. Whereupon, Charming cut off his head before he knew anything about it, and the raven from a tree close by croaked out: 'You see I have not forgotten the good turn you did me in killing the eagle. Today I think I have fulfilled my promise of repaying you.'

'Indeed, I owe you more gratitude than you ever owed me,' replied Charming.

And then he mounted his horse and rode off with Galifron's head.

When he reached the city the people ran after him in crowds, crying: 'Behold the brave Charming, who has killed the giant!' And their shouts reached the princess's ear, but she dared not ask what was happening, for fear she should hear that Charming had been killed. But very soon he arrived at the palace with the giant's head, of which she was still terrified, though it could no longer do her any harm.

'Princess,' said Charming, 'I have killed your enemy; I hope you will now consent to marry the king my master.'

'Oh dear! no,' said the princess, 'not until you have brought me some water from the Gloomy Cavern.

'Not far from here there is a deep cave, the entrance to which is guarded by two dragons with fiery eyes, who will not allow anyone to pass them. When you get into the cavern you will find an immense hole, which you must go down, and it is full of toads and snakes; at the bottom of this hole there is another little cave, in which rises the Fountain of Health and

Beauty. It is some of this water that I really must have: everything it touches becomes wonderful. The beautiful things will always remain beautiful, and the ugly things become lovely. If one is young one never grows old, and if one is old one becomes young. You see, Charming, I could not leave my kingdom without taking some of it with me.'

'Princess,' said he, 'you at least can never need this water, but I am an unhappy ambassador, whose death you desire. Where you send me I will go, though I know I shall never return.'

And, as the Princess Goldilocks showed no sign of relenting, he started with his little dog for the Gloomy Cavern. Everyone he met on the way said: 'What a pity that a handsome young man should throw away his life so carelessly! He is going to the cavern alone, though if he had a hundred men with him he could not succeed. Why does the princess ask impossibilities?' Charming said nothing, but he was very sad. When he was near the top of a hill he dismounted to let his horse graze, while Frisk amused himself by chasing flies. Charming knew he could not be far from the Gloomy Cavern, and on looking about him he saw a black hideous rock from which came a thick smoke, followed in a moment by one of the dragons with fire blazing from his mouth and eyes. His body was yellow and green, and his claws scarlet, and his tail was so long that it lay in a hundred coils. Frisk was so terrified at the sight of it that he did not know where to hide. Charming, quite determined to get the water or die, now drew his sword, and, taking the crystal flask which Pretty Goldilocks had given him to fill, said to Frisk: 'I feel sure that I shall never come back from this expedition;

when I am dead, go to the princess and tell her that her errand has cost me my life. Then find the king my master, and relate all my adventures to him.'

As he spoke he heard a voice calling: 'Charming, Charming!'

'Who calls me?' said he; then he saw an owl sitting in a hollow tree, who said to him: 'You saved my life when I was caught in the net, now I can repay you. Trust me with the flask, for I know all the ways of the Gloomy Cavern, and can fill it from the Fountain of Beauty.' Charming was only too glad to give her the flask, and she flitted into the cavern, quite unnoticed by the dragon, and after some time returned with the flask, filled to the very brim with sparkling water. Charming thanked her with all his heart, and joyfully hastened back to the town.

He went straight to the palace and gave the flask to the princess, who had no further objection to make. So she thanked Charming, and ordered that preparations should be made for her departure, and they soon set out together. The princess found Charming such an agreeable companion that she sometimes said to him: 'Why didn't we stay where we were? I could have made you king, and we should have been so happy!'

But Charming only answered: 'I could not have done anything that would have vexed my master so much, even for a kingdom, or to please you, though I think you are as beautiful as the sun.'

At last they reached the king's great city, and he came out to meet the princess, bringing magnificent presents, and the marriage was celebrated with great rejoicings. But Goldilocks was so fond of Charming that she could not be happy unless he was near her, and she was always singing his praises.

'If it hadn't been for Charming,' she said to the king, 'I should never have come here; you ought to be very much obliged to him, for he did the most impossible things and got me water from the Fountain of Beauty, so I can never grow old, and shall get prettier every year.'

Then Charming's enemies said to the king: 'It is a wonder that you are not jealous: the queen thinks there is nobody in the world like Charming. As if anybody you had sent could not have done just as much!'

'It is quite true, now I come to think of it,' said the king. 'Let him be chained hand and foot, and thrown into the tower.'

So they took Charming, and as a reward for having served the king so faithfully he was shut up in the tower, where he only saw the jailer, who brought him a piece of black bread and a pitcher of water every day.

However, little Frisk came to console him, and told him all the news.

When Pretty Goldilocks heard what had happened, she threw herself at the king's feet and begged him to set Charming free, but the more she cried, the more angry he was, and at last she saw that it was useless to say any more; but it made her very sad. Then the king took it into his head that perhaps he was not handsome enough to please the Princess Goldilocks, and he thought he would bathe his face with the water from the Fountain of Beauty, which was in the flask on a shelf in the princess's room, where she had placed it that she might see it often. Now it happened that one of the princess's ladies in chasing a spider had knocked the flask off the shelf and broken it, and every drop of the water had been spilt. Not knowing what to do, she had hastily swept away the pieces of crystal, and then remembered that in the king's room she had seen a flask of exactly the same shape, also filled with sparkling water. So, without saying a word, she fetched it and stood it upon the queen's shelf.

Now the water in this flask was what was used in the kingdom for getting rid of troublesome people. Instead of having their heads cut off in the usual way, their faces were bathed with the water, and they instantly fell asleep and never woke up any more. So, when the king, thinking to improve his beauty, took the flask and sprinkled the water upon his face, *he* fell asleep, and nobody could wake him.

Little Frisk was the first to hear the news, and he ran to tell Charming, who sent him to beg the princess not to forget the poor prisoner. All the palace was in confusion on account of the king's death, but tiny Frisk made his way through the crowd to the princess's side, and said: 'Madam, do not forget poor Charming.'

Then she remembered all he had done for her, and without saying a word to anyone went straight to the tower, and with her own hands took off Charming's chains. Then, putting a golden crown upon his head, and the royal mantle upon his shoulders, she said: 'Come, faithful Charming, I make you king, and will take you for my husband.'

Charming, once more free and happy, fell at her feet and thanked her for her gracious words.

Everybody was delighted that he should be king, and the wedding, which took place at once, was the prettiest that can be imagined, and Prince Charming and Princess Goldilocks lived happily ever after.

The Prince and the Fakir

There was once upon a time a king who had no children. Now this king went and lay down to rest at a place where four roads met, so that everyone who passed had to step over him.

At last a fakir came along, and he said to the king, 'Man, why are you lying here?'

He replied, 'Fakir, a thousand men have come and passed by; you pass on too.'

But the fakir said, 'Who are you, man?'

The king replied, 'I am a king, fakir. Of goods and gold I have no lack, but I have lived long and have no children. So I have come here to lie at the crossroads. My sins and offences have been very many, so I have come and am lying here that men may pass over me, and perchance my sins may be forgiven me, and God may be merciful, and I may have a son.'

The fakir answered him, 'Oh king! If you have children, what will you give me?'

'Whatever you ask, fakir,' answered the king.

The fakir said, 'Of goods and gold I have no lack, but I will say a prayer for you, and you will have two sons; one of those sons will be mine.'

Then he took out two sweetmeats and handed them to the king, and said, 'King! take these two sweetmeats and give them to your wives; give them to the wives you love best.'

The king took the sweetmeats and put them in his bosom.

Then the fakir said, 'King! in a year I will return,

and of the two sons who will be born to you one is mine and one yours.'

The king said, 'Well, I agree.'

Then the fakir went on his way, and the king came home and gave one sweetmeat to each of his two wives. After some time two sons were born to the king. Then what did the king do but place those two sons in an underground room, which he had built in the earth.

Some time passed, and one day the fakir appeared, and said, 'King! bring me those sons of yours!'

What did the king do but bring two slave-girls' sons and present them to the fakir. While the fakir was sitting there the king's sons were sitting down below in their cellar eating their food. Just then a hungry ant had carried away a grain of rice from their food, and was going along with it to her children. Another stronger ant came up and attacked her in order to get this grain of rice. The first ant said, 'O ant, why do you drag this away from me? I have long been lame in my feet, and I have got just one grain, and am carrying it to my children. The king's sons are sitting in the cellar eating their food; you go and fetch a grain from there; why should you take mine from me?' On this the second ant let go and did not rob the first, but went off to where the king's sons were eating their food.

On hearing this the fakir said, 'King! these are not your sons; go and bring those children who are eating their food in the cellar.'

Then the king went and brought his own sons. The fakir chose the elder son and took him away, and set off with him on his journey, When he got home he told the king's son to go out to gather fuel.

So the king's son went out to gather cow-dung, and when he had collected some he brought it in.

Then the fakir looked at the king's son and put on a great pot, and said, 'Come round here, my pupil.'

But the king's son said, 'Master first, and pupil after.'

The fakir told him to come once, he told him twice, he told him three times, and each time the king's son answered, 'Master first, and pupil after.'

Then the fakir made a dash at the king's son, thinking to catch him and throw him into the caldron. There were about a hundred gallons of oil in this caldron, and the fire was burning beneath it. Then the king's son, lifting the fakir, gave him a jerk and threw him into the caldron, and he was burnt, and became roast meat. He then saw a key of the fakir's lying there; he took this key and opened the door of the fakir's house. Now many men were locked up in this house; two horses were standing there in a hut of the fakir's; two greyhounds were tied up there; two simurgs were imprisoned, and two tigers also stood there. So the king's son let all the creatures go, and took them out of the house, and they all returned thanks to God. Next he let out all the men who were in prison. He took away with him the two horses, and he took away the two tigers, and he took away the two hounds, and he took away the two simurgs, and with them he set out for another country.

As he went along the road he saw above him a bald man, grazing a herd of calves, and this bald man called out to him, 'Fellow! can you fight at all?'

The king's son replied, 'When I was little I could fight a bit, and now, if anyone wants to fight, I would not turn my back. Come, I will fight you.'

The bald man said, 'If I throw you, you shall be my slave; and if you throw me, I will be your slave.' So they began to fight, and the king's son threw him.

On this the king's son said, 'I will leave my beasts here, my simurgs, tigers, and dogs, and horses; they will all stay here while I go to the city to see the sights. I appoint the tiger as guard over my property. And as you are my slave, you, too, must stay here with my belongings.' So the king's son started off to the city to see the sights, and arrived at a pool.

He saw that it was a pleasant pool, and thought he would stop and bathe there, and therewith he began to strip off his clothes.

Now the king's daughter, who was sitting on the roof of the palace, saw his royal marks, and she said, 'This man is a king; when I marry, I will marry him and no other.' So she said to her father, 'My father; I wish to marry.'

'Good,' said her father.

Then the king made a proclamation: 'Let all men, great and small, attend today in the hall of audience, for the king's daughter will today take a husband.'

All the men of the land assembled, and the traveller prince also came, dressed in the fakir's clothes, saying to himself, 'I must see this ceremony today.' He went in and sat down.

The king's daughter came out and sat in the balcony, and cast her glance round all the assembly. She noticed that the traveller prince was sitting in the assembly in fakir's attire.

The princess said to her handmaiden, 'Take this dish of henna, go to that traveller dressed like a fakir, and sprinkle scent on him from the dish.'

The handmaiden obeyed the princess's order, went to him and sprinkled the scent over him.

Then the people said, 'The slave-girl has made a mistake.'

But she replied, 'The slave-girl has made no mistake, 'tis her mistress has made the mistake.'

On this the king married his daughter to the fakir, who was really no fakir, but a prince.

What fate had decreed came to pass in that country, and they were married. But the king of that city became very sad in his heart, because when so many chiefs and nobles were sitting there his daughter had chosen none of them, but had chosen that fakir; but he kept these thoughts concealed in his heart.

One day the traveller prince said, 'Let all the king's sons-in-law come out with me today to hunt.'

People said, 'What is this fakir that he should go a-hunting?'

However, they all set out for the hunt, and fixed their meeting-place at a certain pool.

The newly married prince went to his tigers, and told his tigers and hounds to kill and bring in a great number of gazelles and hog-deer and markhor. Instantly they killed and brought in a great number. Then taking with him these spoils of the chase, the prince came to the pool settled on as a meeting-place. The other princes, sons-in-law of the king of that city, also assembled there; but they had brought in no game, and the new prince had brought a great deal. Thence they returned home to the town, and went to the king their father-in-law, to present their game.

Now that king had no son. Then the new prince told him that in fact he, too, was a prince. At this the king, his father-in-law, was greatly delighted and took him by the hand and embraced him. He seated him by himself, saying, 'O prince, I return thanks that you have come here and become my son-in-law; I am very happy at this, and I make over my kingdom to you.'

The Princess and the Pea

There was once upon a time a prince who wanted to marry a princess, but she must be a true princess. So he travelled through the whole world to find one, but there was always something against each. There were plenty of princesses, but he could not find out if they were true princesses. In every case there was some little defect, which showed the genuine article was not yet found. So he came home again in very low spirits, for he had wanted very much to have a true princess. One night there was a dreadful storm; it thundered and lightened and the rain streamed down in torrents. It was fearful! There was a knocking heard at the palace gate, and the old king went to open it.

There stood a princess outside the gate; but oh, in what a sad plight she was from the rain and the storm! The water was running down from her hair and her dress into the points of her shoes and out at the heels again. And yet she said she was a true princess!

'Well, we shall soon find out!' thought the old queen. But she said nothing, and went into the sleeping-room, took off all the bedclothes, and laid a pea on the base of the bed. Then she put twenty mattresses on top of the pea, and twenty eiderdown quilts on the top of the mattresses. And this was the bed in which the princess was to sleep.

The next morning the queen was asked how she had slept.

'Oh, very badly!' said the princess. 'I scarcely closed my eyes all night! I am sure I don't know what was in

the bed. I lay on something so hard that my whole body is black and blue. It is dreadful!'

Now they perceived that she was a true princess, because she had felt the pea through the twenty mattresses and the twenty eiderdown quilts.

No one but a true princess could be so sensitive.

So the prince married her, for now he knew that at last he had got hold of a true princess. And the pea was put into the Royal Museum, where it is still to be seen if no one has stolen it. Now this is a true story.

Princess Belle-Etoile

Once upon a time there were three princesses, named Roussette, Brunette and Blondine, who lived in retirement with their mother, a princess who had lost all her former grandeur. One day an old woman called and asked for a dinner, as this princess was an excellent cook. After the meal was over, the old woman, who was a fairy, promised that their kindness should be rewarded, and immediately disappeared.

Shortly after, the king came that way, with his brother and the lord admiral. They were all so struck with the beauty of the three princesses, that the king married the youngest, Blondine, his brother married Brunette, and the lord admiral married Roussette.

The good fairy, who had brought all this about, also caused the young Queen Blondine to have three lovely children, two boys and a girl, out of whose hair fell fine jewels. Each had a brilliant star on the forehead, and a rich chain of gold around the neck. At the same time Brunette, her sister, gave birth to a handsome boy. Now the young queen and Brunette were much attached to each other, but Roussette was jealous of both, and the old queen, the king's mother, hated them. Brunette died soon after the birth of her son, and the king was absent on a warlike expedition, so Roussette joined the wicked old queen in forming plans to injure Blondine. They ordered Feintise, the old queen's waiting-woman, to strangle the queen's three children and the son of Princess Brunette, and bury them secretly. But as she was

353

about to execute this wicked order, she was so struck by their beauty, and the appearance of the sparkling stars on their foreheads, that she shrank from the deed.

So she had a boat brought round to the beach, and put the four babes, with some strings of jewels, into a cradle, which she placed in the boat, and then set it adrift. The boat was soon far out at sea. The waves rose, the rain poured in torrents, and the thunder roared. Feintise could not doubt that the boat would be swamped, and felt relieved by the thought that the poor little innocents would perish, for she would otherwise always be haunted by the fear that something would occur to betray the share she had had in their preservation.

But the good fairy protected them, and after floating at sea for seven days they were picked up by a corsair. He was so struck by their beauty that he altered his course, and took them home to his wife, who had no children. She was transported with joy when he placed them in her hands. They admired together the wonderful stars, the chains of gold that could not be taken off their necks, and their long ringlets. Much greater was the woman's astonishment when she combed them, for at every instant there rolled out of their hair pearls, rubies, diamonds and emeralds. She told her husband of it, who was not less surprised than herself.

'I am very tired,' said he, 'of a corsair's life, and if the locks of those little children continue to supply us with such treasures, I will give up roaming the seas.' The corsair's wife, whose name was Corsine, was enchanted at this, and loved the four infants so much the more for it. She named the princess, Belle-Etoile, her eldest brother, Petit-Soleil, the second, Heureux, and the son of Brunette, Cheri.

As they grew older, the corsair applied himself seriously to their education, as he felt convinced there was some great mystery attached to their birth.

The corsair and his wife had never told the story of the four children, who passed for their own. They were exceedingly united, but Prince Cheri entertained for Princess Belle-Etoile a greater affection than the other two. The moment she expressed a wish for anything, he would attempt even impossibilities to gratify her.

One day Belle-Etoile overheard the corsair and his wife talking. 'When I fell in with them,' said the corsair, 'I saw nothing that could give me any idea of their birth.' 'I suspect,' said Corsine, 'that Cheri is not their brother, he has neither star nor neck-chain.' Belle-Etoile immediately ran and told this to the three princes, who resolved to speak to the corsair and his wife, and ask them to let them set out to discover the secret of their birth. After some remonstrance they gained their consent. A beautiful vessel was prepared, and the young princess and the three princes set out. They determined to sail to the very spot where the corsair had found them, and made preparations for a grand sacrifice to the fairies, for their protection and guidance. They were about to immolate a turtle-dove, but the princess saved its life, and let it fly. At this moment a syren issued from the water, and said, 'Cease your anxiety, let your vessel go where it will; land where it stops.' The vessel now sailed more quickly. Suddenly they came in sight of a city so beautiful that they were anxious their vessel should enter the port. Their wishes were accomplished; they landed, and the shore in a moment was crowded with people, who had observed the magnificence of their ship. They ran and told the king the news, and as the grand terrace of the palace looked out upon the sea-shore, he speedily repaired thither. The princes, hearing the people say, 'There is the king,' looked up, and made a profound obeisance. He looked earnestly at them, and was as much charmed by the princess's beauty, as by the handsome mien of the young princes. He ordered his equerry to offer them his protection, and everything that they might require.

The king was so intrigued with these four children that he went into the chamber of the queen, his mother, to tell her of the wonderful stars which shone upon their foreheads, and everything that he admired in them. She was thunderstruck at it, and was terribly afraid that Feintise had betrayed her, and sent her secretary to enquire about them. What he told her of their ages confirmed her suspicions. She sent for Feintise, and threatened to kill her. Feintise, half dead with terror, confessed all; but promised, if she spared her, that she would still find means to do away with them. The queen was appeased; and, indeed, old Feintise did all she could for her own sake. Taking a guitar, she went and sat down opposite the princess's window, and sang a song which Belle-Etoile thought so pretty that she invited her into her chamber. 'My fair child,' said Feintise, 'heaven has made you very lovely, but you yet want one thing – the dancing-water. If I had possessed it, you would not have seen a white hair upon my head, nor a wrinkle on my face. Alas! I knew this secret too late; my charms had already faded.' 'But where shall I find this dancing-water?' asked Belle-Etoile. 'It is in the luminous forest,' said Feintise. 'You have three brothers; does not any one of them love you sufficiently to go and fetch some?' 'My brothers all love me,' said the princess, 'but there is one of them who would not refuse me anything.' The perfidious old woman retired, delighted at having been so successful. The princes, returning from the chase, found Belle-Etoile engrossed by the advice of Feintise. Her anxiety about it was so apparent, that Cheri, who thought of nothing but pleasing her, soon found out the cause of it, and, in spite of her entreaties, he mounted his white horse, and set out in search of the dancing-water. When supper-time arrived, and the princess did not see her brother Cheri, she could neither eat nor drink, and desired he might be sought for everywhere, and sent messengers to find him and bring him back.

The wicked Feintise was very anxious to know the result of her advice; and when she heard that Cheri had already set out, she was delighted, and reported to the queen-mother all that had passed. 'I admit, madam,' said she, 'that I can no longer doubt that they are the same four children: but one of the princes is already gone to seek the dancing-water, and will no doubt perish in the attempt, and I shall find similar means to do away with all of them.'

The plan she had adopted with regard to Prince Cheri was one of the most certain, for the dancing-water was not easily to be obtained; it was so notorious from the misfortunes which occurred to all who sought it, that everyone knew the road to it. He was eight days without taking any repose but in the woods. At the end of this period he began to suffer very much from the heat; but it was not the heat of the sun, and he did not know the cause of it, until from the top of a mountain he perceived the luminous forest; all the trees were burning without being consumed, and casting out flames to such a distance that the country around was a dry desert.

Into this terrible scene he descended, and more than once gave himself up for lost. As he approached this great fire he was ready to die with thirst and perceiving a spring falling into a marble basin, he alighted from his horse, approached it, and stooped to take up some water in the little golden vase which he had brought with him, but just then he saw a turtle-dove drowning in the fountain. Cheri took pity on it, and saved it. 'My Lord Cheri,' she said, 'I am not ungrateful; I can guide you to the dancing-water, which, without me, you could never obtain, as it rises in the middle of the forest, and can only be reached by going underground.' The dove then flew away, and summoned a number of foxes, badgers, moles, snails, ants, and all sorts of creatures that burrow in the earth. Cheri got off his horse at the entrance of the subterranean passage they made for him, and groped his way after the kind dove, which safely conducted him to the fountain. The prince filled his golden vase; and returned the same way he came.

He found Belle-Etoile sorrowfully seated under some trees, but when she saw him she was so pleased that she scarcely knew how to welcome him.

Old Feintise learned from her spies that Cheri had returned, and that the princess, having washed her face with the dancing-water, had become more lovely than ever. Finding this, she lost no time in artfully making the princess sigh for the wonderful singing-apple. Prince Cheri again found her unhappy, and again found out the cause, and once more set out on his white horse, leaving a letter for Belle-Etoile.

In the meanwhile, the king did not forget the lovely children, and reproached them for never going to the palace. They excused themselves by saying that their brother's absence prevented them.

Prince Cheri at break of day perceived a handsome young man, from whom he learned where the singing-apple was to be found; but after travelling some time without seeing any sign of it, he saw a poor turtle-dove fall at his feet almost dead. He took pity on it, and restored it, whereupon it said, 'Good-day, handsome Cheri, you are destined to save my life, and I to do you signal service. You are come to seek for the singing-apple but it is guarded by a terrible dragon.' The dove then led him to a place where he found a suit of armour, all of glass, and by her advice he put it on, and boldly went to meet the dragon. The two-headed monster came bounding along, fire issuing from his throat, but when he saw his alarming figure multiplied in the prince's mirrors he was frightened in his turn. He stopped, and looking fiercely at the prince, apparently laden with dragons, he took flight and threw himself into a deep chasm. The prince then found the tree, which was surrounded with human bones, and breaking off an apple, prepared to return to the princess. She had never slept during his absence, and ran to meet him eagerly.

When the wicked Feintise heard the sweet singing of the apple, her grief was excessive, for instead of doing harm to these lovely children, she only did them good by her perfidious counsels. She allowed some days to pass by without showing herself; and then once more made the princess unhappy by saying that the dancing-water and the singing-apple were useless without the little green bird that tells everything.

Cheri again set out, and after some trouble learnt that this bird was to be found on the top of a frightful rock, in a frozen climate. At length, at dawn of day, he perceived the rock, which was very high and very steep, and upon the summit of it was the bird, speaking like an oracle, telling wonderful things. He thought that with a little dexterity it would be easy to catch it, for it seemed very tame. He got off his horse, and climbed up very quietly. He was so close to the green bird that he thought he could lay hands on it, when suddenly the rock opened and he fell into a spacious hall, and became as motionless as a statue; he could neither stir, nor utter a complaint at his deplorable situation. Three hundred knights, who had made the same attempt, were in the same state. To look at each other was the only thing permitted them.

The time seemed so long to Belle-Etoile, and still no signs of her beloved Cheri, that she fell danger-ously ill; and in the hopes of curing her, Petit-Soleil resolved to seek him. But he too was swallowed up by the rock and fell into the great hall. The first person he saw was Cheri, but he could not speak to him; and Prince Heureux, following soon after, met with the same fate as the other two.

When Feintise was aware that the third prince was gone, she was exceedingly delighted at the success of her plan; and when Belle-Etoile, inconsolable at finding not one of her brothers return, reproached herself for their loss, and resolved to follow them, she was quite overjoyed.

The princess was disguised as a cavalier, but had no other armour than her helmet. She was dreadfully cold as she drew near the rock, but seeing a turtle-dove lying on the snow, she took it up, warmed it, and restored it to life: and the dove reviving, gaily said, 'I know you, in spite of your disguise; follow my advice: when you arrive at the rock, remain at the bottom and begin to sing the sweetest song you know; the green bird will listen to you; you must then pretend to go to sleep; when it sees me, it will come down to peck me, and at that moment you will be able to seize it.'

All this fell out as the dove foretold. The green bird begged for liberty. 'First,' said Belle-Etoile, 'I wish that thou wouldst restore my three brothers to me.'

'Under my left wing there is a red feather,' said the bird: 'pull it out, and touch the rock with it.'

The princess hastened to do as she was instructed; the rock split from the top to the bottom and she entered with a victorious air the hall in which stood the three princes with many others; she ran towards Cheri, who did not know her in her helmet and male

361

attire, and could neither speak nor move. The green bird then told the princess she must rub the eyes and mouths of all those she wished to disenchant with the red feather, which good office she did to all.

The three princes and Belle-Etoile hastened to present themselves to the king; and when Belle-Etoile showed her treasures, the little green bird told him that the Princes Petit-Soleil and Heureux and the Princess Belle-Etoile were his children, and that Prince Cheri was his nephew. Queen Blondine, who had mourned for them all these years, embraced them, and the wicked queen-mother and old Feintise were justly punished. And the king, who thought his nephew Cheri the handsomest man at court, consented to his marriage with Belle-Etoile. And lastly, to make everyone happy, the king sent for the corsair and his wife, who gladly came.

Puss in Boots

There was a miller who left no more estate to the three sons he had than his mill, his ass and his cat. The partition was soon made. Neither scrivener nor attorney was sent for. They would soon have eaten up all the poor patrimony. The eldest had the mill, the second the ass and the youngest nothing but the cat. The poor young fellow was quite comfortless at having so poor a lot.

'My brothers,' said he, 'may get their living handsomely enough by joining their stocks together; but for my part, when I have eaten up my cat, and made me a muff of his skin, I must die of hunger.'

The cat, who heard all this, but made as if he did not, said to him with a grave and serious air: 'Do not thus afflict yourself, my good master. You have nothing else to do but to give me a bag and get a pair of boots made for me that I may scamper through the dirt and the brambles, and you shall see that you have not so bad a portion in me as you imagine.'

The cat's master did not build very much upon what he said. He had often seen him play a great many cunning tricks to catch rats and mice, as when he used to hang by the heels or hide himself in the meal and make as if he were dead; so that he did not altogether despair of his affording him some help in his miserable condition. When the cat had what he asked for he booted himself very gallantly, and putting his bag about his neck, he held the strings of it in his two forepaws and went into a warren where was great abundance of rabbits. He put bran and sow-thistle into his bag, and stretching out at length, as if he had been dead, he waited for some young rabbits, not yet acquainted with the deceits of the world, to come and rummage his bag for what he had put in it.

Scarce was he lain down but he had what he wanted. A rash and foolish young rabbit jumped into his bag, and Monsieur Puss, immediately drawing close the strings, took and killed him without pity. Proud of his prey, he went with it to the palace and asked to speak with his majesty. He was shown upstairs into the king's apartment, and, making a low reverence, said to him: 'I have brought you, sir, a rabbit of the warren, which my noble lord the Marquis of Carabas' (for that was the title which puss was pleased to give his master) 'has commanded me to present to your majesty from him.'

'Tell thy master,' said the king, 'that I thank him and that he does me a great deal of pleasure.'

Another time he went and hid himself among some standing corn, holding still his bag open, and when a brace of partridges ran into it he drew the strings and so caught them both. He went and made a present of these to the king, as he had done before of the rabbit which he took in the warren. The king, in like manner, received the partridges with great pleasure, and ordered him some money for drink.

The cat continued for two or three months thus to carry his majesty, from time to time, game of his master's taking. One day in particular, when he knew for certain that he was to take the air along the river-side, with his daughter, the most beautiful princess in the world, he said to his master: 'If you will follow my advice your fortune is made. You have nothing else to do but go and wash yourself in the river, in that part I shall show you, and leave the rest to me.'

The Marquis of Carabas did what the cat advised him to, without knowing why or wherefore. While he was washing, the king passed by, and the cat began to cry out: 'Help! help! My Lord Marquis of Carabas is going to be drowned.'

'Help! help! My Lord Marquis of Carabas is
going to be drowned.'

At this noise the king put his head out of the coach-window, and, finding it was the cat who had so often brought him such good game, he commanded his guards to run immediately to the assistance of his lordship the Marquis of Carabas. While they were drawing the poor marquis out of the river, the cat came up to the coach and told the king that, while his master was washing, there came by some rogues, who went off with his clothes, though he had cried out: 'Thieves! thieves!' several times, as loud as he could.

This cunning cat had hidden them under a great stone. The king immediately commanded the officers of his wardrobe to run and fetch one of his best suits for the Lord Marquis of Carabas.

The king received him with many compliments, and as the fine clothes he had given him extremely set off his good mien (for he was well made and very handsome in his person), the king's daughter took a secret inclination to him, and the Marquis of Carabas had no sooner cast her two or three respectful and somewhat tender glances but she fell in love with him to distraction. The king would needs have him come into the coach and take part in the airing. The cat, quite overjoyed to see his project begin to succeed, marched on before, and, meeting with some country-men, who were mowing a meadow, he said to them: 'Good people, you who are mowing, if you do not tell the king that the meadow you mow belongs to my Lord Marquis of Carabas, you shall be chopped as small as herbs for the pot.'

The king did not fail asking of the mowers to whom the meadow they were mowing belonged.

'To my Lord Marquis of Carabas,' answered they altogether, for the cat's threats had made them afraid.

*The cat met with some countrymen, who were
mowing a meadow*

'You see, sir,' said the marquis, 'this is a meadow
which never fails to yield a plentiful harvest every
year.'

The Master Cat, who went still on before, met with
some reapers, and said to them: 'Good people, you
who are reaping, if you do not tell the king that all this
corn belongs to the Marquis of Carabas, you shall be
chopped as small as herbs for the pot.'

The king, who passed by a moment after, would
needs know to whom all that corn, which he then
saw, did belong.

'To my Lord Marquis of Carabas,' replied the
reapers, and the king was very well pleased with it,
as well as the marquis, whom he congratulated thereupon. The Master Cat, who went always before, said

the same words to all he met, and the king was astonished at the vast estates of my Lord Marquis of Carabas.

Monsieur Puss came at last to a stately castle, the master of which was an ogre, the richest had ever been known; for all the lands which the king had then gone over belonged to this castle. The cat, who had taken care to inform himself who this ogre was and what he could do, asked to speak with him, saying he could not pass so near his castle without having the honour of paying his respects to him.

The ogre received him as civilly as an ogre could do, and made him sit down.

'I have been assured,' said the cat, 'that you have the gift of being able to change yourself into all sorts of creatures you have a mind to; you can, for example, transform yourself into a lion, or an elephant, and the like.'

'That is true,' answered the ogre very briskly; 'and to convince you, you shall see me now become a lion.'

Puss was so sadly terrified at the sight of a lion so near him that he immediately got into the roof gutter, not without abundance of trouble and danger, because of his boots, which were of no use at all to him in walking upon the tiles. A little while after, when Puss saw that the ogre had resumed his natural form, he came down, and owned he had been very much frightened.

'I have been, moreover, informed,' said the cat, 'but I know not how to believe it, that you have also the power to take on you the shape of the smallest animals; for example, to change yourself into a rat or a mouse; but I must own to you I take this to be impossible.'

'Impossible!' cried the ogre; 'you shall see that presently.'

And at the same time he changed himself into a mouse, and began to run about the floor. Puss no sooner perceived this but he fell upon him and ate him up.

Meanwhile the king, who saw, as he passed, this fine castle of the ogre's, had a mind to go into it. Puss, who heard the noise of his majesty's coach passing over the drawbridge, ran out, and said to the king: 'Your majesty is welcome to this castle of my Lord Marquis of Carabas.'

'What! my Lord Marquis,' cried the king, 'and does this castle also belong to you? There can be nothing finer than this court with all the stately buildings around it; let us go in, if you please.'

The marquis gave his hand to the princess, and

followed the king, who went first. They passed into a spacious hall, where they found a magnificent collation, which the ogre had prepared for his friends, who were that very day to visit him, but dared not enter, knowing the king was there. His majesty was perfectly charmed with the good qualities of my Lord Marquis of Carabas, as was his daughter, who had fallen violently in love with him, and, seeing the vast estate he possessed, said to him, after having drunk five or six glasses: 'It will be owing to yourself only, my Lord Marquis, if you are not my son-in-law.'

The marquis, making several low bows, accepted the honour which his majesty conferred upon him, and forthwith, that very same day, married the princess.

Puss became a great lord, and never ran after mice any more, except for his diversion.

The Red Shoes

There was once a little girl, very nice and very pretty, but so poor that she had to go barefooted all summer. And in winter she had to wear thick wooden shoes that chafed her ankles until they were red, oh, as red as could be.

In the middle of the village lived Old Mother Shoemaker. She took some old scraps of red cloth and did her best to make them into a little pair of shoes. They were a bit clumsy, but well meant, for she intended to give them to the little girl. Karen was the little girl's name.

The first time Karen wore her new red shoes was on the very day when her mother was buried. Of course, they were not right for mourning, but they were all she had, so she put them on and walked bare-legged after the plain wicker coffin.

Just then a large old carriage came by, with a large old lady inside it. She looked at the little girl and took pity upon her. And she went to the parson and said: 'Give the little girl to me, and I shall take good care of her.'

Karen was sure that this happened because she wore red shoes, but the old lady said the shoes were hideous, and ordered them to be burned. Karen was given proper new clothes. She was taught to read, and she was taught to sew. People said she was pretty, but her mirror told her, 'You are more than pretty. You are beautiful.'

It happened that the queen came travelling through the country with her little daughter, who was a princess. Karen went with all the people who flocked to see them at the castle. The little princess, all dressed in white, came to the window to let them admire her. She didn't wear a train, and she didn't wear a gold crown, but she did wear a pair of splendid red morocco shoes.

Of course, they were much nicer than the ones Old Mother Shoemaker had put together for little Karen, but there's nothing in the world like a pair of red shoes!

When Karen was old enough to be confirmed, new clothes were made for her, and she was to have new shoes. They went to the house of a thriving shoemaker, to have him take the measure of her little feet. In his shop were big glass cases, filled with the prettiest shoes and the shiniest boots. They looked most attractive but, as the old lady did not see very well, they did not attract her. Among the shoes there was a pair of red leather ones which were just like those the princess had worn. How perfect they were! The shoemaker said he had made them for the daughter of a count, but that they did not quite fit her.

'They must be patent leather to shine so,' said the old lady.

'Yes, indeed they shine,' said Karen. As the shoes fitted Karen, the old lady bought them, but she had no idea they were red. If she had known that, she would never have let Karen wear them to her confirmation, which is just what Karen did.

Every eye was turned towards her feet. When she walked up the aisle to the chancel of the church, it seemed to her as if even those portraits of bygone ministers and their wives, in starched ruffs and long black gowns – even they fixed their eyes upon her red shoes. She could think of nothing else, even when the pastor laid his hands upon her head and spoke of her holy baptism, and her covenant with God, and her duty as a Christian. The solemn organ rolled, the children sang sweetly, and the old choir leader sang too, but Karen thought of nothing except her red shoes.

Before the afternoon was over, the old lady had heard from everyone in the parish that the shoes were red. She told Karen it was naughty to wear red shoes to church. Highly improper! In the future she was always to wear black shoes to church, even though they were her old ones.

Next Sunday there was holy communion. Karen looked at her black shoes. She looked at her red ones. She kept looking at her red ones until she put them on.

It was a fair, sunny day. Karen and the old lady took the path through the cornfield, where it was rather dusty. At the church door they met an old soldier, who stood with a crutch and wore a long, curious beard. It was more reddish than white. In fact it was quite red. He bowed down to the ground, and asked the old lady if he might dust her shoes. Karen put out her little foot too.

'Oh, what beautiful shoes for dancing,' the soldier said. 'Never come off when you dance,' he told the shoes, as he tapped the sole of each of them with his hand.

The old lady gave the soldier a penny, and went on into the church with Karen. All the people there stared at Karen's red shoes, and all the portraits stared too. When Karen knelt at the altar rail, and even when the chalice came to her lips, she could think only of her red shoes. It was as if they kept floating around in the chalice, and she forgot to sing the psalm. She forgot to say the lord's prayer.

Then church was over, and the old lady got into her carriage. Karen was lifting her foot to step in after her when the old soldier said, 'Oh, what beautiful shoes for dancing!'

Karen couldn't resist taking a few dancing steps, and once she began her feet kept on dancing. It was as if the shoes controlled her. She danced round the corner of the church – she simply could not help it. The coachman had to run after her, catch her and lift her into the carriage. But even there her feet went on dancing so that she gave the good old lady a terrible kicking. Only when she took her shoes off did her legs quieten down. When they got home the shoes were put away in a cupboard, but Karen would still go and look at them.

Shortly afterwards the old lady was taken ill, and it was said she could not recover. She required constant care and faithful nursing, and for this she depended on Karen. But a great ball was being given in the town, and Karen was invited. She looked at the old lady, who could not live in any case. She looked at the red shoes, for she thought there was no harm in looking. She put them on, for she thought there was no harm in that either. But then she went to the ball and began dancing. When she tried to turn to the right, the shoes turned to the left. When she wanted to dance up the ballroom, her shoes danced down. They danced down the stairs, into the street, and out through the gate of the town. Dance she did, and dance she must, straight into the dark woods.

Suddenly something shone through the trees, and she thought it was the moon, but it turned out to be the red-bearded soldier. He nodded and said, 'Oh, what beautiful shoes for dancing.'

She was terribly frightened, and tried to take off her shoes. She tore off her stockings, but the shoes had grown fast to her feet. And dance she did, for dance she must, over fields and valleys, in the rain and in the sun, by day and night. It was most dreadful by night. She danced over an unfenced graveyard, but the dead did not join her dance. They had better things to do. She tried to sit on a pauper's grave, where the bitter fennel grew, but there was no rest or peace for her there. And when she danced towards the open door of the church, she saw it guarded by an angel with long white robes and wings that reached from his shoulders down to the ground. His face was grave and stern, and in his hand he held a broad, shining sword.

'Dance you shall!' he told her. 'Dance in your red shoes until you are pale and cold, and your flesh shrivels down to your skeleton. Dance you shall from door to door, and wherever there are children proud and vain you must knock at the door till they hear you, and are afraid of you. Dance you shall. Dance always.'

'Have mercy upon me!' screamed Karen. But she did not hear the angel answer. Her shoes swept her out through the gate, and across the fields, along highways and byways, forever and always dancing.

One morning she danced by a door she knew well. There was the sound of a hymn, and a coffin was carried out covered with flowers. Then she knew the old lady was dead. She was all alone in the world now, and cursed by the angel of God.

Dance she did and dance she must, through the dark night. Her shoes took her through thorn and briar that scratched her until she bled. She danced

across the wastelands until she came to a lonely little house. She knew that this was where the executioner lived, and she tapped with her finger on his window pane.

'Come out!' she called. 'Come out! I can't come in, for I am dancing.'

The executioner said, 'You don't seem to know who I am. I strike off the heads of bad people, and I feel my axe beginning to quiver.'

'Don't strike off my head, for then I could not repent of my sins,' said Karen. 'But strike off my feet with the red shoes on them.'

She confessed her sin, and the executioner struck off her feet with the red shoes on them. The shoes danced away with her little feet, over the fields into the deep forest. But he made wooden feet and a pair of crutches for her. He taught her a hymn that prisoners sing when they are sorry for what they have done. She kissed his hand that held the axe, and went back across the wasteland.

'Now I have suffered enough for those red shoes,' she said. 'I shall go and be seen again in the church.' She hobbled to church as fast as she could, but when she got there the red shoes danced in front of her, and she was frightened and turned back.

All week long she was sorry, and cried many bitter tears. But when Sunday came again she said, 'Now I have suffered and cried enough. I think I must be as good as many who sit in church and hold their heads high.' She started out unafraid, but the moment she came to the church gate she saw her red shoes dancing before her. More frightened than ever, she turned away, and with all her heart she really repented.

She went to the pastor's house, and begged him to give her work as a servant. She promised to work hard, and do all that she could. Wages did not matter, if only she could have a roof over her head and be with good people. The pastor's wife took pity on her, and gave her work at the parsonage. Karen was faithful and serious. She sat quietly in the evening, and listened to every word when the pastor read the Bible aloud. The children were devoted to her, but when they spoke of frills and furbelows, and of being as beautiful as a queen, she would shake her head.

When they went to church next Sunday they asked her to go too, but with tears in her eyes she looked at her crutches, and shook her head. The others went to hear the word of God, but she went to her lonely little room, which was just big enough to hold her bed and one chair. She sat with her hymnal in her hands, and as she read it with a contrite heart she heard the organ roll. The wind carried the sound from the church to her window. Her face was wet with tears as she lifted it up, and said, 'Help me, O Lord!'

Then the sun shone bright, and the white-robed angel stood before her. He was the same angel she had seen that night, at the door of the church. But he no longer held a sharp sword. In his hand was a green branch, covered with roses. He touched the ceiling with it. There was a golden star where it touched and the ceiling rose high. He touched the walls and they opened wide. She saw the deep-toned organ. She saw the portraits of ministers and their wives. She saw the congregation sit in flower-decked pews, and sing from their hymnals. Either the church had come to the poor girl in her narrow little room or it was she who had been brought to the church. She sat in the pew with the pastor's family. When they had finished the hymn, they looked up and nodded to her.

'It was right for you to come, little Karen,' they said.

'It was God's own mercy,' she told them.

The organ sounded and the children in the choir sang, softly and beautifully. Clear sunlight streamed warm through the window, right down to the pew where Karen sat. She was so filled with the light of it, and with joy and with peace, that her heart broke. Her soul travelled along the shaft of sunlight to heaven, where no one questioned her about the red shoes.

Rapunzel

There were once a man and a woman who had long in vain wished for a child. At length it seemed that God was about to grant their desire.

These people had a little window at the back of their house from which could be seen a splendid garden, which was full of the most beautiful flowers and herbs. It was, however, surrounded by a high wall, and no one dared to go into it because it belonged to an enchantress who had great power and was dreaded by all the world. One day the woman was standing by this window and looking down into the garden, when she saw a bed which was planted with the most beautiful rampion (sometimes called rapunzium), and it looked so fresh and green that she longed for it; she quite pined away, and began to look pale and miserable.

Then her husband was alarmed, and asked: 'What ails you, dear wife?'

'Ah,' she replied, 'if I can't eat some of the rampion which is in the garden behind our house, I shall die.'

The man, who loved her, thought: 'Sooner than let your wife die, bring her some of the rampion yourself, let it cost what it will.'

At twilight, he clambered down over the wall into the garden of the enchantress, hastily clutched a handful of rampion and took it to his wife. She at once made herself a salad of it, and ate it greedily. It tasted so good to her – so very good – that the next day she longed for it three times as much as before. If he was to have any rest, her husband must once more descend into the garden. In the gloom of evening, therefore, he let himself down again; but when he had clambered down the wall he was terribly afraid, for he saw the enchantress standing before him.

'How can you dare,' said she, fixing him with an angry look, 'descend into my garden and steal my rampion like a thief? You shall suffer for it!'

'Ah,' answered he, 'let mercy take the place of justice. I only made up my mind to do it out of necessity. My wife saw your rampion from the window, and felt such a longing for it that she would have died if she had not got some to eat.'

Then the enchantress allowed her anger to be softened, and said to him: 'If the case be as you say, I will allow you to take away with you as much rampion as you will, only I make one condition: you

must give me the child which your
wife will bring into the world; it shall
be well treated, and I will care for it
like a mother.'

The man in his terror consented
to everything, and when the woman
was brought to bed, the enchantress
appeared at once, gave the child the
name of Rapunzel, and took it away
with her.

Rapunzel grew into the most beautiful
child under the sun. When she was
twelve years old, the enchantress shut
her into a tower, which lay in a forest. It
had neither stairs nor door, but quite at
the top was a little window. When the
enchantress wanted to go in, she placed
herself beneath it and cried: 'Rapunzel,
Rapunzel, let down your hair to me.'

Rapunzel had magnificent long hair,
fine as spun gold, and when she heard
the voice of the enchantress she un-
fastened her braided tresses, wound
them round one of the hooks of the
window above, and let the hair fall
twenty metres down, whereupon
the enchantress climbed up by it.

After a year or two, it came to pass that
the king's son rode through the forest
and passed by the tower. Coming from it
he heard a song, which was so charming
that he stood still and listened. This was
Rapunzel, who in her solitude passed
her time in letting her sweet voice

resound. The king's son wanted to climb up to her, and looked for the door of the tower, but none was to be found. He rode home, but the singing had so deeply touched his heart that every day he went out into the forest and listened to it. Once, when he was thus standing behind a tree, he saw that an enchantress came there, and he heard how she cried: 'Rapunzel, Rapunzel, let down your hair to me.' Then Rapunzel let down the braids of her hair, and the enchantress climbed up to her.

'If that is the ladder by which one mounts, I too will try my fortune,' said he, and the next day when it began to grow dark, he went to the tower and cried: 'Rapunzel, Rapunzel, let down your hair to me.' Immediately the hair fell down and the king's son climbed up.

At first Rapunzel was terribly frightened when a man, such as her eyes had never yet beheld, came to her; but the king's son began to talk to her quite like a friend, and told her that his heart had been so stirred that it had let him have no rest, and he had been determined to see her.

Then Rapunzel lost her fear, and when he asked her if she would take him for her husband, and she saw that he was young and handsome, she did not hesitate; she thought: 'He will love me more than old Dame Gothel does;' and she said yes, and laid her hand in his. She said: 'I will willingly go away with you, but I do not know how to get down. Bring with you a skein of silk every time that you come, and I will weave a ladder with it, and when that is ready I will descend, and you will take me away on your horse.' They agreed that until that time he should come to her every evening, for the old woman came by day.

The enchantress remarked nothing of this, until one day Rapunzel thoughtlessly said to her: 'Tell me, Dame Gothel, how it happens that you are so much heavier for me to draw up than the king's young son – he is with me in a moment.'

'Ah! you wicked child,' cried the enchantress. 'What do I hear you say! I thought I had separated you from all the world, yet you have deceived me!'

In her anger she clutched Rapunzel's beautiful tresses, wrapped them twice round her left hand, seized a pair of scissors with the right, and snip, snap, they were cut off, and the lovely braids lay on the ground. And she was so pitiless that she banished poor Rapunzel to a desert where she had to live in great grief and misery.

On the same day that she cast out Rapunzel, however, the enchantress fastened the braids of hair which she had cut off to the hook of the window, and when the king's son came and cried: 'Rapunzel, Rapunzel, let down your hair to me,' she let the hair down.

The king's son ascended, but instead of finding his dearest Rapunzel, he found the enchantress, who gazed at him with wicked and venomous looks.

'Aha!' she cried mockingly, 'you would fetch your dearest, but the beautiful bird sits no longer singing in the nest; the cat has got it, and will scratch out your eyes as well. Rapunzel is lost to you; you will never see her again.'

The king's son was beside himself with pain, and in his despair he leapt down from the tower. He escaped with his life, but the thorns into which he fell pierced his eyes. Then he wandered quite blind about the forest, ate nothing but roots and berries, and did naught but lament and weep over the loss of his dearest wife. Thus he roamed about in misery for some years, and at length came to the desert where Rapunzel, with the twins to whom she had given birth, a boy and a girl, lived in wretchedness.

He heard a voice, and it seemed so familiar to him that he went towards it, and when he approached, Rapunzel knew him and fell on his neck and wept. Two of her tears wetted his eyes and they grew clear again, and he could see with them as before. He led her to his kingdom, where he was joyfully received, and with their children they lived for a long time afterwards, happy and contented.

Ricky of the Tuft

Once upon a time there was a queen who bore a son so ugly and misshapen that for some time it was doubtful if he would have human form at all. But a fairy who was present at his birth promised that he should have plenty of brains, and added that by virtue of the gift which she had just bestowed upon him he would be able to impart to the person whom he should love best the same degree of intelligence which he possessed himself.

This somewhat consoled the poor queen, who was greatly disappointed at having brought into the world such a hideous brat. And indeed, no sooner did the child begin to speak than his sayings proved to be full of shrewdness, while all that he did was somehow so clever that he charmed everyone.

I forgot to mention that when he was born he had a little tuft of hair upon his head. For this reason he was called Ricky of the Tuft, Ricky being his family name.

Some seven or eight years later the queen of a neighbouring kingdom gave birth to twin daughters. The first one to come into the world was more beautiful than the dawn, and the queen was so over-joyed that it was feared her great excitement might do her some harm. The same fairy who had assisted at the birth of Ricky of the Tuft was present, and in order to moderate the transports of the queen she declared that this little princess would have no sense at all, and would be as stupid as she was beautiful. The queen was deeply mortified, and a moment or two later her chagrin became greater still, for the second daughter proved to be extremely ugly.

'Do not be distressed, madam,' said the fairy. 'Your daughter shall be recompensed in another way. She shall have so much good sense that her lack of beauty will scarcely be noticed.'

'May heaven grant it!' said the queen. 'But is there no means by which the elder, who is so beautiful, can be endowed with some intelligence?'

'In the matter of brains I can do nothing for her, madam,' said the fairy, 'but as regards beauty I can do a great deal. As there is nothing I would not do to please you, I will bestow upon her the power of making beautiful any person who shall greatly please her.'

As the two princesses grew up their perfections increased, and everywhere the beauty of the elder and the wit of the younger were the subject of common talk.

It is equally true that their defects also increased as they became older. The younger grew uglier every minute, and the elder daily became more stupid. Either she answered nothing at all when spoken to, or replied with some idiotic remark. At the same time she was so awkward that she could not set four china vases on the mantelpiece without breaking one of them, nor drink a glass of water without spilling half of it over her clothes.

Now although the elder girl possessed the great advantage which beauty always confers upon youth, she was nevertheless outshone in almost all company by her younger sister. At first everyone gathered round the beauty to see and admire her, but very soon they were all attracted by the graceful and easy conversation of the clever one. In a very short time the elder girl would be left entirely alone, while everybody clustered round her sister.

The elder princess was not so stupid that she was not aware of this, and she would willingly have surrendered all her beauty for half her sister's cleverness. Sometimes she was ready to die of grief, for the queen, though a sensible woman, could not refrain from occasionally reproaching her for her stupidity.

The princess had retired one day to a wood to bemoan her misfortune, when she saw approaching her an ugly little man, of very disagreeable appearance, but clad in magnificent attire.

This was the young Prince Ricky of the Tuft. He had fallen in love with her portrait, which was everywhere to be seen, and had left his father's kingdom in order to have the pleasure of seeing and talking to her.

Delighted to meet her thus alone, he approached with every mark of respect and politeness. But while he paid her the usual compliments he noticed that she was plunged in melancholy.

'I cannot understand, madam,' he said, 'how anyone with your beauty can be so sad as you appear. I can boast of having seen many fair ladies, and I declare that none of them could compare in beauty with you.'

'It is very kind of you to say so, sir,' answered the princess; and stopped there, at a loss what to say further.

'Beauty,' said Ricky, 'is of such great advantage that everything else can be disregarded; and I do not see that the possessor of it can have anything much to grieve about.'

To this the princess replied, 'I would rather be as

plain as you are and have some sense, than be as beautiful as I am and at the same time stupid.'

'Nothing more clearly displays good sense, madam, than a belief that one is not possessed of it. It follows, therefore, that the more one has, the more one fears it to be wanting.'

'I am not sure about that,' said the princess; 'but I know only too well that I am stupid, and this is the reason of the misery which is nearly killing me.'

'If that is all that troubles you, madam, I can easily put an end to your suffering.'

'How will you manage that?' said the princess.

'I am able, madam,' said Ricky of the Tuft, 'to bestow as much good sense as it is possible to possess on the person whom I love the most. You are that person, and it therefore rests with you to decide whether you will acquire so much intelligence. The only condition is that you shall consent to marry me.'

The princess was dumfounded, and remained silent.

'I can see,' pursued Ricky, 'that this suggestion perplexes you, and I am not surprised. But I will give you a whole year to make up your mind to it.'

The princess had so little sense, and at the same time desired it so ardently, that she persuaded herself the end of this year would never come. So she accepted the offer which had been made to her. No sooner had she given her word to Ricky that she would marry him within one year from that very day, than she felt a complete change come over her. She found herself able to say all that she wished with the greatest ease, and to say it in an elegant, finished and natural manner. She at once engaged Ricky in a brilliant and lengthy conversation, holding her own so well that Ricky feared he had given her a larger share of sense than he had retained for himself.

On her return to the palace there was amazement throughout the court at such a sudden and extra-ordinary change. Whereas formerly they had been accustomed to hear her give vent to silly, pert remarks, they now heard her express herself sensibly and wittily.

The entire court was overjoyed. The only person not too pleased was the younger sister, for now that she had no longer the advantage over the elder in wit, she seemed nothing but a little fright in comparison.

The king himself often took her advice, and several times held his councils in her apartment.

The news of this change spread abroad, and the princes of the neighbouring kingdoms made many attempts to captivate her. Almost all asked her in marriage. But she found none with enough sense, and so she listened to all without promising herself to any.

At last came one who was so powerful, so rich, so witty, and so handsome, that she could not help being somewhat attracted by him. Her father noticed this, and told her she could make her own choice of a husband. She had only to declare herself. Now the more sense one has, the more difficult it is to make up one's mind in an affair of this kind. After thanking her father, therefore, she asked for a little time to think it over. In order to ponder quietly what she had better do she went to walk in a wood – the very one, as it happened, where she had met Ricky of the Tuft.

While she walked, deep in thought, she heard beneath her feet a thudding sound, as though many people were running busily to and fro. Listening more attentively she heard voices. 'Bring me that boiler,' said one; then another, 'Put some wood on that fire!'

At that moment the ground opened, and she saw below what appeared to be a large kitchen full of cooks and scullions, and all the train of attendants which the preparation of a great banquet involves. A gang of some twenty or thirty spit-turners emerged and took up their positions round a very long table in a path in the wood. They all wore their cook's caps on one side, and with their basting implements in their hands they kept time together as they worked, to the lilt of a melodious song.

The princess was astonished by this spectacle, and asked for whom their work was being done.

'For Prince Ricky of the Tuft, madam,' said the foreman of the gang. 'His wedding is tomorrow.'

At this the princess was more surprised than ever. In a flash she remembered that it was a year to the very day since she had promised to marry Prince Ricky of the Tuft, and was taken aback by the recollection. The reason she had forgotten was that when she made the promise she was still without sense, and with the acquisition of that intelligence which the prince had bestowed upon her, all memory of her former stupidities had been blotted out.

She had not gone another thirty paces when Ricky of the Tuft appeared before her, gallant and resplendent, like a prince upon his wedding day.

'As you see, madam,' he said, 'I keep my word to the minute. I do not doubt that you have come to keep yours, and by giving me your hand to make me the happiest of men.'

'I will be frank with you,' replied the princess. 'I have not yet made up my mind on the point, and I am afraid I shall never be able to take the decision you desire.'

'You astonish me, madam,' said Ricky of the Tuft.

'I can well believe it,' said the princess, 'and undoubtedly, if I had to deal with a clown, or a man who lacked good sense, I should feel myself very awkwardly situated. "A princess must keep her word," he would say, "and you must marry me because you promised to!" But I am speaking to a man of the world, of the greatest good sense, and I am sure that he will listen to reason. As you are aware, I could not make up my mind to marry you even when I was entirely without sense; how can you expect that today, possessing the intelligence you bestowed on me, which makes me still more difficult to please than formerly, I should take a decision which I could not take then? If you wished so much to marry me, you were very wrong to relieve me of my stupidity, and to let me see more clearly than I did.'

'If a man who lacked good sense,' replied Ricky of the Tuft, 'would be justified, as you have just said, in reproaching you for breaking your word, why do you expect, madam, that I should act differently where the happiness of my whole life is at stake? Is it reasonable that people who have sense should be treated worse than those who have none? Would you maintain that for a moment – you, who so markedly have sense, and desired so ardently to have it? But, pardon me, let us get to the facts. With the exception of my ugliness, is there anything about me which displeases you? Are you dissatisfied with my breeding, my brains, my disposition, or my manners?'

'In no way,' replied the princess. 'I like all that you have displayed of the qualities you mention.'

'In that case,' said Ricky of the Tuft, 'happiness will be mine, for it lies in your power to make me the most attractive of men.'

'How can that be done?' asked the princess.

'It will happen of itself,' replied Ricky of the Tuft, 'if you love me well enough to wish that it be so. To remove your doubts, madam, let me tell you that the same fairy who on the day of my birth gave me the power of endowing with intelligence the woman of my choice, gave to you also the power of endowing with beauty the man whom you should love, and on whom you should wish to confer this favour.'

'If that is so,' said the princess, 'I wish with all my heart that you may become the handsomest and most attractive prince in the world, and I give you without reserve the boon which it is mine to bestow.'

No sooner had the princess uttered these words than Ricky of the Tuft appeared before her eyes as the handsomest, most graceful and attractive man that she had ever set eyes on.

Some people assert that this was not the work of fairy enchantment, but that love alone brought about the transformation. They say that the princess, as she mused upon her lover's constancy, upon his good sense, and his many admirable qualities of heart and head, grew blind to the deformity of his body and the ugliness of his face; that his humpback seemed no more than was natural in a man who could make the courtliest of bows, and that the dreadful limp which had formerly distressed her now betokened nothing more than a certain diffidence and charming deference of manner. They say further that she found his eyes shine all the brighter for their squint, and that this defect in them was to her but a sign of passionate love; while his great red nose she found naught but martial and heroic.

However that may be, the princess promised to marry him on the spot, provided only that he could obtain the consent of her royal father.

The king knew Ricky of the Tuft to be a prince both wise and witty, and on learning of his daughter's regard for him, he accepted him with pleasure as a son-in-law.

The wedding took place upon the morrow, just as Ricky of the Tuft had foreseen, and in accordance with the arrangements he had long ago put in train.

Moral:

Here's a fairy tale for you,
Which is just as good as true.
What we love is always fair,
Clever, deft and debonair.

Another Moral:

Nature oft, with open arms,
Lavishes a thousand charms;
But it is not these that bring
True love's truest offering.
'Tis some quality that lies
All unseen to other eyes –
Something in the heart or mind.

Rumpelstiltskin

By the side of a wood, in a country a long way off, ran
a fine stream of water; and upon the stream there
stood a mill. The miller's house was close by, and the
miller, you must know, had a very beautiful daughter.
She was, moreover, very shrewd and clever; and the
miller was so proud of her that he one day told the
king of the land, who used to come and hunt in the
wood, that his daughter could spin gold out of straw.

Now this king was very fond of money; and when
he heard the miller's boast his greediness was aroused,
and he sent for the girl to be brought before him.
Then he led her to a chamber in his palace
where there was a great heap of straw,
and gave her a spinning-wheel, and
said, 'All this must be spun
into gold before morning, if
you love your life.' It was in
vain that the poor maiden
said that it was only a silly
boast of her father's, and
that she could do no such
thing as spin straw into
gold; the chamber door
was locked, and she was
left alone.

She had sat down in one
corner of the room and begun
to bewail her hard fate, when on
a sudden the door opened and a

droll-looking little man hobbled in and said, 'Good-morrow to you, my good lass; why are you weeping?'

'Alas!' said she, 'I must spin this straw into gold, and I know not how.'

'What will you give me,' said the hobgoblin, 'to do it for you?'

'My necklace,' replied the maiden.

He took her at her word, and sat himself down to the wheel, and whistled and sang:

> 'Round about, round about,
> Lo and behold!
> Reel away, reel away,
> Straw into gold!'

And round about the wheel went merrily, the work was quickly done and the straw was all spun into gold.

When the king came and saw this, he was greatly astonished and pleased; but his heart grew still more greedy of gain, and he shut up the poor miller's daughter again with a fresh task. Then she knew not what to do, and sat down once more to weep; but the dwarf soon opened the door, and said, 'What will you give me to do your task?'

'The ring on my finger,' said she. So her little friend took the ring, and began to work at the wheel again, and whistled and sang:

> 'Round about, round about,
> Lo and behold!
> Reel away, reel away,
> Straw into gold!'

till, long before morning, all was done again.

The king was greatly delighted to see all this glittering treasure; but still he had not enough: so he took the miller's daughter to a yet larger heap, and said, 'All this must be spun tonight; and if it is, you shall be my queen.'

As soon as she was alone the dwarf came in and said, 'What will you give me to spin gold for you this third time?'

'I have nothing left,' said she.

'Then say you will give me,' said the little man, 'the first child that you may have when you are queen.'

'Well! That may never be,' thought the miller's daughter; and as she knew no other way to get her task done, she said she would do what he asked.

Round went the wheel again to the old song, and the manikin once more spun the heap into gold. The king came in the morning, and, finding all he wanted, was forced to keep his word; so he married the miller's daughter, and she really became queen.

At the birth of her first little child she was very glad, and forgot the dwarf, and what she had said. But one day he came into her room, where she was sitting playing with her baby, and put her in mind of it. Then she grieved sorely at her misfortune, and said she would give him all the wealth of the kingdom if he would let her off, but in vain; yet at last her tears softened him, and he said, 'I will give you three days' grace, and if during that time you tell me my name, you shall keep your child.'

Now the queen lay awake all night, thinking of all the odd names that she had ever heard; and she sent messengers all over the land to find out new ones. The next day the little man came, and she began with Timothy, Ichabod, Benjamin, Jeremiah, and all the names she could remember; but to all and each of them he said, 'Madam, that is not my name.'

The second day she began with all the comical names she could think of: Bandylegs, Hunchback, Crookshanks, and so on; but the little gentleman still said to every one of them, 'Madam, that is not my name.'

The third day one of the messengers came back, and said, 'I have travelled two days without hearing of any other names; but yesterday, as I was climbing a high hill among the trees of the forest, where the fox and the hare bid each other good-night, I saw a little hut; and before the hut burnt a fire; and round about the fire a funny little dwarf was dancing upon one leg, and singing:

> 'Merrily the feast I'll make,
> Today I'll brew, tomorrow bake;
> Merrily I'll dance and sing,
> For next day will a stranger bring.
> Little does my lady dream
> Rumpelstiltskin is my name!'

When the queen heard this she jumped for joy, and as soon as her little friend came she sat down upon her throne, and called all her court round to enjoy the fun; and the nurse stood by her side with the baby in her arms, as if it was quite ready to be given up. Then the little man began to chuckle at the thought of having the poor child to take home with him to his hut in the woods; and he cried out, 'Now, lady, what is my name?'

'Is it John?' asked she.

'No, madam!'

'Is it Tom?'

'No, madam!'

'Is it Jemmy?'

'It is not.'

'Can your name be Rumpelstiltskin?' asked the lady slyly.

'Some witch told you that – some witch told you that!' cried the little man, and dashed his right foot in a rage so deep into the floor that he was forced to lay hold of it with both hands to pull it out.

Then he made off as best he could, while the nurse laughed and the baby crowed; and all the court jeered at him for having had so much trouble for nothing, and said, 'We wish you a very good-morning, and a merry feast, Mr Rumpelstiltskin!'

The Sagacious Monkey and the Boar

Long, long ago, there lived in the province of Shinshin in Japan, a travelling monkey-man, who earned his living by taking round a monkey and showing off the animal's tricks.

One evening the man came home in a very bad temper and told his wife to send for the butcher the next morning.

The wife was very bewildered and asked her husband: 'Why do you wish me to send for the butcher?'

'It's no use taking that monkey round any longer, he's too old and forgets his tricks. I beat him with my stick all I know how, but he won't dance properly. I must now sell him to the butcher and make what money out of him I can. There is nothing else to be done.'

The woman felt very sorry for the poor little animal, and pleaded for her husband to spare the monkey, but her pleading was all in vain, the man was determined to sell him to the butcher.

Now the monkey was in the next room and overheard ever word of the conversation. He soon understood that he was to be killed, and he said to himself: 'Barbarous, indeed, is my master! Here I have served him faithfully for years, and instead of allowing me to end my days comfortably and in peace, he is going to let me be cut up by the butcher, and my poor body is to be roasted and stewed and eaten? Woe is me! What am I to do. Ah! a bright thought has

struck me! There is, I know, a wild boar living in the forest near by. I have often heard tell of his wisdom. Perhaps if I go to him and tell him the strait I am in he will give me his counsel. I will go and try.'

There was no time to lose. The monkey slipped out of the house and ran as quickly as he could to the forest to find the boar. The boar was at home, and the monkey began his tale of woe at once.

'Good Mr Boar, I have heard of your excellent wisdom. I am in great trouble and you alone can help me. I have grown old in the service of my master, and because I cannot dance properly now he intends to sell me to the butcher. What do you advise me to do? I know how clever you are!'

The boar was pleased at the flattery and determined to help the monkey. He thought for a little while and then said: 'Hasn't your master a baby?'

'Oh, yes,' said the monkey, 'he has one infant son.'

'Doesn't it lie by the door in the morning when your mistress begins the work of the day? Well, I will come round early and when I see my opportunity I will seize the child and run off with it.'

'What then?' said the monkey.

'Why the mother will be in a tremendous state, and before your master and mistress know what to do, you must run after me and rescue the child and take it home safely to its parents, and you will see that when the butcher comes they won't have the heart to sell you.'

The monkey thanked the boar many times and then went home. He did not sleep much that night, as you may imagine, for thinking of the morrow. His life depended on whether the boar's plan succeeded or not. He was the first up, waiting anxiously for what was to happen. It seemed to him a very long time before his master's wife began to move about and open the shutters to let in the light of day. Then all happened as the boar had planned. The mother placed her child near the porch as usual while she tidied up the house and got her breakfast ready.

The child was crooning happily in the morning sunlight, dabbing on the mats at the play of light and shadow. Suddenly there was a noise in the porch and a loud cry from the child. The mother ran out from the kitchen to the spot, only just in time to see the boar disappearing through the gate with her child in its clutch. She flung out her hands with a loud cry of despair and rushed into the inner room where her husband was still sleeping soundly.

He sat up slowly and rubbed his eyes, and crossly demanded what his wife was making all that noise about. By the time the man was alive to what had happened, and they both got outside the gate, the boar had got well away, but they saw the monkey running after the thief as hard as his legs would carry him.

Both the man and wife were moved to admiration at the plucky conduct of the sagacious monkey, and their gratitude knew no bounds when the faithful monkey brought the child safely back to their arms.

'There!' said the wife. 'This is the animal you want to kill – if the monkey hadn't been here we should have lost our child for ever.'

'You are right, wife, for once,' said the man as he carried the child into the house. 'You may send the butcher back when he comes, and now give us all a good breakfast and the monkey too.'

When the butcher arrived he was sent away with an order for some boar's meat for the evening dinner, and the monkey was petted and lived the rest of his days in peace, nor did his master ever strike him again.

Sleeping Beauty

Once upon a time there was a king and a queen, who were very sorry that they had no children – so sorry that it cannot be told.

At last, however, the queen had a daughter. There was a very fine christening; and the princess had for her godmothers all the fairies they could find in the whole kingdom (there were seven of them), so that every one of them might confer a gift upon her, as was the custom of fairies in those days. By this means the princess had all the perfections imaginable.

After the christening was over, the company returned to the king's palace, where was prepared a great feast for the fairies. There was placed before every one of them a magnificent cover with a case of massive gold, wherein were a spoon and a knife and fork, all of pure gold set with diamonds and rubies. But as they were all sitting down at table they saw a very old fairy come into the hall. She had not been invited, because for more than fifty years she had not been out of a certain tower, and she was believed to be either dead or enchanted.

The king ordered her a cover, but he could not give her a case of gold as the others had, because seven only had been made for the seven fairies. The old fairy fancied she was slighted, and muttered threats between her teeth. One of the young fairies who sat near heard her, and, judging that she might give the little princess some unlucky gift, hid herself behind the curtains as soon as they left the table. She hoped that she might speak last and undo as much as she could the evil which the old fairy might do.

In the meanwhile all the fairies began to give their gifts to the princess. The youngest gave her for her gift that she should be the most beautiful person in the world; the next, that she should have the wit of an angel; the third, that she should be able to do everything she did gracefully; the fourth, that she should dance perfectly; the fifth, that she should sing like a nightingale; and the sixth, that she should play all kinds of musical instruments to the fullest perfection.

The old fairy's turn coming next, her head shaking more with spite than with age, she said that the princess should pierce her hand with a spindle and die of the wound. This terrible gift made the whole company tremble, and everybody fell a-crying.

At this very instant the young fairy came from behind the curtains and said these words in a loud voice: 'Assure yourselves, O king and queen, that your daughter shall not die of this disaster. It is true, I have no power to undo entirely what my elder has done. The princess shall indeed pierce her hand with a spindle;

but, instead of dying, she shall only fall into a deep sleep, which shall last a hundred years, at the end of which a king's son shall come and awake her.'

The king, to avoid the misfortune foretold by the old fairy, issued orders forbidding anyone, on pain of death, to spin with a distaff and spindle or to have a spindle in his house. About fifteen or sixteen years after, the king and queen being absent at one of their country villas, the young princess was one day running up and down the palace; she went from room to room, and at last she came into a little garret on the top of the tower, where a good old woman, alone, was spinning with her spindle. This good woman had never heard of the king's orders against spindles.

'What are you doing there, my good woman?' said the princess.

'I am spinning, my pretty child,' said the old woman, who did not know who the princess was.

'Ha!' said the princess, 'this is very pretty; how do you do it? Give it to me. Let me see if I can do it.'

She had no sooner taken it into her hand than, either because she was too quick and heedless, or because the decree of the fairy had so ordained, it ran into her hand, and she fell down in a swoon.

The good old woman, not knowing what to do, cried out for help. People came in from every quarter; they threw water upon the face of the princess, unlaced her, struck her on the palms of her hands, and rubbed her temples with cologne water; but nothing would bring her to herself.

Then the king, who came up at hearing the noise on his return, remembered what the fairies had foretold. He knew very well that this must come to pass, since the fairies had foretold it, and he caused the princess to be carried into the finest room in his palace, and to be laid upon a bed all embroidered with gold and silver. One would have taken her for a little angel, she was so beautiful – for her swooning had not dimmed the brightness of her complexion: her cheeks were carnation and her lips coral. It is true her eyes were shut, but she was heard to breathe softly, which satisfied those about her that she was not dead.

The king gave orders that they should let her sleep quietly till the time came for her to awake. The good fairy who had saved her life by condemning her to sleep a hundred years was in the kingdom of Matakin, twelve thousand leagues off, when this accident befell the princess; but she was instantly informed of it by a little dwarf, who had seven-league boots, that is, boots with which he could stride over seven leagues of ground at once. The fairy started off at once, and arrived, about an hour later, in a fiery chariot drawn by dragons.

The king handed her out of the chariot, and she approved everything he had done; but as she had very great foresight, she thought that when the princess should awake she might not know what to do with herself, if she was all alone in this old palace. This was what she did: she touched with her wand everything in the palace (except the king and queen), governesses, maids of honour, ladies of the bedchamber, gentlemen, officers, stewards, cooks, undercooks, kitchen maids, guards with their porters, pages and footmen; she likewise touched all the horses which were in the stables, the cart-horses, the hunters and the saddle horses, the grooms, the great dogs in the outward court, and little Mopsey, too, the princess's spaniel, which was lying on the bed.

As soon as she touched them they all fell asleep, not to awake again until their mistress did, that they might be ready to wait upon her when she wanted them. The very spits at the fire, as full as they could hold of partridges and pheasants, fell asleep, and the fire itself as well. All this was done in a moment. Fairies are not long in doing their work.

And now the king and queen, having kissed their dear child without waking her, went out of the palace and sent forth orders that nobody should come near it.

These orders were not necessary; for in a quarter of an hour's time there grew up all round about the park such a vast number of trees, great and small, bushes and brambles, twining one within another, that neither man nor beast could pass through; so that nothing could be seen but the very top of the towers of the palace; and that, too, only from afar off. Everyone knew that this also was the work of the fairy in order that while the princess slept she should have nothing to fear from curious people.

After a hundred years the son of the king then reigning, who was of another family from that of the sleeping princess, was a-hunting on that side of the country, and he asked what those towers were which he saw in the middle of a great thick wood. Everyone answered according as they had heard. Some said that it was an old haunted castle, others that all the witches of the country held their midnight revels there, but the common opinion was that it was an ogre's dwelling, and that he carried to it all the little children he could catch, so as to eat them up at his leisure, without anyone being able to follow him, for he alone had the power to make his way through the wood.

The prince did not know what to believe, and presently a very aged countryman spoke to him thus: 'May it please your royal highness, more than fifty years since I heard from my father that there was then in this castle the most beautiful princess that was ever seen; that she must sleep there a hundred years, and that she should be waked by a king's son, for whom she was reserved.'

The young prince on hearing this was all on fire. He thought, without weighing the matter, that he could put an end to this rare adventure; and, pushed on by love and the desire of glory, resolved at once to look into it.

As soon as he began to get near to the wood, all the

great trees, the bushes, and brambles gave way of themselves to let him pass through. He walked up to the castle which he saw at the end of a large avenue; and you can imagine he was a good deal surprised when he saw none of his people following him, because the trees closed again as soon as he had passed through them. However, he did not cease from continuing his way; a young prince in search of glory is ever valiant.

He came into a spacious outer court, and what he saw was enough to freeze him with horror. A frightful silence reigned over all; the image of death was everywhere, and there was nothing to be seen but what seemed to be the outstretched bodies of dead men and animals. He, however, very well knew, by the ruby faces and pimpled noses of the porters, that they were only asleep; and their goblets, wherein still remained some drops of wine, showed plainly that they had fallen asleep while drinking their wine.

He then crossed a court paved with marble, went up the stairs, and came into the guard chamber, where guards were standing in their ranks, with their muskets upon their shoulders, and snoring with all their might. He went through several elegant rooms full of gentlemen and ladies, some standing and others sitting, but all were asleep. He came into a gilded chamber, where he saw upon a bed, the curtains of which were all open, the most beautiful sight ever beheld – a princess who appeared to be about fifteen or sixteen years of age, and whose bright and resplendent beauty had something divine in it. He approached with trembling and admiration, and fell down upon his knees before her.

Then, as the end of the enchantment was come,

the princess awoke, and looking on him with eyes more tender than could have been expected at first sight, said: 'Is it you, my prince? You have waited a long while.'

The prince, charmed with these words, and much more with the manner in which they were spoken, knew not how to show his joy and gratitude; he assured her that he loved her better than he did himself. Their discourse was not very connected, but they were the better pleased, for where there is much love there is little eloquence. He was more at a loss than she, and we need not wonder at it; she had had time to think of what to say to him; for it is evident (though history says nothing of it) that the good fairy, during so long a sleep, had given her very pleasant dreams. In short, they talked together for four hours, and had not said half they had to say.

In the meanwhile all the palace had woken up with the princess; everyone thought upon his own business, and as they were not in love, they were ready to die of hunger. The lady of honour, being as sharp set as the other folks, grew very impatient, and told the princess aloud that the meal was served. The prince helped the princess to rise. She was entirely and very magnificently dressed; but his royal highness took care not to tell her that she was dressed like his great-grandmother, and had a high collar. She looked not a bit the less charming and beautiful for all that.

They went into the great mirrored hall, where they supped, and were served by the officers of the princess's household. The violins and hautboys played old tunes, but they were excellent, though they had not been played for a hundred years; and after supper, without losing any time, the lord almoner married them in the chapel of the castle. They had but very little sleep – the princess scarcely needed any; and the prince left her next morning to return into the city, where his father was greatly troubled about him.

The prince told him that he lost his way in the forest as he was hunting, and that he had slept in the cottage of a charcoal-burner, who gave him cheese and brown bread.

The king, his father, who was a good man, believed him; but his mother could not be persuaded that it was true; and seeing that he went almost every day a-hunting, and that he always had some excuse ready for so doing, though he had been out three or four nights together, she began to suspect that he was married; for he lived thus with the princess above two whole years, during which they had two children, the elder, a daughter, was named Dawn, and the younger, a son, they called Day, because he was a great deal handsomer than his sister.

The queen spoke several times to her son, to learn after what manner he was passing his time, and told him that in this he ought in duty to satisfy her. But he never dared to trust her with his secret; he feared her, though he loved her, for she was of the race of the ogres, and the king married her for her vast riches alone. It was even whispered about the court that she had ogreish inclinations, and that, whenever she saw little children passing by, she had all the difficulty in the world to prevent herself from falling upon them. And so the prince would never tell her one word.

But when the king was dead, which happened about two years afterwards, and he saw himself lord and master, he openly declared his marriage: and he went in great state to conduct his queen to the palace. They made a magnificent entry into the capital city, she riding between her two children.

Soon after, the king made war on Emperor Canta-labutte, his neighbour. He left the government of the kingdom to the queen, his mother, and earnestly commended his wife and children to her care. He was obliged to carry on the war all the summer, and as soon as he left, the queen-mother sent her daughter-in-law and her children to a country house among the woods, that she might with the more ease gratify her horrible longing. Some few days afterwards she went thither herself, and said to her head cook: 'I intend to eat little Dawn for my dinner tomorrow.'

'Oh! Madam!' cried the head cook.

'I will have it so,' replied the queen (and this she spoke in the tone of an ogress who had a strong desire to eat fresh meat), 'and will eat her with a sharp sauce.'

The poor man, knowing very well that he must not play tricks with ogresses, took his great knife and went up into little Dawn's chamber. She was then nearly four years old, and came up to him, jumping and laughing, to put her arms round his neck, and ask him for some sugar-candy. Upon which he began to weep, the great knife fell out of his hand, and he went into the back yard and killed a little lamb, and dressed it with such good sauce that his mistress assured him she had never eaten anything so good in her life. He had at the same time taken up little Dawn and carried her to his wife, to conceal her in his lodging at the end of the courtyard.

Eight days afterwards the wicked queen said to the chief cook, 'I will sup upon little Day.'

He answered not a word, being resolved to cheat her again as he had done before. He went to find little Day, and saw him with a foil in his hand, with which he was fencing with a great monkey: the child was then only three years of age. He took him up in his arms and carried him to his wife, that she might conceal him in her chamber along with his sister, and instead of little Day he served up a young and very tender kid, which the ogress found to be wonderfully good.

All had gone well up to now; but one evening this wicked queen-mother said to her chief cook: 'I will eat the queen with the same sauce I had with her children.'

Now the poor chief cook was in despair and could not imagine how to deceive her again. The young queen was over twenty years old, not reckoning the hundred years she had been asleep: and how to find something to take her place greatly puzzled him. He then decided, to save his own life, to cut the queen's throat; and going up into her chamber, with intent to do it at once, he put himself into as great fury as he possibly could, and came into the young queen's room with his dagger in his hand. He would not, however, deceive her, but told her, with a great deal of respect, the orders he had received from the queen-mother.

'Do it; do it,' she said, stretching out her neck. 'Carry out your orders, and then I shall go and see my children, my poor children, whom I loved so much and so tenderly.' For she thought them dead, since they had been taken away without her knowledge.

'No, no, madam,' cried the poor chief cook, all in tears; 'you shall not die, and you shall see your children again at once. But then you must go home with me to my lodgings, where I have concealed them, and I will deceive the queen once more, by giving her a young hind in your stead.'

Upon this he forthwith conducted her to his room, where, leaving her to embrace her children, and cry along with them, he went and dressed a young hind, which his mistress had for her supper, and devoured with as much appetite as if it had been the young queen. She was now well satisfied with her cruel deeds, and she invented a story to tell the king on his return, of how the queen his wife and her two children had been devoured by mad wolves.

One evening, as she was, according to her custom, rambling round about the courts and yards of the palace to see if she could smell any fresh meat, she heard, in a room on the ground floor, little Day crying, for his mama was going to whip him, because he had been naughty; and she heard, at the same time, little Dawn begging mercy for her brother.

The ogress knew the voice of the queen and her children at once, and being furious at having been thus deceived, she gave orders (in a most horrible voice which made everybody tremble) that, next morning by break of day, they should bring into the middle of the great court a large tub filled with toads, vipers, snakes, and all sorts of serpents, in order to have the queen and her children, the chief cook, his wife and maid, thrown into it, all of whom were to be brought thither with their hands tied behind them.

They were brought out accordingly, and the executioners were just going to throw them into the tub, when the king, who was not so soon expected, entered the court on horseback and asked, with the utmost astonishment, what was the meaning of this horrible spectacle.

No one dared to tell him, but the end came when the ogress, all enraged to see what had happened, threw herself head foremost into the tub, and was instantly devoured by the ugly creatures she had ordered to kill the others. The king was of course very sorry, for she was his mother; but he soon comforted himself with his beautiful wife and his pretty children.

Snow White

It was the middle of winter, when the broad flakes of
snow were falling around, that the queen of a country
many thousand miles off sat working at her window,
the frame of which was made of fine black ebony; and
as she sat looking out upon the snow, she pricked her
finger and three drops of blood fell upon it. Then she
gazed thoughtfully upon the red drops that sprinkled
the white snow, and said, 'Would that my little
daughter may be as white as that snow, as red as that
blood and as black as this ebony window frame!' And
so it was that the little girl really did grow up – her
skin was as white as snow, her cheeks as rosy as the
blood and her hair as black as ebony; and she was
called Snow White.

But this queen died; and the king soon married
another wife, who became queen, and was very
beautiful, but so vain that she could not bear to think
that anyone could be handsomer than she was. She
had a fairy looking-glass, and she would gaze upon
herself in it and say:

> 'Tell me, glass, tell me true!
> Of all the ladies in the land,
> Who is fairest, tell me, who?'

And the glass had always answered: 'Thou, queen,
art the fairest in all the land.'

But Snow White grew more and more beautiful;
and when she was seven years old she was as bright as
the day, and fairer than the queen herself. Then the

glass one day answered the queen, when she went to look in it as usual:

> 'Thou, queen, art fair, and beauteous to see,
> But Snow White is lovelier far than thee!'

When she heard this she turned pale with rage and envy, and called to one of her servants, and said,

'Take Snow White away into the wide wood, that I may never see her any more.'

Then the servant led her away; but his heart melted when Snow White begged him to spare her life, and he said, 'I will not hurt you, thou pretty child.' So he left her by herself; and though he thought it most likely that the wild beasts would tear her in pieces, he felt as if a great weight were taken off his heart when he had made up his mind not to kill her but to leave her to her fate, with the chance of someone finding and saving her.

Then poor Snow White wandered along through the wood in great fear; and the wild beasts roared about her, but none did her any harm. In the evening she came to a cottage among the hills, and went in to rest, for her little feet would carry her no farther. Everything was spruce and neat in the cottage: on the table was spread a white cloth, and there were seven little plates, seven little loaves and seven little glasses with wine in them; and seven knives and forks laid in order; and by the wall stood seven little beds. As she was very hungry, she picked a little piece of each loaf and drank a very little wine out of each glass; and after that she thought she would lie down and rest. So she tried all the little beds; but one was too long, and another was too short, and only the seventh suited her: so there she laid herself down and went to sleep.

By and by in came the masters of the cottage. Now they were seven little dwarfs that lived among the mountains and dug and searched for gold. They lit up their seven little lamps, and saw at once that all was not right.

The first said, 'Who has been sitting on my stool?'

The second, 'Who has been eating off my plate?'

The third, 'Who has been picking my bread?'

The fourth, 'Who has been meddling with my spoon?'

The fifth, 'Who has been handling my fork?'

The sixth, 'Who has been cutting with my knife?'

The seventh, 'Who has been drinking my wine?'

Then the first looked round and said, 'Who has been lying on my bed?' And the rest came running to him, and everyone cried out that somebody had been upon his bed. But the seventh saw Snow White, and called all his brethren to come and see her; and they cried out with wonder and astonishment and brought their lamps to look at her, and said, 'Good heavens! What a lovely child she is!' And they were very glad to see her, and took care not to wake her; and the seventh dwarf slept an hour with each of the other dwarfs in turn, till the night was gone.

In the morning Snow White told them all her story; and they pitied her, and said if she would keep all things in order, and cook and wash and knit and spin for them, she might stay where she was, and they would take good care of her. Then they went out all day long to their work, seeking for gold and silver in the mountains, and Snow White was left at home; but they warned her, and said, 'The queen will soon find out where you are, so take care to let no one in.'

But the queen, now that she thought Snow White was dead, believed that she must be the handsomest lady in the land; and she went to her glass and said:

> 'Tell me, glass, tell me true!
> Of all the ladies in the land,
> Who is fairest, tell me, who?'

And the glass answered:

> 'Thou, queen, art the fairest in all this land:
> But over the hills, in the greenwood shade,
> Where the seven dwarfs their dwelling
> have made,
> There Snow White is hiding her head; and she
> Is lovelier far, O queen! than thee.'

Then the queen was very much frightened; for she knew that the glass always spoke the truth, and was sure that the servant had betrayed her. And she could not bear to think that anyone lived who was more beautiful than she was; so she dressed herself up as an old pedlar, and went her way over the hills, to the place where the dwarfs dwelt. Then she knocked at the door, and cried, 'Fine wares to sell!'

Snow White looked out of the window, and said, 'Good-day, good woman! What have you to sell?'

'Good wares, fine wares,' said she; 'laces and bobbins of all colours.'

'I will let the old lady in; she seems to be a very good sort of body,' thought Snow White, as she ran down and unbolted the door.

'Bless me!' said the old woman, 'how badly your stays are laced! Let me lace them up with one of my nice new laces.'

Snow White did not dream of any mischief, so she stood before the old woman; but she set to work so nimbly, and pulled the lace so tight, that Snow White's breath was stopped, and she fell down as if she were dead.

'There's an end to all thy beauty,' said the spiteful queen, and went away home.

In the evening the seven dwarfs came home; and I need not say how grieved they were to see their faithful Snow White stretched out upon the ground, as if she was quite dead. However, they lifted her up, and when they found what ailed her, they cut the lace; and in a little time she began to breathe, and very soon came back to life again. Then they said, 'The old woman was the queen herself; take care another time, and let no one in when we are away.'

When the queen got home, she went straight to her glass and spoke to it as before; but to her great grief it still said:

'Thou, queen, art the fairest in all this land.
But over the hills, in the greenwood shade,
Where the seven dwarfs their dwelling
                                                          have made,
There Snow White is hiding her head; and she
Is lovelier far, O queen! than thee.'

Then the blood ran cold in her heart with spite and malice to see that Snow White still lived; and she dressed herself up again, but in quite another dress from the one she wore before, and took with her a poisoned comb. When she reached the dwarfs' cottage, she knocked at the door, and cried, 'Fine wares to sell!'

But Snow White said, 'I dare not let anyone in.'

Then the queen said, 'Only look at my beautiful combs!' and gave her the poisoned one. And it looked so pretty that she took it up and put it into her hair to try it; but the moment it touched her head, the poison was so powerful that she fell down senseless.

'There you may lie,' said the queen, and went her way.

But by good luck the dwarfs came in very early that evening; and when they saw Snow White lying on the ground, they guessed what had happened, and soon found the poisoned comb. And when they took it away she got well, and told them all that had passed; and they warned her once more not to open the door to anyone.

Meantime the queen went home to her glass, and shook with rage when she read the very same answer as before; and she said, 'Snow White shall die, if it cost me my life.'

So she went by herself into her chamber, and got

ready a poisoned apple: the outside looked very rosy and tempting, but whoever tasted it was sure to die. Then she dressed herself up as a peasant's wife, and travelled over the hills to the dwarfs' cottage, and knocked at the door; but Snow White put her head out of the window and said, 'I dare not let anyone in, for the dwarfs have told me not to.'

'Do as you please,' said the old woman, 'but at any rate take this pretty apple; I will give it you.'

'No,' said Snow White, 'I dare not take it.'

'You silly girl!' answered the other, 'what are you afraid of? Do you think it is poisoned? Come! Do you eat one part, and I will eat the other.' Now the apple was made up so that one side was good while the other side was poisoned. Then Snow White was much tempted to taste, for the apple looked so very nice; and when she saw the old woman eat, she could wait no longer. But she had scarcely put the piece into her mouth, when she fell down dead upon the ground.

'This time nothing will save thee,' said the queen; and she went home to her glass, and at last it said: 'Thou, queen, art the fairest of all the fair.'

And then her wicked heart was glad, and as happy as such a heart could be.

When evening came, and the dwarfs arrived home, they found Snow White lying on the ground: no breath came from her lips, and they were afraid that she was quite dead. They lifted her up, and combed her hair, and washed her face with wine and water; but all was in vain, for the little girl seemed quite dead. So they laid her down upon a bier, and all seven watched and bewailed her three whole days; and then they thought they would bury her: but her cheeks were still rosy, and her face looked just as it did while she was alive; so they said, 'We will never bury her in the cold ground.' And they made a coffin of glass, so that they might still look at her, and wrote

upon it in golden letters what her name was, and that she was a king's daughter. And the coffin was set beside the cottage among the hills, and one of the dwarfs always sat by it and watched. And the birds of the air came too, and bemoaned Snow White; and first of all came an owl, and then a raven, and at last a dove, and sat by her side.

And thus Snow White lay for a long, long time, and still only looked as though she was asleep; for she was even now as white as snow, and as red as blood, and as black as ebony.

At last a prince came and called at the dwarfs' house; and he saw Snow White, and read what was written in golden letters.

Then he offered the dwarfs money, and prayed and besought them to let him take her away; but they said, 'We will not part with her for all the gold in the world.'

At last, however, they had pity on him, and gave him the coffin; but the moment he lifted it up to carry it home with him, the piece of apple fell from between her lips, and Snow White awoke, and said, 'Where am I?'

And the prince said, 'Thou art quite safe with me.'

Then he told her all that had happened, and said, 'I love you far better than all the world; so come with me to my father's palace, and you shall be my wife.' And Snow White consented, and went home with the prince; and everything was got ready with great pomp and splendour for their wedding.

To the feast was asked, among the rest, Snow White's old enemy the queen; and as she was dressing herself in fine rich clothes, she looked in the glass and said:

'Tell me, glass, tell me true!
Of all the ladies in the land,
Who is fairest, tell me, who?'

And the glass answered:

'Thou, lady, art loveliest here, I ween;
But lovelier far is the new-made queen.'

When she heard this she started with rage; but her envy and curiosity were so great, that she could not help setting out to see the bride. And when she got there, and saw that it was no other than Snow White, who she thought had been dead a long while, she choked with rage and fell down and died; but Snow White and the prince lived and reigned happily over that land many, many years; and sometimes they went up into the mountains, and paid a visit to the little dwarfs, who had been so kind to Snow White in her time of need.

The Steadfast Tin-Soldier

There were once upon a time five-and-twenty tin-soldiers – all brothers, as they were made out of the same old tin spoon. Their uniform was red and blue, and they shouldered their guns and looked straight in front of them. The first words that they heard in this world, when the lid of the box in which they lay was taken off, were: 'Hurrah, tin-soldiers!' This was exclaimed by a little boy, clapping his hands; they had been given to him because it was his birthday, and now he began setting them out on the table. Each soldier was exactly like the other in shape, except just one, who had been made last when the tin had run short; but there he stood as firmly on his one leg as the others did on two, and he is the one that became famous.

There were many other playthings on the table on which they were being set out, but the nicest of all was a pretty little castle made of cardboard, with windows through which you could see into the rooms. In front of the castle stood some little trees surrounding a tiny mirror which looked like a lake. Wax swans were floating about and reflecting themselves in it. That was all very pretty; but the most beautiful thing was a little lady, who stood in the open doorway. She was cut out of paper, but she had on a dress of the finest muslin, with a scarf of narrow blue ribbon round her shoulders, fastened in the middle with a glittering rose made of gold paper, which was as large as her head. The little lady was stretching out both her arms, for she was a dancer, and was lifting up one leg so high in the air that the tin-soldier couldn't find it anywhere, and thought that she, too, had only one leg.

'That's the wife for me!' he thought; 'but she is so grand, and lives in a castle, whilst I have only a box with four-and-twenty others. This is no place for her! But I must make her acquaintance.' Then he stretched himself out behind a snuffbox that lay on the table; from thence he could watch the dainty little lady, who continued to stand on one leg without losing her balance.

When the night came all the other tin-soldiers went into their box, and the people of the house went to bed. Then the toys began to play at visiting, dancing and fighting. The tin-soldiers rattled in their box, for they wanted to be out too, but they could not raise the lid. The nutcrackers played at leapfrog, and the slate-pencil ran about the slate; there was such a noise that the canary woke up and began to talk to them, in poetry too! The only two who did not stir from their places were the tin-soldier and the little dancer. She remained on tiptoe, with both arms outstretched; he stood steadfastly on his one leg, never moving his eyes from her face.

The clock struck twelve, and crack! off flew the lid of the snuff- box; but there was no snuff inside, only a little black imp – that was the beauty of it.

'Hullo, tin-soldier!' said the imp. 'Don't look at things that aren't intended for the likes of you!'

But the tin-soldier took no notice, and seemed not to hear.

'Very well, wait till tomorrow!' said the imp.

When it was morning, and the children had got up, the tin-soldier was put in the window; and whether it was the wind or the little black imp, I don't know, but all at once the window flew open and out fell the little tin-soldier, head over heels, from the third-storey window! That was a terrible fall, I can tell you! He landed on his head with his leg in the air, his gun being wedged between two paving-stones.

The nurserymaid and the little boy came down at once to look for him, but, though they were so near him that they almost trod on him, they did not notice him. If the tin-soldier had only called out, 'Here I am!' they must have found him; but he did not think it fitting for him to cry out, because he had on his uniform.

Soon it began to drizzle; then the drops came faster, and there was a regular downpour. When it was over, two little street boys came along.

'Just look!' cried one. 'Here is a tin-soldier! He shall sail up and down in a boat!'

So they made a little boat out of newspaper, put the tin-soldier in it, and made him sail up and down the gutter; both the boys ran along beside him, clapping their hands. What great waves there were in the gutter, and what a swift current! The paper-boat tossed up and down, and in the middle of the stream it went so quick that the tin-soldier trembled; but he remained steadfast, showed no emotion, looked straight in front of him, shouldering his gun. All at once the boat passed under a long tunnel that was as dark as his box had been.

'Where can I be coming now?' he wondered. 'Oh, dear! This is the black imp's fault! Ah, if only the little lady were sitting beside me in the boat, it might be twice as dark for all I should care!'

Suddenly there came along a great water-rat that lived in the tunnel.

'Have you a passport?' asked the rat. 'Out with your passport!'

But the tin-soldier was silent, and grasped his gun more firmly.

The boat sped on, and the rat behind it. Ugh! how he showed his teeth, as he cried to the chips of wood and straw: 'Hold him, hold him! he has not paid the toll! He has not shown his passport!'

But the current became swifter and stronger. The tin-soldier could already see daylight where the tunnel ended; but in his ears there sounded a roaring enough to frighten any brave man. Only think! at the end of the tunnel the gutter discharged itself into a great canal; that would be just as dangerous for him as it would be for us to go down a waterfall.

Now he was so near to it that he could not hold on any longer. On went the boat, the poor tin-soldier keeping himself as stiff as he could: no one should say of him afterwards that he had flinched. The boat whirled three, four times round, and became filled to the brim with water; it began to sink! The tin-soldier was standing up to his neck in water, and deeper and deeper sank the boat, and softer and softer grew the paper; now the water was over his head. He was thinking of the pretty little dancer, whose face he should never see again, and there sounded in his ears, over and over again: 'Forward, forward, soldier bold! Death's before thee, grim and cold!'

The paper came in two, and the soldier fell – but at that moment he was swallowed by a great fish.

Oh! how dark it was inside, even darker than in the tunnel, and it was really very close quarters! But there the steadfast little tin-soldier lay full length, shouldering his gun.

Up and down swam the fish, then he made the most dreadful contortions, and became suddenly quite still. Then it was as if a flash of lightning had passed through him; the daylight streamed in, and a voice exclaimed, 'Why, here is the little tin-soldier!' The fish had been caught, taken to market, sold, and brought into the kitchen, where the cook had cut it open with a great knife. She took up the soldier between her finger and thumb, and carried him into the room, where everyone wanted to see the hero who had been found inside a fish; but the tin-soldier was not at all proud. They put him on the table, and – no, but what strange things do happen in this world! – the tin-soldier was in the same room in which he had been before! He saw the same children, and the same toys on the table; and there was the same grand castle with the pretty little dancer. She was still standing on one leg with the other high in the air; she too was steadfast. That so touched the tin-soldier, he was nearly going to shed tin-tears; but that would not have been fitting for a soldier. He looked at her, but she said nothing.

All at once one of the little boys took up the tin-soldier, and threw him into the stove, giving no reasons; but doubtless the little black imp in the snuffbox was at the bottom of this too.

There the tin-soldier lay, and felt a heat that was truly terrible; but whether he was suffering from actual fire, or from the ardour of his passion, he did not know. All his colour had disappeared; whether this had happened on his travels or whether it was the result of trouble, who can say? He looked at the little lady, she looked at him, and he felt that he was melting; but he remained steadfast, with his gun at his shoulder. Suddenly a door opened, the draught caught up the little dancer, and off she flew like a sylph to the tin-soldier in the stove and burst into flames – and that was the end of her! Then the tin-soldier melted down into a little lump, and when next morning the maid was taking out the ashes, she found him in the shape of a heart. There was nothing left of the little dancer but her gilt rose, burnt as black as a cinder.

The Three Billy Goats Gruff

Once upon a time there were three billy goats, who were to go up to the hillside to make themselves fat, and the name of all three was 'Gruff'.

On the way up was a bridge over a cascading stream they had to cross; and under the bridge lived a great ugly troll, with eyes as big as saucers, and a nose as long as a poker.

So first of all came the youngest Billy Goat Gruff to cross the bridge.

Trip, trap, trip, trap, went the bridge.

'Who's that tripping over my bridge?' roared the troll.

'Oh, it is only I, the tiniest Billy Goat Gruff, and I'm going up to the hillside to make myself fat,' said the billy goat, with such a small voice.

'I'm coming to gobble you up,' said the troll.

'Oh, no! pray don't take me. I'm too little, that I am,' said the billy goat. 'Wait a bit till the second Billy Goat Gruff comes. He's much bigger.'

'Well, be off with you,' said the troll.

A little while after came the second Billy Goat Gruff to cross the bridge.

Trip, trap, trip, trap, trip, trap, went the bridge.

'Who's that tripping over my bridge?' roared the troll.

'Oh, it's the second Billy Goat Gruff, and I'm going up to the hillside to make myself fat,' said the billy goat, who hadn't such a small voice.

'I'm coming to gobble you up,' said the troll.

'Oh, no! Don't take me. Wait a little till the big Billy Goat Gruff comes. He's much bigger.'

'Very well! Be off with you,' said the troll.

But just then up came the big Billy Goat Gruff.

Trip, trap, trip, trap, trip, trap! went the bridge, for the billy goat was so heavy that the bridge creaked and groaned under him.

'Who's that tramping over my bridge?' roared the troll.

'It's I! The big Billy Goat Gruff,' said the billy goat, who had an ugly hoarse voice of his own.

'I'm coming to gobble you up,' roared the troll.

> 'Well, come along! I've got two spears,
> And I'll poke your eyeballs out at your ears;
> I've got besides two curling-stones,
> And I'll crush you to bits, body and bones.'

That was what the big billy goat said. And then he flew at the troll, and poked his eyes out with his horns, and crushed him to bits, body and bones, and tossed him out into the cascade, and after that he went up to the hillside. There the billy goats got so fat they were scarcely able to walk home again. And if the fat hasn't fallen off them, why, they're still fat; and so, 'Snip, snap, snout, this tale's told out'.

The Three Little Pigs

There was once upon a time a pig who lived with her three children on a large, comfortable, old-fashioned farmyard. The eldest of the little pigs was called Browny, the second Whitey, and the youngest and best looking Blacky. Now Browny was a very dirty little pig, and I am sorry to say spent most of his time rolling and wallowing about in the mud. He was never so happy as on a wet day, when the mud in the farmyard got soft, and thick, and slab. Then he would steal away from his mother's side, and finding the muddiest place in the yard, would roll about in it and thoroughly enjoy himself. His mother often found fault with him for this, and would shake her head sadly and say: 'Ah, Browny! some day you will be sorry that you did not obey your old mother.' But no words of advice or warning could cure Browny of his bad habits.

Whitey was quite a clever little pig, but she was greedy. She was always thinking of her food, and looking forward to her dinner; and when the farm girl was seen carrying the pails across the yard, she would rise up on her hind legs and dance and caper with excitement. As soon as the food was poured into the trough she jostled Blacky and Browny out of the way in her eagerness to get the best and biggest bits for herself. Her mother often scolded her for her selfishness, and told her that someday she would suffer for being so greedy and grabbing.

Blacky was a good, nice little pig, neither dirty nor greedy. He had nice dainty ways (for a pig), and his skin was always as smooth and shining as black satin. He was much cleverer than Browny and Whitey, and his mother's heart used to swell with pride when she heard the farmer's friends say to each other that someday the little black fellow would be a prize pig.

Now the time came when the mother pig felt old and feeble and near her end. One day she called the three little pigs round her and said: 'My children, I feel that I am growing odd and weak, and that I shall not live long. Before I die I should like to build a house for each of you, as this dear old sty in which we have lived so happily will be given to a new family of pigs, and you will have to turn out. Now, Browny, what sort of a house would you like to have?'

'A house of mud,' replied Browny, looking with longing at a wet puddle in the corner of the yard.

'And you, Whitey?' said the mother pig in rather a sad voice, for she was disappointed that Browny had made so foolish a choice.

'A house of cabbage,' answered Whitey, with a mouth full, and scarcely raising her snout out of the trough in which she was grubbing for some potato-parings.

'Foolish, foolish child!' said the mother pig, looking quite distressed.

'And you, Blacky?' turning to her youngest son, 'what sort of a house shall I order for you?'

'A house of brick, please mother, as it will be warm in winter, and cool in summer, and safe all the year round.'

'That is a sensible little pig,' replied his mother, looking fondly at him. 'I will see that the three houses are got ready at once. And now one last piece of advice. You have heard me talk of our old enemy the fox. When he hears that I am dead, he is sure to try and get hold of you, to carry you off to his den. He is very sly and will no doubt disguise himself, and pretend to be a friend, but you must promise me not to let him enter your houses on any pretext whatever.'

And the little pigs readily promised, for they had always had a great fear of the fox, of whom they had heard many terrible tales. A short time afterwards the old pig died, and the little pigs went to live in their own houses.

Browny was quite delighted with his soft mud walls and with the clay floor, which soon looked like nothing but a big mud pie. But that was what Browny enjoyed, and he was as happy as possible, rolling about all day and getting himself in such a mess. One day, as he was lying half asleep in the mud, he heard a soft knock at his door, and a gentle voice said: 'May I come in, Master Browny? I want to see your beautiful new house.'

'Who are you?' said Browny, starting up in great fright, for though the voice sounded gentle, he felt sure it was a feigned voice, and he feared it was the fox.

'I am a friend come to call on you,' answered the voice.

'No, no,' replied Browny, 'I don't believe you are a friend.

You are the wicked fox, against whom our mother warned us. I won't let you in.'

'Oho! Is that the way you answer me?' said the fox, speaking very roughly in his natural voice. 'We shall soon see who is master here,' and with his paws he set to work and scraped a large hole in the soft mud walls. A moment later he had jumped through it, and catching Browny by the neck, flung him on his shoulders and trotted off with him to his den.

The next day, as Whitey was munching a few leaves of cabbage out of the corner of her house, the fox stole up to her door, determined to carry her off to join her brother in his den. He began speaking to her in the same feigned gentle voice in which he had spoken to Browny; but it frightened her very much when he said: 'I am a friend come to visit you, and to have some of your good cabbage for my dinner.'

'Please don't touch it,' cried Whitey in great distress. 'The cabbages are the walls of my house, and if you eat them you will make a hole, and the wind and rain will come in and give me a cold. Do go away; I am sure you are not a friend, but our wicked enemy the fox.' And poor Whitey began to whine and to whimper, and to wish that she had not been such a greedy little pig, and had chosen a more solid material than cabbages for her house. But it was too late now, and in another minute the fox had eaten his way through the cabbage walls, and had caught the trembling, shivering Whitey, and carried her off to his den.

The next day the fox started off for Blacky's house, because he had made up his mind that he would get the three little pigs together in his den, and then kill them, and invite all his friends to a feast. But when he reached the brick house, he found that the door was bolted and barred, so in his sly manner he began, 'Do let me in, dear Blacky. I have brought you a present of some eggs that I picked up in a farmyard on my way here.'

'No, no, Mr Fox,' replied Blacky, 'I am not going to open my door to you. I know your cunning ways. You have carried off poor Browny and Whitey, but you are not going to get me.'

At this the fox was so angry that he dashed with all his force against the wall, and tried to knock it down. But it was too strong and well-built; and though the fox scraped and tore at the bricks with his paws he only hurt himself, and at last he had to give it up, and limp away with his forepaws all bleeding and sore.

'Never mind!' he cried angrily as he went off, 'I'll catch you another day, see if I don't, and won't I grind your bones to powder when I have got you in my den!' and he snarled fiercely and showed his teeth.

Next day Blacky had to go into the neighbouring town to do some marketing and to buy a big kettle. As he was walking home with it slung over his shoulder, he heard a sound of steps stealthily creeping after him. For a moment his heart stood still with fear, and then a happy thought came to him. He had just reached the top of a hill, and could see his own little house nestling at the foot of it among the trees. In a moment he had snatched the lid off the kettle and had jumped in himself. Coiling himself round he lay quite snug in the bottom of the kettle, while with his foreleg he managed to put the lid on, so that he was entirely hidden. With a little kick from the inside he started the kettle off, and down the hill it rolled full tilt; and when the fox came up, all that he saw was a large black kettle spinning over the ground at a great pace. Very much disappointed, he was just going to turn away, when he saw the kettle stop close to the little brick house, and a moment later Blacky jumped out of it and escaped with the kettle into the house; then he barred and bolted the door, and put the shutter up over the window.

'Oho!' exclaimed the fox to himself, 'you think you will escape me that way, do you? We shall soon see about that, my friend,' and very quietly and stealthily he prowled round the house looking for some way to climb on to the roof.

In the meantime Blacky had filled the kettle with water, and having put it on the fire, sat down quietly waiting for it to boil. Just as the kettle was beginning to sing, and steam to come out of the spout, he heard a sound like a soft, muffled step going patter, patter, patter overhead, and the next moment the fox's head and forepaws were seen coming down the chimney. But Blacky very wisely had not put the lid on the kettle, and, with a yelp of pain, the fox fell into the boiling water; before he could escape, Blacky popped the lid on, and the fox was scalded to death.

As soon as he was sure that their wicked enemy was really dead, and could do them no further harm, Blacky started off to rescue Browny and Whitey. As he approached the den he heard piteous grunts and squeals from his poor little brother and sister, who lived in constant terror of the fox killing and eating them. But when they saw Blacky appear at the entrance to the den their joy knew no bounds. He quickly found a sharp stone and cut the cords by which they were tied to a stake in the ground, and then all three started off together for Blacky's house, where they lived happily ever after; and Browny quite gave up rolling in the mud, and Whitey ceased to be greedy, for they never forgot how nearly these faults had brought them to an untimely end.

The Tiger, the Brahman and the Jackal

Once upon a time, a tiger was caught in a trap. He tried in vain to get out through the bars, and rolled and bit with rage and grief when he failed.

By chance a poor Brahman came by. 'Let me out of this cage, oh pious one!' cried the tiger.

'Nay, my friend,' replied the Brahman mildly, 'you would probably eat me if I did.'

'Not at all!' swore the tiger with many oaths; 'on the contrary, I should be for ever grateful, and serve you as a slave!'

Now when the tiger sobbed and sighed and wept and swore, the pious Brahman's heart softened, and at last he consented to open the door of the cage. Out popped the tiger, and, seizing the poor man, cried, 'What a fool you are! What is to prevent my eating you now, for after being cooped up so long I am just terribly hungry!'

In vain the Brahman pleaded for his life; the most he could gain was a promise to abide by the decision of the first three things he chose to question as to the justice of the tiger's action.

So the Brahman first asked a pipal tree what it thought of the matter, but the pipal tree replied coldly, 'What have you to complain about? Don't I give shade and shelter to everyone who passes by, and don't they in return tear down my branches to feed their cattle? Don't whimper – be a man!'

Then the Brahman, sad at heart, went farther afield till he saw a buffalo turning a well-wheel; but he fared no better from it, for it answered, 'You are a fool to expect gratitude! Look at me! While I gave milk they fed me on cotton-seed and oil-cake, but now I am dry they yoke me here, and give me refuse as fodder!'

The Brahman, still more sad, asked the road to give him its opinion.

'My dear sir,' said the road, 'how foolish you are to expect anything else! Here am I, useful to everybody, yet all, rich and poor, great and small, trample on me as they go past, giving me nothing but the ashes of their pipes and the husks of their grain!'

On this the Brahman turned back sorrowfully, and on the way he met a jackal, who called out, 'Why, what's the matter, Mr Brahman? You look as miserable as a fish out of water!'

The Brahman told him all that had occurred. 'How very confusing!' said the jackal, when the recital was ended; 'would you mind telling me over again, for everything has got so mixed up?'

The Brahman told it all over again, but the jackal shook his head in a distracted sort of way, and still could not understand.

'It's very odd,' said he, sadly, 'but it all seems to go in at one ear and out at the other! I will go to the place where it all happened, and then perhaps I shall be able to give a judgement.'

So they returned to the cage, by which the tiger was waiting for the Brahman, and sharpening his teeth and claws.

'You've been away a long time!' growled the savage beast, 'but now let us begin our dinner.'

'*Our* dinner!' thought the wretched Brahman, as his knees knocked together with fright; 'what a remarkably delicate way of putting it!'

'Give me five minutes, my lord!' he pleaded, 'in order that I may explain matters to the jackal here, who is somewhat slow in his wits.'

The tiger consented, and the Brahman began the whole story over again, not missing a single detail, and spinning as long a yarn as possible.

'Oh, my poor brain! oh, my poor brain!' cried the jackal, wringing its paws. 'Let me see! how did it all begin? You were in the cage, and the tiger came walking by –'

'Pooh!' interrupted the tiger, 'what a fool you are! *I* was in the cage.'

'Of course!' cried the jackal, pretending to tremble with fright; 'yes! I was in the cage – no I wasn't – dear! dear! where are my wits? Let me see – the tiger was in the Brahman, and the cage came walking by – no, that's not it, either! Well, don't mind me, but begin your dinner, for I shall never understand!'

'Yes, you shall!' returned the tiger, in a rage at the jackal's stupidity; 'I'll *make* you understand! Look here – I am the tiger –'

'Yes, my lord!'

'And that is the Brahman – '

'Yes, my lord!'

'And that is the cage – '

'Yes, my lord!'

'And I was in the cage – do you understand?'

'Yes – no – Please, my lord – '

'Well?' cried the tiger impatiently.

'Please, my lord! – how did you get in?'

'How! – why in the usual way, of course!'

'Oh, dear me! – my head is beginning to whirl again! Please don't be angry, my lord, but what is the usual way?'

At this the tiger lost patience, and, jumping into the cage, cried, 'This way! Now do you understand how it was?'

'Perfectly!' grinned the jackal, as he dexterously shut the door, 'and if you will permit me to say so, I think matters should remain as they were!'

The Tinderbox

A soldier came marching along the high road – left, right! left, right! He had his knapsack on his back and a sword by his side, for he had been to the wars and was now returning home.

An old witch met him on the road. She was very ugly to look at: her underlip hung down to her breast.

'Good-evening, soldier!' she said. 'What a fine sword and knapsack you have! You are something like a soldier! You ought to have as much money as you would like to carry!'

'Thank you, old witch,' said the soldier.

'Do you see that great tree there?' said the witch, pointing to a tree beside them. 'It is hollow within.

You must climb up to the top, and then you will see a hole through which you can let yourself down into the tree. I will tie a rope round your waist, so that I may be able to pull you up again when you call.'

'What shall I do down there?' asked the soldier.

'Get money!' answered the witch. 'Listen! When you reach the bottom of the tree you will find yourself in a large hall; it is light there, for there are more than three hundred lamps burning. Then you will see three doors, which you can open – the keys are in the locks. If you go into the first room, you will see a great chest in the middle of the floor with a dog sitting upon it; he has eyes as large as saucers, but you needn't trouble about him. I will give you my blue-check apron, which you must spread out on the floor, and then go back quickly and fetch the dog and set him upon it; open the chest and take as much money as you like. It is copper there. If you would rather have silver, you must go into the next room, where there is a dog with eyes as large as mill-wheels. But don't take any notice of him; just set him upon my apron, and help yourself to the money. If you prefer gold, you can get that too, if you go into the third room, and as much as you like to carry. But the dog that guards the chest there has eyes as large as the Round Tower at Copenhagen! He is a savage dog, I can tell you; but you needn't be afraid of him either. Only, put him on my apron and he won't touch you, and you can take out of the chest as much gold as you like!'

'Come, this is not bad!' said the soldier. 'But what am I to give you, old witch; for surely you are not going to do this for nothing?'

'Yes, I am!' replied the witch. 'Not a single farthing will I take! For me you shall bring nothing but an old tinderbox which my grandmother forgot last time she was down there.'

'Well, tie the rope round my waist!' said the soldier.

'Here it is,' said the witch, 'and here is my blue-check apron.'

Then the soldier climbed up the tree, let him-self down through the hole, and found himself standing, as the witch had said, underground in the large hall, where the three hundred lamps were burning.

Well, he opened the first door. Ugh! there sat the dog with eyes as big as saucers glaring at him.

'You are a fine fellow!' said the soldier, and put him on the witch's apron, took as much copper as his pockets could hold; then he shut the chest, put the dog on it again, and went into the second room. Sure enough there sat the dog with eyes as large as mill-wheels.

'You had better not look at me so hard!' said the soldier. 'Your eyes will come out of their sockets!'

And then he set the dog on the apron. When he saw all the silver in the chest, he threw away the copper he had taken, and filled his pockets and knapsack with nothing but silver.

Then he went into the third room. Horrors! the dog there had two eyes, each as large as the Round Tower at Copenhagen, spinning round in his head like wheels.

'Good-evening!' said the soldier and saluted, for he had never seen a dog like this before. But when he had examined him more closely, he thought to himself: 'Now then, I've had enough of this!' and put him down on the floor, and opened the chest. Heavens! what a heap of gold there was! With all that he could buy up the whole town, and all the sugar pigs, all the tin soldiers, whips and rocking-horses in the whole world. Now he threw away all the silver with which he had filled his pockets and knapsack, and filled them with gold instead – yes, all his pockets, his knapsack, cap and boots even, so that he could hardly walk. Now he was rich indeed. He put the dog back upon the chest, shut the door, and then called up through the tree: 'Now pull me up again, old witch!'

'Have you got the tinderbox also?' asked the witch.

'Botheration!' said the soldier, 'I had clean forgotten it!' And then he went back and fetched it.

The witch pulled him up, and there he stood again on the high road, with pockets, knapsack, cap and boots filled with gold.

'What do you want to do with the tinderbox?' asked the soldier.

'That doesn't matter to you,' replied the witch. 'You have got your money, give me my tinderbox.'

'We'll see!' said the soldier. 'Tell me at once what you want to do with it, or I will draw my sword, and cut off your head!'

'No!' screamed the witch.

The soldier immediately cut off her head. That was the end of her! But he tied up all his gold in her apron, slung it like a bundle over his shoulder, put the tinderbox in his pocket, and set out towards the town.

It was a splendid town! He turned into the finest inn, ordered the best chamber and his favourite dinner; for now that he had so much money he was really rich.

It certainly occurred to the servant who had to clean his boots that they were astonishingly old boots for such a rich lord. But that was because he had not yet bought new ones; next day he appeared in respectable boots and fine clothes. Now, instead of a common soldier he had become a noble lord, and the people told him about all the grand doings of the town and the king, and what a beautiful princess his daughter was.

'How can one get to see her?' asked the soldier.

'She is never to be seen at all!' they told him; 'she lives in a great copper castle, surrounded by many walls and towers! No one except the king may go in or out, for it is prophesied that she will marry a common soldier, and the king cannot submit to that.'

'I should very much like to see her,' thought the soldier; but he could not get permission.

Now he lived very gaily, went to the theatre, drove in the king's garden, and gave the poor a great deal of money, which was very nice of him; he had experienced in former times how hard it is not to have a farthing in the world. Now he was rich, wore fine clothes, and made many friends, who all said that he was an excellent man, a real nobleman. And the soldier liked that. But as he was always spending money, and never made any more, at last the day came when he had nothing left but two shillings, and he had to leave the beautiful rooms in which he had been living, and go into a little attic under the roof, and clean his own boots, and mend them with a darning-needle. None of his friends came to visit him there, for there were too many stairs to climb.

It was a dark evening, and he could not even buy a light. But all at once it flashed across him that there was a little end of tinder in the tinderbox, which he had taken from the hollow tree into which the witch had helped him down. He found the box with the tinder in it; but just as he was kindling a light, and had struck a spark out of the tinderbox, the door burst open, and the dog with eyes as large as saucers, which he had seen down in the tree, stood before him and said: 'What does my lord command?'

'What's the meaning of this?' exclaimed the soldier. 'This is a pretty kind of tinderbox, if I can get whatever I want like this. Get me money!' he cried to the dog, and hey, presto! he was off and back again, holding a great purse full of money in his mouth.

Now the soldier knew what a capital tinderbox this was. If he rubbed once, the dog that sat on the chest of copper appeared; if he rubbed twice, there came the dog that watched over the silver chest; and if he rubbed three times, the one that guarded the gold appeared. Now, the soldier went down again to his beautiful rooms, and appeared once more in splendid clothes. All his friends immediately recognised him again, and paid him great court.

One day he thought to himself: 'It is very strange that no one can get to see the princess. They all say she is very pretty, but what's the use of that if she has to sit for ever in the great copper castle with all the towers? Can I not manage to see her somehow? Where is my tinderbox?' and so he struck a spark, and, presto! there came the dog with eyes as large as saucers.

'It is the middle of the night, I know,' said the soldier; 'but I should very much like to see the princess for a moment.'

The dog was already outside the door, and before the soldier could look round, in he came with the princess. She was lying asleep on the dog's back, and was so beautiful that anyone could see she was a real princess. The soldier really could not refrain from kissing her – he was such a thorough soldier. Then the dog ran back with the princess. But when it was morning, and the king and queen were drinking tea, the princess said that the night before she had had such a strange dream about a dog and a soldier: she had ridden on the dog's back, and the soldier had kissed her.

'That is certainly a fine story,' said the queen. But the next night one of the ladies-in-waiting was to watch at the princess's bed, to see if it was only a dream, or if it had actually happened.

The soldier had an overpowering longing to see the princess again, and so the dog came in the middle of the night and fetched her, running as fast as he could. But the lady-in-waiting slipped on india-rubber shoes and followed them. When she saw them disappear into a large house, she thought to herself: 'Now I know where it is;' and made a great cross on the door with a piece of chalk. Then she went home and lay down, and the dog came back also, with the princess. But when he saw that a cross had been made on the door of the house where the soldier lived, he took a piece of chalk also, and made crosses on all the doors in the town; and that was very clever, for now the lady-in-waiting could not find the right house, as there were crosses on all the doors.

Early next morning the king, queen, ladies-in-waiting and officers came out to see where the princess had been.

'There it is!' said the king, when he saw the first door with a cross on it.

'No, there it is, my dear!' said the queen, when she likewise saw a door with a cross.

'But here is one, and there is another!' they all exclaimed; wherever they looked there was a cross on the door. Then they realised that the sign would not help them at all.

But the queen was an extremely clever woman, who could do a great deal more than just drive in a coach. She took her great golden scissors, cut up a piece of silk, and made a pretty little bag of it. This she filled with the finest buckwheat grains, and tied it round the princess's neck; this done, she cut a little hole in the bag, so that the grains would strew the whole road wherever the princess went.

In the night the dog came again, took the princess on his back and ran away with her to the soldier, who was very much in love with her, and would have liked to have been a prince, so that he might have had her for his wife.

The dog did not notice how the grains were strewn right from the castle to the soldier's window, to reach which he ran up the wall with the princess.

In the morning the king and the queen saw plainly where their daughter had been, and they took the soldier and put him in prison.

There he sat. Oh, how dark and dull it was there!

And they told him: 'Tomorrow you are to be hanged.' Hearing that did not exactly cheer him, and he had left his tinderbox in the inn.

Next morning he could see through the iron grating in front of his little window how the people were hurrying out of the town to see him hanged. He heard the drums and saw the soldiers marching; all the people were running to and fro. Just below his window was a shoemaker's apprentice, with leather apron and shoes; he was skipping along so merrily that one of his shoes flew off and fell against the wall, just where the soldier was sitting peeping through the iron grating.

'Oh, shoemaker's boy, you needn't be in such a hurry!' said the soldier to him. 'There's nothing going on till I arrive. But if you will run back to the house where I lived, and fetch me my tinderbox, I will give you four shillings. But you must put your best foot foremost.'

The shoemaker's boy was very willing to earn four shillings, and fetched the tinderbox, gave it to the soldier, and – yes – now you shall hear.

Outside the town a great scaffold had been erected, and all round were standing the soldiers, and hundreds of thousands of people. The king and queen were sitting on a magnificent throne opposite the judges and the whole council.

The soldier was already standing on the top of the ladder; but when they wanted to put the rope round his neck, he said that the fulfilment of one innocent request was always granted to a poor criminal before he underwent his punishment. He would so much like to smoke a small pipe of tobacco; it would be his last pipe in this world.

The king could not refuse him this, and so he took

out his tinderbox, and rubbed it once, twice, three times. And lo, and behold! there stood all three dogs – the one with eyes as large as saucers, the second with eyes as large as mill-wheels, and the third with eyes each as large as the Round Tower of Copenhagen.

'Help me now, so that I may not be hanged!' cried the soldier. And thereupon the dogs fell upon the judges and the whole council, seized some by the legs, others by the nose, and threw them so high into the air that they fell and were smashed into pieces.

'I won't stand this!' said the king; but the largest dog seized him too, and the queen as well, and threw them up after the others. This frightened the soldiers, and all the people cried: 'Good soldier, you shall be our king, and marry the beautiful princess!'

Then they put the soldier into the king's coach, and the three dogs danced in front, crying 'Hurrah!' And the boys whistled and the soldiers presented arms.

The princess came out of the copper castle, and became queen; and that pleased her very much.

The wedding festivities lasted for eight days, and the dogs sat at table and made eyes at everyone.

Titty Mouse and Tatty Mouse

Titty Mouse and Tatty Mouse both lived in a house,
Titty Mouse went a-leasing and Tatty Mouse went a-leasing – so they both went a-leasing.

Titty Mouse leased an ear of corn, and Tatty
Mouse leased an ear of corn – so they both leased an
ear of corn.

Titty Mouse made a pudding, and Tatty Mouse
made a pudding – so they both made a pudding.

And Tatty Mouse put her pudding into the pot to
boil, but when Titty went to put hers in, the pot
tumbled over and scalded her to death.

Then Tatty sat down and wept.

Then a three-legged stool said: 'Tatty, why do you
weep?'

'Titty's dead,' said Tatty, 'and so I weep.'

'Then,' said the stool, 'I'll hop,' so the stool hopped.

Then a broom in the
corner of the room
said, 'Stool, why
do you hop?'
'Oh!' said the
stool, 'Titty's
dead, and Tatty
weeps, and so
I hop.'
'Then,' said the
broom, 'I'll sweep,'
so the broom began
to sweep.

'Then,' said the door, 'Broom, why do you sweep?'

'Oh!' said the broom, 'Titty's dead, and Tatty weeps, and the stool hops, and so I sweep.'

'Then,' said the door, 'I'll jar,' so the door jarred.

'Then,' said the window, 'Door, why do you jar?'

'Oh!' said the door, 'Titty's dead, and Tatty weeps, and the stool hops, and the broom sweeps, and so I jar.'

'Then,' said the window, 'I'll creak,' so the window creaked.

Now there was an old form outside the house, and when the window creaked, the form said: 'Window, why do you creak?'

'Oh!' said the window, 'Titty's dead, and Tatty weeps, and the stool hops, and the broom sweeps, the door jars, and so I creak.'

'Then,' said the old form, 'I'll run round the house,' then the old form ran round the house.

Now there was a fine large walnut tree growing by the cottage, and the tree said to the form: 'Form, why do you run round the house?'

'Oh!' said the form, 'Titty's dead, and Tatty weeps, and the stool hops, and the broom sweeps, the door jars, and the window creaks, and so I run round the house.'

'Then,' said the walnut tree, 'I'll shed my leaves,' so the walnut tree shed all its beautiful green leaves.

Now there was a little bird perched on one of the boughs of the tree, and when all the leaves fell, it said: 'Walnut tree, why do you shed your leaves?'

'Oh!' said the tree, 'Titty's dead, and Tatty weeps, the stool hops, and the broom sweeps, the door jars, and the window creaks, the old form runs round the house, and so I shed my leaves.'

'Then,' said the little bird, 'I'll moult all my feathers,' so he moulted all his pretty feathers.

Now there was a little girl walking below, carrying a jug of milk for her brothers and sisters' supper, and when she saw the poor little bird moult all its feathers, she said: 'Little bird, why do you moult all your feathers?'

'Oh!' said the little bird, 'Titty's dead, and Tatty weeps, the stool hops, and the broom sweeps, the door jars, and the window creaks, the old form runs round the house, the walnut tree sheds its leaves, and so I moult all my feathers.'

'Then,' said the little girl, 'I'll spill the milk,' so she dropped the pitcher and spilt the milk.

Now there was an old man just by on the top of a ladder thatching a rick, and when he saw the little girl spill the milk, he said: 'Little girl, what do you mean by spilling the milk? Your little brothers and sisters must go without their supper!'

Then said the little girl: 'Titty's dead, and Tatty weeps, the stool hops, and the broom sweeps, the door jars, and the window creaks, the old form runs round the house, the walnut tree sheds all its leaves, the little bird moults all its feathers, and so I spill the milk.'

'Oh!' said the old man, 'then I'll tumble off the ladder and break my neck,' so he tumbled off the ladder and broke his neck; and when the old man broke his neck, the great walnut tree fell down with a crash, and upset the old form and knocked down the house, and the house falling knocked the window out, and the window knocked the door down, and the door upset the broom, and the broom upset the stool, and poor little Tatty Mouse was buried beneath the ruins.

The History of Tom Thumb

In the days of the great Prince Arthur, there lived a mighty magician, called Merlin, the most learned and skilful enchanter the world has ever seen.

This famous magician, who could take any form he pleased, was travelling about as a poor beggar, and, being very tired, he stopped at the cottage of a ploughman to rest himself, and asked for some food.

The countryman bade him welcome, and his wife, who was a very good-hearted woman, soon brought him some milk in a wooden bowl, and some coarse brown bread on a platter.

Merlin was much pleased with the kindness of the ploughman and his wife; but he could not help noticing that though everything was neat and comfortable in the cottage, they seemed both to be very unhappy. He therefore asked them why they were so melancholy, and learned that they were miserable because they had no children.

The poor woman said, with tears in her eyes: 'I should be the happiest creature in the world if I had a son; although he was no bigger than my husband's thumb, I would be satisfied.'

Merlin was so much amused with the idea of a boy no bigger than a man's thumb, that he determined to grant the poor woman's wish. Accordingly, in a short time after, the ploughman's wife had a son, who, wonderful to relate! was not a bit bigger than his father's thumb.

The queen of the fairies, wishing to see the little

fellow, came in at the window while the mother was sitting up in the bed admiring him. The queen kissed the child, and, giving it the name of Tom Thumb, sent for some of the fairies, who dressed her little godson according to her orders:

> An oak-leaf hat he had for his crown;
> His shirt of web by spiders spun;
> With jacket wove of thistle's down;
> His trousers were of feathers done.
> His stockings, of apple-rind, they tie
> With eyelash from his mother's eye
> His shoes were made of mouse's skin,
> Tann'd with the downy hair within.

Tom never grew any larger than his father's thumb, which was only of ordinary size; but as he got older he became very cunning and full of tricks. When he was old enough to play with the boys, and had lost all his own cherry-stones, he used to creep into the bags of his playfellows, fill his pockets, and, getting out without their noticing him, would again join in the game.

One day, however, as he was coming out of a bag of cherry-stones, where he had been stealing as usual, the boy to whom it belonged chanced to see him. 'Ah, ah! my little Tommy,' said the boy, 'so I have caught you stealing my cherry-stones at last, and you shall be rewarded for your thievish tricks.' On saying this, he drew the string tight round his neck, and gave the bag such a hearty shake, that poor little Tom's legs, thighs, and body were sadly bruised. He roared out with pain, and begged to be let out, promising never to steal again.

A short time afterwards his mother was making a batter-pudding, and Tom, being very anxious to see how it was made, climbed up to the edge of the bowl; but his foot slipped, and he plumped over head and ears into the batter, without his mother noticing him, so that she stirred him into the pudding-bag and put him in the pot to boil.

The batter filled Tom's mouth, and prevented him from crying out; but, on feeling the hot water, he kicked and struggled so much in the pot that his mother thought that the pudding was bewitched, and, pulling it out of the pot, she threw it outside the door. A poor tinker, who was passing by, lifted up the pudding, and, putting it into his budget, he then walked off. As Tom had now got his mouth cleared of the batter, he began to cry aloud, which so frightened the tinker that he flung down the pudding and ran away. The pudding being broke to pieces by the fall, Tom crept out covered all over with the batter, and walked home. His mother, who was very sorry to see her darling in such a woeful state, put him into a teacup, and soon washed off the batter; after which she kissed him, and laid him in bed.

Soon after the adventure of the pudding, Tom's mother went to milk her cow in the meadow, and she took him along with her. As the wind was very high, for fear of his being blown away, she tied him to a thistle with a piece of fine thread. The cow soon observed Tom's oak-leaf hat, and liking the appearance of it, took poor Tom and the thistle at one mouthful. While the cow was chewing the thistle Tom was afraid of her great teeth, which threatened to crush him in pieces, and he roared out as loud as he could: 'Mother, mother!'

'Where are you, Tommy, my dear Tommy?' said his mother.

'Here, mother,' replied he, 'in the red cow's mouth.'

His mother began to cry and wring her hands; but the cow, surprised at the odd noise in her throat, opened her mouth and let Tom drop out. Fortunately his mother caught him in her apron as he was falling to the ground, or he would have been dreadfully hurt. She then put Tom in her bosom and ran home with him.

Tom's father made him a whip of a barley straw to drive the cattle with, and having one day gone into the fields, he lost his footing and rolled into a furrow. A raven, which was flying over, picked him up, and flew with him over the sea, and there dropped him.

A large fish swallowed Tom the moment he fell into the sea, but was soon after caught, and bought for the table of King Arthur. When they opened the fish in order to cook it, everyone was astonished at finding such a little boy, and Tom was quite delighted at being free again. They carried him to the king, who made Tom his dwarf, and he soon grew a great favourite at court; for by his tricks and gambols he not only amused the king and queen, but also all the Knights of the Round Table.

It is said that when the king rode out on horseback, he often took Tom along with him, and if a shower came on, he used to creep into his majesty's waistcoat-pocket, where he slept till the rain was over.

King Arthur one day asked Tom about his parents, wishing to know if they were as small as he was, and whether they were well off. Tom told the king that his father and mother were as tall as anybody about the court, but in rather poor circumstances. On hearing this, the king carried Tom to his treasury, the place where he kept all his money, and told him to take as much money as he could carry home to his parents, which made the poor little fellow caper with joy. Tom went immediately to procure a purse, which was made of a water-bubble, and then returned to the treasury, where be received a silver threepenny-piece to put into it.

Our little hero had some difficulty in lifting the burden upon his back; but he at last succeeded in getting it placed to his liking, and set forward on his journey. Eventually, without meeting with any accident, and after resting himself more than a hundred times by the way, in two days and two nights he reached his father's house in safety.

Tom had travelled forty-eight hours with a huge silver-piece on his back, and was almost tired to death when his mother ran out to meet him, and carried him into the house. But he soon returned to court. As Tom's clothes had suffered much in the batter-pudding, and the inside of the fish, his majesty ordered him a new suit of clothes, and had him mounted as a knight on a mouse.

> Of butterfly's wings his shirt was made,
> His boots of chicken's hide;
> And by a nimble fairy blade,
> Well learned in the tailoring trade,
> His clothing was supplied.
> A needle dangled by his side;
> A dapper mouse he used to ride,
> Thus strutted Tom in stately pride!

It was certainly very diverting to see Tom in this dress and mounted on the mouse, as he rode out a-hunting with the king and nobility, who were all ready to expire with laughter at Tom and his fine prancing charger.

The king was so charmed with his protégé that he ordered a little chair to be made, in order that Tom might sit upon his table, and also a palace of gold, a span high, with a door an inch wide, to live in. He also gave him a coach, drawn by six small mice.

The queen was so enraged at the honours conferred on Sir Thomas that she resolved to ruin him, and told the king that the little knight had been saucy to her.

The king sent for Tom in great haste, but being fully aware of the danger of royal anger, he crept into an empty snail-shell, where he lay for a long time until he was almost starved with hunger; but at last he ventured to peep out, and seeing a fine large butterfly on the ground, near the place of his concealment, he got close to it and, jumping astride on it, was carried up into the air. The butterfly flew with him from tree to tree and from field to field, and at last returned to the court, where the king and nobility all strove to catch him; but at last poor Tom fell from his

seat into a watering-pot,
in which he was almost
drowned.

When the queen saw him she
was in a rage, and said he should
be beheaded; and he was put into a
mousetrap until the time of his execution.

However a cat, observing something alive in
the trap, patted it about till the wires broke, and set
Thomas at liberty.

The king received Tom again into favour, which
he did not live to enjoy, for a large spider one day
attacked him; and although he drew his sword and
fought well, yet the spider's poisonous breath at last
overcame him.

He fell dead on the ground where he stood, And
the spider suck'd every drop of his blood.

King Arthur and his whole court were so sorry at
the loss of their little favourite that they went into
mourning and raised a fine white marble monument
over his grave with the following epitaph:

Here lies
TOM THUMB
King Arthur's knight,
Who died by a spider's cruel bite.
He was well known in Arthur's court,
Where he afforded gallant sport;
He rode at tilt and tournament,
And on a mouse a-hunting went.
Alive he filled the court with mirth;
His death to sorrow soon gave birth.
Wipe, wipe your eyes, and shake your head
And cry – Alas! Tom Thumb is dead!

Thumbelina

There was once a woman who wanted to have quite a tiny little child, but she did not know where to get one from. So one day she went to an old witch and said to her: 'I should so much like to have a tiny little child; can you tell me where I can get one?'

'Oh, we have just got one ready!' said the witch. 'Here is a barleycorn for you, but it's not the kind the farmer sows in his field or feeds the cocks and hens with, I can tell you. Put it in a flowerpot, and then you will see something happen.'

'Oh, thank you!' said the woman, and gave the witch a shilling, for that was what it cost. Then she went home and planted the barleycorn; immediately there grew out of it a large and beautiful flower, which looked like a tulip, but the petals were tightly closed as if it were still only a bud.

'What a beautiful flower!' exclaimed the woman, and she kissed the red and yellow petals; but as she kissed them the flower burst open. It was a real tulip, such as one can see any day; but in the middle of the blossom, on the green velvety petals, sat a little girl, quite tiny, trim and pretty. She was scarcely half a thumb in height; so they called her Thumbelina. An elegant polished walnut shell served Thumbelina as a cradle, the blue petals of a violet were her mattress and a rose leaf her coverlet. There she lay at night, but in the daytime she used to play about on the table; here the woman had put a bowl, surrounded by a ring of flowers, with their stalks in water, in the middle of which floated a great tulip pedal, and on this Thumbelina sat, and sailed from one side of the bowl to the other, rowing herself with two white horse hairs for oars. It was such a pretty sight! She could sing, too, with a voice more soft and sweet than had ever been heard before.

One night, when she was lying in her pretty little bed, an old toad crept in through a broken pane in the window. She was very ugly, clumsy and clammy; she hopped on to the table where Thumbelina lay asleep under the red rose leaf.

'This would make a beautiful wife for my son,' said the toad, taking up the walnut shell, with Thumbelina inside, and hopping with it through the window into the garden.

There flowed a great wide stream, with slippery and marshy banks; here the toad lived with her son. Ugh! how ugly and clammy he was, just like his mother! 'Croak, croak, croak!' was all he could say when he saw the pretty little girl in the walnut shell.

'Don't talk so loud, or you'll wake her,' said the old toad. 'She might escape us even now; she is as light as a feather. We will put her at once on a broad water-lily leaf in the stream. That will be quite an island for her, she is so small and light. She can't run away from us there, while we are preparing the guest chamber under the marsh where she shall live.'

Outside in the brook grew many water lilies, with broad green leaves, which looked as if they were swimming about on the water.

The leaf farthest away was the largest, and to this the old toad swam with Thumbelina in her walnut shell.

The tiny Thumbelina woke up very early in the morning, and when she saw where she was she began to cry bitterly; for on every side of the great green leaf was water, and she could not get to the land.

The old toad was down under the marsh, decorating her room with rushes and yellow marigold leaves, to make it very grand for her new daughter-in-law; then she swam out with her ugly son to the leaf where Thumbelina lay. She wanted to fetch the pretty cradle to put it into her room before Thumbelina herself came there. The old toad bowed low in the water before her, and said: 'Here is my son; you shall marry him, and live in great magnificence down under the marsh.'

'Croak, croak, croak!' was all that the son could say. Then they took the neat little cradle and swam away with it; but Thumbelina sat alone on the great green leaf and wept, for she did not want to live with the clammy toad, or marry her ugly son. The little fishes swimming about under the water had seen the toad quite plainly, and heard what she had said; so they put up their heads to see the little girl. When they saw her, they thought her so pretty that they were very sorry she should go down with the ugly toad to live. No; that must not happen. They assembled in the water round the green stalk which supported the leaf on which she was sitting, and nibbled the stem in two. Away floated the leaf down the stream, bearing Thumbelina far beyond the reach of the toad.

On she sailed past several towns, and the little birds sitting in the bushes saw her, and sang, 'What a pretty little girl!' The leaf floated farther and farther away; thus Thumbelina left her native land.

A beautiful little white butterfly fluttered above her, and at last settled on the leaf. Thumbelina pleased him, and she, too, was delighted, for now the toads could not reach her, and it was so beautiful where she was travelling; the sun shone on the water and made it sparkle like the brightest silver. She took off her sash, and tied one end round the butterfly; the other end she fastened to the leaf, so that now it glided along with her faster than ever.

A great cockchafer came flying past; he caught sight of Thumbelina, and in a moment had put his arms round her slender waist, and had flown off with her to a tree. The green leaf floated away down the stream, and the butterfly with it, for he was fastened to the leaf and could not get loose from it. Oh, dear! how terrified poor little Thumbelina was when the cockchafer flew off with her to the tree! But she was especially distressed on the beautiful white butterfly's account, as she had tied him fast, so that if he could not get away he must starve to death. But the cockchafer did not trouble himself about that; he sat down with her on a large green leaf, gave her the honey out of the flowers to eat, and told her that she was very pretty, although she wasn't in the least like a cockchafer. Later on, all the other cockchafers who lived in the same tree came to pay calls; they examined Thumbelina closely, and remarked, 'Why, she has only two legs! How very miserable!'

'She has no feelers!' cried another.

'How ugly she is!' said all the lady chafers – and yet Thumbelina was really very pretty.

The cockchafer who had stolen her knew this very well; but when he heard all the ladies saying she was ugly, he began to think so too, and would not keep her; she might go wherever she liked. So he flew down from the tree with her and put her on a daisy. There she sat and wept, because she was so ugly that the cockchafer would have nothing to do with her; and yet she was the most beautiful creature imaginable, so soft and delicate, like the loveliest rose leaf.

The whole summer poor little Thumbelina lived

alone in the great wood. She plaited a bed for herself
of blades of grass, and hung it up under a clover leaf,
so that she was protected from the rain; she gathered
honey from the flowers for food, and drank the dew
on the leaves every morning. Thus the summer and
autumn passed, but then came winter – the long,
cold winter. All the birds who had sung so sweetly
about her had flown away; the trees shed their leaves,
the flowers died; the great clover leaf under which
she had lived curled up, and nothing remained of it
but the withered stalk. She was terribly cold, for her
clothes were ragged, and she herself was so small and
thin. Poor little Thumbelina! she would surely be
frozen to death. It began to snow, and every snow-
flake that fell on her was to her as a whole shovelful
thrown on one of us, for we are so big, and she was
only an inch high. She wrapped herself round in a
dead leaf, but it was torn in the middle and gave her
no warmth; she was trembling with cold.

Just outside the wood where she was now living lay
a great cornfield. But the corn had been gone a long
time; only the dry, bare stubble was left standing in
the frozen ground. This made a forest for her to
wander about in. All at once she came across the
door of a fieldmouse, who had a little hole under a
cornstalk. There the mouse lived warm and snug,
with a storeroom full of corn, a splendid kitchen and
dining-room. Poor little Thumbelina went up to the
door and begged for a little piece of barley, for she
had not had anything to eat for the last two days.

'Poor little creature!' said the fieldmouse, for she
was a kind-hearted old thing at the bottom. 'Come
into my warm room and have some dinner with me.'

As Thumbelina pleased her, she said: 'As far as I

am concerned you may spend the winter with me; but you must keep my room clean and tidy, and tell me stories, for I like that very much.'

And Thumbelina did all that the kind old field-mouse asked, and did it remarkably well too.

'Now I am expecting a visitor,' said the fieldmouse; 'my neighbour comes to call on me once a week. He is in better circumstances than I am, has great big rooms, and wears a fine black velvet coat. If you could only marry him, you would be well provided for. But he is blind. You must tell him all the prettiest stories you know.'

But Thumbelina did not trouble her head about him, for he was only a mole. He came and paid them a visit in his black velvet coat.

'He is so rich and so accomplished,' the fieldmouse told her. 'His house is twenty times larger than mine; he possesses great knowledge, but he cannot bear the sun and the beautiful flowers, and speaks slightingly of them, for he has never seen them.'

Thumbelina had to sing to him, so she sang 'Lady-bird, ladybird, fly away home!' and other songs so prettily that the mole fell in love with her; but he did not say anything as he was a very cautious man. A short time before he had dug a long passage through the ground from his own house to that of his neighbour; in this he gave the fieldmouse and Thumbelina permission to walk as often as they liked. But he begged them not to be afraid of the dead bird that lay in the passage: it was a real bird with beak and feathers, and must have died a little time ago, and now laid buried just where he had made his tunnel. The mole took a piece of rotten wood in his mouth, for that glows like fire in the dark, and went in front, lighting them through the long dark passage. When they came to the place where the dead bird lay, the mole put his broad nose against the ceiling and pushed a hole through, so that the daylight could shine down. In the middle of the path lay a dead swallow, his pretty wings pressed close to his sides, his claws and head drawn under his feathers; the poor bird had evidently died of cold. Thumbelina was very sorry, for she was very fond of all little birds; they had sung and twittered so beautifully to her all through the summer. But the mole kicked him with his bandy legs and said: 'Now he can't sing any more! It must be very miserable to be a little bird! I'm thankful that none of my children are; birds always starve in winter.'

'Yes, you speak like a sensible man,' said the field-mouse. 'What has a bird, in spite of all his singing, in the wintertime? He must starve and freeze, and that must be very pleasant for him, I must say!'

Thumbelina did not say anything; but when the other two had passed on she bent down to the bird, brushed aside the feathers from his head, and kissed his closed eyes gently. 'Perhaps it was he that sang to me so prettily in the summer,' she thought. 'How much pleasure he did give me, dear little bird!'

The mole closed up the hole again which let in the light, and then escorted the ladies home. But Thumbelina could not sleep that night; so she got out of bed, and plaited a great big blanket of straw, and carried it off, and spread it over the dead bird, and piled upon it thistledown, as soft as cotton wool, which she had found in the fieldmouse's room, so that the poor little thing should lie warmly buried.

'Farewell, pretty little bird!' she said. 'Farewell, and thank you for your beautiful songs in the summer,

when the trees were green and the sun shone down warmly on us!' Then she laid her head against the bird's heart. But the bird was not dead: he had been frozen, but now that she had warmed him, he was coming to life again.

In autumn the swallows fly away to foreign lands; but there are some who are late in starting, and then they get so cold that they drop down as if dead, and the snow comes and covers them over.

Thumbelina trembled, she was so frightened; for the bird was very large in comparison with herself – only an inch high. But she took courage, piled up the down more closely over the poor swallow and fetched her own coverlet and laid it over his head.

Next night she crept out again to him. There he was – alive, but very weak; he could only open his eyes for a moment and look at Thumbelina, who was standing in front of him with a piece of rotten wood in her hand, for she had no other lantern.

'Thank you, pretty little child!' said the swallow to

her. 'I am so beautifully warm! Soon I shall regain my strength, and then I shall be able to fly out again into the warm sunshine.'

'Oh!' she said, 'it is very cold outside; it is snowing and freezing! Stay in your warm bed; I will take care of you!'

Then she brought him water in a petal, which he drank, after which he related to her how he had torn one of his wings on a bramble, so that he could not fly as fast as the other swallows, who had flown far away to warmer lands. So at last he had dropped down exhausted, and then he could remember no more. The whole winter he remained down there, and Thumbelina looked after him and nursed him tenderly. Neither the mole nor the fieldmouse learnt anything of this, for they could not bear the poor swallow.

When the spring came, and the sun warmed the earth again, the swallow said farewell to Thumbelina, who opened the hole in the roof for him which the mole had made. The sun shone brightly down upon her, and the swallow asked her if she would go with him; she could sit upon his back. Thumbelina wanted very much to fly far away into the greenwood, but she knew that the old fieldmouse would be sad if she ran away. 'No, I mustn't come!' she said.

'Farewell, dear good little girl!' said the swallow, and flew off into the sunshine. Thumbelina gazed after him with the tears standing in her eyes, for she was very fond of the swallow.

'Tweet, tweet!' sang the bird, and flew into the greenwood. Thumbelina was very unhappy. She was not allowed to go out into the warm sunshine. The corn which had been sown in the field over the fieldmouse's home grew up high into the air, and made a thick forest for the poor little girl, who was only an inch high.

'Now you are to be a bride, Thumbelina!' said the fieldmouse, 'for our neighbour has proposed for you! What a piece of fortune for a poor child like you! Now you must set to work at your linen for your dowry, for nothing must be lacking if you are to become the wife of our neighbour, the mole!'

Thumbelina had to spin all day long, and every evening the mole visited her, and told her that when the summer was over the sun would not shine so hotly; now it was burning the earth as hard as a stone. Yes, when the summer had passed, they would hold the wedding.

But she was not at all pleased about it, for she did not like the stupid mole. Every morning when the sun

was rising, and every evening when it was setting, she would steal out of the house door, and when the breeze parted the ears of corn so that she could see the blue sky through them, she thought how bright and beautiful it must be outside, and longed to see her dear swallow again. But he never came; no doubt he had flown away far into the great greenwood.

By the autumn Thumbelina had finished the dowry.

'In four weeks you will be married!' said the field-mouse; 'don't be obstinate, or I shall bite you with my sharp white teeth! You will get a fine husband! The king himself has not such a velvet coat. His store-room and cellar are full, and you should be thankful for that.'

Well, the wedding day arrived. The mole had come to fetch Thumbelina to live with him deep down under the ground, never to come out into the warm sun again, for that was what he didn't like. The poor little girl was very sad, for now she must say goodbye to the beautiful sun.

'Farewell, bright sun!' she cried, stretching out her arms towards it, and taking another step outside the house; for now the corn had been reaped, and only the dry stubble was left standing. 'Farewell, farewell!' she said, and put her arms round a little red flower that grew there. 'Give my love to the dear swallow when you see him!'

'Tweet, tweet!' sounded in her ear all at once. She looked up. There was the swallow flying past! As soon as he saw Thumbelina, he was very glad. She told him how unwilling she was to marry the ugly mole, as then she would have to live underground where the sun never shone, and she could not help bursting into tears.

'The cold winter is coming now,' said the swallow.
'I must fly away to warmer lands: will you come with
me? You can sit on my back, and we will fly far away
from the ugly mole and his dark house, over the
mountains, to the warm countries where the sun
shines more brightly than here, where it is always
summer, and there are always beautiful flowers. Do
come with me, dear little Thumbelina, who saved
my life when I lay frozen in the dark tunnel!'

'Yes, I will go with you,' said Thumbelina, and got
on the swallow's back, with her feet on one of his
outstretched wings. Up he flew into the air, over
woods and seas, over the great mountains where the
snow is always lying. And if she was cold she crept
under his warm feathers, only keeping her little head
out to admire all the beautiful things in the world
beneath. At last they came to warm lands; there the
sun was brighter, the sky seemed twice as high, and
in the hedges hung the finest green and purple grapes;
in the woods grew oranges and lemons; the air was
scented with myrtle and mint, and on the roads were
pretty little children running about and playing with
great gorgeous butterflies. But the swallow flew on
farther, and it became more and more beautiful.
Under the most splendid green trees beside a blue
lake stood a glittering white marble castle. Vines hung
about the high pillars; there were many swallows'
nests, and in one of these lived the swallow who was
carrying Thumbelina.

'Here is my house!' said he. 'But it won't do for
you to live with me; I am not tidy enough to please
you. Find a home for yourself in one of the lovely
flowers that grow down there; now I will set you
down, and you can do whatever you like.'

'That will be splendid!' said she, clapping her little hands.

There lay a great white marble column which had fallen to the ground and broken into three pieces, but between these grew the most beautiful white flowers. The swallow flew down with Thumbelina, and set her upon one of the broad leaves. But there, to her astonishment, she found a tiny little man sitting in the middle of the flower, as white and transparent as if he were made of glass; he had the prettiest golden crown on his head, and the most beautiful wings on his shoulders; he himself was no bigger than Thumbelina. He was the spirit of the flower. In each blossom there dwelt a tiny man or woman; but this one was the king over the others.

'How handsome he is!' whispered Thumbelina to the swallow.

The little prince was very much frightened at the swallow, for in comparison with one so tiny as himself he seemed a giant. But when he saw Thumbelina, he was delighted, for she was the most beautiful girl he had ever seen. So he took his golden crown from off his head and put it on hers, asking her her name, and if she would be his wife, and then she would be queen of all the flowers. Yes! he was a different kind of husband from the son of the toad and the mole with the black velvet coat. So she said, 'Yes,' to the noble prince. And out of each flower came a lady and gentleman, each so tiny and pretty that it was a pleasure to see them. Each brought Thumbelina a present, but the best of all was a beautiful pair of wings which were fastened on to her back, and now she too could fly from flower to flower. They all wished her joy, and the swallow sat above in his nest and sang the wedding

march, and that he did as well as he could; but he was
sad, because he was very fond of Thumbelina and did
not want to be separated from her.

'You shall not be called Thumbelina!' said the spirit
of the flower to her; 'that is an ugly name, and you
are much too pretty for that. We will call you May
Blossom.'

'Farewell, farewell!' said the little swallow with a
heavy heart, and flew away to farther lands, far, far
away, right back to Denmark. There he had a little
nest above a window, where his wife lived, who can
tell fairy stories. 'Tweet, tweet!' he sang to her. And
that is the way we learnt the whole story.

Tom Tit Tot

Once upon a time there was a woman, and she baked
five pies. And when they came out of the oven, they
were that overbaked the crusts were too hard to eat.
So she says to her daughter: 'Darter,' says she, 'put
you them there pies on the shelf, and leave 'em there
a little, and they'll come again.' She meant, you know,
the crust would get soft.

But the girl, she says to herself: 'Well, if they'll
come again, I'll eat 'em now.' And she set to work
and ate 'em all, first and last.

Well, come suppertime the woman said: 'Go you,
and get one o' them there pies. I dare say they've
come again now.'

The girl went and she looked, and there was nothing
but the dishes. So back she came and
says she: 'Noo, they ain't come
again.'

'Not one of 'em?' says
the mother.

'Not one of 'em,'
says she.

'Well, come again,
or not come again,'
said the woman 'I'll
have one for supper.'

'But you can't, if they
ain't come,' said the girl.

'But I can,' says she. 'Go
you, and bring the best of 'em.'

484

'Best or worst,' says the girl, 'I've ate 'em all, and you can't have one till that's come again.'

Well, the woman she was done, and she took her spinning to the door to spin, and as she span she sang:

> My darter ha' ate five, five pies today.
> My darter ha' ate five, five pies today.

The king was coming down the street, and he heard her sing, but what she sang he couldn't hear, so he stopped and said: 'What was that you were singing, my good woman?'

The woman was ashamed to let him hear what her daughter had been doing, so she sang, instead of that:

> My darter ha' spun five, five skeins today.
> My darter ha' spun five, five skeins today.

'Stars o' mine!' said the king, 'I never heard tell of anyone that could do that.'

Then he said: 'Look you here, I want a wife, and I'll marry your daughter. But look you here,' says he, 'eleven months out of the year she shall have all she likes to eat, and all the gowns she likes to get, and all the company she likes to keep; but the last month of the year she'll have to spin five skeins every day, and if she don't I shall kill her.'

'All right,' says the woman; for she thought what a grand marriage that was. And as for the five skeins, when the time came, there'd be plenty of ways of getting out of it, and likeliest, he'd have forgotten all about it.

Well, so they were married. And for eleven months the girl had all she liked to eat, and all the gowns she liked to get, and all the company she liked to keep.

485

But when the time was getting over, she began to think about the skeins and to wonder if he had 'em in mind. But not one word did he say about 'em, and she thought he'd wholly forgotten 'em.

However, the last day of the last month he takes her to a room she'd never set eyes on before. There was nothing in it but a spinning-wheel and a stool. And says he: 'Now, my dear, here you'll be shut in tomorrow with some victuals and some flax, and if you haven't spun five skeins by the night, your head'll go off.'

And away he went about his business.

Well, she was that frightened, she'd always been such a gatless girl, that she didn't so much as know how to spin, and what was she to do tomorrow with no one to come nigh her to help her? She sat down on a stool in the kitchen, and law! how she did cry!

However, all of a sudden she heard a sort of a knocking low down on the door. She upped and oped it, and what should she see but a small little black thing with a long tail. That looked up at her right curious, and that said: 'What are you a-crying for?'

'What's that to you?' says she.

'Never you mind,' that said, 'but tell me what you're a-crying for.'

'That won't do me no good if I do,' says she.

'You don't know that,' that said, and twirled that's tail round.

'Well,' says she, 'that won't do no harm, if that don't do no good,' and she upped and told about the pies, and the skeins, and everything.

'This is what I'll do,' says the little black thing, 'I'll come to your window every morning and take the flax and bring it spun at night.'

'What's your pay?' says she.

That looked out of the corner of that's eyes, and that said: 'I'll give you three guesses every night to guess my name, and if you haven't guessed it before the month's up you shall be mine.'

Well, she thought she'd be sure to guess that's name before the month was up. 'All right,' says she, 'I agree.'

'All right,' that says, and law! how that twirled that's tail.

Well, the next day, her husband took her into the room, and there was the flax and the day's food.

'Now there's the flax,' says he, 'and if that ain't spun up this night, off goes your head.' And then he went out and locked the door.

He'd hardly gone, when there was a knocking against the window.

She upped and she opened it, and there sure enough was the little old thing sitting on the ledge.

'Where's the flax?' says he.

'Here it be,' says she. And she gave it to him.

Well, come the evening a knocking came again to the window. She upped and she opened it, and there was the little old thing with five skeins of flax on his arm.

'Here it be,' says he, and he gave it to her.

'Now, what's my name?' says he.

'What, is that Bill?' says she.

'Noo, that ain't,' says he, and he twirled his tail.

'Is that Ned?' says she.

'Noo, that ain't,' says he, and he twirled his tail.

'Well, is that Mark?' says she.

'Noo, that ain't,' says he, and he twirled his tail harder, and away he flew.

Well, when her husband came in, there were the five skeins ready for him. 'I see I shan't have to kill you tonight, my dear,' says he; 'you'll have your food and your flax in the morning,' says he, and away he goes.

Well, every day the flax and the food were brought, and every day that there little black impet used to come mornings and evenings. And all the day the girl sat trying to think of names to say to it when it came at night. But she never hit on the right one. And as it got towards the end of the month, the impet began to look so maliceful, and that twirled that's tail faster and faster each time she gave a guess.

At last it came to the last day but one. The impet came at night along with the five skeins, and that said, 'What, ain't you got my name yet?'

'Is that Nicodemus?' says she.

'Noo, t'ain't,' that says.

'Is that Sammle?' says she.

'Noo, t'ain't,' that says.

'A-well, is that Methusalem?' says she.

'Noo, t'ain't that neither,' that says.

Then that looks at her with that's eyes like coals o' fire, and that says: 'Woman, there's only tomorrow night, and then you'll be mine!' And away it flew.

Well, she felt that horrid. However, she heard the king coming along the passage. In he came, and when he sees the five skeins, he says, says he,

'Well, my dear,' says he, 'I don't see but what you'll have your skeins ready tomorrow night as well, and as I reckon I shan't have to kill you, I'll have supper in here tonight.' So they brought supper, and another stool for him, and down the two sat.

Well, he hadn't eaten but a mouthful or so, when he stops and begins to laugh.

'What is it?' says she.

'A-why,' says he, 'I was out a-hunting today, and I got away to a place in the wood I'd never seen before And there was an old chalk-pit. And I heard a kind of a sort of a humming. So I got off my hobby, and I went right quiet to the pit, and I looked down. Well, what should there be but the funniest little black thing you ever set eyes on. And what was that doing, but that had a little spinning-wheel, and that was spinning wonderful fast, and twirling that's tail. And as that span that sang:

> 'Nimmy nimmy not,
> My name's Tom Tit Tot.'

Well, when the girl heard this, she felt as if she could have jumped out of her skin for joy, but she didn't say a word.

Next day that there little thing looked so maliceful when he came for the flax. And when night came, she heard that knocking against the window panes. She oped the window, and that come right in on the ledge. That was grinning from ear to ear, and Oo! that's tail was twirling round so fast.

'What's my name?' that says, as that gave her the skeins.

'Is that Solomon?' she says, pretending to be afeard.

'Noo, t'ain't,' that says, and that came farther into the room.

'Well, is that Zebedee?' says she again.

'Noo, t'ain't,' says the impet. And then that laughed and twirled that's tail till you couldn't hardly see it.

'Take time, woman,' that says; 'next guess, and you're mine.' And that stretched out that's black hands at her.

Well, she backed a step or two, and she looked at it, and then she laughed out, and says she, pointing her finger at it:

> 'Ninny, Ninny not,
> Your name's *Tom Tit Tot*.'

Well, when that heard her, that gave an awful shriek and away that flew into the dark, and she never saw it any more.

490

The Twelve Dancing Princesses

There was a king who had twelve beautiful daughters. They slept in twelve beds all in one room; and when they went to bed, the doors were shut and locked up; but every morning their shoes were found to be quite worn through as if they had been danced in all night; and yet nobody could find out how it happened, or where they had been.

Then the king made it known to all the land that if any man could discover the secret, and find out where it was that the princesses danced in the night, he should have the one he liked best for his wife, and should be king after his death; but whoever tried and did not succeed, after three days and nights should be put to death.

A king's son soon came. He was well entertained, and in the evening was taken to the chamber next to the one where the princesses lay in their twelve beds. There he was to sit and watch where they went to dance; and, in order that nothing might pass without his hearing it, the door of his chamber was left open. But the king's son soon fell asleep; and when he awoke in the morning he found that the princesses had all been dancing, for the soles of their shoes were full of holes. The same thing happened the second and third night, so the king ordered his head to be cut off. After him came several others; but they had all the same luck, and all lost their lives in the same manner.

Now it chanced that an old soldier, who had been wounded in battle and could fight no longer, passed through the country where this king reigned, and as he was travelling through a wood, he met an old woman, who asked him where he was going. 'I hardly know where I am going, or what I had better do,' said the soldier; 'but I think I should like very well to find out where it is that the princesses dance, and then in time I might be a king.'

'Well,' said the old dame, 'that is no very hard task, only take care not to drink any of the wine which one of the princesses will bring to you in the evening; and as soon as she leaves you pretend to be fast asleep.' Then she gave him a cloak, and said, 'As soon as you put that on you will become invisible, and you will then be able to follow the princesses wherever they go.'

When the soldier heard all this good counsel, he determined to try his luck: so he went to the king, and said he was willing to undertake the task. He was as well received as the others had been, and the king ordered fine royal robes to be given him; and when the evening came he was led to the outer chamber.

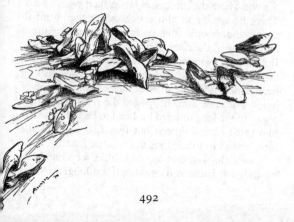

Just as he was going to lie down, the eldest of the princesses brought him a cup of wine; but the soldier threw it all away secretly, taking care not to drink a drop. Then he laid himself down on his bed, and in a little while began to snore very loud as if he was fast asleep.

When the twelve princesses heard this they laughed heartily; and the eldest said, 'This fellow too might have done a wiser thing than lose his life in this way!'

Then they rose up and opened their drawers and boxes, and took out all their fine clothes, and dressed themselves at the glass, and skipped about as if they were eager to begin dancing. But the youngest said, 'I don't know why it is, but while you are all so happy I feel very uneasy; I am sure some mischance will befall us.'

'You simpleton,' said the eldest, 'you are always afraid; have you forgotten how many kings' sons have already watched in vain? And as for this soldier, even if I had not given him his sleeping draught, he would have slept soundly enough.'

When they were all ready, they went and looked at the soldier; but he snored on, and did not stir hand or foot, so they thought they were quite safe; and the eldest went up to her own bed and clapped her hands, and the bed sank into the floor and a trap-door flew open. The soldier saw them going down through the trap-door one after another, the eldest leading the way; and thinking he had no time to lose, he jumped up, put on the cloak which the old woman had given him, and followed them; but in the middle of the stairs he trod on the gown of the youngest princess, and she cried out to her sisters, 'All is not right; someone took hold of my gown.'

'You silly creature!' said the eldest, 'it is nothing but a nail in the wall.'

Then down they all went, and at the bottom they found themselves in a most delightful grove of trees; and the leaves were all of silver, and glittered and sparkled beautifully. The soldier wished to take away some token of the place; so he broke off a little branch, and there came a loud noise from the tree. Then the youngest daughter said again, 'I am sure all is not right – did not you hear that noise? That never happened before.'

But the eldest said, 'It is only our princes, who are shouting for joy at our approach.'

Then they came to another grove of trees, where all the leaves were of gold; and afterwards to a third, where the leaves were all glittering diamonds. And the soldier broke a branch from each; and every time there was a loud noise, which made the youngest sister tremble with fear; but the eldest still said, it was only the princes, who were crying for joy. So they went on till they came to a great lake; and at the side of the lake there lay twelve little boats with twelve handsome princes in them, who seemed to be waiting there for the princesses.

One of the princesses went into each boat, and the soldier stepped into the same boat as the youngest. As they were rowing over the lake, the prince who was in the boat with the youngest princess and the soldier said, 'I do not know why it is, but though I am rowing with all my might we do not get on so fast as usual, and I am quite tired: the boat seems very heavy today.'

'It is only the heat of the weather,' said the princess. 'I feel very warm too.'

On the other side of the lake stood a fine illuminated castle, from which came the merry music of horns
and trumpets. There they all landed, and went into
the castle, and each prince danced with his princess;
and the soldier, who was all the time invisible, danced
with them too; and when any of the princesses had a

cup of wine set by her, he drank it all up, so that when she put the cup to her mouth it was empty. At this, too, the youngest sister was terribly frightened, but the eldest always silenced her. They danced on till three o'clock in the morning, and then all their shoes were worn out, so that they were obliged to leave off. The princes rowed them back again over the lake (but this time the soldier placed himself in the boat with the eldest princess); and on the opposite shore they took leave of each other, the princesses promising to come again the next night.

When they came to the stairs, the soldier ran on before the princesses, and laid himself down; and as the twelve sisters slowly came up, very much tired, they heard him snoring in his bed; so they said, 'Now all is quite safe;' then they undressed themselves, put away their fine clothes, pulled off their shoes, and went to bed. In the morning the soldier said nothing about what had happened, but determined to see more of this strange adventure, and went again the second and third night; and everything happened just as before; the princesses danced each time till their shoes were worn to pieces, and then returned home. However, on the third night the soldier carried away one of the golden cups as a token of where he had been.

As soon as the time came when he was to declare the secret, he was taken before the king with the three branches and the golden cup; and the twelve princesses stood listening behind the door to hear what he would say. And when the king asked him, 'Where do my twelve daughters dance at night?' he answered, 'With twelve princes in a castle under-ground.' And then he told the king all that had happened, and showed him the three branches and the golden cup which he had brought with him. Then the king called for the princesses, and asked them whether what the soldier said was true; and when they saw that they were discovered, and that it was of no use to deny what had happened, they confessed it all.

And the king asked the soldier which of them he would choose for his wife; and he answered, 'I am not very young, so I will have the eldest.' And they were married that very day, and the soldier was chosen to be the king's heir.

The Ugly Duckling

The country was lovely just then; it was summer. The heat was golden and the oats still green; the hay was stacked in the rich low-lying meadows, where the stork was marching about on his long red legs, chattering Egyptian, the language his mother had taught him.

Round about field and meadow lay great woods, in the midst of which were deep lakes. Yes, the country certainly was delicious. In the sunniest spot stood an old mansion surrounded by a deep moat, and great dock leaves grew from the walls of the house right down to the water's edge; some of them were so tall that a small child could stand upright under them. In amongst the leaves it was as secluded as in the depths of a forest, and there a duck was sitting on her nest. Her little ducklings were just about to be hatched, but she was nearly tired of sitting, for it had lasted such a long time. Moreover, she had very few visitors, as the other ducks liked swimming about in the moat better than waddling up to sit under the dock leaves and gossip with her.

At last one egg after another began to crack. 'Cheep cheep!' they said. All the chicks had come to life, and were poking their heads out.

'Quack! quack!' said the duck; and then they all quacked their hardest, and looked about them on all sides among the green leaves; their mother allowed them to look as much as they liked, for green is good for the eyes.

'How big the world is to be sure!' said all the young ones; for they certainly had ever so much more room to move about now than when they were inside the egg.

'Do you imagine this is the whole world?' said the mother. 'It stretches a long way on the other side of the garden, right into the parson's field: but I have never been as far as that! I suppose you are all here now?' and she got up. 'No! I declare I have not got you all yet! The biggest egg is still there; how long is it going to last?' and then she settled herself on the nest again.

'Well, how are you getting on?' said an old duck who had come to pay her a visit.

'This one egg is taking such a long time,' answered the sitting duck, 'the shell will not crack; but now you must look at the others; they are the finest ducklings I have ever seen! they are all exactly like their father, the rascal! he never comes to see me.'

'Let me look at the egg which won't crack,' said the old duck. 'You may be sure that it is a turkey's egg! I was cheated like that once, and I had no end of trouble and worry with the creatures, for I may tell you that they are afraid of the water. I could not get them into it. I quacked and snapped at them, but it was no good. Let me see the egg! Yes, it is a turkey's egg! You just leave it alone and teach the other children to swim.'

'I will sit on it a little longer. I have sat so long already, that I may as well go on till the Midsummer Fair comes round.'

'Please yourself,' said the old duck, and she went away.

At last the big egg cracked. 'Cheep, cheep!' said the

young one and tumbled out; how big and ugly he was! The duck looked at him.

'That is a monstrous big duckling,' she said; 'none of the others looked like that; can he be a turkey chick? well we shall soon find that out; into the water he shall go, if I have to kick him in myself.'

Next day was gloriously fine, and the sun shone on all the green dock leaves. The mother duck with her whole family went down to the moat. Splash, into the water she sprang. 'Quack, quack!' she said, and one duckling plumped in after the other. The water dashed over their heads, but they came up again and floated beautifully; their legs went of themselves, and they were all there; even the big ugly grey one swam about with them.

'No, that is no turkey,' she said; 'see how beautifully he uses his legs and how erect he holds himself: he is my own chick! after all, he is not so bad when you come to look at him properly. Quack, quack! Now come with me and I will take you into the world, and introduce you to the duckyard; but keep close to me all the time, so that no one may tread upon you, and beware of the cat!'

Then they went into the duckyard. There was a fearful uproar going on, for two broods were fighting for the head of an eel, and in the end the cat took it.

'That's how things go in this world,' said the mother duck, and she licked her bill for she had wanted the eel's head herself.

'Use your legs,' said she; 'mind you quack properly, and bend your necks to the old duck over there! She is the grandest of them all; she has Spanish blood in her veins and that accounts for her size; and, do you see? she has a red rag round her leg; that is a wonderfully fine thing, the most extraordinary mark of distinction any duck can have. It shows clearly that she is not to be parted with, and that she is worthy of recognition both by beasts and men! Quack now! don't turn your toes in, a well-brought-up duckling keeps his legs wide apart just like father and mother; that's it, now bend your necks, and say quack!'

They did as they were bid, but the other ducks round about looked at them and said, quite loud: 'Just look there! now we are to have that tribe! just as if there were not enough of us already, and, oh dear! how ugly that duckling is, we won't stand him!' and a duck flew at him at once and bit him in the neck.

'Let him be,' said the mother; 'he is doing no harm.'

'Very likely not, but he is so ungainly and queer,' said the biter; 'he must be whacked.'

'They are handsome children mother has,' said the old duck with the rag round her leg; 'all good-looking except this one, and he is not a good specimen; it's a pity you can't make him over again.'

'That can't be done, your grace,' said the mother duck; 'he is not handsome, but he is a thorough good creature, and he swims as beautifully as any of the others; nay, I think I might venture even to

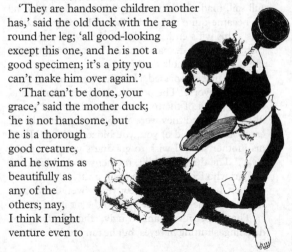

501

add that I think he will improve as he goes on, or perhaps in time he may grow smaller! He was too long in the egg, and so he has not come out with a very good figure.' And then she patted his neck and stroked his down. 'Besides he is a drake,' said she; 'so it does not matter so much. I believe he will be very strong, and I don't doubt but he will make his way in the world.'

'The other ducklings are very pretty,' said the old duck. 'Now make yourselves quite at home, and if you find the head of an eel you may bring it to me!'

After that they felt quite at home. But the poor duckling who had been the last to come out of the shell, and who was so ugly, was bitten, pushed about, and made fun of both by the ducks and the hens. 'He is too big,' they all said; and the turkey-cock, who was born with his spurs on, and therefore thought himself quite an emperor, puffed himself up like a vessel in full sail, made for him, and gobbled and gobbled till he became quite red in the face. The poor duckling was at his wit's end, and did not know which way to turn; he was in despair because he was so ugly, and the butt of the whole duckyard.

So the first day passed, and afterwards matters grew worse and worse. The poor duckling was chased and hustled by all of them; even his brothers and sisters ill-used him and they were always saying, 'If only the cat would get hold of you, you hideous object!' Even his mother said, 'I wish to goodness you were miles away.' The ducks bit him, the hens pecked him and the girl who fed them kicked him aside.

Then he ran off and flew right over the hedge, where the little birds flew up into the air in a fright.

'That is because I am so ugly,' thought the poor duckling, shutting his eyes, but he ran on all the same.

Then he came to a great marsh where the wild ducks lived; he was so tired and miserable that he stayed there the whole night.

In the morning the wild ducks flew up to inspect their new comrade.

'What sort of a creature are you?' they enquired, as the duckling turned from side to side and greeted them as well as he could. 'You are frightfully ugly,' said the wild ducks; 'but that does not matter to us, so long as you do not marry into our family!' Poor fellow! he had no thought of marriage, all he wanted was permission to lie among the rushes, and to drink a little of the marsh water.

He stayed there two whole days, then two wild geese came, or rather two wild ganders; they were not long out of the shell, and therefore rather pert.

'I say, comrade,' they said, 'you are so ugly that we have taken quite a fancy to you; will you join us and be a bird of passage? There is another marsh close by, and there are some charming wild geese there; all sweet young ladies, who can say quack! You are ugly enough to make your fortune among them.' Just at that moment, bang! bang! was heard up above, and both the wild geese fell dead among the reeds, and the water turned blood red. Bang! bang! went the guns, and whole flocks of wild geese flew up from the rushes and the shot peppered among them again.

There was a grand shooting party, and the sportsmen lay hidden round the marsh; some even sat on the branches of the trees which overhung the water; the blue smoke rose like clouds among the dark trees and swept over the pool.

The water-dogs wandered about in the swamp, splash! splash! The rushes and reeds bent beneath their tread on all sides. It was terribly alarming to the poor duckling. He twisted his head round to get it under his wing and just at that moment a frightful big dog appeared close beside him; his tongue hung right out of his mouth and his eyes glared wickedly. He opened his great chasm of a mouth close to the duckling, showed his sharp teeth – and – splash – went on without touching him.

'Oh, thank heaven!' sighed the duckling. 'I am so ugly that even the dog won't bite me!'

Then he lay quite still while the shot whistled among the bushes, and bang after bang rent the air. It only became quiet late in the day, but even then the poor duckling did not dare to get up; he waited several hours more before he looked about and then he hurried away from the marsh as fast as he could. He ran across fields and meadows, and there was such a wind that he had hard work to make his way.

Towards night he reached a poor little cottage; it was such a miserable hovel that it could not make up its mind which way to fall even, and so it remained standing. The wind whistled so fiercely round the duckling that he had to sit on his tail to resist it, and it blew harder and harder; then he saw that the door had fallen off one hinge and hung so crookedly that he could creep into the house through the crack and by this means he made his way into the room. An old woman lived there with her cat and her hen. The cat, which she called Sonnie, could arch his back, purr, and give off electric sparks, that is to say if you stroked his fur the wrong way. The hen had quite tiny short legs and so she was called Chuckie-Low-Legs. She laid good eggs, and the old woman was as fond of her as if she had been her own child.

In the morning the strange duckling was discovered immediately, and the cat began to purr and the hen to cluck.

'What on earth is that!' said the old woman looking round, but her sight was not good and she thought the duckling was a fat duck which had escaped. 'This is a capital find,' said she; 'now I shall have duck's eggs if only it is not a drake! we must find out about that!'

So she took the duckling on trial for three weeks, but no eggs made their appearance. The cat was the master of the house and the hen the mistress, and they always spoke of 'we and the world', for they thought that they represented the half of the world, and that quite the better half.

The duckling thought there might be two opinions on the subject, but the cat would not hear of it.

'Can you lay eggs?' she asked.

'No!'

'Have the goodness to hold your tongue then!'

And the cat said, 'Can you arch your back, purr or give off sparks?'

'No.'

'Then you had better keep your opinions to yourself when people of sense are speaking!'

The duckling sat in the corner nursing his ill-humour; then he began to think of the fresh air and the sunshine, an uncontrollable longing seized him to float on the water, and at last he could not help telling the hen about it.

'What on earth possesses you?' she asked; 'you have nothing to do, that is why you get these freakish ideas into your head. Lay some eggs or take to purring, and you will get over it.'

'But it is so delicious to float on the water,' said the duckling; 'so delicious to feel it rushing over your head when you dive to the bottom.'

'That would be a fine amusement,' said the hen. 'I think you have gone mad. Ask the cat about it, he is the wisest creature I know; ask him if he is fond of floating on the water or diving under it. I say nothing about myself. Ask our mistress yourself, the old woman, there is no one in the world cleverer than she is. Do you suppose she has any desire to float on the water, or to dive underneath it?'

'You do not understand me,' said the duckling.

'Well, if we don't understand you, who should? I suppose you don't consider yourself cleverer than the cat or the old woman, not to mention me. Don't make a fool of yourself, child, and thank your stars for all the good we have done you! Have you not lived in this warm room, and in such society that you might have learnt something? But you are an idiot, and there is no pleasure in associating with you. You may believe me – I mean you well, I tell you home truths, and there is no surer way than that of knowing who are one's friends. You just see about laying some eggs, or learn to purr or to emit sparks.'

'I think I will go out into the wide world,' said the duckling.

'Oh, do so by all means,' said the hen.

So away went the duckling; he floated on the water and ducked underneath it, but he was looked at askance by every living creature for his ugliness. Now the autumn came on, the leaves in the woods turned yellow and brown; the wind took hold of them, and they danced about. The sky looked very cold, and the clouds hung heavy with snow and hail. A raven stood on the fence and croaked Caw! Caw! from sheer cold; it made one shiver only to think of it; the poor duckling certainly was in a bad case.

One evening, the sun was just setting in wintry splendour, when a flock of beautiful large birds appeared out of the bushes; the duckling had never seen anything so beautiful. They were dazzlingly white with long waving necks; they were swans, and uttering a peculiar cry they spread out their magnificent broad wings and flew away from the cold regions to warmer lands and open seas. They mounted so high, so very high, and the ugly little duckling became strangely uneasy; he circled round and round in the water like a wheel, craning his neck up into the air after them. Then he uttered a shriek so piercing and so strange, that he was quite frightened by it himself. Oh, he could not forget those beautiful birds, those happy birds, and as soon as they were out of sight he ducked right down to the bottom, and when he came up again he was quite beside himself. He did not know what the birds were, or whither they flew, but all the same he was more drawn towards them than he had ever been by any creatures before. He did not envy them in the least; how could it occur to him even to wish to be such a marvel of beauty? He would have been thankful if only the ducks would have tolerated him among them – the poor ugly creature!

The winter was so bitterly cold that the duckling was obliged to swim about in the water to keep it from freezing, but every night the hole in which he swam got smaller and smaller. Then it froze so hard that the surface ice cracked, and the duckling had to use his legs all the time, so that the ice should not close in round him; at last he was so weary that he could move no more, and he was frozen fast into the ice.

Early in the morning a peasant came along and saw him; he went out on to the ice and hammered a hole in it with his heavy wooden shoe, and carried the duckling home to his wife. There it soon revived. The children wanted to play with it, but the duckling thought they were going to ill-use him, and rushed in his fright into the milk pan, and the milk spurted out all over the room. The woman shrieked and threw up her hands, and in its confusion it flew into the butter cask, and down into the meal tub and out again. Just imagine what it looked like by this time! The woman screamed and tried to hit it with the tongs, and the children tumbled over one another in trying to catch it, and they screamed with laughter; by good luck the door stood open, and the duckling flew out among the bushes and the new-fallen snow – and it lay there thoroughly exhausted.

It would be too sad to mention all the privation and misery it had to go through during that hard winter. When the sun began to shine warmly again, the duckling was in the marsh, lying among the rushes; the larks were singing and the beautiful spring had come.

Then all at once it raised its wings and they flapped with much greater strength than before, and bore him off vigorously. Before he knew where he was, he found himself in a large garden where the apple trees were in full blossom, and the air was scented with lilacs, the long branches of which overhung the indented shores of the lake! Oh! the spring freshness was so delicious!

Just in front of him he saw three beautiful white swans advancing towards him from a thicket; with rustling feathers they swam lightly over the water. The duckling recognised the majestic birds, and he was overcome by a strange melancholy.

'I will fly to them, the royal birds, and they will hack me to pieces, because I, who am so ugly, venture to approach them! But it won't matter; better be killed by them than be snapped at by the ducks, pecked by the hens or spurned by the henwife, or suffer so much misery in the winter.'

So he flew into the water and swam towards the stately swans; they saw him and darted towards him with ruffled feathers.

'Kill me, oh, kill me!' said the poor creature, and bowing his head towards the water, he awaited his death. But what did he see reflected in the transparent water?

He saw below him his own image, but he was no longer a clumsy dark grey bird, ugly and ungainly, he was himself a swan! It does not matter in the least having been born in a duckyard, if only you come out of a swan's egg!

He felt quite glad of all the misery and tribulation he had gone through; he was the better able to appreciate his good fortune now, and all the beauty which greeted him. The big swans swam round and round him, and stroked him with their bills.

Some little children came into the garden with corn

and pieces of bread, which they threw into the water; and the smallest one cried out: 'There is a new one!' The other children shouted with joy, 'Yes, a new one has come!' And they clapped their hands and danced about, running after their father and mother. They threw the bread into the water, and one and all said that 'the new one was the prettiest; he was so young and handsome'. And the old swans bent their heads and did homage before him.

He felt quite shy, and hid his head under his wing; he did not know what to think; he was so very happy, but not at all proud; a good heart never becomes proud. He thought of how he had been pursued and scorned, and now he heard them all say that he was the most beautiful of all beautiful birds. The lilacs bent their boughs right down into the water before him, and the bright sun was warm and cheering, and he rustled his feathers and raised his slender neck aloft, saying with exultation in his heart: 'I never dreamt of so much happiness when I was that ugly duckling!'

The Valiant Little Tailor

One summer's morning a little tailor was sitting on his table by the window; he was in good spirits, and sewed with all his might.

Then came a peasant woman down the street crying: 'Good jams, cheap! Good jams, cheap!'

This rang pleasantly in the tailor's ears; he stretched his delicate head out of the window, and called: 'Come up here, dear woman; here you will sell your goods.'

The woman came up the three steps to the tailor with her heavy basket, and he made her unpack all the pots for him.

He inspected each one, lifted it up, put his nose to it, and at length said: 'The jam seems to me to be good, so weigh out four ounces, dear woman, and if it is a quarter of a pound that is of no consequence.'

The woman who had hoped to find a good sale, gave him what he desired, but went away quite angry and grumbling.

'Now, this jam shall be blessed by God,' cried the little tailor, 'and give me health and strength;' so he brought the bread out of the cupboard, cut himself a piece right across the loaf and spread the jam over it. 'This won't taste bitter,' said he, 'but I will just finish the jacket before I take a bite.'

He laid the bread near him and sewed on, in his joy making bigger and bigger stitches. In the meantime the smell of the sweet jam rose to where the flies were sitting in great numbers, and they were attracted and descended on it in hosts.

'Hi! Who invited you?' said the little tailor, and drove the unbidden guests away.

The flies, however, who understood not a word, would not be turned away, but came back again in ever-increasing companies. The little tailor at last lost all patience, and drew a piece of cloth from the hole under his work-table, and, saying: 'Wait, and I will give it to you,' struck it mercilessly on them.

When he drew it away and counted, there lay before him no fewer than seven dead and with legs stretched out.

'Are you a fellow of that sort?' said he, and could not help admiring his own bravery. 'The whole town shall know of this!' And the little tailor hastened to cut himself a girdle, stitched it, and embroidered on it in large letters: 'Seven at one stroke'.

'Why stop at the town?' he continued. 'The whole world shall hear of it!' and his heart wagged with joy like a lamb's tail.

The tailor put on the girdle, and resolved to go forth into the world, because he thought his workshop was too small for his valour. Before he went away, he sought about in the house to see if there was anything which he could take with him; however, he found nothing but an old cheese, and that he put in his pocket. In front of the door he observed a bird which had caught itself in the thicket. It had to go into his pocket with the cheese. Now he took to the road boldly, and as he was light and nimble, he felt no fatigue. The road led him up a mountain, and when he had reached the highest point of it, there sat a powerful giant looking peacefully about him.

The little tailor went bravely up, spoke to him and said: 'Good-day, comrade, so you are sitting there

overlooking the widespread world! I am just on my
way thither, and want to try my luck. Have you any
inclination to go with me?'

The giant looked contemptuously at the tailor, and
said: 'You ragamuffin! You miserable creature!'

'Oh, indeed?' answered the little tailor and,
unbuttoning his coat, showed the giant the girdle.
'There may you read what kind of a man I am!'

The giant read:
'Seven at one
stroke', and
thought that
they had been
men whom the
tailor had killed,
and began to

feel a little respect for the tiny fellow. Nevertheless, he wished to try him first, and took a stone in his hand and squeezed it together so that water dropped out of it. 'Do that likewise,' said the giant, 'if you have strength.'

'Is that all?' said the tailor; 'that is child's play with us!' and put his hand into his pocket, brought out the soft cheese, and pressed it until the liquid ran out of it. 'Faith,' said he, 'that was a little better, wasn't it?'

The giant did not know what to say, and could not believe it of the little man. Then the giant picked up a stone and threw it so high that the eye could scarcely follow it. 'Now, little mite of a man, do that likewise.'

'Well thrown,' said the tailor; 'but after all the stone came down to earth again; I will throw you one which shall never come back at all,' and he put his hand into his pocket, took out the bird, and threw it into the air. The bird, delighted with its liberty, rose, flew away and did not come back. 'How does that shot please you, comrade?' asked the tailor.

'You can certainly throw,' said the giant; 'but now we will see if you are able to carry anything properly.'

He took the little tailor to a mighty oak tree which lay there felled on the ground, and said: 'If you are strong enough, help me to carry the tree out of the forest.'

'Readily,' answered the little man; 'take you the trunk on your shoulders, and I will raise up the branches and twigs; after all, they are the heaviest.' The giant took the trunk on his shoulder, but the tailor seated himself on a branch, and the giant, who could not look round, had to carry away the whole tree, and the little tailor into the bargain; he, behind, was quite merry and happy, and whistled the song

'Three tailors rode forth from the gate', as if carrying the tree were child's play.

The giant, after he had dragged the heavy burden part of the way, could go no farther, and cried: 'Hark you, I shall have to let the tree fall!'

The tailor sprang nimbly down, seized the tree with both arms as if he had been carrying it, and said to the giant: 'You are such a great fellow, and yet cannot even carry the tree!'

They went on together, and as they passed a cherry tree, the giant laid hold of the top of the tree where the ripest fruit was hanging, bent it down, gave it into the tailor's hand, and bade him eat. But the little tailor was much too weak to hold the tree, and when the giant let it go, it sprang back again, and the tailor was tossed into the air with it.

When he had fallen down again without injury, the giant said: 'What is this? Have you not strength enough to hold a weak twig?'

'There is no lack of strength,' answered the little tailor. 'Do you think that could be anything to a man who has struck down seven at one blow? I leapt over the tree because the huntsmen are shooting down there in the thicket. Jump, as I did, if you can do it.'

The giant made the attempt but he could not get over the tree, and remained hanging in the branches, so that in this also the tailor kept the upper hand.

The giant said: 'If you are such a valiant fellow, come with me into our cavern and spend the night with us.'

The little tailor was willing, and followed him. When they went into the cave, other giants were sitting there by the fire, and each of them had a roasted sheep in his hand and was eating it. The little tailor looked round and thought: 'It is much more spacious here than in my workshop.' The giant showed him a bed, and said he was to lie down in it and sleep. The bed, however, was too big for the little tailor; he did not lie down in it, but crept into a corner.

When it was midnight, and the giant thought that the little tailor was lying in a sound sleep, he got up, took a great iron bar, cut through the bed with one blow, and thought he had finished off the grasshopper for good.

With the earliest dawn the giants went into the forest, and had quite forgotten the little tailor, when all at once he walked up to them quite merrily and boldly. The giants were terrified, they were afraid that he would strike them all dead, and ran away in a great hurry.

The little tailor went onwards, always following his own pointed nose. After he had walked for a long time, he came to the courtyard of a royal palace, and as he felt weary, he lay down on the grass and fell asleep.

While he lay there, the people came and inspected him on all sides, and read on his girdle: 'Seven at one stroke'.

'Ah!' said they, 'what does the great warrior want here in the midst of peace? He must be a mighty lord.' They went and announced him to the king, and gave it as their opinion that if war should break out, this would be a weighty and useful man who ought on no account to be allowed to depart. The counsel pleased the king, and he sent one of his courtiers to the little tailor to offer him military service when he awoke. The ambassador remained standing by the sleeper, waited until he stretched his limbs and opened his eyes, and then conveyed to him this proposal.

'For this very reason have I come here,' the tailor replied. 'I am ready to enter the king's service.'

He was therefore honourably received, and a special dwelling was assigned him.

The soldiers, however, were set against the little tailor, and wished him a thousand miles away. 'What is to be the end of this?' they said among themselves. 'If we quarrel with him, and he strikes about him, seven of us will fall at every blow; not one of us can stand against him.'

They came therefore to a decision, betook themselves in a body to the king, and begged for their dismissal. 'We are not prepared,' said they, 'to stay with a man who kills seven at one stroke.'

The king was sorry that for the sake of one he should lose all his faithful servants, wished that he had never set eyes on the tailor, and would willingly have been rid of him again. But he did not venture to give him his dismissal, for he dreaded lest he should strike him and all his people dead and place himself on the royal throne. He thought about it for a long time, and at last found good counsel. He sent to the little tailor and caused him to be informed that, as he was a great warrior, he had one request to make to him.

In a forest of his country lived two giants, who caused great mischief with their robbing, murdering, ravaging and burning, and no one could approach them without putting himself in danger of death. If the tailor conquered and killed these two giants, he would give him his only daughter to wife, and half of his kingdom as a dowry, likewise one hundred horsemen should go with him to assist him. 'That would indeed be a fine thing for a man like me!' thought the little tailor. 'One is not offered a beautiful princess and half a kingdom every day of one's life!'

'Oh, yes,' he replied, 'I will soon subdue the giants, and do not require the help of the hundred horsemen to do it; he who can hit seven with one blow has no need to be afraid of two.'

The little tailor went forth, and the hundred horsemen followed him. When he came to the outskirts of the forest, he said to his followers: 'Just stay waiting here, I alone will soon finish off the giants.' Then he bounded into the forest and looked about right and left.

After a while he perceived both giants. They lay sleeping under a tree, and snored so that the branches waved up and down. The little tailor, not idle, gathered two pocketfuls of stones, and with these climbed up the tree. When he was halfway up, he slipped down by a branch until he sat just above the sleepers, and then let one stone after another fall on the breast of one of the giants. For a long time the giant felt nothing, but at last he awoke, pushed his comrade, and said: 'Why are you knocking me?'

'You must be dreaming,' said the other. 'I am not knocking you.'

They laid themselves down to sleep again, and then the tailor threw a stone down on to the second. 'What is the meaning of this?' cried the other. 'Why are you pelting me?'

'I am not pelting you,' answered the first, growling. They disputed about it for a time, but as they were weary they let the matter rest, and their eyes closed once more.

The little tailor began his game again, picked out

the biggest stone, and threw it with all his might on the breast of the first giant.

'That is too bad!' cried he, and springing up like a madman, he pushed his companion against the tree until it shook. The other paid him back in the same coin, and they got into such a rage that they tore up trees and belaboured each other so long that at last they both fell down dead on the ground at the same time.

Then the little tailor leapt down. 'It is a lucky thing,' said he, 'that they did not tear up the tree on which I was sitting, or I should have had to sprint on to another like a squirrel; but we tailors are nimble.'

He drew out his sword and gave each of them a

couple of thrusts in the breast, and then went out to the horsemen and said: 'The job is done; I have finished both of them off, but it was hard work! They tore up trees in their sore need, and defended themselves with them, but all that is to no purpose against a man like myself, who can kill seven at one blow.'

'But are you not wounded?' asked the horsemen.

'You need not concern yourself about that,' answered the tailor, 'they have not bent one hair of mine.' The horsemen would not believe him, and rode into the forest; there they found the giants swimming in their blood, and all round about lay the torn-up trees.

The little tailor demanded of the king the promised reward; he, however, repented of his promise, and again bethought himself how he could get rid of the hero. 'Before you receive my daughter, and half of my kingdom,' said he, 'you must perform one more heroic deed. In the forest roams a unicorn which does great harm, and you must catch it first.'

'I fear one unicorn still less than two giants. Seven at one blow is my kind of affair.'

He took a rope and an axe with him, went forth into the forest, and again bade those who were sent with him to wait outside. He had not long to seek. The unicorn soon came towards him, and rushed directly on the tailor, as if it would gore him with its horn without more ado. 'Softly, softly; it can't be done as quickly as that,' said he, and stood still and waited until the animal was quite close, and then sprang nimbly behind the tree.

The unicorn ran against the tree with all its force and stuck its horn so fast in the trunk that it had not strength enough to draw it out again, and thus it was caught. 'Now, I have got the bird,' said the tailor, and came out from behind the tree and put the rope round its neck, and then with his axe he hewed the horn out of the tree, and when all was ready he led the beast away and took it to the king.

The king still would not give him the promised reward, and made a third demand. Before the wedding the tailor was to catch him a wild boar that made great havoc in the forest, and the huntsmen should give him their help.

'Willingly,' said the tailor, 'that is child's play!' He did not take the huntsmen with him into the forest, and they were well pleased that he did not, for the wild boar had several times received them in such a manner that they had no inclination to lie in wait for him.

When the boar perceived the tailor, it ran on him with foaming mouth and whetted tusks, and was about to throw him to the ground, but the hero fled into a chapel which was near and in one bound sprang out again by the window. The boar ran after him, but the tailor ran round outside and shut the door behind it, and then the raging beast, which was much too heavy and awkward to leap out of the window, was caught.

The little tailor called the huntsmen thither that they might see the prisoner with their own eyes. The hero, however, went to the king, who was now, whether he liked it or not, obliged to keep his promise and give him his daughter and half his kingdom. Had he known that it was no warlike hero but a little tailor who was standing before him, it would have grieved him still more than it did. The wedding was held with great magnificence and small joy, and out of a tailor a king was made.

After some time the young queen heard her husband say in his dreams at night: 'Boy, make me the doublet, and patch the pantaloons, or else I will rap the yard-measure over your ears.' Then she discovered in what state of life the young lord had been born, and next morning complained of her wrongs to her father, and begged him to help her to get rid of her husband, who was nothing else but a tailor.

The king comforted her and said: 'Leave your bed-room door open this night, and my servants shall stand outside, and when he has fallen asleep shall go in, bind him, and take him on board a ship which shall carry him into the wide world.' The woman was satisfied with this; but the king's armour-bearer, who had heard all, was friendly with the young lord, and informed him of the whole plot. 'I'll put a screw into that business,' said the little tailor.

At night he went to bed with his wife at the usual time, and when she thought that he had fallen asleep, she got up, opened the door, and then lay down again. The little tailor, who was only pretending to be asleep, began to cry out in a clear voice: 'Boy, make me the doublet and patch me the pantaloons, or I will rap the yard-measure over your ears. I smote seven at one blow. I killed two giants, I brought away one unicorn and caught a wild boar, and am I to fear those who are standing outside the room?' When these men heard the tailor speaking thus, they were overcome by a great dread, and ran as if the wild huntsman were behind them, and none of them would venture any-thing further against him. So the little tailor was and remained a king to the end of his life.

The Well at the World's End

Once upon a time, and a very good time it was, though it wasn't in my time, nor in your time, nor anyone else's time, there was a girl whose mother had died, and her father married again. And her step-mother hated her because she was more beautiful than herself, and she was very cruel to her. She used to make her do all the servant's work, and never let her have any peace. At last, one day, the stepmother thought to get rid of her altogether; so she handed her a sieve and said to her: 'Go, fill it at the Well of the World's End and bring it home to me full, or woe betide you.' For she thought she would never be able to find the Well of the World's End, and, if she did, how could she bring home a sieve full of water?

Well, the girl started off, and asked everyone she met to tell her where was the Well of the World's End. But nobody knew, and she didn't know what to do, when a queer little old woman, all bent double, told her where it was, and how she could get to it. So she did what the old woman told her, and at last arrived at the Well of the World's End. But when she dipped the sieve in the cold, cold water, it all ran out again. She tried and tried again, but every time it was the same; and at last she sat down and cried as if her heart would break.

Suddenly she heard a croaking voice, and she looked up and saw a great frog with goggle eyes looking at her and speaking to her.

'What's the matter, dearie?' it said.

'Oh, dear, oh dear,' she said, 'my stepmother has sent me all this long way to fill this sieve with water from the Well of the World's End, and I can't fill it no how at all.'

'Well,' said the frog, 'if you promise me to do whatever I bid you for a whole night long, I'll tell you how to fill it.'

So the girl agreed, and the frog said:

> 'Stop it with moss and daub it with clay,
> And then it will carry the water away';

and then it gave a hop, skip and jump, and went flop into the Well of the World's End.

So the girl looked about for some moss, and lined the bottom of the sieve with it, and over that she put some clay, and then she dipped it once again into the Well of the World's End; and this time, the water didn't run out, and she turned to go away.

Just then the frog popped its head out of the Well of the World's End, and said: 'Remember your promise.'

'All right,' said the girl; for thought she, 'What harm can a frog do me?'

So she went back to her stepmother, and brought the sieve full of water from the Well of the World's

End. The stepmother was angry as angry, but she said nothing at all.

That very evening they heard something tap-tapping at the door low down, and a voice cried out:

> *Open the door, my hinny, my heart,*
>   *Open the door, my own darling;*
> *Mind you the words that you and I spoke,*
>   *Down in the meadow, at the World's End Well.*

'Whatever can that be?' cried out the stepmother, and the girl had to tell her about it, and what she had promised the frog.

'Girls must keep their promises,' said the stepmother. 'Go and open the door this instant.' For she was glad the girl would have to obey a nasty frog.

So the girl went and opened the door, and there was the frog from the Well of the World's End. And it hopped, and it hopped and it jumped, till it reached the girl, and then it said:

> *Lift me to your knee, my hinny, my heart;*
>   *Lift me to your knee, my own darling;*
> *Remember the words you and I spoke,*
>   *Down in the meadow, by the World's End Well.*

But the girl didn't like to, till her stepmother said: 'Lift it up this instant, you hussy! Girls must keep their promises!'

So at last she lifted the frog up on to her lap, and it lay there for a time, till at last it said:

> *Give me some supper, my hinny, my heart,*
>   *Give me some supper, my darling;*
> *Remember the words you and I spoke,*
>   *In the meadow, by the Well of the World's End.*

Well, she didn't mind doing that, so she got it a bowl of milk and bread, and fed it well. And when the frog had finished, it said:

> *Go with me to bed, my hinny, my heart,*
> *Go with me to bed, my own darling;*
> *Mind you the words you spoke to me,*
> *Down by the cold well, so weary.*

But that the girl wouldn't do, till her stepmother said: 'Do what you promised, girl; girls must keep their promises. Do what you're bid, or out you go, you and your froggie.'

So the girl took the frog with her to bed, and kept it as far away from her as she could. Well, just as the day was beginning to break what should the frog say but:

> *Chop off my head, my hinny, my heart,*
> *Chop off my head, my own darling;*
> *Remember the promise you made to me,*
> *Down by the cold well, so weary.*

At first the girl wouldn't, for she thought of what the frog had done for her at the Well of the World's End. But when the frog said the words over again she went and took an axe and chopped off its head, and lo! and behold, there stood before her a handsome young prince, who told her that he had been enchanted by a wicked magician, and he could never be unspelled till some girl would do his bidding for a whole night, and chop off his head at the end of it.

The stepmother was surprised indeed when she found the young prince instead of the nasty frog, and she wasn't best pleased, you may be sure, when the prince told her that he was going to marry her stepdaughter because she had unspelled him. But married they were, and went away to live in the castle of the king, his father, and all the stepmother had to console her was that it was all through her that her stepdaughter was married to a prince.